Sentence of a Somat©

David Dh.

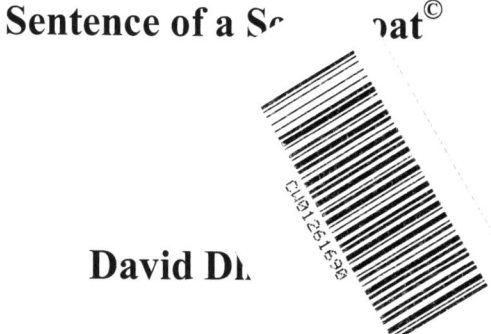

Copyright © 2024 by David Dhekelia
All rights reserved. This book or any portion thereof may not be reproduced or used in any manner whatsoever without the express written permission of the publisher except for the use of brief quotations in a book review.

This is a work of fiction. Names, characters, businesses, places, events and incidents are either the products of the author's imagination or used in a fictitious manner. Any resemblance to actual persons, living or dead, or actual events is purely coincidental.

Other titles in this series by David Dhekelia

The Robe of Iniquity
The Pemberton Legacy
Dark Eucharist
Death Comes of Age
The Curse of Samael's Grimoire

Prologue

It's been a while since I last caught up with my friends Alan and Sue Baylock. I'm aware that not everybody who has picked up this book will have read the previous four novels, so I thought a little introduction and background information would be helpful in giving you some context to this story since it began with "***The Robe of Iniquity***."

Let's start with the two main characters in this story (lord only knows if I didn't give Sue Baylock the introduction she feels she deserves, I would be in serious trouble). Alan and Sue Baylock are a married couple in their mid-to-late fifties who have a daughter called Ruth. Ruth is 30 years old and married to Chris.

In the first novel, we learned that Alan and Sue sold their house in order to downsize, without realising that there was something a bit odd about an item of clothing that had been left in a wardrobe in the new house. When Sue tried it on, after a long tingling sensation, she discovered that she was 30 years younger. Well who can blame a lady of mature years for taking advantage of this new vixen personae and going out to paint the town red? Oh, the broken hearts she left along the way with wild abandon shouldn't even be mentioned. There was one broken heart she left that she was truly sorry for – and that was her son-in-law Chris. Unbeknownst to him, he met Sue in a bar and let's just say one thing led to another. Since that time, Chris has seen old photographs of Sue holding Ruth as a baby and couldn't help noticing the resemblance between the younger Sue and the young woman he met at the bar. This has caused him to wonder.

Then there's Phyllis. What's not to love about dear old Phyllis? Slightly older than Sue, she was a real child of the sixties and boy did she have some fun!!! She listened to all the best music, took all the wrong drugs and generally did what people did back then. She may have put a bit of weight on and her long hair is now greying, but when she smiles, she excudes sincerity, warmth and honesty and she's intensely loyal to her closest friends, one of which is Sue. If ever an individual embodied the spirit of mother earth, it's dear Phyllis.

Then there's Robert. Robert's an interesting character. By profession, he is a clinical psychologist who lost his wife several years ago. He doesn't talk about it a lot – it's probably still quite painful for him. But his acquaintance with Sue and Alan began late one night when he was hiding in their back garden, trying to find the man who had killed a very good friend of his, Professor Ian Pemberton. Alan thought he was a burglar and tackled him to the ground. It was only when he called the police he found out that Robert Whitehead was no burglar, but according to the police just a 'meddling fool who should let the police do their work without his interference'. Since that time they have become good friends. Oh, and at one point, Robert and Phyllis almost became close but for whatever reason, it wasn't to be.

Talking of Ian Pemberton, the man was a veritable genius who created a device which could not only cause age reversal in people by 30 years (though it would only last six hours at a time), but could also read the DNA within a blood sample when injected into another person's arm who shared the same blood group. It does sound unbelievable but there has long been the idea that so called 'junk DNA' has a lot more to tell us than is presently known and Ian Pemberton always adhered to this theory. The four friends have used the device several times to 'read' DNA and discover all sorts of information pertaining to criminal activity.

Then there's Ophelia. A very close friend of Phyllis, she's something of an enigma. We don't know a great deal about her background, but she does have a strong connection with all things metaphysical and spiritual. She doesn't necessarily adhere to the new age movement, but she does have her own beliefs and philosophy, some of which run along similar lines to the aforementioned.

I hope this has given you some background information. Sue is now glaring at me, telling me to 'get on with the story' so without further ado, I shall leave you in peace to read "Sentence of a Scapegoat." I hope you enjoy reading this book as much as I enjoyed writing it.

David Dhekelia

Chapter One

"Jesus, this heat is killing me. What the hell are they waiting for? We were supposed to take off over an hour ago." Sue pulled at her top as if trying to loosen it. "I'm sure there's no air conditioning on this bloody thing."

One of the cabin crew walked down the aisle of the 'plane and Sue caught her attention. "Excuse me, have you got any idea what the hold up is?"

"I'm very sorry, we've been told we've got to wait to be given clearance. It shouldn't be too long now." She smiled reassuringly at Sue as she went to address the complaints of other passengers.

"I hope there's nothing wrong with the plane. I've heard all sorts of horror stories about engines setting alight, wings and tails falling off before the plane nosedives into a crash."

"Oh Sue, we've just had a great holiday. Don't finish it off with tales of doom and gloom" said Alan as he cast her a sideways glance.

"Well it wouldn't be so bad if they at least told us what the problem is. We haven't got a clue and we've got no idea how long they intend to keep us here" she moaned.

"Well if it is a technical issue, I find it at least reassuring that they won't let the plane take off before they know it's totally safe to fly."

"They said the Titanic was unsinkable but ...."

"Enough! There's nothing we can do about it. With any luck we'll be on our way soon!"

Suddenly they heard a woman's voice from the seat behind them. "I've got a good idea what the problem is."

Alan and Sue both turned their heads to look at the woman expectantly. She lowered her head as she moved forward and whispered between the space of the seats "drugs!"

"Drugs?" said Sue, rather louder than she realised.

The woman frowned at her. "Shhh! Don't say it out loud. But it's definitely drugs. They're checking the plane in front because it just came in an hour ago. It's got to be drugs!"

"How do you know?" asked Sue surprised, not sure that

she believed this crazy woman.

"Oh I can't prove it, but there's been a big drug smuggling problem for a long time. I think there's some big drug cartel over here they're trying to crack down on. It's been going on for years!"

Sue wasn't sure whether she wanted to continue this conversation. For all she knew, as normal as she seemed, this woman could be some bat-shit lunatic looking for attention and concocting stories just to get an audience. From the look on the woman's face, it seemed to Sue that she could read her mind.

"Oh I know it probably seems a bit far fetched. I mean it's a great family holiday destination after all". She lowered her voice again. "But I've been coming over here for years. I've got friends here and they've told me all about it. Believe me, they've got no reason to lie about something like that."

Sue took this in before considering whether she wanted to carry on the conversation. "Well if that's the case, have they caught anybody yet?"

The woman sat back, an exasperated look on her face. "Of course not!" She made it seem as though it was the most obvious answer in the world.

"But surely security is pretty tight at airports now, especially after 911!" Sue gestured.

The woman laughed, a sarcastic laugh. "That's because they haven't got the bloody brains to realise that no idiot would try smuggling drugs onto an aeroplane. Shit, we've all seen the film 'Midnight Express'."

"Well how do they get them in then?" For a minute Sue could see by the incredulous look the woman gave her that she thought she was at best naive, at worst an idiot.

"You have seen Cyprus on a map, haven't you?" The woman's voice had a slight tone of condescenion.

"Of course I have" Sue almost snapped back.

"So you know that it's an island which means it has a wide coastline with no borders."

"Well yes" said Sue as she suddenly realised what the woman was getting at.

"And with a 400-mile coastline, with the best will in the world there's no way the Cypriot authorities can guard the entire coast."

"Oh, I didn't think of that" said Sue.

"And when you have Turkey to the North and the Middle East right next door, you've got a whole series of routes coming in from everywhere with everything from hash to heroin." The woman seemed to be enjoying her informative lecture.

"Blimey, I wish I'd known that before we came over. I'm not sure I would have chosen to have a holiday here if that's the case." Sue seemed a little unsettled.

"Oh, you've got nothing to worry about. Cyprus is perfectly safe for families. Hell, it's safer than England. Every country has its drugs problems. You don't honestly think the UK is drug free do you?"

"Well no, of course not" said Sue. "But I just wouldn't have thought ....."

"That a holiday location would be a haven for drug smugglers. I mean of course you don't see it on the streets. But there are specific areas and the authorities have been trying to weed out the heads of the cartels for years. The trouble is they're too bloody clever!"

Sue suddenly wondered how this woman knew so much about these cartels. She'd mentioned that her friends had told her. Could it be that her friends were involved somehow?

Again the woman seemed to know what Sue was thinking. "Oh don't look so worried, I wouldn't know one end of a joint from another. Hell, I threw up the first time I tried a cigarette and never did it again. My boyfriend thought it was hysterically funny."

"Funny?" said Sue. "Why?"

"Because he was the swine who persuaded me to have a cigarette. He'd smoked a couple of times and told me it was fine. He said I'd enjoy it."

"And then he laughed at you? Sounds like a bit of a shit to me" said Sue, almost with a tone of disgust in her voice.

"Oh he was lovely really. He just used to like winding me up. Oh I gave him as good as I got though. We were always winding each other up."

"Are you still in touch with him?" quizzed Sue.

The woman's facial expression suddenly changed. She looked sad, she looked weary. "Sadly no, I lost touch with him years ago."

"You don't know if he still lives in the same area?" asked Sue.

"Oh no, he won't. We met out here. Both our Dads were in the RAF – so we were what was known as scaly brats".

"Scaly brats?" said Sue, puzzled.

"Yes, it was a name they gave RAF kids. Something about how the Father would go up the scales when they started a family."

"And you said you met him here, in Cyprus?"

"Yes, thats' right". The woman's demeanour seemed to perk up a bit. "This was in the early seventies. Our Dads were both stationed at Akrotiri, but we lived in Limassol. We went to school together at St. Johns. He was in the year above me. Dear old Alan, I wonder where he is now. Probably got a wife and kids. Hell, he could even have grandkids."

Sue suddenly looked thoughtful. "Oh that's interesting."

"Interesting?" the woman quizzed.

"Yes. It's a strange coincidence, but Alan's Dad was in the RAF and they were stationed in Cyprus as well at one point. I'm sure it was in the early seventies wasn't it Alan? Where was your Dad stationed?"

There was a moment's silence. Alan spoke quietly. "Akrotiri."

Although Alan was hidden behind his seat, the woman looked curiously toward him. "That's funny. I only knew one Alan in the whole school" she said. "Alan Baylock was his name."

Alan turned around and looked at the woman. "Hello Becky."

Alan couldn't tell who looked more surprised, Sue or the woman he called Becky.

"Alan? Alan? Is it really you? My god, it is. You look older obviously, but I'd recognise you anywhere."

"How have you been?" Alan's voice seemed almost remorseful.

"Oh my god, I can't believe it. After all this time. Who'd have thought?" The woman seemed to ignore his question. "How have you been? Sorry, we haven't been introduced properly."

Alan seemed a little hesitant but felt obliged to carry out the necessary introductions. "This is my wife Sue. Sue, this is Becky." He decided that using the term ex-girlfriend might not be the best thing to do in front of Sue. "We knew each other in Cyprus."

Becky seemed to pick up on Alan's hesitancy to use the phrase 'girlfriend' and nodded in agreement. "Yes, that's right. We did."

Sue didn't seem to be particularly perturbed to learn of the history between Alan and Becky and came out with the proverbial elephant in the room. "You were boyfriend and girlfriend? Well there's no need to hide it. We've all had previous boyfriends and girlfriends before we tied the knot."

Even though Sue seemed to accept this situation, both Alan and Becky picked up on a slight hint of jealousy.

"Well it was a long time ago" she said.

"Yes" added Alan, that regretful tone in his voice again. "We did write to each other for a while, but then you suddenly stopped."

Perhaps this last statement gave Sue some comfort, thinking that Becky had lost interest in Alan, but she was soon to learn that this was not the case.

Becky sighed and looked as forlorn as Alan sounded. "I'm sorry Alan. Truly I am. It's just that .... well .... something happened and ..... well it just threw me a bit."

"You don't have to explain" said Alan, although the tone in his voice begged an answer to a long unanswered question.

"It was Tom. You remember Tom."

Alan's look suddenly changed. "Oh yes, I remember Tom".

Sue looked at the two puzzled, as if expecting somebody to let her in on the secret as to who this mysterious Tom character was.

"Oh I know he could be a bit of a pain in the arse at times. He was loud and gobby, but he wasn't vicious Alan. He really didn't have a bad bone in his body."

"Who's Tom?" asked Sue.

"That was my older Brother" replied Becky, her tone definitely changing – the sadness in her voice couldn't be disguised.

"I won't deny he used to get on my nerves at times" said Alan.

"I know you didn't like him, but he really wasn't as bad as you thought he was. I think he was a bit jealous of you to be honest. You were always so bright and hey, you weren't bad looking in those days". Her tone picked up as she gave Alan a quick smile.

"Well he sure didn't make any secret of the fact that he didn't like me" said Alan.

"I think he resented the fact that Dad seemed to like you more than him. Dad was always on at him, asking him why couldn't he get his head down in his school books like you. I know it sounds like a corny thing to say, but I think I was the only one who really understood him. He had a good heart, he was just a bit misguided."

Alan was about to say something but a little voice in his head told him to curb his consternation.

"Anyway" continued Becky. "It's all water under the bridge now." She paused a moment and Alan detected a break in her voice. "He's dead". She lowered her head, determined that Sue and Alan wouldn't see the tears.

"Oh god, I'm sorry Becky, I didn't realise ....."

"It's ok Alan. You weren't to know."

"What happened to him?"

Becky had her head down and both Sue and Alan could hear her softly weeping. Between her sobs they both heard her say "he died in prison!"

Neither Alan or Sue knew what to say. The usual comment to make at a time like this was "I'm really sorry to hear that" and whilst they both thought it, there was a slight feeling of judgment after what they'd just learned.

"Oh you don't have to say anything" said Becky, drying her eyes with the tissue she was holding. "I know you're going to think I'm biased because I was his sister, but I swear to you Alan he was innocent." There was almost a tone of determined fury in her voice.

"What was he in prison for?" asked Alan.

Becky seemed to hesitate for a moment, as if she knew how her next statement would be taken. "Murder" she stammered. "But he didn't do it. I'm telling you now, he didn't do it. Nick was his best friend. They'd been friends for years."

"Murder?" said Sue, unable to hide her shock.

"Yes murder, and I've never seen such an example of a bloody kangeroo court! Evidence was withheld throughout the entire trial. I swear some of the defence team were receiving back-handers. Even my Dad knew he didn't do it, and Dad could be hard on Tom at the best of times."

This was a lot to take in, for both Sue and Alan. Sue because she was still in shock to discover an old flame of Alan's sitting behind them on a plane and then to be told that her Brother had died in prison. For Alan it stirred a lot of memories of happier times and subsequent unanswered questions as to why the girl he fell in love with all those years ago suddenly stopped writing to him. He always felt that Tom was a big mouth and a bit of a trouble maker but murder was a strong word and he wasn't sure that it fit the profile of this loud and petulant teenager that he'd known all those years ago.

Suddenly one of the cabin crew emerged from the front of the plane to announce that they would be taking off shortly and would everybody fasten their seat belt before going through the usual safety routine.

Once the plane was airborne, the conversation continued, but in a lighter manner.

"Look, I'm not going to bore you with the ins and outs of what happened to Tom. It's not fair on Sue as she's only just met me" said Becky. "Suffice to say that since he died, I've been speaking to a few people and following leads to see what I can find."

"But if he is innocent" replied Alan, "surely it's not going to help you now. It's only going to make you more resentful."

"Alan, I made a promise to Tom before he died that I'd find out who killed Nick. I'm not going to let him down."

"But what if .... what if ....."

"What if all roads lead to him still being guilty? I have pondered that but he's not. I've found a few snippets of information and I just need to put them together. God knows I've got enough time on my hands to pursue it now."

The next two hours were spent in superficial conversation about the holiday and what parts they enjoyed.

Becky seemed mindful of the fact that Sue might not appreciate her nose being put out of joint by this woman who'd previously had a history with Alan. If Alan veered off into a conversation that just included Becky and himself, she made sure to bring it right back to the present and a wife who had been sitting there trying to take in a whole new side to Alan's life.

The plane flew over London and as it almost skimmed the M25, the passengers sat making sure their seatbelts were firmly on, anticipating the screech of tyres on tarmac. A few slight jolts and gradually the plane slowed to a smooth stop. A few brief instructions from the cabin crew and the passengers began to get up from their seats. As Sue sat in the aisle seat, she got up before Alan and began to walk towards the front of the plan. Alan followed and suddenly felt a piece of paper being shoved into his hand. Becky had made sure to find the opportune moment when Sue wasn't looking. Alan gripped it tightly and put it into his pocket without looking.

They waited patiently in the airport lounge baggage reclaim for the suitcases to be taken off the plane and put onto the carousel, picking up their luggage before heading their separate ways.

"Well it's been lovely to see you again Alan, and to meet you Sue. You're a very lucky woman." Becky smiled.

"Nice to meet you too" said Sue, a slightly icy tone in her voice.

"Goodbye Becky. I hope you're right about Tom and find the answers you're looking for" said Alan.

"Don't you worry. I will. Take care." Becky looked at Alan before turning, quickly so he wouldn't see the tears in her eyes. Alan stared after her for a brief moment.

"Well" Sue interrupted. "That was a turn up for the books. Any other women you've got hidden away from me?"

"Oh Sue, don't be ridiculous, that was decades ago."

"Well she still seems to hold a flame for you."

"Nonsense. There's only one man she's focussed on – and he's dead."

"Perhaps" said Sue. "But a woman's intuition is never wrong."

They walked silently back to the car. Sue got into the passenger seat while Alan loaded the cases into the boot. As he was doing so, he quickly took the piece of paper out of his pocket and unfolded it. It read "It was so good to see you again Alan. I understand if you don't want to stay in contact, especially after what happened, but I'd love to speak to you again." She'd given an email address rather than a phone number. Well perhaps it was more discreet. Alan put the paper back into his pocket. Could this be the opportunity to get some real answers to the questions he'd asked all those years ago?

Chapter Two

"I won't be too long. Are you sure you don't want to come with me?" said Alan as he walked towards the front door.

"Don't be silly Alan, I told you that Phyllis and Ophelia are coming over today. I haven't seen them for ages and we're way overdue a good catch up." Sue's answer was brusque.

"I thought that neither of them drove. Oh no wait, let me guess, they're flying here on their broomsticks."

"I'll treat that remark with the contempt it deserves and not dignify it with a response."

"Oooooh, get her – been working for a law firm so long she's all wrapped up in lawyer speak."

"Yes, and I can get a good solicitor to throw the book at you. Now bugger off and leave me some space for a girly afternoon. If you're nice to me, I might not ask Phyllis for a voodoo doll of you that I can stick pins in."

"You can stick it to me anytime, honey child."

"Alan – get out!"

"I'm going – but I'll be back."

"Yes like a bad virus."

"Always the compliments with you Sue Baylock."

"And always the sarcasm with you AL-AN Baylock!"

"But I do it so well. Anyway, I'm off now. Enjoy your witchy meeting and erm, please, no bat soup for dinner – I tend to find the wings get stuck between my teeth."

Alan closed the front door before he could hear Sue's retort of "I'll stick something between your teeth – a bunch of fives!"

The house went quiet and Sue suddenly realised that she'd been having niggling little thoughts over the last few days. What was it? That woman, Becky. She and Alan had been an item way back in the early seventies. But they'd still kept in contact for a while. Yes, contact had been lost but that wasn't due to any diminished feelings between them – it was because Becky's Brother had been sent to prison for murder. Murder – that was such a strong word. How much could Sue believe of what she'd said? All this talk of drug cartels and real murderers lurking in the shadows all seemed a bit far fetched. Yet it had somehow managed to hook Alan back in. He hadn't been the same since they'd come back from holiday. Today was the first time he'd been slightly more upbeat, but even so, he didn't seem to talk to Sue as much these days. He'd go onto his computer for hours and – had she imagined it – when she walked into his work room, he seemed to switch screens quickly. Could he have found Becky online? Of course it was possible – anything was possible. Sue tried to distract herself by thinking about other things. She glanced at the clock. She knew the bus would be due along in five minutes and it was a short walk to the bus stop from the house. Sue had offered to go and pick Phyllis and Ophelia up, but they insisted that they came on the bus.

"It's such strange energy these days Sue" Phyllis had said to her. "People are so different, I should stay away from it but I feel I need to observe it to see if the planet is evolving."

As much as Sue loved Phyllis, she took her new age ideas with a pinch of salts. Once in a while though, Phyllis would pull a couple of her tarot cards and tell Sue things that she was unaware of which eventually transpired, but then again, as Alan said, Phyllis and Sue had known each other a long time and it wouldn't be that difficult to second guess what was going on in Sue's life.

Sue heard a car pull up outside. Surely Alan hadn't forgotten something only to return. She looked outside, not to see Alan's car, but another car that she was very familiar with. It was Robert. What was he doing here? Neither she nor Alan had spoken to Robert for a long time. She looked on as she realised that both Phyllis and Ophelia were with him. So they hadn't taken the bus after all. How strange. What was going on? As she saw Phyllis walking down the garden path towards the door, she awaited the familiar sound of the doorbell as she went to welcome her guests in. As she opened the door, there stood Phyllis in one of her traditional long dresses, very colourful, and not necessarily the product of a bygone 60s age with the fashions ever changing, coming back in and going out.

"Hello sweetheart" said Phyllis as she gave Sue a big hug. Sue held onto Phyllis tightly.

"God, I didn't realise how much I've missed you" said Sue, fighting back a tear.

"Tell me about it, it's been too long. I haven't seen you since you went on holiday. How did it go?"

"Oh come in and I'll tell you all about it. Hello Ophelia, how are you?"

A second round of hugs as Sue seemed to notice Ophelia giving her an unusually tight hug and looking her in the eye. "Are you ok Sue?"

Sue was taken aback. "Well of course I am. Why ever wouldn't I be?"

Ophelia said nothing but gave Sue a concerned look.

"Come inside. I'll put the kettle on."

As Ophelia followed Phyllis into the lounge, Robert came towards Sue and gave her his usual semi-formal hug. "Hello Sue. How are you?"

"Well I'm fine Robert, but I wasn't expecting to see you. What brings you here?"

"Well I'd been speaking to Phyllis who told me she and Ophelia were coming over to see you and I thought I'd pop round to see how you were both doing." He seemed to hesitate for a moment. "I just wanted to make sure you were ok as well, you know, after what happened in Cornwall."

"Oh Robert, don't be silly, I'm fine. I haven't had any symptoms since then."

Sue and Alan had been on holiday in Cornwall when Sue had acquired a strange virus that nearly threatened her life and shortly afterwards, she'd been kidnapped, only to be found frighteningly close to death.

"I was just concerned about any long term effects, that's all."

"I promise you, I haven't had any. Now come in and I'll put the kettle on."

Robert made his way into the lounge and Sue prepared some tea. Fortunately she'd remembered to keep a small variety of herbal teas in the cupboard as both Ophelia and Phyllis only drank the "hippie variety" as Alan called it.

"Well I must say, this is really nice. It does seem a long time since we've met up like this. It's just a shame Alan wasn't here. I'm sure he'll be sorry he missed you." Sue's comment wasn't directed at anybody in particular although Phyllis and Ophelia both knew that it would have been aimed mainly at

Robert as they instinctively knew how Alan felt about their 'spiritual eccentricities' as he described them to Sue.

"How is Alan? Has he finally given up work yet?" asked Robert.

"Not yet, but he's got a retirement date in mind, though god knows what he's going to do with himself all day if he does retire. Then again ....." Sue's voice fell away.

"Then again?" Robert picked up where Sue had trailed off.

"He may find certain things to keep him occupied."

"Like what? Gardening? DIY? Hacking into the Kremlin to discover all sorts of nefarious secrets." Robert's mood was jovial, trying to make light of what he felt seemed a strange uncertainty for Sue.

"Well maybe. Then again, he could go chasing after long lost loves." The sentence completely slipped off Sue's tongue – she hadn't meant to say that.

"Oh?" Robert frowned.

Sue smiled, a false smile. "Just joking. No he'll probably get himself entangled with the lawnmower. I swear he doesn't know one end from the other."

"That was a strange thing to say Sue" observed Ophelia. "I wonder what made you say that?"

"Nothing honestly. Just a joke about him getting older. You know what men are like when they get older. Start realising they're not young anymore."

Phyllis looked at Sue. "Sweetheart, I've known you a long time and I've got to say, it's not like you to say something so off the cuff without it having some sort of connotation. What's going on?"

Sue suddenly felt extremely uncomfortable. She felt as though she was in the middle of the Spanish Inquisition with three of the most notorious Conquistadors present, psychologically grilling her over hot embers.

"Honestly, take no notice of me. It's just a silly thing I said" she protested.

"But you did say it" persisted Phyllis. "Tell me the truth Sue, is Alan seeing somebody?"

"No Phyllis he's not honestly. Honestly."

"Did something happen in Cyprus while you were on

holiday?" Phyllis was like a dog with a bone.

"No, honestly no."

"So when then?" Ophelia added.

"My goodness, this seems to be turning into a murder enquiry." Sue suddenly went cold as she heard herself saying the word 'murder'.

Robert, Ophelia and Phyllis all observed this reaction and looked at each other.

"Oh for goodness sake it's nothing" said Sue, becoming more flustered. "We just met this strange woman on the plane coming home."

Three pairs of ears pricked up and Sue could feel six eyes piercing into hers.

"Oh alright. I'll tell you the story, but really there's absolutely nothing to tell." She then proceeded to discuss the incident on the plane coming home when they had seemingly bumped into an old flame of Alan's called Becky. She described Becky's fanciful story about a major drug cartel in Cyprus and then about her Brother dying in prison after serving a life sentence, allegedly as an innocent man.

There was a slight pause as the three others took all this information in.

"Well that's quite a story" said Phyllis. "I would hardly call it nothing. And you say that she and Alan were old flames?"

"Oh yes, but we're talking about the early 70s. I mean they did lose contact."

"They lost contact" echoed Robert, "but you said it was because of what happened to this Becky's Brother."

"Yes, that's right" said Sue. She was beginning to curse herself for her slip of the tongue in mentioning all of this.

"How long ago did you say this incident occured?" asked Robert.

"Oh I don't know exactly. I know that Alan's family came back from Cyprus in '73 and her family returned in '74, just before the outbreak of the war there."

"War?" said Phyllis startled.

"Oh yes" said Robert. The Turkish invasion in July 1974. It's what caused the island to be split between Turkey and Greece. It's still like that today, sadly.

"Yes it is sad" agreed Sue. "It's a lovely country. I must admit I would have been more than happy to go back there on holiday if it wasn't for this drugs cartel thing she mentioned. It did put me off a bit."

"Oh Sue, that sort of thing is happening everywhere, it's not peculiar to Cyprus" Robert reassured her. "Still, this murder story intrigues me. That is of course if she's not making it up."

"That's the thing, I honestly don't think she was. She got really upset when she mentioned it. I honestly don't think she was putting it on."

"And you think that she and Alan may still be in contact?" asked Robert.

"Well I didn't seem them exchange any phone numbers, but let's be honest, it's easy enough to track people down on the internet these days if you know what you're doing."

"That's true" said Robert. "I would like to look into it a little bit more, though obviously I'd be discreet. Sounds intriguing. I wonder if her Brother really was innocent or whether she's just kidding herself because she doesn't want to face the truth."

"That's what I thought" agreed Sue. "Whatever the case, Alan's definitely been different since we got back."

"I'd like to do some energy work with him, but I know he'd refuse to work with us" said Ophelia.

"Well yes, I can't argue with that" said Sue. "Alan's life view is definitely on the concrete and matter-of-fact school of thought. No time for the abstract."

"Well if he ever comes around, let me know and I can do a reading on him."

"Try doing one on Chris as well if you like Ophelia. He's suddenly gone all middle distance on us too."

"Oh?" Ophelia looked puzzled.

"Ruth tends to come and visit us on her own these days. We haven't seen Chris for ages. She always makes excuses for him, says he's busy with 'projects', although she did confide in me that she thought something was wrong."

"I hope he's not ill" said Phyllis, not wanting to think the worst.

"I don't know. Present company aside, I'm beginning to think that all men are a total mystery and I seem to repel them these days" said Sue semi-jokingly.

"Oh rubbish" said Phyllis. "You're a fabulous babe magnet and what man wouldn't want you?"

"I love your support Phyllis, but I'm in my late fifties for god's sake, I'm hardly likely to turn heads anymore."

"Look, if this Becky can still find Alan attractive after all this time, what's stopping you?"

Sue couldn't argue with Phyllis's line of reasoning, but decided that she'd had enough flattery for one day.

The conversation took a lighter tone until Robert, Ophelia and Phyllis decided it was time to go.

"Oh by the way Sue, didn't you mention something about dropping off something at Ruth's?" said Phyllis upon getting up to leave.

"Oh yes, that's right. There was an old law book I managed to 'obtain' from work that she wanted to look at. I can take it round tomorrow."

"Well it's only a short diversion of the route home" said Robert. "We could drop it off for you."

"Oh I don't want you going out of your way" protested Sue.

"Don't be silly" insisted Robert. "It's less than half a mile away from the route I take. We can drop it off for you."

"Well if it's not too much trouble" said Sue. "But please don't feel obliged."

"No trouble at all" Robert reassured her.

Sue took a book from a cabinet drawer and handed it to Robert. He observed the title.

"That looks like exciting reading I've got to say" said Robert.

"Something to do with her new job. All legal jargon, means nothing to me, but she seemed very keen to get hold of it."

"And you acquired it from work?" Phyllis looked dubious.

"Don't look at me like that Phyllis. Working for a London law firm doesn't pay as well as it used to, so I allow myself certain perks like letting books fall into my handbag and non-stop use of their printers. They bloody owe me that much".

Phyllis chuckled. "Good for you kiddo. Down with the

establishment!" Phyllis began to re-enact the protests of her sixties mis-spent youth which lifted the previously somber mood considerably. They all said their goodbyes and Sue closed the door, with a sense of sadness, at her three friends. The people she felt she could depend on more than anybody.

Ophelia slunk into the back seat as both Robert and Phyllis got into the front of the car and Robert started the engine.

"I think you turn second right as we go along the main road" said Phyllis. "I'm sure Chris and Ruth live down that road somewhere."

After a few minor wrong turns, they finally found the house where Chris and Ruth lived. As before, Phyllis was the first to get out of the car and promptly walked towards Ruth's front door and rang the bell. Ophelia and Robert followed shortly.

Ruth answered the door and seemed surprised to see them. "Oh hello" she said. "I'm sorry, I've just got out of the shower. Do come in."

The three followed Ruth into the living room and she wrapped the towel around her head more firmly.

"Sorry to intrude on you" said Phyllis. "We haven't come to stop. We've just come from your Mum's and she said she had a book that you wanted." Phyllis handed the book to Ruth.

"Oh that's fabulous" she said, as she took it gratefully from Phyllis. "That'll come in so useful for my new job."

"How is the new job?" asked Phyllis. "And how's Chris doing?"

Ophelia darted Phyllis a look as if to say "that was a sneaky move."

"Oh the job's going fine. A lot to learn and very different from what I was doing before. But it's a nice team of people and the work's more interesting."

Robert, Ophelia and Phyllis noticed that Ruth didn't follow up on the enquiry about Chris. Ophelia persisted.

"Is Chris ok?"

Ruth's eyes dropped. Was that a small sigh she let out? "Oh he's fine."

"That didn't sound very convincing" said Phyllis, trying

to phrase it in a joking way.

"Oh, has Mum said something to you?"

"No ......" Phyllis began.

"Oh Phyllis you don't have to hide it. I know he hasn't been exactly, shall we say, very present these days when it comes to visiting Mum and Dad. I've got to admit he has been very quiet recently, I mean more quiet than usual. Not the most talkative of men, my Chris at the best of times, but he does seem to be keeping himself to himself these days."

"He's not ill is he?" asked Phyllis.

Ophelia darted Phyllis a disapproving look as if to say "that was tactless". The look definitely wasn't missed by Phyllis.

"I don't know. I don't think so. I'm sure I'd pick up on it if something was physically wrong. It's just .... it's just .... I don't know".

"Oh, has somebody had an accident?" said Ophelia, almost as if to divert the subject from Ruth's obvious discomfort.

"An accident? What do you mean?" asked Ruth.

"Well there's a tissue here with blood on it by the sofa" observed Ophelia.

"Oh lord, I forgot to pick that up and throw it away. Chris has been having nose bleeds recently. He seems to get them when he's stressed. It must have dropped on the floor."

Ruth picked up the bloody tissue and took it to the kitchen to discard it in the bin.

"Oh, while I remember" she said, walking back into the living room. "Mum asked me to get some soap from that craft shop in town for you Phyllis. Wait here, it's upstairs. I'll just go and get it."

Ruth walked upstairs and Ophelia suddenly disappeared swiftly into the kitchen. Robert and Phyllis looked at each other in puzzlement, awaiting Ophelia's return. Shortly afterwards, she returned with a semi-guilty, semi-self-satisfied look on her face.

Phyllis was just about to ask her what she'd been doing when Ruth came downstairs again.

"I must admit, it was so lovely I even bought some for myself." She gave several bars of soap to Phyllis.

"Oh Ruth, that's so kind of you. I love this soap. You can't get it anywhere except that shop and I rarely get to go down there. How much do I owe you?"

"Oh don't be silly Phyllis. I don't want anything."

"But it's not cheap I must give you something."

"Phyllis, please, take it as a gift from me. A thank you for being an absolute rock for Mum. You have no idea how much you've done for her. You've been there way more than I have, which I do feel guilty about."

"Oh thank you Ruth." Phyllis gave Ruth a big hug. "It will definitely be used in my self-indulgent pampering moments, I can tell you. Smell this Ophelia, it's absolutely gorgeous."

Ophelia took a sniff of the soap and the expression on her face was one of approval.

"Don't worry Robert" said Ruth. "We won't ask you to sniff it. I know you think it's probably very girly."

"I'm not saying a word" said Robert, giving out a light chuckle.

The three companions said goodbye to Ruth as she saw them to the front door. She waved as they got into the car and Robert beeped on the horn before heading off.

"Ophelia" said Phyllis.

"Yes?" replied Ophelia.

"Why did you sneak off to the kitchen like that?"

Ophelia said nothing but proceeded to open her handbag. She took out a tissue and carefully unwrapped it, only to reveal a bloody tissue hidden inside.

"Is that the tissue that Ruth threw into the bin?" said Phyllis, puzzled.

"It is indeed" said Ophelia.

"But why would you want to take that?" asked Phyllis.

"Well, I know it's probably not very moral, and I'm not saying we would do anything with it ....." Ophelia began.

"But?" quipped Phyllis.

"Well, if Chris has been out of sorts recently, we could put our moral objectives aside and use the tissue to dissolve the blood and use it with Robert's machine to see if we can get any answers as to his recent odd behaviour."

"Ophelia, that's very naughty" said Phyllis.

"But bloody brilliant" added Robert. It wasn't often

Robert swore and the two women looked at him in surprise.

"I'm not saying we would" he added. "But at least it gives us the option".

Perhaps they would get to the bottom of Chris's reclusive behaviour and find out if anything was really wrong.

Chapter Three

"Hello Alan,

It was so lovely to receive your email yesterday. I must admit, I wasn't sure whether you'd contact me when I gave you my email address and I would have understood fully if you didn't want to. I really am sorry that I stopped writing to you but as I mentioned to you, Tom's best friend had just been murdered and he was actually standing over Nick's dead body. I know you're going to assume the worst and I can understand why, but if you knew all the details of the case, you'd know that Tom was completely innocent. I'm sure you can understand that it was a pretty horrendous time for all of us. Mum was absolutely devastated and I'm sure it sent her to an early grave. Even Dad took it really badly, even though he and Tom had their differences. I tried to support Tom in every way I could. I know you didn't like him, but he always looked after me as his kid sister. After I received your last letter, I was determined I was going to write to you but by the time I eventually did, my letter was sent back in the post. I think you must have moved and they didn't have a forwarding address for you. I explained everything in that letter but I realised it was too late, and to my absolute despair, I knew that it would be difficult to find you. I did ask Dad if he could ask around to see if you'd moved to another RAF camp but I learned that your Dad had done his 22 years service and retired. Who knows what might have happened if circumstances had been different. I never stopped loving you in all that time. I appreciate you might not want to stay in contact, being that you're married – I did get the impression your wife wasn't too keen on me, that's why I tried to keep the conversation casual.

I would love to speak to you again Alan. If you do want to talk, you can contact me on the number at the top of this email. Again, I know it might be awkward as you're married, but it was such a strange twist of fate that we met on the plane like that. What are the odds. Anyway Piggy, I'll love you and leave you for now.

Always in my heart.

Becky.

The word 'Piggy' struck Alan like a bolt of lighting and brought with it a host of memories cascading into his mind. That was Becky's pet name for him back in Cyprus. Didn't she write it on something? What was it now? He suddenly remembered. Sue was in the kitchen preparing dinner but he closed the email down just in case. He walked up the hallway and took the staircase up to the spare room. In the wardrobe where they had found Ian Pemberton's device, he'd stored an old case of his vinyl singles. He pulled the box out and searched through the records – and there – he found it. He pulled the record out and written in small and neat handwriting on the centre of the record "You win smart arse. Love you always Piggy. Your Becky xxx" Alan suddenly remembered. They'd had a bet on two records going to number one and said that whoever lost the bet would have to buy the winning record for the other person. Alan won the bet and this was his prize. He chuckled slightly as he remembered the event.

"Alan, dinner's ready."

He heard Sue calling, although her voice was faint. She must have gone into his work room to look for him. He was relieved that he'd closed his emails down. He slipped the record back into the box and closed the lid.

"Just coming". He walked downstairs and helped Sue put the food out.

Suddenly the phone began to ring.

"I'll get it" said Sue.

"Oh just ignore it Sue. Whoever it is can leave a message and we can call them back."

"But it might be urgent" said Sue. She looked at the number on the call display. "Oh it's Phyllis."

"Well then it can't be urgent unless that stupid bloody cat of hers has got itself stuck in the toilet."

"Not funny Alan. You never know. Go on, you start eating, I'll be with you in a minute."

Alan rolled his eyes. No doubt Phyllis was calling Sue to tell her she'd found this really amazing crystal that took you into the fifth, sixth, seventh or eighth dimension of supreme consciousness where you can park your arse on a big lotus petal and contemplate your toe nails in shamanic bliss for eternity. He heard Sue give the occasional "uh-huh – yes – uh-huh. Oh really? Oh, ok. Oh well – uh-huh. Well possibly." When she finally hung up and came through to eat, Alan couldn't help feeling that she looked a bit stunned.

"What's wrong? Has the supreme feline from another galaxy finally slipped off it's mortal coil and used it's final ninth life?"

Sue looked at Alan puzzled and then realised what he had said. "Er, oh no."

"Well what is it then?"

"Nothing, honestly. Just Phyll talking about the usual stuff."

"So she hasn't managed to tempt you into taking some guided meditation where you can meet your power insect?"

"Don't be like that Alan." Sue seemed to snap at Alan.

"Sorry, I was just joking."

"It's ok. Let's just eat."

Alan instinctively felt that something was wrong but couldn't work out what it was.

Unbeknownst to him, Phyllis had called Sue to tell her that Ophelia had whisked away a bloody tissue belonging to Chris and Robert, Ophelia and her had been debating as to whether they should use the device to find out why he was acting so strange. Ophelia and Robert had discussed the moral problem of prying into Chris and Ruth's private affairs, but Phyllis was of the view that if it was a serious issue that was bothering him, the sooner they got to the bottom of it, the better. She'd asked Sue's opinion and Sue had responded that she was of the same view as Robert and Ophelia. What Phyllis didn't realise was that Sue was worried about them finding out that she'd shared an intimate night with Chris and if it all came out into the open, the ramifications all around would be devastating. How could she persuade Robert not to pursue this line of inquiry? If she was too vocal, Robert might instinctively know that "the lady doth protest too much" and see a big red flag in Sue's concerns. How could she deal with this situation. Could she get hold of the tissue somehow and destroy it? Who had it? Robert? Ophelia? Certainly Phyllis didn't.

"Did you hear me?"

"What?" Sue looked up at Alan.

"What's wrong Sue? You haven't been listening to a word I've said. You're mind's totally somewhere else?"

"Oh sorry, I'm just a bit tired, that's all."

Again, Alan found Sue's excuse hard to believe but knew that if he pursued it further, it would probably lead to an argument. They began to clear the dinner plates up and Sue began taking them into the kitchen. Just then the phone rang again.

"I'll get it this time" said Alan. Sue almost protested but as she had plates in her hand and Alan was nearest to the phone, it seemed reasonable that he should be the one to take the call. "Oh hello Robert. How are you?" Sue was preoccupied in the kitchen and didn't hear the conversation. Robert had just told Alan exactly the same thing that Phyllis had told Sue, although Alan was unaware of it at the time. "Listen Robert, I don't know what's happened, but Phyllis called Sue a while ago and when she hung up, she was acting very strange. I don't know what Phyllis told her, but if it's exactly the same as what you've just told me, why would Sue be so concerned? I would have thought she'd be relieved at the chance of getting to the bottom of what's bothering Chris."

"Yes, that's what I would have thought" said Robert. "I can understand the moral dilemma, but Sue's reaction does seem odd if it's just the moral issue she's worried about." Robert paused for a minute and then spoke again. "Look Alan, I think it's probably best that you don't mention what I've just told you to Sue. Just tell her I was asking you if she was still feeling ok. Don't mention any of this."

"Ok, but I can't help feeling a bit bemused by it all. She might be worried about finding out that Chris is cheating on Ruth. I could understand why she'd be upset if that's the case."

"Maybe" said Robert. "Best not to say anything just in case."

They said goodbye and Robert put the phone down. He then picked up the phone again and dialed a number. He waited as he heard the tone and then a woman's voice answered.

"Hello?"

"Hello Ophelia. It's Robert."

"Oh hello Robert."

"Look, something strange has just happened. I just called Alan to tell him and Sue about the bloody tissue that you took out of Ruth's kitchen bin. He told me that Phyllis had already called Sue earlier to tell her the same thing and after the call, Sue was acting very strange. Alan thought it might be that she was worried that Chris was having an extra-marital affair, but I've got a niggling feeling that something's not right."

"Funny you should say that. I know that you don't follow mine and Phyllis's belief, but the other night when you dropped me off I shuffled my tarot cards and three fell out. The Moon, The Queen of Swords reversed and the Seven of Swords. To me that indicates deception – and an older woman is at the centre of it. I don't want to cast aspersions but ......"

"Well I'll be honest and say I don't believe in things like tarot, but I did have the same feeling as you. I'm not sure what's happened but Chris seems to be avoiding Sue and Alan at the moment and there's got to be a reason for it."

"But what can we do Robert? We've both discussed the moral issue of Chris and Ruth's privacy. I know Phyllis is keen to look into it, but that doesn't sit easily with me."

"I agree with you Ophelia, but I can't help feeling curious about the whole business."

"The only thing I can suggest is that we go ahead and try to find somebody who has Chris's blood group who we can trust and see what we can find out."

"Well I have to say I'm one step ahead of you there."

"Oh?"

"When you gave me the tissue, I had it tested and Chris is the same blood group as me."

Ophelia paused for a moment. Then she used that tone of voice which sounded like the wise female oracles of the ages. "Robert, I can't help thinking that we're meant to look into it.

What we do with the information, if anything is another matter. But fate seems to have provided us with the opportunity to investigate this."

"You might be right, but I would add one caveat" said Robert.

"Which is?"

"I know you're not going to like me for saying this, but we don't tell Phyllis. Don't get me wrong, I have great affection for Phyllis and I know that she is both yours and Sue's best friend, but I feel she's too close to Sue and she may say something inadvertantly without thinking. I'd rather keep the lid on this until we've had a chance to investigate."

"I think you're right Robert. I definitely think you're right. Which begs the question ....."

"Where and when do we carry this out?"

"Are you free at all this week?"

"I'm free on Wednesday evening."

"I could come and pick you up and bring you to my house. You know how to use the device don't you?"

"I recall vaguely but I know that once you take me through the instructions again I'll pick it up fairly quickly."

"Good. Ok, let's say Wednesday then. Obviously don't let Phyllis or Sue know. Or even Alan for that matter. Let's keep this under wraps until we've found something."

"Right, I've put Wednesday in the diary."

"There's also another line of enquiry I'm following which is more to do with Alan."

"Oh?"

"It's about this Becky and her Brother. I haven't told Alan but I'm going to see if I can find out anything about this murder. I want to see if this woman is just trying to play the sympathy card with Alan or whether there's anything in it."

"Good idea. I'll use my own methods to see if I can find anything out."

"Just as long as you don't come floating through my walls after midnight."

Ophelia laughed. "Only on the full moon Robert, only on the full moon."

Robert laughed and bade Ophelia farewell. "Ok, until Wednesday, take care and I'll see you then."

"Goodnight Robert, see you then."

Chapter Four

Alan turned into the car park that was just off the town centre. He felt slightly guilty as well as nervous as he'd spoken to Becky on the phone and they had arranged to meet up for a coffee in town when Sue was at work. He felt paranoid that somebody who knew him would walk by and see him with Becky. Sue had told him that Ophelia and Phyllis were attending a workshop on healing remedies and so that was two people he didn't have to worry about. Both Ruth and Chris were at work, so who else could bump into him? Robert perhaps? Possibly, although highly unlikely as Robert had mentioned several times in the past that he didn't like town centres, especially if they had big shopping malls. He walked towards the coffee shop where he could see Becky waiting for him.

"Hello Becky, it's good to see you again although I do feel a bit guilty."

"I'm sorry Alan. I really wanted to see you again too – I just wanted to put you in the picture about what happened with Tom. Not just for that reason of course, but nobody will listen to my side of the story, and with Mum and Dad both dead now, I'm the only one who can really carry on looking for the truth."

"Look, I'll be honest with you. I'll listen to what you have to say but I'm going to keep an open mind. If I think there's enough to convince me in what you tell me, then I'll give it serious consideration. On the other hand ....."

"Don't worry Alan, I'll be truthful with you, I won't embelish a thing and I'll see what conclusion you come to."

"Sounds fair to me. Now let's go and get caffeine to wake up the brain cells."

They found a small table in the corner of the coffee shop with two chairs and sat down with their coffee.

"I can't tell you how much I regret not writing to you sooner. I could have explained everything back then but things were such a haze for a long time. I felt as though I was living in a dream, no, a nightmare, and what with trying to support Tom and Mum, things got a bit frenetic. Dad wasn't much help. Said he'd complain to this party and that party, but he didn't really have a clue and in the end, Tom only really had me."

"I'm sorry to hear about your Mum and Dad. I can understand it must have been a hell of a shock for them."

"Not just the shock, the sheer unbelievability of it. It was a complete farce. The whole trial ..... the defence team were incompetent, the Judge was an idiot, the ...."

"Hang on, hang on" said Alan, "let's just start at the beginning. Give me some context."

"Yes of course" said Becky. "Sorry, I did go off on one a bit but it's just been so frustrating all these years."

"Ok, what actually happened?"

"Right, well first of all I'll tell you about the murder of a girl called Lesley. Apparently she was Nick's girlfriend, though I never met her. Well one night she turns up dead by the side of a row of garages near the park. Of course Nick was upset. Well, upset would be too mild a word for it. He was bloody furious. He told Tom that he knew who'd done it but wouldn't say anymore."

"Was this a long time before this Nick was murdered?"

"Only about three weeks. The thing was that one night Nick was in the pub and he'd been drinking quite a bit. Tom came in to join him later and Nick started getting mouthy about how he was going to get the person who did it. He'd mentioned something about somebody who was dealing drugs and before she was murdered, this Lesley had told Nick that she'd found out about this drug ring and she was going to spill the beans on whoever was at the head of it. Next thing, she's dead. Nick then tells Tom that he knew who the person was and he was going to get his revenge. At some point the conversation got a bit heated and Tom was heard saying to Nick "if you're not careful, you're going to end up dead" before leaving the pub. The thing is Alan, as Tom told me, he wasn't threatening Nick, he was trying to warn Nick to be careful. He was his best friend for God sake, there's no way he'd ever do anything to harm Nick."

"So I'm assuming that Lesley told Nick about the drug ring and that's how he knew who was involved."

"Yes, that's right."

"But how did she find out about it?"

"That I don't know. Tom never got to the bottom of it.

But the next thing is, a few days after they'd had that conversation in the pub, Tom got a phone call from Nick one evening and he was terrified. He told Tom to come around as soon as he could because, and I quote "they're going to fucking kill me Tom". He told Tom that he daren't leave the house because they'd be outside waiting for him. He said he couldn't call the police but he didn't say why. Anyway, Tom could tell by the sound of Nick's voice that he was terrified. So he got in his car and raced around there. But here's the problem with the police's story about Tom committing the murder. Nick's house was about a 30-minute drive from Tom and on the way, he got pulled in by the police for speeding. They gave him a breathalyser test, and when that was negative, they gave him a speeding fine. This all added a further ten minutes to his journey. He told them about the telephone call but apparently one of the policeman said that if they believed every cock and bull story about somebody getting murdered, they'd end up chasing their own tails and getting a bollocking from the Sarge for allowing some yobbo to waste police time. So he took his speeding ticket and went on his merry way. When he got to Nick's place, the front door was wide open. There were a few people standing outside as they'd heard a commotion. Tom asked them what had happened and they said they didn't know but somebody had called the police as they saw someone running out of the house. Tom then went in to find Nick's dead body on the floor. Literally within minutes of that happening, the police turned up and pretty much nailed him for the murder."

"But didn't the neighbours tell the police that he'd just got there?"

"Oh yes" said Rebecca, with a flash of anger. "And do you know what bullshit story they came up with? They said he'd fled the scene to clean himself up only to drive back to the scene of the crime and pretend he was innocent. It was an absolute bloody joke. Apparently Nick had been cut to pieces and there was blood everywhere. But as Tom's Solicitor said right from the beginning, there wasn't a spot of blood on Tom's clothes, but if he had been responsible, he would have been covered in it. Also they found traces of blood on Nick's body that didn't belong to him and when they tested it, it was O Positive. This was obviously the blood of the murderer. Well

Tom was A Negative."

Alan frowned. "But surely this all came up in the trial didn't it?"

"No!!!" Rebecca's face now looked like thunder. "The Solicitor collected a whole bundle of evidence that pretty much proved Tom couldn't have done it, but shortly before the whole thing went to trial, he stepped down and another Solicitor stepped in. Well, first or all, it was strange why this guy suddenly stepped down, but worse than that, the new Solicitor was a complete idiot. When the defence put up their argument in court, the prosecution ripped them to pieces and made them look like total morons. Mum and Dad had to be taken out of the court because Mum was shouting at the Judge and calling him all sorts of names. It was pretty bloody harrowing, I can tell you. Oh I forgot to mention, the person who killed Lesley also had O positive blood and both murders had virtually identical MO's. It was obvious it was the same person who killed both Nick and his girlfriend. Which again goes in Tom's favour. Tom had an absolute rock solid concrete alibi for the night Lesley was murdered. He was in the Isle of Wight witnessed by hundreds. His team were playing a friendly match against a local football team. He was there for four days. There's no way he could have committed Lesley's murder. It all stinks Alan, totally stinks."

Alan frowned. "I must admit, I'm not committing myself either way at the moment, but it does sound very suspect."

"Suspect? That's an understatement. Even Nick's Mum and Dad didn't believe he did it. Tom got on really well with Nick's parents. They even said that Tom was the only one who could get through to Nick and make him see sense over anything. Yes, I know you find that hard to believe after what you remember of Tom, but he'd really started to calm down and when Nick tried to encourage him to go back to their old stupid ways, Tom would put him right. They were more like Brothers than mates."

"But didn't Tom ever try to appeal the conviction?" asked Alan.

"Oh Alan, we were always trying to appeal it. Each time it was overturned, evidence had been conveniently lost and as for the Solicitor who originally represented Tom, well he may as well have left the bloody planet for all we knew – he just seemed to disappear off the face of the earth."

"But what about the policemen who issued Tom with the speeding ticket. Didn't anybody track them down? Surely it must have been fairly easy to find out who was on duty that night."

"Oh they found them alright, no problem at all. And when they asked them about this speeding ticket – they denied all knowledge of even stopping Tom, let alone giving him a bloody speeding ticket."

Alan frowned. "I've got to admit, it all sounds strange.

"Not just strange, but downright bloody suspicious. I can't help feeling that the police knew who it was, but they were covering up for them."

"Oh come on Becky, now you're just being paranoid, you ...."

"Alan, I'm telling you. They weren't even interested in looking at the evidence. They found the witness in the pub who heard Tom telling Nick that if he wasn't careful, he'd end up dead, and that was the sole piece of evidence they used to convict him. Jesus, it was a kangeroo court on steriods!"

"The thing is Becky, let's just say you're right."

"I know I'm right Alan."

"I know you believe you are and I'm not refuting that. But what I'm trying to say is that if you've been pursuing this all these years, where do you think you're going to find the evidence to overturn the conviction? First of all, and I don't mean this to sound in any way disrespectful to Tom, but the police aren't going to be interested in investigating an old case like this, especially if the person they've convicted of murder has died. It doesn't serve their own interests because it shows them up for incompetent idiots if it's discovered that Tom was innocent all along."

"Ok, I wasn't going to say this but I've been having these strange dreams recently. A few have been of Tom, begging me to keep going. He kept mentioning the name of somebody who could help me. I didn't get the name of the person, but I could see him clearly in my dreams. It was so vivid. I don't know why I'm so certain, but I honestly think that if I met this person in real life, he'd be able to help me."

"Now you're starting to sound like Ophelia and Phyllis".

"Who?"

"Oh, just two friends of Sue. They're both a bit 'new agey'" said Alan as he made the sign of speech marks with his fingers.

"Well maybe they could lead me to this guy. Are they psychics?"

"Now Becky, I'm sorry, but I don't want to go down that route. It's bad enough listening to Sue talking about all their new age bullshit. I honestly think they'd only lead you up the garden path and get your hopes up, then deliver absolutely nothing."

"But Alan, I'm so desperate I'm willing to give anything a try. I need to do this for Tom."

"I just ..... I just feel so sad that this has consumed your whole life. From what I can gather you've sacrificed your own need for a relationship to give Tom your support. That's a noble thing to a certain degree, but what about you?"

Becky let out a deep sigh. "Oh Alan, don't think I haven't had relationships. I have. I've been married twice. The first one was a total bastard. I had three miscarriages with him and all he could do was joke about the fact that I had probably been Katharine of Aragon in a previous life to have had so many miscarriages. The guy was a total ... well, I won't say the word. Suffice to say, it's a word that not a lot of women like to hear. Then there was Bob, the second one. Total disaster right from the start. I gave up on marriage after that and decided the only man I could focus on was Tom. Well let's face it, the only other man I'd wanted to focus on I'd lost contact with ...... years ago."

"We can't change the past Becky. What happened happened. I love Sue to bits but I can't pretend that our marriage was based on romance and bliss. More like oops I forgot to wear a condom and we'd better do something about it."

Becky giggled. "I'm sorry Alan, I shouldn't have done that. It's just the way you said it, made it seem so ...... comical."

"Well it wasn't funny at the time. I had high hopes for pursuing my career and we'd only been going out for a short time. We just got taken by the heat of the moment and ...... well no thought of precaution had been taken. Thing is I love Ruth to bits so I've got no regrets. She's a smart one that Daughter of mine. Bloody proud of her I am."

"And what about Sue?" Becky looked at Alan straight in the eyes.

"We get by" Alan smiled weakly.

"Get by .... sounds a bit ..... vague."

"It's fine, honestly. Anyway, this isn't helping with finding out what happened with Tom."

Becky noted the quick change of subject but decided to drop it.

"I've been having a lot of strange dreams lately. Some have even come to pass. That's why I'm convinced I've got to meet this guy who can help me."

"Oh? What things have come to pass in your dreams? I'm intrigued."

Becky looked down. "Don't be."

"Oh?" Alan suddenly felt concerned.

"A few times I've had a dream about Mum. She kept coming to me looking really upset. A Freudian psychoanalyst would probably say it's because of her concern about Tom. But this was after he died."

"What were the dreams about then?"

"She kept pleading with me to go to see a doctor."

"Really?" Alan didn't like the way this conversation was going.

"Yes. I had been feeling very tired and I'd had a few pains in my stomach. I thought nothing of it at first, I just thought all the stress over the years had taken their toll. Little did I realise how true that was."

"Oh? Go on."

"No, sorry. I shouldn't have mentioned it. That's not fair."

"Come on Becky, you've come this far. Don't clamp down on me now."

"Alan, you've got your own life to lead. God, I wish I hadn't contacted you now."

"That's not fair Becky. We lost touch all those years ago, maybe those two bat shit crazy women Phyllis and Ophelia would say something like it was fated that we should meet up again .... and who knows .... perhaps maybe they'd be right."

Becky looked into the dregs of her coffee. "Oh well, I may as well tell you." She looked up at Alan "but let me make this clear, I'm not looking for any sympathy. I've survived all my life without anybody and I sure as shit can survive for the rest of it."

"Ok little miss Boudica, point taken. But please ...... tell me."

"Well I don't know how to say this so I'll just come out and say it outright." Becky paused.

"Go on." Alan suddenly had a sick feeling in his stomach, though he didn't know why.

"Alan .... I've got cancer .... and it's terminal. I haven't got long left. That's why I need to do this for Tom."

Chapter Five

Robert walked down the front path to Ophelia's small, tucked away house and knocked on the door. He could hear shuffling from the other side of the door and shortly it was opened by a tall, slim elderly woman with dark hair, penetrating eyes and slender fingers that would sit comfortably on the keys of a piano, playing soft and soothing music. But tonight the goal was not to partake of such indulgent past-times.

"Good evening Robert" said Ophelia with a quiet tone.

"Good evening Ophelia. Are you sure you want to do this?"

"Wanting to do it probably isn't how I'd describe it, more like feeling an obligation to do it, only if it can help to get to the bottom of the problem."

Robert and Ophelia had arranged for them to use Ian Pemberton's device to access the DNA Genetic Memory Modulation function. This was a function that, when used in collaboration with a sample of somebody's blood, could allow the user to experience past memories of the blood donor as if they were their own. They had used it several times in the past and this evening they had decided to use the bloody tissue in order to try and ascertain why Chris was being so evasive towards Ruth's parents.

"How much do you honestly think we'll find out?" asked Ophelia.

"To be honest, I'm really not sure. That blood was totally dry and although I soaked the tissue in a specific solvent, I'm not sure if we'll gain any clear information."

Ophelia nodded. "A bit like dried vegetables. You can re-hydrate them again but I've always believed the vital nutrients can never be replaced."

Robert had a sinking feeling. He thought that Ophelia might be right. "Still" he said, "we can but try."

They drove in silence to Robert's house. When they went inside, Robert had already set the device up in preparation for the session.

"Do you want a drink before we start?" asked Robert.

"No, I'm fine thanks Robert. I think we should just proceed with the session to see what we can find out."

Ophelia sounded determined. She came across as quite a demure woman, but she had a steely determination that would cause anybody who crossed her path to walk on by.

"I agree. Right, I'll just talk you through the functionality and the modalities again." Robert began to go through the various functions of the device and as he talked Ophelia through the procedure, she began to remember how they'd used it before and how they would adjust the dials to tap into the correct frequencies. Before long she was nodding her assurance that she knew how to operate the device.

"I injected myself with a sample of the blood before I picked you up, so it should be well immersed in my blood stream now" said Robert. He put the attachments onto his head – two on the front of his forehead and two just to the front of his ears by his temples.

Ophelia adjusted the dials. "I feel like I'm teaching my granny to suck eggs by saying this Robert, but just sit back and try to relax."

Although he had his eyes closed, Robert smiled gently, acknowledging Ophelia's suggestion. He sat further back in his chair and rested his arms on the arm rests of the chair.

"Now, I'm going to adjust the dials a bit more so let me know if you need me to change the frequency."

"Ok" Robert almost whispered. His eyes flickered behind his eyelids and he frowned several times. "Just a bit lower" he said in a whisper, although Ophelia was able to hear clearly what he said. She adjusted the dials while watching him closely.

"Very nearly there" Robert muttered. "That's it!"

Ophelia sat back, trying to make as little noise as possible. She knew that Robert was accessing memories and needed to concentrate to make sense of the information he was receiving. A few times he muttered and she was concerned that he was telling her to adjust the modulation. When she asked if this is what he wanted her to do, he gently shook his head.

Robert continued to breathe steadily, occasionally opening and closing his mouth and then looking slightly puzzled. At one point his eyes squinted and they half opened.

Shortly after this, they closed again. This seemed to go on for what seemed like hours, although forty minutes had passed by before Robert gestured for Ophelia to adjust the dials to bring him back into full consciousness. When he opened his eyes, Ophelia handed him a glass of water. This was standard practice in her meditation workshops. She insisted it helped to ground the clients again and bring them back fully into the present.

A few minutes passed in silence. This was something that Ophelia was very familiar with when running past life therapy sessions. People needed time to process the information when they 'returned' from their experience and she allowed Robert plenty of silence so that he could process what he'd just experienced properly.

"Well, that was interesting, although slightly puzzling too" said Robert when he finally spoke.

Ophelia said nothing. Her training had taught her to allow the client to talk without interruption so that they could express what they needed to say without interference or suggestion.

Robert was obviously not playing the role of the typical client as he expected Ophelia to respond. When she didn't he repeated what he'd said. "That's answered one question, but it's left another one."

"Oh?" This time Ophelia responded.

"Ok, I can't say for certain that my theory is true about what I experienced, but I'll run it by you and see what you think."

"Ok" said Ophelia.

"So when I finally accessed the memory we were looking for, I experienced being Chris in some sort of pick up bar. It was full of older guys and young women. I don't think it was a knocking shop, it was just somewhere that young women would go to in order to meet an older guy who would spoil them a bit."

"Not the sort of place I'd expect Chris to be" commented Ophelia, although she was trying not to talk as she wanted to hear what Robert had to say.

"Quite. My thoughts exactly. Anyway, he was sitting on his own when this attractive young woman came up and started chatting to him. I don't need to go into the details but it was obvious that Chris found her extremely attractive. They got talking and agreed to meet again." Robert paused for a moment, as if recalling the exact details. "As it transpired, they did meet again and it went a bit further – quite a bit further. I don't think either of them planned for it to happen, it was a spur of the moment thing. Afterwards, I could feel what Chris was feeling – deep remorse at cheating on Ruth." Robert could see the look of surprise on Ophelia's face and could almost hear what she was thinking. "Oh yes, this wasn't that long ago. I believe Ruth was working overtime a lot. He felt lonely so he went to this bar, though he didn't really think he would meet anybody. But he did – and the rest, as they say, is history."

"What else?" said Ophelia, expectantly.

"They met one final time and realised that it was a mistake to pursue things any further and decided not to contact one another again. The trouble is that Chris felt more for this woman than he wanted to admit." Robert suddenly went quiet.

"Robert, I don't want to jump to conclusions but ..... do you think this might be around about the time that Sue discovered the device?"

Robert looked directly at Ophelia. "Yes!" There was no mistake in his voice. The implication was obvious to both Ophelia and himself.

"I think I know where you're going with this Robert, but I'd prefer it if you said it direct."

"Let's put it this way" said Robert. "I wouldn't mind betting that if you took 30 years off Sue's age, this is exactly what she'd look like!"

Ophelia looked at Robert and gave a semi-nod. The cat was out of the bag.

"Oh dear" she said.

"Yes, oh dear indeed."

"And you think Chris knows or at least suspects?"

"Yes. I was seeing another time when Ruth and Chris were both round at Sue and Alan's house after this happened. Ruth pulled out a photo album because she promised Chris that she would show him some of her baby photos. As soon as he saw the pictures of Sue holding Ruth as a baby, he went into shock. I can only describe the experience as confusion, denial and sheer puzzlement, all at the same time. From that point on he's been battling with these thoughts and that's why he doesn't want to go round there anymore."

"So we were right in our assumption then" said Ophelia. "The trouble is, it's all very well having this information, but what can we do with it?"

"That's the million dollar question" replied Robert. "Obviously we can't tell Phyllis, and it goes without saying that we can't disclose this to Alan, Sue, Ruth or Chris. It's going to be a tough one. I think we'll have to give it careful consideration."

"I've had some challenging clients in my time Robert, but I've always managed to help them find solutions to their problems, but I have to say, for the first time in a very long time, I'm totally stumped with this one." Ophelia's facial expression reflected her comment perfectly.

"You and me both Ophelia. I have no idea how to handle this. But that's not the only problem."

"Oh?" Ophelia looked at Robert not knowing if she wanted to hear what he was going to say next.

"Something else was niggling at the back of my mind. Nothing to do with what happened between him and Sue. Just something else."

Ophelia looked puzzled. "What do you mean?"

"I don't know. I honestly think it was vague because the blood was of poor quality, being as it had dried on the tissue and had probably sat there for days. But I was getting a snippet of a conversation between two men when Chris was at the bar after first entering the place. He was ordering a drink and two men off to his left were having a conversation, almost a whisper, and yet, I felt that I could hear what they were saying and it really caught my attention. I could hear snippets of the conversation."

"Did you get the gist of what it was about?"

"No, not really, but I got the distinct impression I didn't like these men and didn't want to be near them too long. I think Chris was afraid that they might see him eavesdropping on their conversation and take action."

"I don't like the sound of that" agreed Ophelia. "But what sort of things were they saying?"

"Something about one of them having to disappear years

ago and nobody knew he was back in the country. He didn't actually say that he had a new identity, but that's the impression I got from the conversation. He said something about a woman being a threat and that he wanted to shut her up once and for all."

"That doesn't sound good at all. What if somebody's in danger? How can we find out who it is and warn them?"

"They didn't mention a name – they just kept referring to 'her' – she'd been a thorn in his side for a long time. He wanted her gone in case she recognised him. I think there was more but I couldn't make it out."

"You know what I'm going to say next don't you Robert" said Ophelia.

"Well, I would guess that you're going to tell me we really need a better sample of Chris's blood, but then I'm going to say to you in response, how do we even begin to go down that route? We can't exactly pop over to Ruth and Chris's house and say "Oh by the way Chris, could we just have a sample of your blood, we need to find out if somebody's going to be murdered?""

Ophelia sighed. "You're right, but we can't just sit and do nothing."

"For the time being I think that's exactly what we're going to have to do until we can work out – that's IF we can work out – what that conversation was all about."

"Oh there must be a way" said Ophelia, although she knew in her heart of hearts that Robert was right.

Even if they asked Chris for a blood sample for some completely made up medical reason, he would probably be suspicious. One thing that Robert had learned about Chris from experiencing his genetic memory was that he was very quiet but he took everything in and didn't miss a trick.

"He's a smart boy that's for sure" said Robert. "He's going to be a challenge."

Chapter Six

Alan felt guilty that he seemed to be so underhanded in his actions around Sue of late, but he felt it better to keep things under wraps until such time as he could work out how best to deal with Becky's situation. Although she had told him that she wasn't looking for sympathy and could handle things on her own, he couldn't help feeling that he needed to help her in whatever way he could, though he knew that if Sue found out that they'd met up, she would be non-too pleased, even though it was only for a coffee.

"Thanks for coming over Robert., I'm sorry to bother you, but I just needed to talk to somebody about a situation that's arisen and I can't talk to Sue about it."

"Oh?"

"Well, something happened on the way back from holiday. We've been to Cyprus for a couple of weeks."

"Go on" encouraged Robert. He had an idea what this was about, but didn't tell Alan that Sue had already spoken to him about it.

"Well, I met an old flame on the plane, a woman called Becky who I knew back in the seventies."

"Ok" said Robert. "I think it only fair to tell you that Sue's already mentioned her."

"Really? When?"

"It was the day that Phyllis and Ophelia came over to visit. I thought I'd drop by as well to see how she was doing after what happened in Cornwall."

"And?"

"She mentioned that you're thinking about retiring and wondered how you'd fill your time. That's when she made some sort of light joke about you pursuing long lost loves."

Alan rolled his eyeballs. "Oh for goodness sake, she really is making a big deal out of nothing. This was all a long time ago."

"Ok, so what is it you wanted to see me about?" asked Robert.

Alan suddenly realised that by continuing with the

subject of Becky, he was slightly contradicting himself as he had obviously met her for a coffee. He looked guiltily at Robert.

"Look, I did meet up with her again, but only for a coffee. There's nothing going on. That's why I don't want to tell Sue. She'll think the worst and all I'm trying to do is help Becky."

"How exactly?"

"How much has Sue told you?"

"She mentioned something about Becky discussing some drug cartel in Cyprus and how her Brother had died in prison after serving a life sentence for a crime he allegedly didn't commit."

"Ok, so you've got the bare bones of it. Well I met up with Becky as I told you and she filled me in with more detail. I have to say, she told a convincing story about her Brother's innocence."

"Now Alan, I don't want to come across as if I'm lecturing you but ......"

"I know, I know. Because I had a connection with her in the past, it leaves me wide open to believing anything she says. But she did put across a pretty good argument. Look, I have no dog in this fight, I never got on with Becky's brother. Frankly, I thought he was a loud-mouthed pain in the arse, but Becky tried to convince me that he had changed and that there was no way he could have committed the murder."

"How so?"

Alan told Robert the entire story as quoted to him by Becky. Robert raised his eyebrows at certain points and frowned at others. When Alan had finished telling him the story, he sat silently for a moment.

"Well?" said Alan. "What do you think?"

"Without meeting this Becky, it's hard to tell. When I've worked with clients in the past, I can pick up nuances in their voice, facial expressions, body language. I can usually tell if they're lying or telling the truth."

"But you've got to admit from what I've told you it does seem pretty compelling evidence?"

"On the surface yes, but we don't know if she's withheld any information. Now I'm not saying she has, but she's obviously biased towards her brother and even if he didn't commit the murder, I would need to find out more around the entire situation. I can't make a judgment based purely on what I've heard. No disrespect to you Alan, you've given me a very comprehensive account of your meeting with Becky, but it's like the old game of Chinese whispers, certain things can get lost in translation and I would really like to hear it from the horse's mouth."

"Do you mean you'd like to meet her?"

"Let's put it this way, I could glean more information from a one-to-one talk with her."

"Ok. So let's just say for arguments sake you believe her story. Where could we go from there? Do you know anybody in the legal profession who could look at the evidence with a fresh pair of eyes?"

"Due to the nature of my job I do work with solicitors on a regular basis, so I know one or two. The thing is, I'm not sure how helpful they would be as their time would be precious and quite understandably, they might not want to give up some of that time gratis."

"To be honest, I think Becky would be more than happy to pay for whatever help we could find."

"The trouble is they'd have to do some serious digging going back a long way and that's not going to be a quick job. We don't really even know where to start. You mentioned that this Nick's girlfriend was murdered first. If there was a connection between Nick and her, we'd need to get some context to see what the motive could be. It's going to be a tricky one."

"I understand. All I'm saying is that if we can at least try to get some leads for Becky, I'm sure she'd be very grateful."

"Well let me make a few phone calls and see what I can come up with. In the meantime, I'd be more than happy for you to set up a meeting between her and I."

"You don't know how much I appreciate it Robert, I really do. There was another piece of information she shared with me when I met her."

"Oh? What's that?"

"She's got terminal cancer. She's dying. She promised her brother she'd get to the bottom of this whole case before she died."

"Oh god ...... I'm sorry Alan."

"Yes, so am I."

For the second time, Robert saw emotional vulnerability in Alan. In many ways they had much in common – both were very matter-of-fact people, firmly stoic in any given situation, but he recalled that when Sue had been abducted, the fragility that Alan tried to hide so carefully and now, to a slightly lesser degree, he could see the same sense of helplessness.

"The thing is I feel so guilty doing this behind Sue's back. I would never cheat on her, but in a way, even having a coffee with Becky feels like I'm being dishonest."

Robert felt the strong urge to say, "Alan, I wouldn't worry about it considering that Sue has already slept with your son-in-law" but realised he had to be careful in case he slipped up. Alan had no idea what he and Ophelia had found out about the meeting Sue had had with Chris, using the pseudonym of Sam.

"Well you haven't done anything thus far, so let's just focus on helping Becky with this case and Mum's the word."

"Thanks Robert."

Robert was about to say something when voices flashed into his mind. Who were they? What were they saying? He suddenly remembered the conversation that the two men had had within earshot of Chris before he met 'Sam' at the bar. What had they said? One of them was talking about getting rid of 'her' because she posed a direct threat. Who was he referring to? Why did he suddenly think of that? Something in his mind wouldn't let it go but he couldn't understand why.

"Are you alright?" asked Alan.

"Er yes, of course" replied Robert.

"Are you sure? You just looked a bit taken aback."

"No, just having a thought." Robert didn't want to give Alan any more concern than he already had. "So if you'd like to let me know when Becky is free and I can look at my diary, we can sort something out and meet up."

"I won't take offence if you don't want me to be there" said Alan.

"Don't be silly, she'll probably open up more if you're there. She might not feel very comfortable speaking to a complete stranger on her own."

"I suppose that's a fair point. Ok, I'll give you a call Robert and we can sort something out."

* * *

It was several days later when Alan and Becky met Robert in a quiet little pub on the outskirts of town.

"Oh this is nice" said Becky. "What a lovely relaxed atmosphere and not too busy either."

"It was Robert's idea to meet here. I don't think he's a fan of town centres so he suggested this place."

"Very nice. I'm slightly nervous about meeting him, I don't know why. Maybe it's because I'm getting my hopes up and he might not be able to help us."

"I've known Robert for a while now and I can tell you he will be completely honest with you. If he doesn't think there's a case to pursue, he'll let you know. On the other hand ......"

"If there is" continued Becky, "do you think he can really help me Alan?"

"I can't make any promises either way. All I know is that he'll have a much better idea than I do."

"Well if that's your opinion of him, it's good enough for me" said Becky with a smile. Alan hadn't seen that smile for years.

"Would your Piggy lie to you?" said Alan.

Becky laughed. "Bloody hell, it's been decades since I've heard that name."

"Oink! Oink!"

Just at that point one of the bar tenders came up to serve them and upon hearing Alan, gave him a funny look. Becky giggled.

"What would you like?"

Becky couldn't resist. "A vodka and coke for the piglet, and a lager for the porcine papa" she said pointing to Alan.

The woman behind the bar looked at them oddly. "Right" she said and proceeded to get their drinks.

"Will you stop that! You'll get us both sectioned" said Alan, a wry smile on his face.

"Oh Alan, it's just like the good old days. We were

always laughing and clowning around."

"Indeed we were" replied Alan, as he recalled those long hot summer days in Cyprus when they were both care-free teenagers.

"Do you remember that bet we had" continued Becky. "I was convinced that The Jean Jeanie was going to get to number one and you said it would be Blockbuster. We promised that the loser would have to buy the winner the number one record."

"It's funny you should say that" said Alan. "I pulled the record out only the other night."

"Oh behave, you're making that up" quipped Becky.

"No I'm not. I can even tell you what you'd written on the centre of the label. Alan paused a moment to recall what the message was. "You win smart arse. Love you always Piggy. Your Becky kiss kiss kiss."

Becky looked at him, slightly taken aback. "You remembered. You still have the record."

"How could I ever get rid of it?"

The short silence between them as they looked at each other was interrupted by the sound of somebody walking into the pub. "I'm really sorry I'm a bit late Alan, I had a bit of a problem trying to get rid of a client." Robert looked at Becky. "Ah, you must be Becky. Is that right?"

For a few moments there was what Alan thought was an awkward silence. Instead of reciprocating the greeting, Becky just stared at Robert ...... and stared ...... and stared.

Robert suddenly felt a bit awkward. "Sorry, have I made a mistake?"

"No" said Alan, trying to break the awkward silence. "Becky, this is Robert, the person I told you about. Robert, this is Becky."

Becky still stood staring for a moment, but still no words came.

"Are you feeling ok?" asked Robert. "Is something wrong?"

Becky finally found her voice. "Erm, er, er, no, I'm sorry. Erm, can we sit down?"

This sudden change in behaviour puzzled Alan and he wasn't quite sure how to deal with this turn of events. Had

Becky met Robert before? Surely she couldn't have been a client.

"Becky, what's the matter? This is Robert, he's a friend" Alan said, trying to reassure her.

"I'm sorry Alan, it's just that ... it's just ....."

"If you'd rather call the meeting off I'd understand" said Robert. "You seem to be a bit apprehensive."

"No, no, honest. It's fine. I'm just ..... I'm just .... I'm just in shock."

"I don't understand Becky, what is it?" There was a slight impatience in Alan's voice now.

"I'm sorry Alan." She looked at Robert again. "It's you. It is you."

"You know me?" said Robert puzzled.

"Yes, well no, but yes, in a way."

Neither Alan nor Robert knew how to deal with this new situation. Becky seemed to be talking in riddles and they couldn't make out what she was trying to say.

"Have you read one of my papers?" enquired Robert.

"No, no, you don't understand." Becky had managed to get back some of her composure. "I don't know you but ..... but Alan, remember, I told you I had a dream about a man who would help me?"

"Yes" said Alan, suddenly realising where the conversation was leading.

Becky pointed straight at Robert. "It's you. You're the man in my dreams."

Robert seemed taken aback by this strange turn of events. He'd studied body language with great interest in order to understand his clients better and he could see that Becky wasn't acting or lying. Her whole countenance was one of total shock.

"Dreams?" said Robert. "What dreams?"

"Oh erm, that's one thing I didn't mention to you when we spoke Robert" said Alan. "Becky mentioned that she'd been having odd dreams and that in one of them she met a man who she believed could help her."

Robert looked at Becky directly. "And you believe that man is me?"

Becky looked directly back at Robert. "Without a

shadow of a doubt. Tom told me I'd meet you." She picked up her glass and drank her vodka and coke in one gulp.

Chapter Seven

Several days after this strange meeting between Robert, Alan and Becky, Ophelia had contacted Robert to see if he'd had any more thoughts on what they could do concerning the situation with Chris.

"To be honest Ophelia, I haven't given it any more thought after what happened the other day. I've been so preoccupied trying to think about how to tackle this situation with Becky and Alan that it completely slipped my mind."

"Don't worry Robert, it can go on the back burner for now. It seems that this new situation is transpiring to be a more pressing issue."

"Yes, I think it is. But it was so strange. She said she'd foreseen me in her dreams. Well you know that's not my field at all, I deal very much with the here and now. But it's just the way she said it – I knew she wasn't lying. She was in complete shock."

"And what about the story of her brother being innocent? What do you make of that?" Ophelia was careful to choose her words. She didn't want to put any suggestions into Robert's mind. She wanted him to give her his unbiased opinion.

"Well she went through the case with me as she had done with Alan, and I have to say, it's pretty compelling. Now I don't know all the facts but if she's telling the truth about the parking ticket and the lack of blood splatter on her Brother's clothes, it doesn't make sense that he was convicted. I mean yes, I know he was standing over the body, but then the door was apparently wide open so any of the neighbours could have gone in before him. It's all very strange."

"Do you think we'd be able to help her in any way?"

"I know a few solicitors who I've had dealings with in the past. I could make some enquiries and see what they come up with. I've asked her to write down a full account of the events in chronological order, starting with the murder of this Lesley. That was Nick's girlfriend. Then there's the problem of the witness in the pub who overheard Tom seeming to threaten Nick, but Becky swears he wasn't threatening him, he was warning him. The trouble is, all the key players in this story are dead."

"Apart from Becky" added Ophelia.

"Well yes, but that's the other tragedy."

"Oh?"

"She's got cancer and it's terminal."

"Oh Robert, no!" The tone in Ophelia's voice was one of horror.

"I know. Life is so cruel .... and always it seems to the nicest people."

"Isn't it" added Ophelia. "Look, I know that you don't believe in what Phyllis and I do, and if Alan even got a whiff of the suggestion, I know he'd protest from the highest mountain. But why don't you bring Becky round to see Phyllis and I? We could try and do some energy work on her."

"Well, I've got to say that with all due respect I'm not totally on board with all this new age philosophy, but to be honest, I don't think it would do any harm. The poor woman has nobody. She's virtually dedicated her life to finding this elusive murderer, two bad marriages and three miscarriages being thrown into the mix. By all accounts, it sounds as though she's had a pretty lousy life."

"It sounds to me as though she could do with some strong supportive feminine energy. I'd love to meet her."

"Well I can certainly suggest it to her, though I'd be reluctant to tell Alan."

"What he doesn't know doesn't hurt him".

"That's true. It does seem as though there's a lot of sneakiness going around at the moment."

"What do you mean?"

"Well obviously what we found out about Sue and Chris having a brief fling and then Alan telling me he felt guilty about meeting Becky behind Sue's back."

Robert could hear a light chuckle over the phone.

"Well it's hardly on the same level as somebody having sex with her son-in-law is it?"

Ophelia's bluntness even surprised Robert. "Well I wouldn't have expected you to come out with it so pointedly" he said.

"But it's true Robert. I have no quarrel with Sue, but

you witnessed the entire event and I hardly think that Alan having a coffee with an old flame and trying to help her clear her brother's name has the same level of duplicity."

"My goodness, I've never heard you being so forthright, Ophelia. Whatever happened to talk of us all being of one spirit?"

"We are indeed all of one spirit ultimately Robert, but as droplets of the ocean we are all responsible for returning to that ocean untarnished."

"Hmmm, if I didn't know any better I'd say you were being slightly judgmental."

"Oh please don't misunderstand me Robert. Many people have extra-marital flings. It's just that normally people don't do it in their own back yard. If Sue had been seeing somebody at work I could understand it, but the ramifications to all concerned if it ever came to light would be horrendous."

"I know exactly what you're saying Ophelia and you are right. I do think we need to put the situation between Chris and Sue on the backburner for now and focus on Becky."

"Yes, I agree."

"One thing that's been niggling me though."

"Oh? What's that?"

"It doesn't seem to have any connection at all, but when I met Becky the other day and she was telling me the story of what happened to her brother, I couldn't help remembering the conversation that the two men in the bar had that Chris overheard. I don't understand what triggered that."

"Do you think there might be a connection?"

"I wouldn't have thought so but ...."

"I know your line of work has trained you to deal with the facts in hand, but maybe once in a while you should trust your instincts."

"Oh believe me I have. I knew for certain that Ian Pemberton had been murdered long before we found his body."

"Well there you are then" added Ophelia. "If your intuition is trying to tell you something, just let it sit for a while and see where it takes you."

"Well right now it needs to take me to my study to write a few notes and make a few phone calls. I'm quite behind on some of my work and adding the Becky case to my file is going to swallow up a lot of spare time, but I can't let Alan down."

Ophelia paused for a minute. "Robert?"

"Yes?"

"Do you .... do you ....."

"What is it Ophelia?"

"Do you get the impression that Alan still has feelings for Becky?"

"You see, you accuse me of being so matter of fact and not listening to my intuition."

"And?"

"That's where you're wrong. My intuition tells me it's a very big 'yes'."

Chapter Eight

"Now look Alan, I know you're going to protest, but I honestly think it wouldn't do any harm for Becky to pay Phyllis and Ophelia a visit. I'm just as skeptical as you are about all this crystal healing and meditative pathwork they keep talking about, but I can't help thinking that it would be like a placebo effect just for Becky to see them. Apart from you, who does she have in the world?"

"She has friends in Cyprus. She goes over to see them a few times a year."

"That's all well and good" protested Robert. "But she spends a lot more time in England and she's got no other relatives from what you can gather, so it might be good for her to spend an evening with the pair of them. Let's be honest, from what you've told me, Sue wouldn't exactly be over the moon to meet Becky again so that's not really an option."

"Well I'm sure Phyllis would slip up and tell Sue that Becky had been to see them."

"I think if she's aware how Sue feels about Becky, she'd probably be more discreet."

"And how would she feel anyway? For all my perception of Phyllis's faults, there's one thing I can't take away from her. She's been a bloody loyal friend to Sue and I know she'd probably even give her own life for Sue. So wouldn't she feel compromised?" said Alan.

"You don't give her enough credit" said Robert. "Phyllis is adult enough to realise that if she's just helping to give somebody a bit of reassurance, she's not deceiving her best friend. It's not as if you're going to go around there and you and Becky are going to have a full on orgy in front of them."

"There's no need for that Robert."

"I'm sorry, it's an extreme example, but all I'm trying to say is that Phyllis isn't deceiving Sue in any way just by offering to do some sort of healing session. It's what she does all the time with her clients."

Alan was torn between wanting to give Becky as much support by as many people as possible, but feeling that Phyllis and Ophelia might lead her on and get her hopes up."

Robert could see the torment on his face. "Look, let's just try one meeting. If Becky's not happy or if, as Ophelia and Phyllis describe it, the energy isn't right, it won't happen again. Just give it a try."

Alan muttered something under his breath. "Oh alright, but please don't let Sue know about this. It's bad enough trying to sneak around behind her back as it is. The other day she asked me why I hadn't been working in the garden and I had to make some lame excuse that I had a shooting pain in my back, after which she insisted I should call the doctors. It's a bloody nuisance trying not to slip up and keep all evidence of my meetings with Becky private."

"I know Alan and I can appreciate it's going to be difficult for you. But I promise, I'm going to make a few calls later to see if I can find a solicitor who might be able to help. In the meantime, a relaxing session with soft music and two crazy new age woman fussing over Becky might be just what she needs to take her mind off things. Bloody hell, I hardly know the woman and even I can sense she's had a rotten life."

Alan paused. "Oh ok then, but will you promise to make some calls for me? After what she's said and what you've observed, I'm becoming more convinced that Tom was innocent. To be honest, I don't think we've got a hope in hell of finding the real murderer, but we can't stop trying. Especially as ...... especially as ....." Alan's voice broke off and he blinked quickly.

"I know Alan, you don't have to say it. That's why I think it's important for Becky to get some sort of support – and let's be honest, as much as you care about her, sometimes the company of other women is probably going to be just what the doctor ordered."

"What, you mean I didn't convince you with my drag act" said Alan, trying to bring some humour into a solemn situation.

"Well I didn't want to say anything" grinned Robert, "but those high heels really don't suit you and as for that eye shadow, god, which bargain bucket store did you get that from?"

Both men laughed at the thought of Alan in drag and Alan came around to Robert's way of thinking. "Ok, let's arrange for Becky to see the two bat crazy cat ladies, but if I see the first whiff of bodies being thrown into cauldrons, I'm pulling her out of there!"

"It's a deal!"

* * * * *

When Robert suggested arranging a get together with Becky, Phyllis and Ophelia were only too happy to organise a meeting. They were already getting their diaries out when Robert interjected.

"There are a couple of things I need to make really clear though" he said.

"Oh, what's that Robert?" said Phyllis, slightly concerned by the sombre tone of his voice.

"I know you both genuinely want to help Becky as much as you can, but she's got terminal cancer and I don't want you giving her false hope with any promises of miraculous healings."

"Robert, I think you know us well enough to realise that we wouldn't do that. For one thing, it's not ethical and for another, I think Becky has had more than enough disappointments in her life to present her with another one in the guise of a false promise" said Ophelia.

"Thank you Ophelia, I do appreciate your understanding of the situation."

Ophelia nodded.

"The other thing" he said turning to Phyllis, "and I have to confess, this concerns mainly you Phyllis."

"Me?" Phyllis looked worried. "What have I done?"

"You haven't done anything, and that's precisely the point."

Phyllis looked puzzled.

"I know that Sue is your best friend and you would never lie to her or do anything to upset her."

"Certainly not!" said Phyllis defiantly.

"However, I think the subject of Becky is a bit of a sensitive one between Alan and Sue right now, so I would really appreciate it if you didn't mention this meeting to Sue, or indeed, anything to do with Becky."

Phyllis looked a little sad. "But surely Sue's not jealous of an old flame of Alan's?"

"Well talking of flames, let's just not fan any ok? I get the impression from speaking to Alan – and if you dare repeat this I will have your guts for garters – but I get the impression that Sue is a little resentful of the meeting on the plane with Becky, and ...." Robert paused.

"And?" Phyllis looked at Robert expectantly.

"Well, let's put it this way. Due to the circumstances surrounding the sudden cut off of communication between Becky and Alan all those years ago, I believe there is still unfinished business between them."

Phyllis looked incredulous. "You mean .... you mean after all these years ....?"

"It happens Phyllis, it happens."

"Oh my goodness."

"So I hope you can understand me asking for your discretion. Not a word to Sue. I've spoken to Alan and I can promise you, there's nothing going on between him and Becky, but as I've got to know Alan more and more, he is a gentleman and right now, he's trying to help Becky in her hour of need. And god knows, it is an hour of need."

"Well yes, definitely" agreed Phyllis. "I must admit, it's going to be difficult not talking to Sue about it but ...."

"Phyllis, I really need you to be very careful around this situation. I know it's going to feel like treading on egg shells but we don't want to encourage a situation where accusations and misunderstandings can be thrown around."

"Ok Robert, I understand." Phyllis's voice had a sad quality to it.

"Another thing – please don't go scaring the hell out of her with doom and gloom tarot card readings. No, I know you wouldn't deliberately do it Phyllis" said Robert, before Phyllis had the chance to interrupt. "But if you did see something unfavourable, sometimes the old foot in mouth scenario can happen before you have the chance to stop it."

"I feel like I'm being lectured to by a school teacher, but yes, I do understand what you mean."

"Good. Right, that's settled. If you can let Becky know when you're both free, I can pick her up and bring her around."

"Are you sure Robert?" said Ophelia. "I feel guilty that you have to do all this running around. I know you have a lot of work on your plate at the moment and this is just adding to the load."

"I have my father's genes Ophelia, I can keep going when the rest of the army have all fallen in battle."

"Even so, you don't want to suffer burn out."

"Aye captain!" Robert winked at Ophelia.

"Ok" she laughed. "Get back to your bunker private and report back on duty when you have some news!"

* * * * *

"Oh what a lovely house" said Becky as she walked into the hallway of Ophelia's house. Robert was just locking the door and followed behind her.

"Let me introduce you ladies properly. Becky, this is Ophelia and this is Phyllis. I'll be leaving you in their gentle hands while I go and make some phone calls. I'll be back in about three hours if that's ok. Are you ok with that?"

"Oh Robert, that's fine. I'm really pleased to meet both of you. Robert has told me so much about you."

"It's good to meet you too" said Ophelia. "Come on in and I'll make some tea. We can have a chat and Phyllis and I can do some healing on you with the crystals."

"Sounds fascinating. You know, I've heard a few of my friends talking about all of this stuff, but I don't really know a lot about it."

"Well there's nothing to be concerned about. It's very gentle and it will help you to relax. Take a seat over here." Ophelia pointed to her comfiest chair and Becky sat down and rested her head.

"Oh I feel more relaxed already."

"Right, I'm off now, but I'll see you later." Robert gave Ophelia a quick look as if to say "remember that we agreed – no false promises, no scary readings." Ophelia gave Robert a reassuring look and with that, he walked up the path back to his car, closing the gate behind him. Now he had to follow up some leads he'd been given. He didn't want to leave it too late as he didn't think the various solicitors names he'd been given would appreciate phone calls coming late into the night, especially if they had heavy workloads.

Although Ophelia had promised that she wasn't going to do any 'scary readings' as Robert had put it, she decided that whilst her and Phyllis arranged some soft cushions and pillows for Becky to lie on, she would pull a few cards while Becky had her eyes closed and Phyllis was doing the healing work with her crystals. Gentle music filled the air, the scent of soft musk incense wafted throughout the room and Becky could feel warm tingling sensations as Phyllis used her hands and crystals to float above specific areas of Becky's body. Several times, Becky let out gentle sighs and Ophelia couldn't help feeling that she looked more relaxed than she probably had done in a very long time. Ophelia looked on, admiring Phyllis's touch – she did seem to have the ability of making her clients feel totally relaxed, almost as if they were floating downstream in a small boat on a bright sunny day. Ophelia took some cards from her tarot deck but didn't turn them over straight away. She didn't want to spoil the atmosphere with turning over negative cards. She would wait until Becky had gone. Even so, already she was getting feelings and impressions from the cards.

"I'm going to bring you back now Becky" said Phyllis softly. "I want you to allow yourself to come back into the present very slowly, perhaps having a little stretch and taking a few nice deep breaths."

Becky murmured something and then gradually parts of her body began to twitch. After a few more subtle movements, she began to take deeper breaths and then gently stretch her arms. Her eyes flickered and eventually opened. She looked at Phyllis and smiled.

"Welcome back" said Phyllis with her warmest smile.

"That was marvellous. I can't remember when I've felt so relaxed."

"Good" said Phyllis. "Now take your time and slowly sit up when you feel ready."

Becky arose and before long was sitting up.

"Here, have a glass of water." Phyllis offered her a glass of water.

Becky took the glass and drank several gulps of water. "Thank you."

The rest of the evening passed with Becky telling them the story of what had happened to her brother, although Robert had already told both of them everything that he knew of the story. Ophelia and Phyllis told Becky about their acquantance with Robert and Alan. Phyllis was very careful not to discuss Sue too much as she recalled what Robert had said about Alan still holding a flame for Becky and Sue not being overly-keen on the situation. They were both particularly interested in hearing how Becky had foreseen Robert in her dreams and how she was convinced that he was the man who could help her.

"Well if anybody can help you it will be Robert" said Ophelia assuringly. "He's a very rare breed indeed. Very quiet most of the time, but don't let that fool you. He knows what he's doing."

As coincidence would have it, at that moment there was a knock on the door. Ophelia looked up at the clock. "Oh my goodness, is that the time already? That must be Robert."

Sure enough, when she opened the front door, there stood Robert. He looked a little tired but he also had a look of victory on his face.

"Come in Robert. Can I get you some tea?"

"No thanks Ophelia. I had some coffee back home. How did it go?"

"Very well. How about you?"

"Yes, very well indeed. I think I have at least two very good leads."

"That's wonderful news. Come on in."

Even Robert could see how much more relaxed Becky looked after the evening's session and he was glad that he'd suggested to Alan that she should pay a visit to Phyllis and Ophelia.

"Hello Robert. I've had a wonderful evening. I feel so relaxed I'm not sure I want to get up and go home" joked Becky.

"Well I think Ophelia's cat might take offence at you pinching his favourite chair" Robert laughed.

"Oh no, you should have told me Ophelia, I don't want to upset your cat."

"Oh don't worry, Grimaulkin has several favourite spots that he likes to call his own. I told him you were coming tonight and he was fine about you using his chair."

This was the type of conversation that made Alan squirm and even Robert found it hard to accept somebody having a full blown conversation with a cat.

"Well anyway, let's not push our luck and outstay our welcome on Grimaulkin's chair otherwise he may look at you with the evil eye" said Robert.

"Yes, I think you're right" said Becky. "Did you have any luck tonight?"

"Yes I did" said Robert, with a positive tone. "There are two solicitors I'm going to contact tomorrow. I don't want to get your hopes up too much Becky, but I think they may be able to point us in the right direction in terms of getting some information."

"Oh that sounds great" said Becky, her smile lighting up her face.

Robert couldn't help feeling that he knew why Alan found this woman so attractive. He could imagine that before all of this tragedy that befell her, she was somebody who had a very bubbly personality and could probably befriend anybody.

"Anyway, I'm sure both of these ladies have things to wrap up as have I, so we shall take our leave now. Becky, are you ready to go?"

"Yes, of course." She turned to Ophelia and gave her a big hug. She then did the same with Phyllis. "Thank you both so much. You really have no idea what a wonderful evening I've had. It really has helped tremendously."

"You're more than welcome my love" said Phyllis. "You know you're very welcome to come back again anytime, and I mean that."

Phyllis excuded her earth mother energy like a beacon of light that could beckon all the sick and the helpless to her. Sue always said she would have made an excellent mum. "You're far more bloody maternal than I am Phyllis. Oh of course I love Ruth, but I really don't have much patience with other kids." Phyllis had laughed at Sue's comment.

Becky and Robert said their final farewells and walked down the garden path towards Robert's car. Ophelia and Phyllis gave them a final wave before they closed the door.

"Well I think that went really well" said Phyllis. "I

could feel the blockage inside of her stomach and I was really trying to shift it, but it wouldn't budge. I think I helped to sooth it but it's not going anywhere soon."

"I know Phyllis. You did your very best – more than anybody else could have done."

"I just wish I could have done more. I do feel torn. I love Sue to bits, but I am worried about Becky and we really do need to give her as much support as we can. Trouble is if I told Sue, she may feel I was being disloyal to her."

"Phyllis, you need to put such thoughts out of your mind. You're deceiving no-one and in fact you're doing a great deal of good. Isn't that what we were put on this earth for?"

"Well yes, but sometimes it just doesn't feel like enough."

"Phyllis, trust me it is. Now I don't want to put a dampener on the evening but ...."

"What's wrong?" There was a tone of panic in Phyllis's voice.

"Don't get uptight. I just need to show you something."

"What is it?" Still that tone of panic.

"While you were carrying out your healing work on Becky – and doing an excellent job, I have to say ...... I decided to pull a few cards. Now I promised Robert that I wouldn't do any 'scary readings' as he put it, that's why I did it out of sight of Becky. I haven't looked at them yet but I did get a feeling as I was pulling them. I want us both to look at the cards together and see what we both think.

"Ok" said Phyllis.

"I pulled four cards to ask for helpful influences, and then four cards to warn against negative influences."

"Good thinking Ophelia. Ok, let's turn them over."

Ophelia began to turn the cards over.

"'The Emperor' as the first card" observed Ophelia. "I think that's Robert. He's very much in the driving seat in this situation and is definitely a force for good. I'm not surprised Becky saw him in her dreams."

She turned the second card. "'King of Swords'. Interesting. Robert did say he was contacting a few solicitors who may be able to help him – well this is our man, whoever he is."

Third card. "'Six of Cups'." Ophelia paused. "Interesting. I always associate that card with past connections, memories of times gone by. Emotional links with the past. There seems to be a strong connection between that card and the King of Swords. How odd."

Ophelia pulled the fourth of the positive cards. Both she and Phyllis smiled. "'Justice'" they said together. "What a perfect card in this situation" added Ophelia. "I really do think that Alan and Becky's meeting on the plane was fate."

"Ok" said Phyllis. "Now we've got to look at the other cards.

"Yes, we have" agreed Ophelia. "I have to say though Phyllis, I didn't get a good feel from these cards at all. She turned the first card. "'The Devil!' Oh dear, I had a feeling that would turn up.

"Oh really? Why?" said Phyllis, looking worried.

Ophelia was about to tell Phyllis about the session she and Robert had had had using Ian Pemberton's device but then realised that Robert had sworn her to secrecy as he didn't want Phyllis knowing that Sue had seduced Chris.

"There's a man in the background. I don't want to jump to conclusions, but he's a very negative influence. The card describes how I feel about him very well."

"Well let's turn over the others" said Phyllis, almost hoping that by doing so, they may see better cards.

Ophelia turned the other card over. "Wow!" they both exclaimed. "Judgment!"

"Well that ties in with the justice card don't you think?" asked Phyllis.

"It certainly does Phyllis. Let's look at the others."

"Jeeeeeeeeeeeeeeeeeeeeeeeeesus!" Phyllis exclaimed as they turned the next card over. "'The Tower!' Three major arcana cards, one after the other. She didn't allow Ophelia any time to turn the last card. She turned it over and the reaction of both of them was the same. "'The World'. Completion."

"Oh my word, I don't even know what to say" said Phyllis. "I honestly wasn't expecting that. There are bigger ramifications to this whole thing than just Becky's brother."

"Much bigger" said Ophelia. "We can only sit on this for now, but I am worried about who 'The Devil' card represents. Not my favourite card at the best of times, but I just had a really negative feeling as soon as I touched it."

"Let's pull one more for Becky" said Phyllis.

"Ok" said Ophelia, though she felt a little reluctant to do so. She shuffled the pack and one card fell out onto the floor. Phyllis bent down to pick it up and turned it over. They both looked at the card and then at each other.

Chapter Nine

Robert stood waiting patiently in the foyer whilst the receptionist was talking to a client on the phone. She looked up at him, gesturing for him to take a seat while she continued talking to the client. Finally, she put the receiver down.

"I'm sorry about the wait. I just need to get some information for a client and they gave me very specific instructions. How can I help you?"

Robert smiled. "That's no problem. I'm here to see Michael Parks. He's expecting me."

"And can I take your name please?"

"Robert, Robert Whitehead."

"Thank you. I'll just let him know you're here." The receptionist picked up her phone and tapped an extension number. "Hello Michael? I have a Mr Robert Whitehead in reception for you. Yes, yes, ok." She put down the receiver. "If you just take the lift to the third floor, his office is no. 5, he's waiting for you."

"Thank you" said Robert and walked towards the lift. He pressed the button and shortly he could see the numbers descending on the display above the door. When the doors opened he walked into the lift and pressed the button marked 3. The lift door closed slowly and it began to ascend as the numbers went up from ground floor, first floor, second floor ..... third floor. Robert got out of the lift and looked at the numbers on the door. There was the door with the number five on it. Robert knocked softly.

"Come in" said a voice from behind the door. Robert walked into the office and a man arose from his chair to greet him. "Hello Robert. Long time no see. How are you doing?"

"I'm fine thanks Mike. Busy as ever, interesting clients."

The other man chuckled. "That's what I love about you Robert, you're always too polite to say that somebody's a difficult pain in the butt. 'Interesting' is a word that covers a multitude of sins and psychopaths."

"Now Mike, you're being a typical cynical solicitor.

They're not really all that bad."

"No? What about that one you had a couple of years ago. Wanted to send messages to Mars on his radio. Thought that they were sending him secret messages through the white noise."

"We do have a few exceptional cases but for the most part they're people with serious problems who just need assistance in getting through their difficulties."

"Well I've got to give it to you, after all this time the humanitarian in you shines through. I'm not as tolerant as you I'm afraid."

"That's why you're a solicitor and not a clinical psychologist" joked Robert.

"Touché my friend, touché. Anyway, enough of the small talk. Let me get you a coffee. Black, no sugar as usual?"

"Actually I don't usually have coffee when I'm out on visits, but yes please."

"So how can I help you old friend?" asked the solicitor as he poured Robert a coffee.

"I have an unusual case and I'd like to see if you could give me any help."

"Well I'm fresh out of alien baby sitters, but maybe I can rustle you up a zombie killer somewhere in my files."

"I'm being serious Mike. This is an old case, you may have heard of it. Happened quite a few years ago now. Does the name Thomas Collerton ring a bell at all?"

The other man squinted his eyes, as if trying to recall something. "Not sure. The name seems to ring a bell, but I couldn't tell you why."

"Let me help you" said Robert. He took the satchell from under his arm and pulled out some papers. "He was convicted of murder and sentenced to life in prison around '79/'80."

Robert produced various newspaper clippings, showing the victim and the suspect, together with other items relating to the case.

"I'm not sure to be honest. Back then the big story was The Yorkshire Ripper. All the other cases melted into the background. What's so special about this one?"

"I've recently been acquainted with his sister through a

friend. Nice lady. She wants me to help her do some digging into the case. She's determined that her brother was innocent."

The other man smiled. "Oh come on Robert, you haven't fallen for the old "woz nuffin' to do wiv me guv' – I wasn't ever there" routine, have you? That's what they all say."

"Yes, and in most cases, they're blatantly lying. But I've listened to the details she's provided and I'm convinced he was innocent too."

"Robert, you're not getting a little soft in your old age? Perhaps this lady has turned her charm on you?"

"It's not like that Mike. She was going out with a friend of mine way back in the 70s before this happened. He asked me if I could help her. I've done some research myself, although there's scant information out there, that's for sure. But from what she's told me, it does seem to put a question mark on the validity of his conviction."

"So these so-called facts. Can you give me a couple?"

"Ok, first off, he was found over the body of the victim but ...."

The other man burst out laughing. "Oh, but he just happened to be there making house calls?"

"Just hear me out Mike." Robert's voice was a little bit sharp. "As I was saying, whilst he was found standing over the victim, despite the fact the victim had been literally slashed to death with blood all over the crime scene, there wasn't one drop of blood on the alleged killer."

The solicitor paused. "Ok. Interesting point, but not conclusive."

"Maybe. But Becky, that's his sister's name, said that he'd been stopped by the police en route to the victim's house after he'd received a call from the victim telling him that 'they' were going to come and kill him. They made him use a breathalyser and then gave him a speeding ticket before sending him on his way. When he arrived, there were neighbours standing outside the house, the front door wide open and several of the neighbours said they saw somebody running off about ten minutes before he arrived."

"Well there you are. He ran off, took off the bloody clothing, came back and pretended to be the good Samaritan."

"Which is plausible – until you learn that the person seen

running away was at least six foot, fairish hair and Thomas Collerton was just under 5 foot 9, dark hair and of much smaller stature. The police arrested him and put him in an identity parade, and none of the witnesses who were there picked him out. It was only weeks later when he was put into the identity parade again and an individual picked him out as the suspect, but this witness disappeared into the mist."

The solicitor sat quietly. "It's sort of circumstantial evidence Robert, but I'm not sure it would stand up very well in court."

"Maybe, but here's another fact. Three weeks before the victim was killed, his girlfriend was also killed. The autopsy suggested a virtually identical MO for both murders. In the case of the first murder, Thomas Collerton was on the Isle of Wight playing football. Oh, the other thing I forgot to mention – and most important of all. Both victims had defence marks as if warding off the attacker. In both cases, blood was found under the finger nails and in both cases it tested O Positive." Robert paused a few seconds, as if to give his next statement dramatic effect. "But Thomas Collerton was A Negative."

The solicitor sat, frowning. He looked at Robert. "Are you sure?"

"Yes. A lot of the evidence around the case seemed to disappear mysteriously. The original solicitor representing him said it was obvious that he hadn't done it, but then he was quickly replaced with another solicitor who by all accounts, didn't know one end of a witness statement from the other. He was a laughing stock in court and chances are, an innocent man served a life sentence for a crime he didn't commit."

"And you want to open the case and get another solictor to represent him?"

"No" said Robert. "He died in prison several years ago."

"Hang on, I don't understand. He's dead – but what purpose will re-opening the case serve?"

Robert sighed. "His sister promised him that she would track down the real killer and get him released, but sadly she never managed to do that before he died."

"Ok, I can see why that would be upsetting for her but ....."

"But she's now got terminal cancer and she wants to do

this for him before she dies."

The solicitor's face froze. "Oh, I see."

"Now I know I'm probably asking for a miracle and I've made it quite clear to her that I can't make her any promises, but I did say I would do my best to find out any fresh information wherever possible."

"Well Robert, I don't want to bring your day down, but you've really got your work cut out for you there. I think the only place you could start was by getting access to the original police file but I'm not sure they'd be too keen to allow that."

"To be honest, I doubt if there is a police file. I know you're going to think I sound conspiratorial, but from what Becky told me, she thinks all the original evidence was destroyed."

"Now hang on Robert. Isn't that being a bit paranoid? I mean, why would they want to destroy the evidence?"

"Well you're the solicitor, what would you suggest?"

"Well I'm not exactly sure what you're getting at. Cold cases get put away in storage for years, even if they're not solved. They get archived. Buried in some vault. Boxes of them. Are you sure this one hasn't been archived? Have you checked?"

"I've already ran some preliminary investigations but from the information I've gleaned so far, I've been told it can't be found. Now my work allows me certain access privileges and usually if I have a client who's had a colourful past, I can get access to records going back right to their childhood. But this one – I've met nothing but dead ends. It does make me very suspicious."

"What are you saying exactly?"

"What if they knew who the real murderer was, but didn't want that information disclosed?"

"Oh come on Robert, that's preposterous!"

"Is it?"

"For god's sake, we don't have a bloody mafia in this country."

"No, but we do have prominent people who might have certain privileges that make them exempt from prosecution."

"Look Robert, I was willing to listen to your story and help out wherever I could, but this is a step too far. I don't see how I can help you if you're going to go down this route."

"What a shame. Two dead people and possibly others, and the killer has got away scot free."

"Robert, we're just going to go round in circles here."

"Look, all I'm asking is for you to point me in the direction of any possible leads. Where might I get hold of the type of information I'm looking for?"

"I don't know. I'm not a bloody fortune-teller."

"No Mike, but you know how the system works. Don't tell me you haven't come across people pulling favours, taking bribes, asking for the law to look the other way."

"I'm sorry Robert, I really think you're barking up the wrong tree. Look, I would love to help you but this is way out of my sphere of expertise. The cases I deal with are very dull, matter-of-fact, it's obvious the client did it and I have to do my best to convince the jury that they didn't. After that, I'm not interested. It's just not something I've ever even done before."

"There's a first time for everything."

"Not in this case. Look ..... I may know someone who may be able to help you. I'm making no promises but he's a damn good criminal lawyer and he might be able to give you advice on how to do your own research. But apart from that, I really can't help you."

Robert sat in silence for a short period. "Ok. Let me know when I can talk to him – and I will chase you until you do put me onto him. You know I will."

"I've known you long enough Robert. You're like a dog with a bloody bone. But in this instance, I honestly think there's no meat left on that bone. You've picked it right down to the marrow."

"Marrow has it's uses."

"Always got to have the last word, haven't you Robert."

"Always Mike, always. I'll be expecting your call."

As Robert left the office, the solicitor stared at the door. He'd known Robert for several years and had frequently given him advice on how to deal with difficult clients who had a criminal past. This was something totally different. A dead convict. No physical evidence. Witnesses who disappeared in the middle of the night. Well it wasn't his line of work that was for sure. What to do? He knew that Robert would hound him until he gave him some sort of a lead. He sat for a moment, thinking. He looked through his Rolodex. His PA kept all his client details on the computer system but he kept all his contacts in his Rolodex as he didn't trust technology and was afraid of losing such vital information. He shuffled through a few names, then stopped. There he was. He found the details of the person he'd mentioned to Robert. He picked up his phone.

"Hello, can I speak to Martin please? Yes, it's Mike, Mike Parks." He waited until he was put through to a familiar voice. "Hi Martin, it's Mike. How are you? Listen, I've had an unusual request from a business acquaintance and I've no idea how I can help him. I thought you might be able to. Would you mind having a word with him if I give you his number?"

After the call had finished, Mike Parks put the receiver down and he sat back in his chair.

"Well, at least it's out of my hands now. Good luck Martin, you're going to bloody need it!"

Chapter Ten

"Hello Ophelia. It's Robert. Can you talk?"

The voice on the other end of the line answered in the affirmative.

"Listen. I visited a solicitor the other day who I've known for a long time now. He's helped me with some of my clients where there've been legal issues to deal with. Anyway, I asked him if he could give me any advice on Becky's case and he flipped. Virtually said I didn't stand a chance of getting anywhere with it."

Ophelia expressed her disappointment on the other end of the line.

"All is not lost though. He put me into contact with another solicitor that he knows. I received a call from him this morning and asked if he could help me. I didn't give him too many details as I thought he'd also blow me out. I just said I was trying to help a friend look into a murder conviction for me." Robert paused a second. "At first he didn't seem too helpful, but I just said if I could have half an hour of his time and it came to nothing, I would let it go."

"That's all you can do Robert, you've tried your best" replied Ophelia.

"He seemed a bit cagey at first – he didn't want me to come over to his office. I don't know why. He did say that he would meet me at a quiet pub. I know just the place – it's where I met with Alan and Becky the other day."

"Good idea – he may feel more relaxed in those surroundings and be more willing to help."

"Thing is Ophelia ……." Robert paused. "I can't help feeling that it would look less formal if I had somebody with me, and somebody who might not seem threatening."

"You want me to come along Robert?"

"I'd understand if you said no."

"I'd be more than happy to. Let me know when and I'll be there."

"But you might have clients. I know you're busy."

"I can re-schedule clients. I feel this is too important to

ignore."

"Thank you Ophelia. I really appreciate it."

"You're more than welcome. I have a feeling it's going to lead us in the right direction."

If only Robert could be as sure. "Ok, I'll arrange the time and day and I'll come and pick you up before we meet him."

"That's fine. What's his name?"

"Erm …. Martin. Martin Smithson."

"I look forward to meeting this Mr. Smithson."

* * * * *

Robert and Ophelia arrived at the quiet little pub a few days later and Robert ordered them both drinks and asked Ophelia to find a discrete little corner where they could sit. Fortunately it was just after lunch and there were only a few people in the pub.

"I thought this looked like a nice little spot" said Ophelia and Robert agreed.

"Yes, no prying eyes, though I don't even know why I'm saying that. I honestly can't believe anybody would be interested in a murder trial that took place decades ago."

"Even so, it's best to err on the side of caution" commented Ophelia.

"Yes, it certainly is, you just don't know who's ……….." Robert suddenly looked up at a man who was walking into the pub. Was he just another customer or was he the solicitor that they were expecting to meet?

The man looked around the bar and noticed Robert and Ophelia. He spoke to the barman and waited. Robert wasn't sure whether he should approach him and waited for a few moments. The man then walked over to where he and Ophelia sat.

"Are you Robert Whitehead?" he said.

"Yes I am, you must be Martin Smithson."

The man nodded.

"Thank you for coming. Let me get you a drink."

"I shouldn't really drink at lunchtime, I've still got a few reports I need to get finished today so I'm afraid I won't be able to stay very long."

"I understand" said Robert. "This is a friend of mine, Ophelia."

"Hello" said Martin and smiled at Ophelia. "Nice to meet you."

"And likewise Mr. Smithson. I've heard you're very good at your job."

Whether Ophelia was paying a genuine compliment or just using her charm to win the solicitor over, it seemed to work. He smiled at her again.

"I'll do what I can to help you but I'm not sure how possible that might be. I hear you're investigating a murder case."

"Yes, that's correct" said Robert. "What did Mike Parks tell you about it so that I don't repeat it all again?"

"Not a lot to be honest. I got the impression he felt it wasn't worth pursuing but said that he'd let me make my own mind up once I'd heard your story."

"Well that's fair enough" said Robert. "At least he's allowing you to listen objectively rather than with a pre-conceived idea of what's happened."

"And what would that be?" asked the solicitor.

Robert proceeded to tell the story of Becky and her brother's murder trial. He highlighted the evidence of the differing blood groups, the lack of blood splatter and the fact that the police who issued Tom Collerton a speeding ticket completely denied any knowledge of him when they were brought forward as witnesses. He finished off the story on a slightly manipulative note by saying that Becky had terminal cancer and wanted to fulfil her promise to her brother before she died.

The solicitor sat for a moment and took a careful sip of his drink. "To be honest, I'm not sure what to suggest. If, as you have suggested, the original evidence has been destroyed, you don't really have much of a case."

Robert was quite taken aback by the solicitor's blunt response. He was hoping that he would obtain some information as to how he could go about finding out where to obtain some fresh evidence. "You mean you can't suggest anything? Give us any advice?"

"Not really. You say that the man convicted of the murder is now dead. I should imagine a lot of the original witnesses probably are as well. Even if some of them were still alive, many will have moved on. I'm sorry but I honestly don't know what to suggest."

Robert was struggling to make sense of this response and for once was lost for words. Ophelia just sat silently, very silently, watching this man.

"I'm sorry that I can't be of more help Mr Whitehead but a solicitor needs some tangible evidence to work with and it would appear that in this case, there isn't anything to go on."

Before Robert had a chance to speak, Ophelia chimed in. "Never mind Robert. Thank you for your time Mr. Smithson. If you do think of anything, you can either reach Robert on the phone or if you wanted to speak to Miss Collerton direct, she's currently residing at this address." Ophelia quickly wrote down Becky's address and gave him the piece of paper.

The solicitor seemed surprised at Ophelia's reaction. "Oh well, if that's it, I'd best get back to work."

"Thank you Mr. Smithson for your time. I'm sorry we appear to have wasted it but we're quite happy to compensate you financially if you would like to send us an invoice." Ophelia seemed to be playing a very strange game.

"Oh that won't be necessary. Getting out for a bit of fresh air was quite the tonic. Good day to you both." With that he arose from his seat and walked out of the pub.

"Ophelia, what did you do that for? I was going to ask him a few more questions."

"Robert, trust me, you weren't going to get any more information out of him, but believe me, we haven't seen or heard the last of our Mr. Smithson. I got a very strong feeling he was hiding something."

"What do you mean?" quizzed Robert.

"Something that's been around for centuries called a woman's intuition was positively screaming at me throughout that entire, albeit brief meeting. I had to struggle to keep my composure, I can tell you."

"Well you could have fooled me Ophelia, you looked as calm as a cucumber."

"Thank you Robert. But please trust me. The only thing

we can do now is sit and wait. We haven't seen the last of our Mr. Smithson."

If only Robert could be as sure. Despite what Ophelia said about her intuition, he couldn't help feeling that it was 'case closed' in all directions. How could he argue with what Martin Smithson said? They had no evidence apart from copies of the original statements that Becky had held onto so dearly for years. But a lot of the vital evidence was missing from them. No mention of blood groups, no lack of blood spatter, nothing that could even begin to resemble a smoking gun. Not even the slightest whiff of a clue. To Robert it felt as though they were walking into dead end after dead end.

* * * * *

Several days later Robert received a frantic call from Becky. "I've been burgled. My flat has been broken into."

"What?" exclaimed Robert. "Have you called the police?"

"Yes of course but I wanted to let you know. I know it sounds crazy but I wondered if it had anything to do with this case."

"Well I wouldn't have thought so" said Robert. "Nobody knows about it. Have there been any other burglaries in that area recently?"

"I did ask the police when they came round, but they said they hadn't heard of any."

"Has anything been taken?"

"No, that's what's so strange."

"How did they manage to break in?"

"Oh the kitchen window is pretty lousy. You can easily open the small window at the top and then reach down to the handle of the main window. They didn't exactly have security in mind when these places were built."

"Well I think you should stay somewhere else. You don't know if the would-be burglar has any intention of coming back."

Becky didn't like the sound of what Robert had just said. She didn't think in her heart of hearts that the burglary had anything to do with her researching her brother's trial and felt that if they'd realised she wasn't harbouring the crown jewels, they'd go elsewhere for richer pickings.

"Surely you don't think they'd come back?" she protested.

Robert felt uncomfortable at this sudden turn of events. He was just about to say something when Becky interrupted his train of thought.

"Sorry Robert, can you hold on a minute. One of the policemen wants to talk to me."

Robert waited for what seemed like ages until Becky finally came back onto the phone. "They've basically told me that whoever's done this must be some sort of pro. They're going to take several items back with them, but it appears that our thief has left no clues as to who they are. I wouldn't mind betting there are no finger prints to be found anywhere."

Robert really didn't like the sound of this. "Look Becky, I'm going to come and pick you up. I don't want you staying there tonight. You can either stay at my house, or if you're not comfortable with that I'm sure Phyllis or Ophelia would be happy to put you up."

"Don't be silly Robert, I'm quite capable of …."

"I insist!" Robert snapped. "I'm sorry, I'm sorry, I didn't mean to snap but I just want you out of harm's way. Until we know exactly what's going on, I won't feel safe with you being there on your own."

Becky felt torn. On the one hand she had always been fiercely independent – more out of necessity than choice, but she'd learned to rely on nobody and fend for herself. Now, here was somebody offering her a safe port in what could turn out to be a very nasty storm.

"Well if it's all the same to you Robert, and please don't take offence, but if Phyllis or Ophelia wouldn't mind – just for tonight, I'd be happy to stay with one of them."

* * * * *

"Of course she can stay with me Robert" said Phyllis when he called her. Robert had actually mentioned that either Ophelia or Phyllis would be an ideal host, but Phyllis took it on herself to play the fussing earth mother – even if it was to a woman almost her own age.

"Thank you Phyllis. I just don't like the way things are turning out and I do feel responsible for Becky's safety."

"I totally understand Robert. We all do. Well, most of us do."

"What do you mean?" enquired Robert.

"Well, I'm sorry Robert, but I was chatting to Sue the other day and I mentioned Becky's name. Oh don't worry, I didn't tell her very much, but I did notice a slightly icy tone when I mentioned her name, so I changed the subject quickly."

"Yes, somehow I don't think Sue is too keen on her."

"But I don't understand why" replied Phyllis. "She really is lovely and I really feel she's had a rotten life. I can't understand why anybody wouldn't want to help her."

"Yes but Phyllis you have to understand that Becky is an old flame of Alan's."

"But that was decades ago Robert. Surely he doesn't still feel the same way about her?"

"You'd be surprised Phyllis. People who suddenly come back to us from our past can still have a profound effect on us."

"Oh that's just plain silly" said Phyllis, as she chuckled at the thought. Little did she realise that her mockery would come back to haunt her.

Chapter Eleven

"I understand you're helping this Becky with her murder enquiry" said Sue to Robert when he popped round one afternoon to see Alan.

"Oh I didn't realise you were home Sue."

"Yes, I took the day off. You wanted a quiet word with Alan?" The statement was loaded.

Robert could feel the subtle iciness, even standing yards away. He felt awkward as he had indeed popped round to give Alan an update on the situation thinking that Sue would be at work.

"I just wanted to ask him some questions about this Tom character. I understood that he wasn't too keen on him and wanted to see if he really thought he was capable of murder." Robert skipped around a sensitive subject and made it seem as though he wanted to know more about Tom than Becky.

"From what I know, he didn't like him very much. As for whether he did turn out to be a murderer, I'm not sure even Alan could answer that. He'll be back in five minutes anyway, he's just popped out to get something from the DIY shop." Sue paused as she walked to the kitchen. "At least that's what he told me he was doing."

Robert decided to challenge Sue. "What is that supposed to mean Sue?" He hadn't intended it to sound as confrontational as it had, but he wanted to hear exactly how Sue felt about the whole affair.

"Well, for all I know he could have arranged a little tête-à-tête with this Becky. She certainly didn't try to hide the fact that she still held a flame for Alan when we met her on the plane."

"Oh Sue, don't be ridiculous. Alan wouldn't go cheating behind your back."

"Wouldn't he?" Sue flashed at Robert. "They certainly seemed quite chatty on the plane. I'm sure he could have tracked her down on the internet if he'd wanted to."

"Why are you so insecure Sue?"

"I'm not insecure, I just think that Alan's stupid enough

to fall for her lies – especially that part about her dying of cancer. Give me a break, what a heart-wrenching tale of bullshit."

Robert was starting to become irritated with Sue's coldness. He could understand a little spousal jealousy, but to accuse Becky of making up a story like that was beyond his comprehension.

"Ok, I'm going to be totally honest with you Sue. I've met Becky a few times now and I've heard her story. The fact is she has got terminal cancer and from the evidence I've collected so far has definitely lead me to believe that her brother was innocent. If I can help her find some closure before her sad and untimely demise, I'm only to happy to assist, and perhaps Alan is as well, because you can't just turn off somebody's history. It doesn't mean that they're screwing all over the place."

The last statement jolted Sue. Robert was usually too much of a gentleman to use language like that. Little did she realise he hadn't finished. He was just about to play his ace card.

"Not only that Sue, I wasn't going to mention this as I felt it was stooping a bit low, but just so that we have a level playing field, I find that a bit rich coming from somebody who slept with her own son-in-law!"

Even Robert was shocked at how that last statement seemed to slip out of his mouth.

"What did you say?" replied Sue, feigning shock at such a thought.

"I'm sorry Sue, you can pretend all you like, but I know about you and Chris. Frankly I think it was a pretty despicable thing to do when he was at such a low ebb in his life."

"The tissue. It was the tissue wasn't it? You used it with Ian Pemberton's device."

"Yes I did, but it wasn't to pry. Ruth was seriously concerned about Chris's behaviour and I thought we might get some insight as to what was bothering him, but I wasn't expecting that. Suffice to say I have no intention of ever mentioning this to either Alan, Ruth or Chris because I don't want to be responsible for the destruction of two perfectly good relationships. All I will say though is that it's a bit bloody rich of you to accuse Alan of having an affair with a woman who's not only dying of cancer, but trying to bring some closure to what up to now has been a pretty awful life when you've had a little fling with Chris, and for no other reason than to alleviate your boredom while Alan was working all hours to meet a deadline for a firm that couldn't care less about him."

Again, Sue was shocked. Robert's diction was always so careful and considered but this spontaneous outburst made her realise there was another side to Robert. She wasn't sure if she liked it or not.

By this time Robert had cooled down and reflected on what he'd just said. "I'm sorry for that outburst, I just wanted to point out that as somebody apparently said quite some time ago, people who are without blemish should feel free to throw stones. Can anyone of us say that this applies to us?"

There was a silence for a moment .... a silence that was broken only by the sound of Alan's key turning in the door.

"Let's not speak of this ever again" said Robert. "It's history now. Let it stay in the past where it belongs. In the meantime, try not to be so hard on Alan because I don't think you realise what a bloody nice guy he is."

Alan walked into the living room to observe what almost looked like a stand-off.

"Oh hello Robert, is something wrong?"

"Hello Alan. Erm, no, well, yes, but look, it's probably not the best time to talk. I've got a few things I need to do. I just wanted to pop in and ask you a few questions but time's pressing on. I'll catch up with you soon." With that, Robert walked towards the door and patted Alan on the shoulder on his way out – almost as a gesture to Sue to reiterate what he'd said.

When he closed the door, Alan looked at Sue. "What was all that about?"

"Oh nothing." She tried to shake it off.

"Well something happened. You could cut the atmosphere with a knife when I walked in here."

"I'm sorry Alan. I think I got the wrong end of the stick about something and Robert's put me right on it."

"About what?"

"Let's not discuss it. I'll go and see what to do for dinner."

Sue walked past Alan and he stared after her, the puzzled

look on his face almost fixed.

* * * * *

The following day, Robert called in to see Phyllis and make sure that Becky was ok.

"Did she sleep ok last night?" he asked Phyllis who was bustling around in her kitchen.

"Oh yes" said Phyllis as she gently picked up her beloved Pywackit from the chair in order to allow Robert to sit down. "Come over here sweetheart, this cushion is so good for your chakras."

Robert had a silent chuckle as he watched Phyllis treating her feline companion as if he was some ancient Egyptian god.

"I made her a warming drink with relaxing herbs and soothing blends of tea. She's still asleep at the moment so I don't want to wake her. She really has been through the wars, poor love."

"Thanks Phyllis. I really appreciate you looking after her."

"Oh don't be silly, Robert, it's my pleasure. Anyway, how are things going? Have you made any further progress in finding out about her brother?"

"No not really." Robert sounded dispirited. "I don't actually even know where to begin."

"There's got to be something we can do. Surely it's not a lost cause?"

"I don't want to think so Phyllis, but we're just hitting brick wall after brick wall."

"Have you got any idea who broke into Becky's flat?" Phyllis lowered her head and almost spoke in a whisper. "Do you think it has got anything to do with Becky's investigation?"

"I don't want to think that Phyllis, but I can't help feeling that there is a connection. I mean who else knows? You, me, Ophelia, Alan, Sue. The two solicitors. Well both of those solicitors showed absolutely no interest, Sue doesn't really want to know and neither you, me, Ophelia or Alan would do anything like that. Which begs the questions – why?"

They were interrupted by the sound of the phone ringing.

Phyllis walked over to pick up the receiver. "Oh hello love, how are you?" It was Ophelia at the other end of the line.

"Oh she's had a good night's sleep. I made her a special herbal tea and she's still in bed. Robert's just popped round. What? You want a word with him? Of course."

Phyllis handed over the phone to Robert.

"Hello Ophelia." Phyllis busied herself in the kitchen while Robert chatted to Ophelia. "Are you sure?" Robert frowned. "I'm not sure if he would though, especially after what happened the other day. Well ok, I can pick you up if that's alright. Ok, see you soon."

Robert put the receiver down and Phyllis looked at him expectantly.

"What was all that about?" she asked.

"It was about the burglary. As far as we know, nobody knows where Becky lives except for us .... and the solicitor we saw the other day."

"And ...... surely he couldn't have been responsible for the burglary. I thought he said you didn't have a case."

"That's right, but Ophelia had a feeling he was hiding something."

"Really? But if he did have anything to do with it, how did he know where she lived?"

"Ophelia gave him Becky's address and told him to call her if he did change his mind."

"Ophelia did what? Why on earth would she do something like that?"

"I don't know, but she seemed certain that he was holding something back."

"Well I do find that surprising, but I've always trusted Ophelia's intuition so if she feels that he's hiding something, then I'm more than willing to believe she's right."

"Well there's only one way to find out. I'm going round to pick her up and we're going to pay a visit to this solicitor."

"Is that a good idea though? I mean he's already given you the cold shoulder once and if you start accusing him of breaking into Becky's house, well ...... even if he did do it, he's hardly likely to admit it, is he?"

"Everything you say makes perfect sense Phyllis and I can't believe that he did break in. But he was the only other person who knows where she lives so maybe if we start putting pressure on him, he might start telling us what he knows ..... if he knows anything."

"Ok, well let me know what happens won't you?"

"I will Phyllis. In the meantime, are you ok to look after Becky for a while longer?"

"My pleasure." Phyllis gave him a smile.

Robert smiled back. "See you later." With that he left, and headed straight over to Ophelia's house.

Ophelia opened the door and rather than inviting Robert in, she closed the door behind her and started walking towards Robert's car. "Come on Robert, we've no time to lose. I just know there's something we need to find out ..... and our Mr. Smithson seems to by our King of Swords."

"King of what?"

"Swords." Ophelia stated it as if it was the most obvious thing in the world.

"Sorry, you've lost me."

"The man in the reading that Phyllis and I did the other night. We knew that we'd make contact with somebody who could help us get to the bottom of the murder case, and I'm convinced he's our King of Swords."

Robert decided the best thing to do was just focus on going to meet Martin Smithson to see if they could get any more out of him than they did the other day. He still wasn't convinced. They found a side road to park the car in and then walked towards the small firm of solicitors where Martin Smithson practiced. They walked into the foyer and were greeted by the receptionist.

"Can I help you?"

"We've come to see Mr. Smithson" said Ophelia, in her calmest, black-widow-is-about-to-bite tone.

"Do you have an appointment?"

"Not at the moment, but we will do with the police if he refuses to see us."

The receptionist looked shocked. "What's it about?"

"Well let's put it this way. A close friend of ours has her house broken into the other day and nobody knows where she lives apart from us .... although I did give your Mr. Smithson her address, which makes it a strange coincidence that she was burgled so soon afterwards."

Robert had to supress a smirk as he heard Ophelia's cool delivery, as if giving somebody the most delicious piece of chocolate cake that was laden with arsenic.

"Erm, can you wait here. I'll just go and see him."

"That's fine." Ophelia smiled. "Take your time, we're in no rush. We can sit here all day if necessary."

The receptionist disappeared and five minutes came back with Martin Smithson following behind her.

"What's this about?" he said in an agitated voice.

"Oh just the matter of a burglary – we just want to clear your name Mr. Smithson." Now it was Robert's turn to use the deadly-but-calm tone.

"Look, I'll ring the police if you don't leave."

"Please do Mr. Smithson" said Robert. "We'd be more than happy to speak to them, considering we gave you the victim's address the other day and her house was then coincidentally burgled."

The receptionist looked at Martin Smithson, shocked.

"You can't go round accusing people of things like that. I can ......"

"Oh, we're not accusing you at all Mr. Smithson" said Robert, calmly. "We just want to clarify details ... you know .... verify where you were at the time ..... no accusations, just ...... clarification."

Martin Smithson looked flustered and was not best pleased by this turn of events, especially with the receptionist bearing witness to the entire conversation.

"Come into my office. Janet, hold all calls for the next five minutes. This lady and gentleman will be leaving very shortly."

The receptionist nodded while Robert and Ophelia followed the solicitor into his office.

"I do NOT appreciate you coming here uninvited, making me look like a criminal in front of my staff. Now what the hell are you two playing at?"

"This isn't a game Mr. Smithson. I don't believe for one minute that you commited the burglary, but that doesn't mean to say you don't know who did."

"I told you the other day that I couldn't help you. Now

why don't you just go off and play the detective elsewhere? I've got enough on my plate at the moment, what with the cases I'm trying to deal with and I don't need people coming to my office and harrassing me with absolutely no justification whatsoever."

Ophelia looked directly at Mr. Smithson. "Mr. Smithson" she said. "I like you. You seem like a nice man to me. Honest, upright, hard working, a little too formal perhaps but ..... you see, I like to study people's body language and when we sat talking with you the other day, I couldn't help noticing some nervous twitches here and there. Eyes flickering a bit too much around certain subjects. Something just didn't seem right to me. Now as my good friend here has said, we're not accusing you of anything, but a little birdie tells me you're not being totally honest with us."

"Well unless that little birdie can prove your point, this canary has no intention of singing." Martin Smithson decided he was going to use the same tone as Ophelia and Robert to meet them head on.

"Touché Mr. Smithson. I like your style" said Ophelia. "But here's the deal. My friend and I are going to leave you ...... for now .... but you really haven't heard the last of us."

Robert was surprised by Ophelia's comment. He had no intention of leaving just yet but Ophelia looked at him as if to say "come on, it's time to go now." He wasn't sure what else he could say so just gave a brief "we'll be in touch" and followed Ophelia out.

When they got to the car he looked at Ophelia with puzzlement. "Why did you do that? I was just going to press him further. I'm sure he would have snapped."

"Robert, trust me. It's a bit like a bad stitch. If you just pull on it, you only make it worse. The best way to deal with it is to tease it out gently. Trust me, our Mr. Smithson might seem calm and collected on the surface, but something's worrying him."

"How can you tell? I didn't see any traces of anxiety in him at all. Irritation yes, but not anxiety."

"Patience Robert, patience. Trust me, things are going to plan."

As he drove away, Robert still wasn't convinced. He

couldn't help feeling that Ophelia was too confident in her own ability to read the situation.

Later that night he went to bed but couldn't sleep. He tossed and turned, and mulled over the situation again and again. He looked at the picture on his bedside cabinet of his deceased wife. "Oh Maria, if you were still alive, you'd know what to do." The woman in the picture smiled back at him. He continued to stare at her as he drifted off to sleep.

"Off the case .... they put the heat on him .... nothing to worry about now. Just move abroad and everything will be fine. Nobody will ever find out. I visited the local graveyard .... found just what I needed. Piece of cake. Just disappear into the sunset and nobody's any the wiser. Wants to see his kids grow up. He won't give anybody any trouble. The new one is much more compliant. It's handy when your old man has the right connections. We still hate each other but it's as much to protect him as it is me and he knows it. Putty in my hands."

Robert woke up with a start. He turned the light on. His deceased wife was still there smiling back at him. He'd had a dream – or so he thought – what were those voices talking about? He'd heard them before. What were they saying? It didn't make any sense and yet he got the feeling that all he needed to do was fill in the missing blanks and the puzzle would be solved.

Chapter Twelve

"Honestly, I'll be fine. I really appreciate what you've all done for me but I really just want to go home now and get back to normal." Becky looked back at the three anxious faces staring at her.

"But Becky, we still don't know if it was just a burglary or ......" Robert couldn't finish the sentence.

"Honestly Robert, I think we've all over-reacted. The police contacted me to say that a neighbour saw somebody breaking into the kitchen but they were literally out in five minutes flat. They called the police but by the time the police got there, the burglar had long gone. Then I turned up half an hour later.

Ophelia and Phyllis shared Robert's concern.

"But sweetheart, I'd feel better if you stayed with me for a while longer. It's really no trouble at all and Pywackit really likes your energy."

Becky laughed. "I've become very fond of Pywackit too and I'd love to come and see him again. I just need to live as normal a life as possible. I can put some new locks on the windows and it'll be like a fortress. Honestly."

Robert, Ophelia and Phyllis tried to persuade Becky to stay with Phyllis a little longer but their efforts were in vain. In the end, Robert resigned himself to the fact that she wasn't going to budge. "Ok" he said. But we want you to phone us regularly to tell us you're ok. If we don't hear from you we'll be round there like a shot."

"I promise Robert. I really do appreciate your concern. I just need some time to think and work out what I need to do next. Besides, if it wasn't just a straightforward burglary and somebody really was after me, it just proves to me I'm getting closer to the target." Becky laughed.

"That's not funny Becky. What if you're right? It just puts you in more danger" said Robert.

"Robert, I don't know how long I've got to live, so I'm determined to live the rest of my life in as normal a way as possible. I can't keep running away from things. I ran away from two bad marriages, I don't want to run away from Tom .... or Alan."

"Tom I can understand" said Phyllis. "But I'd be a bit wary of Alan – I don't think Sue is too keen on you going down that Avenue."

"Totally understandable" said Becky. "She caught herself a good one there." She looked down. "My loss, her gain."

Robert decided to change the subject. "Well look, if you are determined to go back home, I'll give you a lift and we'll pop by a DIY store en route to pick up some locks. I'll fit them myself."

"Oh no Robert you don't ......"

"I insist!!!"

"Please Becky, let Robert do it" added Ophelia.

"Ok, but you've all gone out of your way to help me and I feel guilty. You've all got your own lives to lead."

"Yes but you know how it is. It's like having that pesky kid sister who keeps getting under your feet, but you know you've just gotta look after her!" Phyllis winked at Becky.

Becky laughed. "Thanks Phyllis. I'll try not to be such a pesky kid sister."

"That's alright, just make sure you don't go nicking my best mate's fella, ok?"

"Understood."

Robert helped Becky carry her bags to the car and put them in the boot. Shortly, they were driving off, waving to a very worried Phyllis and Ophelia.

"I don't like it Ophelia, I can tell you. It all feels wrong. Trouble is we don't know what we're up against ..... or who."

"I know Phyllis. I feel the same way as you. If only I could pin that solicitor down. He knows something, I can just feel it. Trouble is .... what?"

"What if we put some cards down?" suggested Phyllis.

"No, I don't think that would do any good. He's put a psychic barrier up."

"Oh, you think he's a sensitive like us?" wondered Phyllis.

"No I don't. But people who don't believe in what we do can still put mental barriers up – and his is like a huge brick wall."

"Well the Berlin wall eventually came down" observed Phyllis.

"Indeed it did Phyllis. And as with the Berlin wall, we just have to find the weakest link."

* * * * *

Robert carried Becky's bags into her house.

"Look you don't have to do that for me, I'm quite capable ...."

" ..... of carrying them yourself. Yes I know but it'll take me two minutes and then I'll put those locks on."

"I feel so guilty – you're all running around after me and ....."

"Don't be silly Becky. I'm still not happy about you coming home, but I'm determined to do what I can to make this house as safe as possible. Now where did I put those locks. Ah, here they are in this bag." Robert took out the locks he'd bought and headed straight for the kitchen window.

"Can I get you a coffee or tea?" asked Becky.

"No thanks I'm fine. I'm going to crack on with putting these locks on and then I need to get home to make a phone call."

"Look, why don't you let me put them on, you can go home and ....."

"Oh no madam, I intend to make sure this place is 100% burglar proof before I leave."

"Well I honestly don't think he'll come back now."

"Even so."

Robert secured the locks on the windows. "I'll put the keys in this draw here so you know where they are. Suffice to say I would recommend that you don't leave them in the window lock at any time."

"Oh you don't have to worry about that, I'll make sure they're well out of sight." Becky put the kettle on and proceeded to pour herself a coffee.

Robert gave the locks a hard tug to make sure they were bolted on thoroughly. "Nice and secure. Good job, even if I do say so myself." He smiled.

"I can't argue with you there. I don't think an elephant could break through that window."

"Well fortunately there aren't too many elephants around here so let's just worry about potential burglars for now. I think they might find this one a bit of a challenge."

Becky tested all the keys in the locks to make sure she could open and close the windows. "All very secure" she said.

"Right, I'll be on my way now but I'll give you a quick call when I get home to make sure you're ok" said Robert.

"Honestly Robert, you don't have to ..."

"I insist. Now make sure you lock the door behind me ok?"

"I will. Thanks Robert, for everything. Oh, one last thing if I could ask."

"Yes, what's that?"

"Would you take my spare front door key? I just think I'd feel safer knowing you have it."

"Of course I will – I think it's a good idea."

Becky gave Robert her spare front door key and he proceeded to walk down the path and then got into his car. He started the engine and gave Becky a quick beep of the horn before he set off. As instructed, she locked the door behind her. Suddenly without Robert there she didn't feel as brave. She took a sip of coffee and sat down in her armchair.

Robert had barely unlocked his own front door when his mobile phone rang. He looked at the display. It was Becky. "Becky, are you ok?"

At the other end all he could hear was somebody gasping for breath, trying to say "Robert help me."

Panic set in. His heart started racing and he knew he had to get back there. He slammed his front door and literally ran to his car. He started the engine with the wheels screeching as he turned and drove back towards Becky's house. He completely ignored the seatbelt warning tone as he began to call 999. It was difficult to hear the voice at the other end of the line with the car engine racing and he had to repeat his request several times to make himself understood.

"I need a police car and an ambulance right now. It's an emergency!" He must have said this at least five times and eventually the voice at the other end of the line acknowledged that she'd understood his message and that a police car and ambulance would be despatched to Becky's address straight away.

When Robert's car pulled up outside Becky's house there was no sign of the police or an ambulance. "Oh come on, where the hell are they? I knew I shouldn't have let her come back."

He raced towards the front door and fumbled for the spare key in his pocket. His hands were shaking but he managed to put the key in the lock and turn it. The door opened. He raced in to see Becky lying on the floor of the lounge, barely conscious. She managed to look up.

"It's ok Becky, I'm here. Don't try to say anything. The ambulance is on it's way."

Shortly the ambulance arrived and was followed a few moments later by the police car. Robert raced out and almost shouted for them to come in. "She's through here. I don't know what the hell's happened but she's barely conscious. She needs to be rushed to A&E straight away."

The ambulance crew acted swiftly, opening the back door of the vehicle and pulling out the stretcher bed. They took it through and one of them began carrying out the standard tests.

"I can't tell for sure what it is but we need to get her to hospital right away" he said.

"She's got terminal cancer but I can't believe this is what's caused it. I only left her half an hour ago and she was fine."

"You were the last person to see her?" quizzed the paramedic.

"Yes, and I'm willing to come with you and give you the full story, but right now the priority is to get her to a hospital" insisted Robert.

"That's exactly what we're going to do. Unfortunately you won't be able to come with us but you might need to speak to the police."

"Yes, yes" Robert agreed.

The paramedics continued to secure Becky on the stretcher, trying to make her as comfortable as possible.

"Don't you worry my love, we're going to take care of you" said the female paramedic.

Becky seemed to understand and tried to vocalise something, but the paramedic shook her head. "No my love, I just want you to keep calm ok. Don't try and say anything. We're going to look after you."

One of the policeman approached Robert. "Good evening sir, are you the person who called for the ambulance?"

"Yes I am. My name's Robert Whitehead and I'll be more than happy to answer your questions once I know that Becky's ok."

"Is this your wife sir?"

"No, it's not my wife. She's a friend of a friend. Look, it's too complicated to explain here. Can you just let me go to the hospital – I want to make sure she's ok."

"She's in the best hands sir. I'd prefer it if you come down to the station with us."

The officer's voice was firm but not without concern.

"Hang on. Before I go." He walked up to one of the paramedics and gave him his mobile number, insisting they call him to keep him up to date. The paramedic nodded. Whether he would actually be able to do that was highly unlikely, but seeing how distressed Robert was, he felt he just wanted to give him that added reassurance.

The police took Robert down to the station in the police car. He told them the full story of what Becky was trying to do and how he'd become acquainted with her.

"For someone who doesn't know this lady very well, you do seem to be quite concerned about her" commented one of the interviewing officers.

"She has a history with a very good friend of mine and we both want to help her as much as we can."

"This friend of yours. Are they still an item?"

"No, that was years ago. He's happily married." Even Robert could hear the slight doubt in that last sentence.

"Really? You don't seem so sure."

Robert became frustrated. All he wanted to do was make sure that Becky was going to be ok, and here he was, having to answer ridiculous questions on the validity of Alan and Sue's marriage. "Look, I'm not going to get into the intricacies of relationships between married couples. Suffice to say that my friend and Becky were very close decades ago and they happened to bump into each other on a flight back from Cyprus. That's it."

For the next two hours Robert answered question after question. He knew he was well within his rights not to have to say anything, but he wanted to get the truth out into the open and hopefully these over-zealous police officers would be able to see that he wasn't some psychotic murderer. "Look, I'm a clinical psychologist and I've had training in body language. I know for certain that you have and you can tell that I'm not making this up."

"Well sir, if it's true you've had training in reading body language, perhaps that enables you to supress any give away signs of guilt."

"Oh come on officer, don't be ridiculous. You know for a fact that you can't have that much control of your body under circumstances like this. Now I'd be more than happy to give you the telephone numbers of people who could vouch for my innocence."

"We're just following procedure sir."

Robert muttered under his breath. "That was the lame excuse the Nazis used in slaughtering millions of innocent people."

"What's that sir?"

"Nothing" muttered Robert.

"I can assure you we're not Nazis and we have no intention of slaughtering innocent people."

Damn – the officer heard every word he said.

Eventually Robert was allowed to go, though he was advised that the police would appreciate it if he didn't "disappear" as they may need to speak to him further.

As soon as he got back to his car he called the hospital, asking which ward Becky had been taken to, how she was, could he see her and what was the diagnosis. The nurse on the other end of the line tried to placate him, although she advised that he couldn't come to see her now. She asked him to call back in the morning. This was too much. He wanted answers and he wanted them now. The nurse at the other end of the line could hear how worried he was. "It's too early to tell and I can't really disclose any information to a member of the public. All I will say is that it's not connected to the cancer diagnosis you mentioned."

"Well that doesn't really tell me a great deal" Robert protested.

"All I can say is they're running toxicity tests, now I must go. I've said more than I should." With that, the line went dead.

Toxicity tests. That could only mean one thing ..... Becky had been poisoned. But how? He'd only just brought her back from Phyllis's house. His mind raced back and forth at the events of the last couple of hours. He and Becky had left Ophelia and Phyllis, they'd gone to the DIY store to pick up some locks, he'd taken her home and secured the locks. It didn't make sense. Then suddenly he froze in his tracks. Becky had offered him a cup of coffee. He'd refused as he wanted to get back home to make a call. She'd then proceeded to make herself one. What had the neighbour said? They'd seen a burglar break in through the kitchen window and very shortly come out again. Robert began to put the pieces together. So the person breaking in hadn't done so to take anything, but to bring something. Poison. They'd most probably poisoned the milk. It would be so easy. If Becky already had a bottle or carton of milk open, all they need do is add an odourless and flavourless poison and Becky would no longer be able to continue with this case. Suddenly he shuddered. He may have secured Becky's house but the danger was already in the house, sitting in her fridge.

"No, no, no, please Becky, be ok." He sat in his car. He wouldn't be able to sleep tonight. He didn't want to phone Ophelia or Phyllis as they'd only worry as well and that wouldn't help anybody. All he could do tonight was drive home and call the hospital in the morning.

Chapter Thirteen

"Poisoned you say? Oh no!" Phyllis's voice on the other end of the line was trembling. "Robert, how?"

"I don't know Phyllis. All I know is that it was definitely poison. When I called the ward they weren't going to give me any information but I told them that I wanted to speak to Dr. Baxter. I've known him for years. Luckily he was doing his rounds and he told me what the cause was. Thankfully she'd only had a few sips of the coffee so she hadn't managed to have a lethal dose. She's going to be in hospital for a good week or so. They're not allowing visitors in. They're keeping her in a secure ward and I doubt we'll be allowed to see her but we can get messages to her through Dr. Baxter."

"Oh Robert, that's horrible. How did it happen?"

"Well I'm assuming the burglar must have put the poison into the milk when he broke in. She made herself a coffee and that's how she was poisoned."

"But shouldn't the police be called ... I mean to get somebody to test the milk."

"Already sorted Phyllis, don't you worry. I've made numerous calls this morning and that was one of them."

"Have you told Alan yet?"

"No, not yet. I'm not sure it's a good idea, though he'd certainly want to know. Trouble is I think things are a bit awkward between him and Sue at the moment. I think with Becky coming back onto the scene, it's highlighted a few issues they may have been having for a while and ....."

"..... and?" Phyllis waited for Robert to finish.

He nearly let slip that he had found out about Chris and Sue's fling and that it changed the dynamics with Sue possibly feeling exposed. Although Alan clearly didn't know, Sue now realised that it was no longer her little secret. When she'd spoken to Phyllis after Robert's disclosure, it was apparent that Phyllis didn't know as she was not very good at keeping secrets and Sue had a knack of gleaning information out of people without them realising it. She surmised that Ophelia also knew, but assumed that neither of them would disclose anything to anybody.

"God Robert, this is serious." Phyllis interrupted his thoughts. "It proves that Becky is right and that she's definitely onto something."

That statement punched Robert in the stomach. He knew that Phyllis was correct in her assumption, but they were still nowhere near getting any clues as to where they needed to look. How did this person know where Becky lived? Why had this only happened now? So many questions and no answers. If only they could find out what Martin Smithson was trying to hide. Was he trying to hide something? Ophelia seemed so sure – but was it just her imagination? No, of course it wasn't. Even if Robert didn't claim to be as intuitive as Ophelia, he could read the solicitor's body language on both occasions when they met and he lost count of the nervous tics and twitches that the solicitor displayed.

* * * * *

"We need to step up to the plate Phyllis" said Ophelia when they met up later that day.

"But Robert's doing everything he can Ophelia, I can't see what else he can do."

"Oh, please don't take what I've said the wrong way. You're absolutely right, Robert is going way beyond the call of duty to resolve this problem. But I just wonder if there's something we can do."

"Like what?"

"I don't know. For some reason I just feel we should go back to see this solicitor. You and me."

"Just us two? But what about Robert?"

"I think he's quite intimidated by Robert. Let's face it, Robert can be quite the tour de force when he puts his mind to it. I'm just wondering if a more subtle womanly approach might not work."

"Do you think?" Phyllis didn't seem convinced.

"Are you busy today?" asked Ophelia.

"Well no, but ....."

"Come on, there's a bus going into town in ten minutes. Let's catch it. The solicitors office isn't far from the town centre."

With one spontaneous swift movement, Phyllis had picked up her shoulder bag and the two women headed towards the bus stop.

"I must admit it's not as comfortable as driving in Robert's car, but we can't always depend on Robert to be there as our personal chauffeur" said Ophelia.

"More's the pity" commented Phyllis.

When they alighted the bus, Ophelia pointed in the direction of the law firm's premises and they walked stridently towards the building. When they entered the building, the same receptionist greeted them and when she saw Ophelia, her face dropped.

"No need to be like that my dear. We've just come to see your Mr. Smithson again."

"He's busy all morning and doesn't have time to see you" replied the receptionist. Her response was quite curt.

"Well in that case" said Ophelia, in that irritatingly calm, cool tone with the undercurrent of a pick axe, "we'll just have to call the police on the possible charge of attempted murder by poisoning."

The receptionist didn't know how to take this. Was Ophelia bluffing? Possibly, but she wasn't sure.

"Oh if you don't believe me, you can call the hospital. Our friend is on a secure ward, but if you ask for a Dr. Baxter and ask him how Becky Collerton is after the attempt on her life by poisoning, I'm sure he'd be only to happy to tell you. Now do be a dear and run along and fetch Mr. Smithson."

The receptionist felt trapped. If she went through and alerted Martin Smithson, he would be particularly angry, especially if this claim turned out to be false. On the other hand, police arresting a solicitor would not look good for the firm.

"Wait here a minute" she said, just as curtly as before.

A minute later Martin Smithson walked into reception, following the receptionist. He looked directly at Ophelia.

"What's all this nonsense about an attempted murder? Why do you keep hounding me when I've told you I don't know anything about this Becky whatever her name is. And who is this person you've dragged off the street?" He looked pointedly at Phyllis.

"Oh sorry Mr. Smithson, how rude of me. This person who I definitely did NOT drag off the street is a very dear friend of mine called Phyllis. Phyllis, let me introduce you to this very rude solicitor. His name is Martin Smithson."

For a moment there was a stunned silence. Phyllis looked at Martin Smithson and he in turn looked back at her.

"Martin?" she said. "Martin Smithson? Is it really you?"

"Who are you?" asked Mr. Smithson, though there was something about Phyllis that seemed vaguely familiar.

"It's Phyllis. You don't remember me? We went out together back in the sixties when you were at university."

Both Ophelia and the receptionist looked first at each other, then back at Martin and Phyllis.

"Phyllis Brewer? My god, you've ..... cha ......"

"Oh you don't have to be polite Martin. Yes, I've put weight on over the years and the hair is greying now. But you've kept in shape I have to say."

"You two knew each other?" Ophelia asked, although she'd already heard about the pair's previous acquaintance.

Phyllis blushed slightly. "Erm yes, well it was a long time ago."

Martin Smithson stood in silence for a while.

"How's your wife?" asked Phyllis. "I did enquire through the grapevine as to what happened to you and I found out you'd got married. Do you have children?"

"We're divorced and we have two children."

"Oh I'm sorry about the former, but congratulations on the latter." Phyllis smiled and Martin suddenly recognised that this was indeed the same Phyllis Brewer who he had dated in the sixties.

"And you?" he asked. "Still with that biker you ran off with?" His tone was accusatory.

"Well no, but we are still good friends."

"As long as you're happy" he replied, again with that tone.

"Looks like you've done well for yourself Martin. I always knew you would. Always conscientious and studious."

"What were the words you and your friends used back then? Let me see now – a nerd and a geek."

Phyllis blushed again. "I was young and foolish then. I did and said stupid things. I am sorry Martin, I didn't mean it."

"It's ancient history now" replied Martin. "We've led our own lives."

Phyllis was about to reply when Ophelia interjected. "Um, this is all quite fascinating, a strange coincidence indeed, but with all due respect to both of you, we've come here about a very important matter."

Martin's face, having previously mellowed slightly, stiffened up again. "Look I told you the other day, I don't know anything about your friend." His tone wasn't quite as harsh as it had been on their previous visit. Ophelia couldn't help feeling that the re-acquaintance between he and Phyllis may have had something to do with this.

"Well possibly Mr. Smithson, but there's been a very sinister turn of events" Ophelia replied. She didn't tell him what those events were. She wanted him to interact and ask what had happened.

"Sinister?" he questioned.

"Yes. Well Becky, that is, Phyllis and my friend – the lady in question – somebody tried to kill her with poison the other night. She's currently on a secure ward in the hospital. I'm afraid it's gone from a simple burglary to a full blown murder attempt."

Martin Smithson couldn't hide the look of shock on his face. He stuttered several times. "But surely, you're not accusing me of being involved? I had nothing to do with it – and I can provide solid alibis for the last few evenings. I've been working here late with two of my colleagues."

"Oh there's no question in my mind as to your innocence Mr. Smithson" said Ophelia. She was about to use 'that' voice again. A soothing tone of Spanish Inquisitorial delight. "As to your lack of knowledge about this situation .... well, that's a totally different matter altogether."

"Now hang on ...." the solicitor interjected.

Ophelia looked at him with daggers. "Hang on nothing Mr Smithson." Her voice was deadly quiet. "I know that you have some knowledge – I don't quite know what it is, but I'm determined to get to the bottom of it. Phyllis and I haven't known Becky very long but we've become very fond of her ....

and very protective. If you think I'm going to sit by and let people make attempts on her life when I know that other people are withholding vital information, you have me very much mistaken."

Even Phyllis shuddered as she heard her dear friend speak in such a way. It was enough to make anybody confess to murder straight away, regardless of whether they'd commited it or not.

"And what exactly am I supposed to know?"

"You tell me, Mr. Smithson, you tell me. My friend Mr Whitehead is very good at reading body language and between us, we both managed to ascertain that you're hiding something. Now all you have to do is give us some information and we promise we'll leave you alone."

"Please Martin" added Phyllis softly. "If not for me for being a total jerk back then, please do it for Becky. She doesn't deserve this – first of all doors closing in on her from all directions when she's been looking for answers and now this – an attempt on her life."

The solicitor shuffled uncomfortably. "Look, I can't talk to you right now. Leave your number with me and I'll endeavour to call you if I can."

Ophelia walked closer to the solicitor. She was slightly taller than he and her eyes pierced into him. "Make sure you endeavour in earnest Mr. Smithson. I will be waiting to hear from you. If I don't, my friend Mr. Whitehead might have to use a method he's found very effective for obtaining information from people." It sounded like a threat but Phyllis knew that Ophelia was referring to Ian Pemberton's device. How they were going to extract a sample of blood out of the solicitor was anybody's conjecture, but if Ophelia could happen upon a bloody tissues lying on a floor, only to find out that Sue had been having a fling with her son-in-law, it shouldn't be too difficult to find ways of obtaining some lovely little particles of DNA from Mr. Smithson.

"If you're threatening me ...." he blurted.

"Oh, I never threaten people" said Ophelia in her softest voice. "Violence and blackmail are so vulgar and so base." She walked up close out of earshot of Phyllis and whispered to him "I recently found out that a mutual friend of mine and Phyllis had taken her son-in-law to bed, and here's the thing. We didn't have to ask either of them to confess. We found out by quite unconventional means. It's fascinating Mr. Smithson, absolutely fascinating." She moved away.

The solicitor shuddered. He didn't like what Ophelia might be implying – mainly because he wasn't sure exactly what she was implying.

"Come on Phyllis. We need to go now but I'm sure our journey hasn't been wasted. We'll be hearing from you Mr. Smithson. Goodbye."

"Goodbye Martin, it's good to see you again. I just wish it was in more pleasant circimstances. Take care" said Phyllis, a tone of sadness in her voice.

Chapter Fourteen

"Come on Phyllis, spill the beans. I want to know all about you and Martin Smithson. What an absolute turn up for the books."

As Phyllis and Ophelia sat on the bus taking them home, Ophelia coaxed her friend to tell her the whole story.

"Oh Ophelia, I'm not exactly proud of myself."

"Why, what happened?"

Phyllis sighed. "It was such a long time ago now ....."

"Phyllis, we all have pasts and we've all made mistakes. You know I wouldn't tell anybody. I couldn't help noticing how your demeanour changed when you saw Mr Smithson, er, Martin again. Now something significant must have happened to make you react in that way."

Phyllis let out another sigh. "It was back in the sixties." She looked reflective. "They say that what happened in the sixties stayed in the sixties ..... but it didn't."

There was a short pause until Ophelia encouraged her to go on.

"And?"

"I was still quite innocent when I met Martin. I was doing a college course in art and he'd just started at university. We met in a coffee bar and got chatting. Anyway, one thing led to another and we decided to go out together." Phyllis paused again, her gaze looking into the distance. "We had a great time. We used to go to dances, out for long walks, discussing philosophy, all sorts. He really did have a sharp mind. We were really happy."

"So what happened?" asked Ophelia.

"Well, a friend of mine encouraged me to smoke a bit of grass. Nothing serious, just a bit here and there. It was a giggle. Then I met some of her friends and got involved with them. I took a couple of hits of acid as well." Phyllis let out a chuckle. "Well it was the sixties after all. That's when I met Tony and his gang. Oh, they've never been into any trouble. Always a good bunch of guys. But it was the allure of the dangerousness associated with them that attracted me. Well, I fell for Tony big time. I started seeing less and less of Martin. At first he couldn't understand why and asked what was wrong. I just gave him some feeble excuse like my college work was starting to take up all my time. Until .... that night." Phyllis let out a huge sigh.

"That night?"

"Yes. I told Martin I couldn't see him because I was studying. I was really out on the town with Tony and his biker friends. We'd all had a bit of weed. Anyway, guess who should happen along."

"Oh dear, let me guess - Martin."

Phyllis nodded. "Oh dear indeed. When he saw me he made a slightly sarcastic remark, something like 'I see you're studying hard Phyllis.' Well, Tony didn't like his tone and he told Martin to get lost. Martin replied back with an equally sarcastic remark, something about Tony being welcome to me, but his tone was so derisory and it was obviously aimed at me. This didn't go down well with Tony and he went towards Martin as if he was going to beat him up. I shouted at Tony to leave him alone. Trouble was I was in a bit of a giggly mood due to the acid and a few of the bikers were stoned. Well, there was a water fountain in the town centre that formed into a sculptured shell so it was quite shallow. Anyway ..... Tony and a few of his friends decided to get hold of Martin, take all his clothes off and throw him in the fountain. Of course, because I was on acid I just laughed my head off. I mean at the time I thought it was hysterically funny." Phyllis let out a loud long sigh. "I never saw Martin again ...... until today."

"Oh" said Ophelia.

"Exactly" said Phyllis. "Oh. I treated him abominably and he didn't deserve it. He was such a nice guy. Always so polite, so considerate, never tried anything funny on. We really had some good times and I blew it."

Ophelia stayed silent. This was not the time for feedback.

"I mean you could say it didn't work out too disastrously. You know how it is with me and Tony. I love him to bits but I could never go out with him, he's just a serial gang-bang merchant. But Martin .... well he was a true gentleman. I must say as well, after seeing him today, he's aged very well."

Ophelia could have interjected at this point that Phyllis was lovely just as she was and indeed, she did actually feel that way about Phyllis. But she knew that Phyllis felt that she hadn't taken care of herself .... whereas Martin obviously had.

"I don't know what to say Phyllis." Now it was Ophelia's turn to speak with a tone of sadness. "I can't argue, he is distinguished looking. I mean Robert's distinguished looking but Martin is ......"

"Oh come on Ophelia, don't mince with your words ..... he's more beddable."

Ophelia blushed. "Well I wouldn't quite have used that expression Phyllis, but ....."

Phyllis laughed. "That's why I love you Ophelia. You're far more subtle than I'll ever be."

Both women laughed.

"I did think about him occasionally and wondered how his life turned out" said Phyllis.

"Well, divorced with two children" observed Ophelia.

"And a PA with a serious attitude problem."

Again, both women laughed. They talked a little more about their respective histories when the subject turned again back to the present situation.

"I just don't know what we're going to do. You seem certain that he's hiding something Ophelia, and I don't doubt you for one minute. But you don't honestly think he was somehow involved in ....."

"Oh no Phyllis, I don't imagine for one minute that he had anything to do with Becky being poisoned. But I just know he's holding something back. He always seems so twitchy and nervous."

"But couldn't that just be his default position? Some people are naturally nervous."

"Well you knew him before I did, was he like this back then?"

"Well no. Quite the opposite. Always so calm and reassuring."

"There you are then. So something is obviously bothering him about this case. Which begs the question, what does he know about it?"

"Well what can he know about it."

"Oh Phyllis, he's a criminal lawyer! Of course he could know about it. You know how they're always reading up on historic legal cases to see how the system dealt with similar situations in the past. I've no doubt that he's familiar with this case." Ophelia paused a second and then frowned. "I just wonder .... how famiiar?"

"Oh my god, you don't think he was working for the prosecution do you?" Phyllis couldn't hide the shock in her voice.

Ophelia frowned again. "I hate to say it Phyllis but ..... you might have something there."

"Oh no! I hope not. How would Becky feel if she knew we'd met somebody who was responsible for sentencing her brother to life in prison."

"I don't like the direction this is starting to take. The trouble is ..... you could have a point."

The two women had been so engrossed in conversation that they nearly missed their stop.

"Oh god Ophelia, look, we're supposed to get off here!"

Luckily another passenger had rung the bell for the bus to stop so it came to a halt and this alerted both Phyllis and Ophelia to the fact that they'd reached their destination. They thanked the driver, alighted from the bus and started heading towards Phyllis's house. As they got nearer, they noticed a car parked outside. The driver was just about to drive off when he spotted the two women. It was turning to dusk and they couldn't see clearly who it was.

"What's that car doing outside my house?" said Phyllis apprehensively.

Ophelia stopped and looked. She saw that the man in the car was also looking at them – more quizzically than anything. They then heard a familiar voice.

"Ophelia? Phyllis? Is that you?"

Both women let out a sigh of relief.

"It's Robert" said Ophelia. "Yes Robert" she called. "It's us."

"I popped round to your house earlier, but when I realised you weren't in I assumed you'd come over to see Phyllis so I thought I'd drop by to share what I've found out."

"Oh good" said Ophelia. "We have some interesting

news too."

Phyllis walked up her garden path and unlocked her door. Even though she had no incence alight in the house, the smell of its remnants hit you as you walked in the door.

"You two go and make yourself comfortable. I'll put the kettle on and make a drink. I'll get something for Pywackit as well."

Pywackit looked up at Phyllis as if to say "where have you been? I've been neglected and you're not treating me the way royalty should be treated."

"Oh I'm sorry darling, we got carried away. You know I wouldn't deliberately leave you on your own for so long."

Phyllis gave Pywackit some of his treats and he took them disdainfully as if to say, "don't let it happen again."

Phyllis carried the tray of drinks into the living room, taking the seat opposite Ophelia and Robert.

"Don't worry Phyllis, I haven't told Robert anything. I thought I'd let you."

"Me? Why?"

"Oh come on, a disclosure like that – only you can tell Robert" replied Ophelia, as if it was a big moment for Phyllis.

"Well really it's no great revelation" she said as she observed Robert's expectant expression.

"Go on" he said.

"Well as we told you, we went to visit the solicitor today to see if we could glean any further information out of him. Well, I certainly gleaned more information than I was expecting."

"And what was that?" asked Robert.

"I only went out with him for a while back in the sixties."

Robert looked at Phyllis, stunned.

"Are you sure? I mean, you're sure it's the same person."

Phyllis sighed ..... she'd been doing a lot of that today. "Yes Robert, it's the very same one. Only when we parted ways back then, it wasn't in very pleasant circumstances."

"Oh?" Robert looked cautious, as if he didn't want to bring back any raw memories for her.

Phyllis proceeded to tell Robert how she'd gone out with

Martin in the sixties, how nice he was too her and how she suddenly started mixing more with her friends who had discovered things like hash and acid. She then told him about the incident where Tony and his friends had stripped Martin naked and thrown him into the fountain while she stood by laughing hysterically.

Robert sat quietly.

"It's ok Robert, you don't have to say anything, the look on your face says it all. I can't justify what I did. I treated him terribly – but when you're off your tits on acid, something like that can seem hysterically funny. It was like something out of a cartoon at the time. It was only when I came off the trip that I realised how badly I'd treated him, but it was too late by then. I never saw him again after that."

"Well we all do things we're not proud of Phyllis ...."

"Yes, yes, Ophelia has already told me that. But there's a difference between doings things we're not proud of and then being a total jerk. God it was rotten! So mean – in the so-called world of love and peace." Phyllis's tone seemed slightly bitter.

"Ok, but on a practical level you can't turn back the clock and undo what's been done" Robert tried to reassure her.

"I know" she said. "But had I known who this solicitor was going to turn out to be, I never would have agreed to meet him."

"I'm sorry Phyllis, that was my idea" said Ophelia.

"Oh don't be silly Ophelia, we were bound to meet up sooner or later with this case going on. It was just a case of it being sooner rather than later."

Neither Robert nor Ophelia replied as they both realised that Phyllis had just made a valid point. As this case developed further, paths were bound to cross and undoubtedly Phyllis and Martin would have re-acquainted at some point.

"The thing to do now" continued Phyllis, "is to put my stuff behind me and focus on what's most important. That's Becky's well being and trying to solve this riddle."

"So you didn't manage to get anymore information out of him?" asked Robert.

"No" said Ophelia. "But I did tell him that we weren't going to leave him alone until he gave us some information and I did warn him that we had persuasive means of gaining such information."

"Oh?" said Robert.

"Well" said Ophelia. "I did think about using Ian's device to find out what he knew, but of course I realised it would mean we'd have to get a blood sample from him and he's hardly likely to go offering it freely is he. A bit silly of me, but my enthusiasm got the better of me."

"But you were good" Phyllis giggled. "Bless him, he looked seriously worried when you told him that violence and blackmail were vulgar and that I'd found out a snippet of very interesting information concerning two people I knew and I didn't have to ask either of them to disclose it."

Robert shot a look at Ophelia and she suddenly realised that she nearly let slip the fact that Chris and Sue had slept together.

"Oh, what information was that?" asked Phyllis, completely innocently.

Robert flashed another look at Ophelia.

"Oh, it was er, just some information about two separate clients of mine. One of them had some information that she was withholding but it became apparent that things were not quite as they seemed between them."

Robert looked at Ophelia as if to say "that was too close but well done, you squirmed your way out of that one nicely."

Ophelia felt a wave of relief when she saw Robert's reaction.

"Well maybe you could use the same method with Martin."

"I don't think it would work Phyllis." Ophelia was choosing her words carefully – she wasn't lying as such, she was just skirting around the facts.

"Well" said Robert, "I can't deny it's an interesting coincidence that you should meet him again after all this time ...."

"A bit like Alan and Becky" interrupted Phyllis.

"Yes indeed" agreed Robert. "But we're still no further on with him than we were originally, though I appreciate your effort for trying. I just hope we don't frighten him off."

"I don't think so Robert, he took my number and said that he might get in touch. I have a strange feeling he will."

"Well if he doesn't we're going to have to press him now that Becky's life's in danger."

"Yes, you're right" said Ophelia. "What about you Robert? What did you find out today?"

"Well not as much as I would have liked to but I did manage to confirm all of the details that Becky told us. For example, the blood group of the killer was different to Tom's – in both murders."

"You mean the girlfriend and Tom's friend?" asked Ophelia.

"Yes, that's right. Not only that, Tom was indeed on the Isle of Wight the night that his friend's girlfriend was murdered and one more important fact."

"Which is?" asked Phyllis. Both she and Ophelia looked at Robert expectantly.

"Several of the original witnesses said that they saw somebody running out of Nick's house – that's the name of Tom's friend – just after 7.30 pm. They were quite certain of it as Coronation Street had just started and they heard somebody banging loudly on a front door and went to see what the commotion was. They noticed the door was open and heard some screams coming from inside the house. They were too scared to go and investigate and the next thing they saw was this person running out of the house and down the street. Shortly after that Tom turned up."

"We know this already, but the police made the lame excuse that Tom had just run round the block, cleaned himself up and came back pretending he was innocent" said Ophelia.

"Yes they did" said Robert. "But I've found a photocopy of the speeding ticket" said Robert.

"Where did you get that!" exclaimed Phyllis.

"I know a couple of people in the force that could lead me to the information, although I was led to believe that the original ticket was destroyed before the trial began.

"But why?" Phyllis looked baffled.

"To cover up Tom's innocence Phyllis" said Ophelia.

Robert then produced the photocopy of the speeding ticket. It clearly had Tom's name on it, the date of the fine and more importantly, the time. 7.30 pm.

"That's our smoking gun!" exclaimed Phyllis. "That

proves he wasn't there when the murder occured."

"Absolutely Phyllis!" agreed Robert.

"Well this is great news, but how can we use it going forward?" she quipped.

"I found out another piece of information which may or may not prove useful" replied Robert.

"Which is?" Phyllis was virtually hanging on the edge of her seat and nearly spilt her tea.

"I found the name of the Judge who took the case. Luckily he's still alive though I understand he's not in the best of health. I've tracked him down and I've decided I'm going to pay him a visit."

"Is that wise?" asked Ophelia. "You need to be careful Robert, you don't want somebody accusing you of harrassing an elderly man."

"Don't worry Ophelia, I'll use my usual gentlemanly subtlety."

"Well if it's anything like Ophelia's today, I'd rather take on a shark" laughed Phyllis.

Even Ophelia found that funny.

"So where do we go from here?" asked Phyllis.

"Well, the final piece of news is that the police confirmed that Becky's milk had indeed been poisoned" said Robert.

Phyllis and Ophelia couldn't hide their shock, even though they were expecting this news.

"I've been advised that Becky is well enough to come out of hospital but the police have suggested that she stay with friends and so if you don't mind Phyllis, I'd like her to stay with you for a while again."

"Absolutely!" said Phyllis. "As long as she likes."

"Thanks Phyllis. It means a lot. In the meantime, I need to go and ask this judge some questions and see if I can get some answers out of him."

Chapter Fifteen

Speaking to the judge who oversaw the original trial was not as easy as Robert thought it would be. Although he'd used his powers of persuasion to obtain his home address, he realised that if he were to go round to the judge's house, he could quite easily slam the door on Robert and possibly even call the police. He needed to find out the judge's movements to see if there was somewhere he could have a quiet word where the judge couldn't slam the door closed so easily.

"Old man Eldridge?" said one of Robert's colleagues. "Oh yes, I know where you can find him."

"Oh yes? Where's that?"

"Why the interest?"

"Just interested in one of his cases."

Robert's colleague looked at him. "What are you up to Robert?"

"Nothing Jerry, just want to have a chat."

"I know what your chats consist of" chuckled Jerry.

"Well, up to you, if you don't want to tell me, I'll find out some other way."

"Nice one Robert, always the classic 'treat it with indifference' routine. Good reverse psychology. But what if I call your bluff."

"Go ahead." Robert smiled. "Been nice chatting to you Jerry. Got to go now, things to do, places to go, people to meet." Robert was about to walk off.

"Hang on a minute, come back here." Had Jerry fallen for the bait?

Robert turned back to face his friend. "Better make it quick, I'm a busy man."

"Come on Robert, what's the low down? Why is this judge of interest to you?"

"Well I figured that if he's in poor health, he may just want to clear his conscience before he meets the big boss judge in the sky."

"Oh please, spare me Robert."

"Stranger things have happened at sea."

"Do you think you're honestly going to make that pompous old prick feel guilty about all the poor bastards he's sent down?"

"If one of them was innocent and he knew it, I'll give it a go."

"One of them? Oh Robert, you really are naive. I wouldn't be surprised if at least 50% of the people he sent down were innocent. Do you think old man Eldridge would give a shit?"

"He might if he knew the circumstances and the impact it's had on the people close to those he sent down."

"Oh Robert, Robert, Robert." Jerry patted him on the back. "You have this mistaken, nay, deluded idea that just because you are a man of principle, that everybody else is. It doesn't work like that in the real world."

"You mean I wouldn't be able to trust you?"

Jerry laughed. "Of course you would, you old sod. But I don't hold any position of authority. People don't treat me with that kind of reverence. Can you imagine being addressed as 'Your Honour' all the time? That's got to make you feel as though you're something special. Fact is, turds come out of his ass just like the rest of us."

"Jerry you're an old friend, but why do you have to stoop to vulgarity every time we have a conversation like this?"

"Just telling it like it is old chum. I met him once – thoroughly dislikable character. Most of the judges on the circuit around that time were pretty decent people. They went by the rule of law, tried to do their job properly, researched all the facts – all above board. Then there's old man Eldridge. Firmly up his own posterior. He loved sending what he called 'the little people' down. Facts were almost irrelevant. If he didn't like the look of them, he'd use his poisonous little tongue to sway the jury in whatever way he could."

"But if the facts were laid before them, they could make their own judgment, surely."

"Oh Robert, for god's sake, be real man. Facts could be twisted, evidence could be destroyed, people could be bribed. I wouldn't mind betting that if he didn't get laid the night before, the next day the poor bugger in the dock was going to go down even if he was a bloody saint!"

This comment came like a punch in the gut. He thought about the speeding ticket that was clear evidence proving that Tom Collerton couldn't have murdered his friend.

"And as for that prick of a son of his, Jesus, if ever there was a bigger crook on this planet, I'd be surprised. That's what was so funny. I bet he was a real thorn in his old man's side. Can you imagine, His Honour Judge Eldridge, the mighty magistrate having a son that everybody knew was a pilfering, thieving, no good liar. Sent to all the rights schools, expensive private education – and look how he turned out."

"Really?" said Robert with interest. Perhaps he could add this to his armoury of weapons when speaking to the judge.

"Well you're the bloody clinical psychologist Robert. I don't need to tell you about good ol' fashioned Freudian transference. Couldn't bear to think that his little Tristran – I mean Jesus, pretentious name or what – was anything less than perfect, coming from his seed. So what does he do – transfer all of darling little Tristran's imperfections onto the public. God knows how many scrapes he dragged him out of."

"Oh yes? And where is this Tristran now?"

"He disappeared years ago. Nobody knows where he went. Probably ended up running some seedy little brothel somewhere. Never did an honest day's work in his life so he would have some other mug or mugs to do his bidding for him."

"You do realise you're only giving me more ammunition to use against our Mr. Eldridge if I do get to meet him."

"Why do you think I'm feeding this all to you Robert. I'd love to see the old goat squirm when he hears that everybody knows about his sordid little shit of a son."

"You're a harsh man Jerry."

"Difference is Robert, it's all talk in my case – I'm not responsible for sending some poor sucker to prison for something they didn't do."

"Ok, so if you would like to imagine me feeding all this back to our honourable judge, where can I find him?"

"You drive a hard bargain Mr Whitehead, but buy me a drink next time we catch up and I'll tell you."

"I haven't got that much time Jerry."

"That's ok old man. I'll take the drink in lieu, but right now, your Mr Eldridge can be found at the local bowls club on

Tuesday mornings, weather permitting of course. I'm not sure if non-members are allowed in but you could just say you've come to give your condolensces as his son was found hanging from a barbed wire with a cucumber stuck up his jacksie."

Robert looked at his friend incredulously. "Jerry, you really do need to get out more often."

"Don't I know it old chum. But the lady indoors won't let me. Keeps my nose to the grind."

"Well, as long as she keeps you on a leash and gives you your rabies shot regularly, I'm sure the public are safe."

Jerry laughed. "Humour as dry as ever. Let me know how you get on Robert – and I want to hear all the graphic details of how the old man squirms when you give it to him in the gut."

"Goodbye Jerry, give your wife my sympathies."

"Always old man, always."

* * * * *

The following Tuesday Robert decided to venture down to the bowls club to see if Judge Eldridge was indeed where Jerry said he would be. He made sure that he was appropriately suited and booted to add an air of respectability which would make his demeanour non-threatening to the receptionist. He used his powers of persuasion to assure her that he needed to see Mr Eldridge about some pressing business but that it wouldn't take long.

"He's in that group over there" said the receptionist. She pointed to a group of members shuffling around the lawn.

"Thank you" said Robert. He headed towards the group of elderly men.

"Can I speak to Mr Eldridge?" he enquired as he approached them. One person looked at him quizzically.

"What's it about?"

Robert smiled at him, his friendliest smile, trying to reassure the elderly man that he was no threat.

"Just a quiet word if that's ok. It'll only take five minutes."

The elderly man looked suspiciously at Robert but agreed to speak to him and indicated a quiet table at the edge of the lawn. They both sat down.

"What is it?" The man's voice was abrupt.

"I'm interested in one of your cases Mr Eldridge. I wondered if you wouldn't mind sharing some information with me?"

"I've overseen thousands of cases. You expect me to remember each of them?" That curt tone again.

"It might help if I show you a picture of the defendant to see if it triggers any memories." Robert pulled out the picture from the newspaper clipping that Becky had given him and showed it to the judge.

"Vaguely remember. Can't say I can recall what the case was about. Why do you want to know?"

"Well it's like this Mr Eldridge. You gave this man a life sentence several decades ago now for a crime he didn't commit. The worst part of it was there was enough evidence to prove he was innocent."

"What rot! Who's put you up to this? Haven't you got anything better to do?"

"Oh I'm a very busy man Mr Eldridge. But you see, this man died in prison several years ago and a close relative of his made him a promise that she would find the guilty party to clear his name."

"If I've heard that line once, I've heard it a thousand times."

"Well, perhaps in some cases, that line happens to be true."

"What are you, one of those bleeding-heart liberals? You're all the same, you can't accept that some people are just out and out evil."

Robert moved forward and looked directly at the judge. "And what about your son, dear Tristran." He smiled. "Bit of a pompous name really isn't it? What is he doing these days for a living? I hear he was a bit of a scallywag back in the day."

"Keep him out of this, I can't be held responsible for his actions."

"No, you never could, could you? Even when he was younger you were having to pull him out of fights, use your position to cover up for him. Not bad having a father who can wash away all your misdemeanours."

"If you think you're going to use blackmail against me you can forget ......"

Oh Mr Eldridge, I would never stoop so low as to blackmail somebody." Robert paused. "But then again, if I could dig up some juicy information, I could go to the press. You know how those leftie papers love a good 'how the mighty are fallen' headline. They just love dragging the names of the well-to-do and upper crust through the mud. Keeps them in work, you know."

"Oh really? And what are you going to tell them with no evidence?"

"Well as a matter of fact I'm collecting quite a bit of evidence. I'm sure you're aware of the advances of DNA evidence. I understand that the blood group of the murderer and the convicted man were completely different. The timelines don't match. Goodness, he was accused of two murders and he wasn't even in the country at the time of the first murder. A bit inconvenient these facts, wouldn't you say?"

"If you can find the evidence, you go ahead."

"You seem very sure that the evidence doesn't exist. Could that be because you helped to have it destroyed?"

"That's one hell of an accusation to make – and without substance."

"Oh it's not the only thing around here that has no substance – I'm looking at such an entity as we speak!" Robert's voice was harsh. He was beginning to tire of this man's pomposity.

"Insult me all you like. It makes no difference to the fact that you're making accusations with no evidence. If you can come forward with some real evidence and facts – that's what cases rest on – evidence and facts, then maybe I might be prepared to give you the time of day. In the meantime, I have more important things to tend to – like joining my friends for a game of bowls. Now be on your way." The elderly man stood up and flicked his hand towards Robert as if shooing him away like an irritating fly.

Robert could feel his anger rising, but he knew that the cantankerous old man was right. He wasn't prepared to leave without having the final word though.

"Like father like son I should imagine. I wouldn't be

surprised if any offspring of yours was living off the ill-gotten gains of some poor possie of drug-dependent sex workers to keep him in the lifestyle which he arrogantly assumes to be his birthright. I shouldn't think for one minute that all the private education he undertook did him any good." Robert's comments were well below the belt and he knew he'd dropped his standards – but there was something about this old man that infuriated him.

The retired judge turned his back and ignored Robert, although he was getting some interested looks from the group that were playing.

Robert left the club and thanked the receptionist politely for her help. She smiled and said "you're welcome", completely oblivious to the less than pleasant exchange of words that had just taken place. If Robert had been determined to help Becky before today's meeting, he was even more determined now.

Chapter Sixteen

"What an arrogant prick" hissed Phyllis. "So typical of the establishment!"

"Phyllis, this isn't the sixties. You can't go blackening the name of the entire 'establishment' because of a few bad apples" Robert replied. "I must admit though ... whilst I wouldn't have put it in quite those words, I share your sentiment."

"I hope he gets his dick caught in his zip after he's been for a pee!" she added.

Robert laughed. "You do bring light relief to the situation Phyllis. I've now got an image in my head of such an occurence. I can't say I'm not enjoying it."

Phyllis hadn't meant to bring myrth to the table but it did help to lighten the tension.

"I wish you'd told me all that's happened Robert. Why did you keep it from me?" asked Alan.

"I'm sorry Alan, but I just get the feeling that Sue's not overly-enamoured with Becky and probably doesn't share your sympathy for her predicament."

"I think there may be a little jealousy there" added Ophelia in a quiet tone.

"I don't like us talking behind Sue's back like this" said Phyllis. "It makes me feel disloyal and she's my best friend, that is, alongside you Ophelia."

"I know Phyllis" said Ophelia, trying to reassure her friend. "We're not badmouthing Sue, we're just pointing out the facts as they are and this is why we can't always share the information with you Alan, because it might upset Sue."

"I understand" said Alan. "She has been different since we met Becky on the plane. I can't help feeling that something else is bothering her as well, but she won't talk to me about it. You know my Sue, always so bossy, always barking orders at me. She's been very subdued recently and I don't know why. I can't imagine it's just because of Becky."

Robert and Ophelia shot each other a sly glance out of eyesight of both Alan and Phyllis. They knew exactly why Sue had suddenly become subdued – her little liaison with Chris had been exposed and not only did it make her feel embarrassed and ashamed, but it also made her look like a hypocrite if she started accusing Alan of having an affair with Becky behind her back. Even if he was seeing her intimately, it had an air of conventionality to it in as much as this was an old flame of Alan's and the age gap was minimal. It didn't hold quite the same reactionary disgust value as a married woman having sex with her son-in-law.

"Maybe you just need to give her a bit of time Alan" suggested Ophelia. "She may be trying to untangle a few different feelings that are going on inside her right now."

"Possibly." Alan smiled at Ophelia. Normally he wasn't overly-keen on this crazy new age witch as he often described her to Sue, but he knew she was only trying to help the situation.

"I don't wish to sound cold Alan, but I would like to bring the conversation back to Becky."

"Oh quite" said Alan. "I am concerned about her."

Both Phyllis and Ophelia sensed that Alan was concerned about Becky and that perhaps old feelings hadn't quite gone away.

"She's coming out of hospital tomorrow and we've agreed that she's coming here to stay with Phyllis" said Robert. "Ophelia's staying here as well so that there's always somebody around her. I'm going to do shopping trips and if any of the three ladies need to get out, I can provide a taxi service."

"I still don't think it's fair that you're taking all of this on Robert" said Ophelia.

"It's the only practical thing to do right now. We need to keep her safe. Now I've gone all around this place to make sure all the locks are secure and trust me, nobody will be able to break in here."

"But in the meantime, we're no nearer solving this case" said Phyllis. "You can't take on the role of a 24-hour guard and investigate this case as well Robert" Phyllis pointed out.

"Look, I'll help out in whatever way I can. Sue seems to be wrapping herself up in work at the moment. I know she might be jealous if she thinks I'm helping in any way, but if she knows that Becky is staying with Phyllis at least she'll know that we're not having an affair. She knows that Phyllis wouldn't stand for such a thing under her roof."

"Damn right I wouldn't" said Phyllis. "I've grown extremely fond of Becky but I would never betray Sue's confidence and trust and if I even suspected that you were coming round here to have your wicked way with Becky Mr Baylock, I'd cut your balls off while you were in the act."

Robert and Alan both laughed at Phyllis's bluntness.

"Now don't hold back Phyllis, you tell it like it is. Put me straight right from the outset" chuckled Alan.

"You know it!" Phyllis had that determined look on her face. "You don't double-cross my friend Sue if you value your life!"

"Horror of horrors that you would set Pywackit onto me!"

"If you're making fun of my cat I swear I'll put a hex on you!"

"Now Alan, behave yourself. Stop winding Phyllis up or I'll personally pour catnip all over you and let Pywackit run amok!"

"Sorry Robert" said Alan, trying hard to suppress a smirk.

"Now come on, we've got to get down to some serious business. Mainly where do we go from here?" Robert ruminated over the events of the past few days.

"Well we're certainly not going to get any joy out of that judge" said Phyllis. "The arrogant prick obviously doesn't want to admit that he's done any wrong."

"Then there's Martin Smithson" said Robert, although he was reluctant to mention his name in front of Phyllis.

"Oh it's ok Robert, you can't tread on eggshells around me. It's ancient history now."

"Ancient history? What's this about?" asked Alan. He hadn't been told about Martin and Phyllis's past liaison. When Phyllis told him the story of her relationship with Martin, he looked astonished.

"God almighty, it seems as though everybody is meeting up with their long lost lovers."

"Not all of us" corrected Ophelia. Robert and I have not – and are not likely to have such an encounter."

"Well I wouldn't be surprised if you do, the way things

are going" he said.

"Sorry to cut into the conversation, but can we come back to the matter in hand" said Robert.

"Sorry Robert, yes of course" said Phyllis.

"Ophelia, you seem certain that Martin knows something, but even if he does, how do you propose to get anything out of him?" quizzed Robert.

"That's a good question Robert. He did say he may call me back at some point."

"We can't rely on that though can we?" asked Alan.

"No we can't" said Robert.

"The only way we could get information out of him is to stab him, get a sample of his blood and run it through Ian Pemberton's device."

Alan, Ophelia and Robert all looked at Phyllis with raised eyebrows.

"Oh I'm just kidding of course, but that's what we need. A sample of his blood. You know, in the same way that we got a sample of Chris's blood the other week."

Alan looked up at Phyllis and frowned. "I didn't know you'd done that. How did that happen?"

"That's a story for another day Alan, we keep going off subject" Ophelia jumped in.

"Nice work Ophelia" said Robert under his breath, out of earshot.

"Would it work with any sample of DNA or just blood?" asked Ophelia.

"I don't really know" said Robert. "Why?"

"Well, I was at a friend's house the other week and she was watching one of those forensic programmes. You know, the ones they have on late at night. Quite fascinating actually. Anyway, they were talking about how they could pick up DNA from an empty cup, a disguarded soft drink can or a cigarette butt. If we could get something like that of Martin's, would that work?"

"It's a possibility" said Robert. "Although with the blood, we're able to inject it directly into a person's arm and allow the DNA to flow through the veins of the person undergoing the experience. I'm not sure we could do the same with DNA from a cup or a can."

"There's another option, but it's a bit of a longshot" said Ophelia.

"What's that?" asked Robert.

"Remember when we used that drug on Simon Forester to find out where Ruth was?" said Ophelia.

She didn't have to finish the sentence.

"Scopolamine?" said Robert.

"Exactly."

'Scopolamine' or 'Devil's Breath' as the drug was more commonly known was a drug they had used to obtain information from an individual by the name of Simon Forester a year ago when Ruth, Sue and Alan's daughter, had been kidnapped. The individual who ingested it had no choice but to obey any suggestions or commands given to them. It had been used historically as a truth serum.

"The trouble is" commented Robert, "it's risky using it if the dose is wrong. It can be dangerous."

"Let me sleep on it tonight" said Ophelia. "I'll speak to my guides and see what they can come up with."

Alan remained quiet as he didn't have a very high opinion of Phyllis and Ophelia's 'other wordly' interests but Robert nodded at Ophelia's suggestion.

"I'm willing to explore all options at the moment. We need all the help we can get!"

The party decided to call it a night and the three said goodnight to Phyllis.

"I'll send you some extra thought energy tonight before I go to bed" said Phyllis as she hugged Ophelia.

"Thanks Phyllis. I know we'll find an answer once we've slept on it" replied Ophelia.

"Let me know if you need me to do anything Robert" said Alan.

"Thanks Alan. I'm sure it's going to be a case of all hands on deck to resolve this one."

Chapter Seventeen

"Come on in love, let me take your things and get you settled in properly." Phyllis fussed around Becky like a clucking hen as she walked through the door. Robert had just picked her up from the hospital and had taken her straight round to Phyllis's house.

"Thanks Phyllis. Again I seem to be in debt to you" replied Becky.

"Absolute nonsense. I told you before – you're like my pesky kid sister who keeps getting into mischief and still needs looking after."

"You don't have to be that polite. I'm becoming a complete pain in the arse for everybody" noted Becky.

"Well this time we're going to make sure you don't get into any trouble. Ophelia is staying here overnight to sleep for a while, although she will have to make sure Grimalkin is ok, otherwise he will have a major strop."

"Grimalkin?"

"Yes, I'm afraid he and Pywackit don't get along, otherwise he'd come and stay here. The few times they have met there's been stand offs and out-and-out hissing matches."

Becky was unsure at first as to who Grimalkin could be and then realised what Phyllis meant. "Oh, he's Ophelia's cat".

"Cat? He's her spiritual mentor, just like Pywackit is mine. You know they used to persecute so called witches in the old days for having familiars, but they were spiritually wise women and they shared a special relationship with their cats. They weren't evil, they were very wise."

Robert caught the tail end of the conversation as he brought more of Becky's bags into the lounge. "Now Becky, I must warn you, as fond as I am of both Phyllis and Ophelia, some of their ideas are a tad unconventional and I can't say that I follow their philosophy, so don't feel obliged to fall in with their ideas."

"What's he's trying to say politely is 'don't listen to those two bat shit crazy cat ladies'."

Becky burst out laughing. "Oh Robert, don't be so cruel.

I'm becoming very fond of Pywackit."

"Yes, and no doubt he'll be showing you how to cast spells on people and turning their food into fur balls as they eat it."

"Now that's enough Robert" said Phyllis. "I don't expect you to follow our philosophy, but I'll have more respect towards Pywackit under my roof."

"Sorry ma'am. Won't do it again ma'am." Robert doffed a pretend hat to Phyllis.

"Anyway, what's the situation with the police?" asked Phyllis.

"Well they're a bit scarce of resources but said they can have one person standing guard by the house for the next couple of nights. After that we'll have to be extra vigilant." Robert's tone dropped on his last few words.

"The thing that worries me" said Phyllis "is that surely having somebody standing outside the house is going to be obvious."

"Oh they won't be standing outside the house. They'll be tucked away parked in a car very discreetly just over the road."

"But what about the back of the house?"

"The back is far more secure than the front. A would be intruder would cause a hell of a racket trying to break in that way, so it's the front they're going to focus on."

"I suppose they're right" said Phyllis.

"I'm sure it'll be fine Phyllis. You've got a street light virtually at the end of your garden. I would have thought that would discourage anybody from trying to break in" said Becky.

"I'm sure you're right Becky" said Robert. He glanced at his watch. "Now unfortunately I'm going to have to leave you in Phyllis's capable clucking mother-hen hands as I have some papers to catch up on. I'll pop round tomorrow so Phyllis, if you want to make a shopping list I can pick it up then."

"Thanks Robert" said Phyllis. "There are a few things I need, although I hope we are going to be able to go out. It won't do either of us any good to be stuck inside the house all the time."

"Quite" replied Robert. "We'll definitely organise a few trips out but we will have to be careful."

"I don't like this. It makes you feel paranoid that somebody is watching you all the time" said Phyllis.

"I honestly don't think that's likely, but we can't be too careful after what's happened" replied Robert.

"Certainly not" said Phyllis.

"Right I must go. I'll see you both tomorrow. I'll have my phone switched on at all times and I want you to promise me you'll call me if you need to ok?"

"I promise Robert" said Phyllis solemnly. She escorted Robert to the door.

"Don't worry Phyllis" he whispered out of Becky's ear shot. "We're going to find whoever is trying to get to Becky." He then walked towards his car, got in and drove into the night.

What Phyllis didn't know was that he was going to meet Ophelia. She had received a call from Martin Smithson saying he would agree to meet Robert and Ophelia again, but this time in a location of his choosing. A small pub situated down a quiet country lane. He too was suffering bouts of paranoia and selected this pub so that he could see if anybody followed him.

When Ophelia and Robert arrived they scanned the sedate lounge of the pub. There were only a few customers in that night and it had a relaxing atmosphere and a huge lurcher that was sprawled out on the floor just by the entrace to the pub's kitchen.

Robert was the first to recognise the solicitor. He saw him sitting in a quiet corner at a small table. "He's over there" whispered Robert to Ophelia. He didn't want to make it obvious that he had seen him, just to be on the safe side. He saw that Martin Smithson had a drink and so bought one for himself and Ophelia. They chatted briefly and then slowly walked over to the table. Martin Smithson looked around nervously.

"I don't want to stay too long. I've been apprehensive all day long about this. I keep looking around to see if anybody has spotted me. You have no idea how this has made me feel opening all this up again" he said.

"Ok Mr Smithson, in your own time, why don't you tell us what's bothering you?"

Ophelia smiled across at Robert. She liked Robert's delivery – making it sound as though they were concerned about what was bothering him rather than just trying to force information out of him.

He started shaking again and his breathing was shallow.

"Let me get you a brandy" said Robert. "Do you drink brandy?"

"I'm driving."

"One won't hurt you and it will steady your nerves."

The solicitor accepted and Robert went back to the bar to buy a large brandy. When he returned, Ophelia was speaking softly to the obviously frightened man.

"Look, whatever's worrying you, we're trying to get to the bottom of it as well and if we bring it out into the open, maybe we can deal with whoever it is you're frightened of and expose them."

"If you can find him and good luck with that!" hissed the solicitor.

"Who? Who is it you're frightened of?"

"Oh it's not him, it was the connections he had. I don't know if he's still got them now but he'll always have somebody do his dirty work for him."

Robert felt they weren't making any headway and everytime they tried to coax the identity of this mysterious person out of the solicitor, he only began talking in riddles.

"Look, why don't you start from the beginning? None of this makes any sense to us at all. The only thing we know is that Becky Collerton is trying to clear her dead brother's name and by some weird twist of fate, your story seems to interlink with hers. Am I right?"

Martin Smithson let out a deep sigh and took a large swig of brandy. "Yes" he said finally. "Yes".

"Ok" said Robert calmly. "Perhaps you can help us to fill in the pieces of the puzzle because right now I'm very confused."

Martin took another sip of his brandy, not seeming to be aware or even care that he might be going over the limit. He needed something to calm his nerves.

"Jesus, I'm not proud of myself, but what else could I do?" He looked at Robert pleading. "I had no choice, my hands were tied. My kids were in danger." He fought back tears as his voice went higher.

Ophelia interjected. "It's ok. Just take your time" she

whisphered. Her voice seemed to have a soothing effect on Martin Smithson.

He rocked back a little in his chair and then sat still. He looked at them both.

"I haven't told anybody this story, apart from my ex-wife." He paused.

"Go on" said Ophelia, gently coaxing him.

"So Thomas Collerton was seen standing over the body of Nicholas Putterill."

"That was his friend wasn't it?" asked Robert.

Martin Smithson nodded. "I'm sure that Rebecca Collerton has already told you that her brother had been stopped for speeding and given a speeding ticket with the date and time on it. He then arrived at his friends house, not that long after somebody was seen running out of the house in bloodstained clothes. Several witnesses confirmed the time because .....

"..... Coronation Street had just started and they heard all this banging" Robert interrupted.

"Right, right". Martin Smithson nodded. "So Thomas Collerton arrives shortly after that and finds his friend's body literally ripped to pieces. Jesus, I saw the photos – it was horrific." The solicitor grimaced as he recalled the images. "Shortly afterwards, the police arrive and think they've got their murderer."

"Yes, that much we do know" said Robert.

"That's where I come into the story" said Martin. Was he expecting Robert and Ophelia to look shocked? If so, they had perfectly fine poker faces as they gave nothing away but just looked at him expectantly.

"He needed a solicitor and at that time I was a newby at criminal law and I was assigned to him under legal aid. I can't help thinking that because I was inexperienced they thought I wouldn't be very good at representing him." There was a sense of bitterness in his voice. "Oh how wrong they were!"

Robert and Ophelia were virtually on the edge of their seats but they tried to look as cool and collected as they could whilst Martin Smithson was about to drop bombshell after bombshell onto them.

"So I made some preliminary enquiries and right from the outset, it was blatantly obvious to an idiot that he was innocent."

"Yes?" asked Robert.

"Yes! The speeding ticket was his concrete alibi. Not only that, they took scrapings from the victims finger nails, he had so many defence wounds and obviously had fought for his life, the poor bastard!" Martin took a deep breath. "Well there was quite a bit of blood evidence,not just of the victim, but of the assailant. Obviously we didn't have DNA back then but we knew that the blood group was O positive, whereas Thomas Collerton's blood group was A negative. They also tried to pin the murder of Nicholas Putterill's girlfriend onto him. She was murdered a couple of weeks before."

Robert knew all of this information already and was desperate to hear the new evidence but decided to let Martin Smithson continue talking in case there was any additional information that he hadn't heard.

"Thomas Collerton was playing football on the Isle of Wight the night that she was murdered. And surprise, surprise, she had similar defensive wounds to her boyfriend, they found the attacker's blood under her finger nails and guess what?"

"O positive" said Robert.

"Exactly!" said Martin. "Same MO, same style of attack, the whole shebang. The only feeble evidence they had against Thomas Collerton was that somebody overheard him in a pub saying to Nicholas 'if you're not careful you're going to end up dead.' Of course I questioned him about this and he explained to me – and I believed him – that he was trying to warn his friend to back off from a situation because he was worried that he'd be killed, he wasn't threatening him."

"What was he warning him about?"

"There was a drugs ring going around. I'd heard about it but didn't know a great deal of who operated it or where they got their supplies from. It turns out the quality of the drugs was horrendous. Most street drugs are anyway – they mix them with so much rubbish, no wonder so many people end up dead. Anyway, a close friend of the girlfriend had got some sort of hallucinogenic off this dealer. It wasn't LSD but something not disimilar. She had a bad trip and ended up running across the road terrified that something was chasing her ..... right into the path of a car. She died virtually instantly."

Robert couldn't help letting out a little "woah".

Martin nodded. "Woah indeed." So it transpired that this girlfriend knew who the drug dealer was and was going to go to the police about him. I don't really think I need to tell you the rest, apart from the fact that she ended up dead."

"And Nicholas?" quizzed Ophelia.

"Oh yes, his girlfriend told him who it was and when she was murdered, he was determined to get his revenge. The trouble was he wasn't discreet about it. He made it well known that he was going to track the culprit down and 'get him'. That's when Thomas Collerton told him he was an idiot and that he should back off or he'd get himself killed."

"Which is exactly what happened" added Robert.

"Indeed."

"But why were they so eager to pin the murder on Thomas Collerton if they knew he was innocent?"

"Because they knew who the real murderer was."

Ophelia's eyes nearly popped out of her head. "You know who it was?"

"Oh yes" hissed Martin, "me and a few of my colleagues knew who it bloody well was."

"Well why couldn't you convict him?"

Martin Smithson let out a bitter laugh. "Oh yes, of course!" His tone was sarcastic.

"Well why not?" persisted Ophelia.

"Because dear lady, our murderer was one Tristran Eldridge." He was about to explain who this was when Robert interjected.

"Jesus! Godfrey Eldridge's son!"

"You've heard of him then?" asked Martin.

"I met our Mr Godfrey Eldridge the other day. I found out who the judge was on the case and it turned out to be him. A colleague of mine said he was an obnoxious piece of work and my god, was he right. I knew his son had been trouble, but I had no idea about this."

"So now you know" said Martin, looking slightly relieved, as if the sharing of his story had unburdened him somewhat.

"Well I understand that he wouldn't have convicted his own son, but surely couldn't you have gone to another judge or told somebody else?"

"No!" Martin's voice was flat.

"Why not?" Ophelia was baffled.

Martin didn't move his head but his eyes darted across at her. "Because I was a newly qualified solicitor, married a few years – this was quite some time after I knew Phyllis. I had two young children." He suddenly stopped.

"Yes?" said Robert, although he had a good idea what was coming next.

"And I was told quite plainly that if I wanted to see my children grow up to be healthy happy individuals and not have either of them end up six feet under, then maybe I should drop the case."

The three sat in silence for a minute or two.

"So you dropped the case ....." said Robert.

"And they gave it to somebody else who was a completely incompetent idiot which is just what they were looking for." The bitterness in his voice was overwhelming.

"And so an innocent man served a life sentence to protect Tristran Eldridge" said Robert, his tone almost matching Martin's.

Martin took another swig of his brandy, not realising that he'd drunk the entire glass. "Don't believe this crap that solicitors have no conscience. Everytime I felt guilty about letting an innocent man go to prison, I had to look at my children to remind myself why I did it. The means did indeed justify the end, but what a lousy thing to be forced into."

"I don't blame you, I don't envy you and I certainly don't judge you" said Robert.

"I've done enough judging of myself over the years. I nearly quit law but my wife said it was a good career and paid well and we wanted to make sure the kids had a decent start in life."

"Nobody can blame you for wanting that" commented Robert.

"No, that's true, but I'm sure that Thomas Collerton wanted a good life as well; and then you come into my life telling me his sister is looking for answers." Martin looked at Robert with lifeless eyes. "What the hell am I supposed to tell her? 'Sorry Miss Collerton, but I had my own agenda. I didn't want to see my kids ending up on a mortuary slab so I had to throw your brother under the bus. Shit!"

Ophelia sat silently. Fortunately she was sitting in a shaded part of the room as a tear started to trickle down her cheek. She discreetly wiped it away.

They sat in silence for what seemed like a lifetime, processing this new information when Robert finally spoke up. "So where is Tristran Eldridge now?"

"Nobody knows" said Martin somberly. "He just seemed to disappear off the face of the earth. No doubt daddy dearest paid for him to bugger off somewhere until the heat died down. I wouldn't be surprised if he's still dealing drugs. I only met him once and I didn't like the look of him."

"So where do we go from here?" asked Ophelia to nobody in particular.

Robert shook his head. "I don't know. First of all we need to track down this Tristran Eldridge but he could be anywhere."

"Can't you ask his father where he is?" asked Ophelia.

Robert and Martin both laughed, but in both cases, it was a bitter laugh.

"After what happened the other day, I can't help thinking he'd only delight in the fact that his lousy offspring got off scot free" said Robert.

"I concur!" added Martin.

"So we have a woman who is dying of cancer, looking for answers and we can't give her any." Ophelia's tone was resigned.

"I'm not sure I'd agree with that Ophelia" said Robert, a look of deep thought on his face.

"Oh?"

"Well look at it this way. Somebody has already tried to poison her, and as far as I'm aware she has no enemies, which leads me to conclude that it may be our murderer who is trying to stop her in her tracks."

Ophelia thought for a moment. "Yes, yes, that would make sense."

"So somehow we need to tease him out of his hiding hole" added Robert.

"Yes, but how?" asked Ophelia.

"Well before you even start thinking of doing that, I'd warn you to seriously consider it. He is one dangerous indivdual. He had connections then and I wouldn't mind betting that he has connections now" warned Martin.

Robert knew that Martin had a very good point. He had to find someway of setting a trap for him. Ophelia seemed to read his thoughts.

"Robert, I don't want us to put Becky's life in jeopardy in any way, even if it means letting him get away with it."

"I know Ophelia, I know. But there's got to be something we can do."

Chapter Eighteen

After what Ophelia had heard tonight, she felt as if she was in no fit state to see anybody.

"Are you sure you're going to be alright on your own Ophelia?" asked Robert as he dropped her off.

"Yes Robert, please don't worry. I'm just still reeling from the entire story. So much to take in. What a horrible situation for Martin to be forced into. I really do feel for him."

"Same here Ophelia. I couldn't blame anybody for choosing between the lives of their own children and the life of somebody they hardly knew, however innocent they might be."

"We can't share this with Becky. I'm worried about telling Phyllis as well. I know she wouldn't say anything deliberately but bless her, something might slip out."

"I agree to be honest Ophelia. I think we should let this go no further until we get some answers."

"That could take a long time. I can't help feeling deceitful about harbouring all these secrets. First the fling between Sue and Chris and now this."

"The trouble is, no good could come of disclosing either story."

"I know. What a horrible situation."

"Are you sure you're going to be ok?"

"Yes, yes honestly. I'll call Phyllis and tell her I want to stay here tonight."

"Ok, but if you need to speak to me, please call me."

"Thanks Robert. I'll say goodnight now."

"Goodnight Ophelia. Try to get some sleep."

Ophelia closed the door and Robert walked back to his car. The first thing she did was call Phyllis.

"Hello Phyllis? It's Ophelia. Listen sweetheart are you ok?"

Phyllis affirmed over the phone that she and Becky were fine and they felt completely safe with the police car sitting on the opposite side of the road watching over them.

"I feel really guilty for saying this but would you mind if I slept at my place tonight? I'm not feeling great and I need some time on my own."

Phyllis's concerned voice wanted to know what was wrong.

"I'm fine Phyllis, honestly. I'll come over tomorrow. I just need to do a bit of a cleansing tonight and make a nice cup of camomile."

Phyllis agreed that she understood and they both ended the call.

But Ophelia was not fine. The story of Thomas Collerton's wrongful conviction, brought about only by a man who was desperately trying to protect his family, had disturbed her more than she thought. What would Phyllis think if she knew what Martin had done? Worst of all, how would Becky feel if she met the man who helped to convict her brother simply by remaining quiet? And how were they going to track Tristran Eldridge down? Robert certainly had a point when he said that it could most likely be he who had tried to kill Becky. But Ophelia was not prepared to allow Becky or Phyllis to be put in any danger as bait to set a trap. It was far too risky, and whilst she felt genuinely sad for Becky and her dead brother, she prioritised the well-being of the living over the dead. How else could they do it? She would just have to sleep on it – if sleep would come. She'd had several cups of camomile tea and added a few of her own special herbs. Whilst she certainly felt more relaxed than she had before, she was still restless. She lay down on her bed and closed her eyes. "Come on guides, I need your help. How can we find a resolution to this problem?" She gradually began to drift off with images flashing in her mind. A murderer standing over a dead body. No, no, no! An innocent man standing over a dead body. A murderer running out of a house. A woman lying dead by a row of garages. The images came one after another, no matter how much Ophelia's unconscious mind tried to shun them away. She woke up and sat bolt upright, her eyes wide. She stared at the wall. Was that a shadow? Did she hear a noise downstairs? She was sure she heard something. She quietly stepped towards the bedroom door and softly pulled it open. She could definitely hear something downstairs. She held her breath, terrified. The noise was soft, but it was definitely there. It seemed to be getting nearer but still as soft. Suddenly she let out a scream as something brushed against her legs. She looked down and then breathed a heavy sigh of relief. "Grimalkin, why did you frighten me like that? Surely you know I'm already on edge."

Grimalkin looked up at her with his pale green eyes, brushed past her and jumped onto the bed.

"Well at least one of us is going to get a good night's sleep tonight."

* * * * *

Robert had been equally as restless all night although he managed to get some sleep. When he woke up the following morning he made himself a strong cup of coffee in the hope of bringing him back into the 'real' world – a world full of murderers, victims and wrongful convictions. He almost questioned himself as to why he had bothered. As he sat on his sofa, his eyes gazed slightly out of focus until they rested on a device sitting in the corner of his lounge on a shelf. Ian's device. He'd used it several times to seek out murderers, kidnap victims and …… unfaithful marital partners. But something was niggling at the back of his mind. Ophelia had suggested that somehow they could obtain a sample of Martin's blood and find out all the information they needed, but that was now unnecessary. Martin had disclosed all that he knew – or as much as they thought he would know. It wasn't Martin they needed a sample from, it was Nick Putterill, the victim who was found dead lying in a pool of his own blood, albeit mixed with some of the murderer's blood. But this all happened years ago.

"No point thinking about it now old man" he said to himself. "I'll leave it until later." In the meantime, he decided to call Ophelia to see how she was feeling.

"Oh good morning Robert" she said, the tiredness in her voice impossible to disguise.

"It sounds like you didn't have a very good night's sleep last night" he said.

"I'm not going to lie to you, I didn't. I just kept having micro-dreams, images flashing in my mind. But one image kept coming up time after time."

"What was that?" asked Robert.

"A woman's bloody dress. It was horrible. I kept trying

to push the image away but it persisted. I wouldn't mind so much, but I'd asked my guides for help before I tried to go to sleep but this was the only thing that kept coming to mind."

Robert went quiet. He was thinking.

"Hello? Robert, are you still there?"

"Er, yes, sorry Ophelia, I was just thinking."

"Oh, penny for them?"

"I'm not even sure they're worth h'penny, but I'll share them anyway. I wonder if all the evidence from the murder has been archived. They usuall do archive all material. If there's any of the murderers blood on Nick Putterill's clothes ....."

"..... we could run them through Ian's machine" finished Ophelia.

"Precisely" added Robert.

"But the only way we could find out is to ask Martin and I'm not sure he'd be best pleased if we turned up at his offices, especially as he was so helpful last night."

"I know, I think you're right."

"On the other hand ......" Ophelia tailed off.

"Yes?"

"Look, I don't wish to sound vain, but I did get the impression he and I had a rapport last night."

"Go on" said Robert.

"Well what if I pop by his office on my own? I could use some excuse such as apologising for us forcing him to dredge up all those memories last night and ....."

"And?"

"And just slip in the question of where could we find the evidence."

"Ooh Ophelia, you really are a crafty old minx – but I do like your style" Robert chuckled.

"Look Robert, there are times when the 'softly softly' approach works much better than the bull in a china shop method, so why don't I go round there today and speak to him?"

"But you must be shattered. Why don't you try to get some sleep?"

"I'm too wired to be honest."

"Well I can pick you up and drive you round there. I could stay out of sight while you go and see him."

"I'd rather you went to see how Phyllis and Becky are."

"I've got an idea. I know that Alan's on his own with Sue out at work. I could ask him to go round and check on them while I take you to go and see Martin."

Ophelia wasn't overly-keen on this idea, although she knew that Alan would be only too pleased to see Becky, and she rather felt that the feeling was mutual.

"Ok then, but remember to warn Alan of what Phyllis said if he tried to get all amorous with Becky. She'd have kitchen knives at the ready and meatballs for dinner!"

Robert let out a loud laugh. "See Ophelia, I always knew that underneath that dark, mysterious, brooding high priestess there was a woman with a sense of humour."

"Who says I'm joking?" said Ophelia, trying to sound as deadpan as she could.

"Right, I'll call Alan and ask him to check on Phyllis and Becky. Then I'll come and pick you up."

"Ok Robert, I'll go and try to make myself look semi-awake."

It wasn't long before Robert turned up at Ophelia's front door.

"Ready?" he said when she opened it.

"As I'll ever be."

Despite what she'd said about feeling and looking like a zombie after a restless night, Ophelia looked as polished and turned out as always. She seemed to be able to read Robert's thoughts.

"If I'm going to turn on the charm with Martin, I can hardly turn up to his offices looking like a drowned rat."

Robert laughed as they both got into his car and drove off. After a short drive, he pulled into a side street just around the corner from Martin's office. "Before you get out" he said to Ophelia, "I just want to see if there's anybody about who looks suspicious." He scanned both sides of the road, paying particular attention to a couple of cars that were parked not far away from his.

"I know we need to be careful Robert, but I shouldn't think anybody would be expecting someone to turn up looking for Martin."

"Even so" said Robert. "He looked extremely nervous when we met him last night. I don't want to put anybody's life in danger."

"I understand" said Ophelia.

They waited a few minutes and Robert gave it the all clear. Ophelia opened the door and got out of the car. "See you in a bit" she said.

Robert watched her as she walked down the street and turned the corner. He didn't like even losing sight of her for one minute, but it couldn't be helped.

Ophelia walked into the foyer of Martin's law firm and the receptionist remembered her from her last visit. Before she had a chance to say anything, Ophelia spoke first.

"No, I don't have an appointment, but I do believe Mr Smithson will be interested to hear what I have to say."

The receptionist eyed her suspiciously. "Wait here" she said in her usual curt tone.

A minute or so later she was back with Martin following her. He did not look very pleased to see Ophelia. He gestured for her to follow him into his office.

"What are you doing here? I told you all I know last night."

Rather than retaliate, Ophelia's demeanour was gentle and empathic. "I know Mr Smithson, and I haven't slept a wink as I felt so guilty for putting you through all that again. I appreciate it must have been very difficult. I just wanted to come and apologise in person."

Martin Smithson's defensive posture softened a little.

"Ok, but I really would appreciate it if you didn't keep coming back here. I know it was years ago but I still feel the need to look over my shoulder even now. I'm about to become a grandfather and I feel as concerned for the life of my grandchild as I do for when my children were young."

"I can imagine you were a good father" said Ophelia. She was really turning on the charm now.

"I tried to be, though my ex-wife would tell you otherwise."

"Well I'm sure your current lady is very happy with the relationship." Oops, careful Ophelia, don't go too far, she thought to herself.

"There is no current lady, there is work, worry and concern for my children and my soon to be grandchild."

"What a shame" said Ophelia. "You've obviously looked after yourself, I'm sure you'd have no problems meeting somebody and after all, there has to be more to life than work."

"Thank you for the compliment but I'm happy enough at present" replied Martin.

Ophelia said nothing but smiled. "Look after yourself Mr Smithson. I sincerely wish you and your family every happiness." Ophelia turned to go and then stopped. "Oh, there was one thing I wanted to ask you."

"Yes?"

"After what we discussed last night, I forgot to ask you if the evidence from Nick Putterill's murder had been archived. I've watched a few of these cold case documentaries and you hear about how they re-open the file many years later, using DNA to find murderers."

"Well I'm sorry to disappoint you but all the evidence was destroyed. When I was 'persuaded' to drop the case, the people who 'persuaded' me made sure that there wasn't a trace of evidence left. No speeding ticket, no blood samples, no clothes, nothing. All gone."

"Oh". Ophelia couldn't hide the disappointment in her tone. She was about to turn around again and then stopped. She turned to look at Martin again. "What about the other murder?"

"The girl you mean?" asked Martin.

"Yes, I know you said they tried to pin that one on Thomas Collerton, but surely the fact that he was in the Isle of Wight would have made it difficult to convict him of that murder when there were so many witnesses who saw him playing football?"

"It was only suggested that he murdered her, he was never formally convicted of it. Now that you mention it yes, I should imagine the evidence for that murder is still in a box somewhere, archived away."

"Interesting" said Ophelia. "I wonder if it would be possible to obtain that evidence."

"Ok, ok, I'll make you a deal. If I give you a contact to follow up, will you promise that neither your nor your friend ever come here or contact me again?" His defensive armour was up again.

"I will. I have to say though, it would be a great shame

because I meant what I said Mr Smithson."

The solicitor pulled out a book from his desk drawer and flicked through it's pages. He scribbled a name and number down on a piece of paper and handed it to Ophelia.

"There you are, you've got what you obviously came for, but we now have a deal."

"I won't lie Mr Smithson, I did indeed come to obtain some information from you and I am truly grateful for it. But I do find you very attractive." Ophelia walked slowly over to the pensive solicitor and gave him a soft peck on the cheek. "Goodbye Mr Smithson ...... for now."

Ophelia turned and walked, seemingly gliding across the carpet, opened the door, took one look back at Martin Smithson and closed the door.

Robert heaved a sigh of relief when he saw Ophelia walking around the corner towards his car. She opened the door and sat down, closing the car door with a soft 'clunk'.

"How did it go?" he asked.

"Well sadly, the evidence from the murder of Nick Putterill was all destroyed. He told me that when he was warned to drop the case, the people involved made sure that all the evidence was destroyed."

"Oh no, back to square one then" said Robert, disappointed.

"Not necessarily. I remember what happened last night when I asked my guides for help. I just kept getting those images of a bloody dress. Well I asked him if that evidence had been archived. I know they pointed the finger at Thomas Collerton, but he said they couldn't definitely accuse him due to him being outside of the mainland. It's been archived and he gave me a contact number to obtain information as to where we can find it."

"You really are a charmer Ophelia, good work!" said Robert.

"However, it did come with a condition."

"Oh?" Robert looked slightly concerned.

"He doesn't want us to contact him ever again" added Ophelia.

"Well, that's fair enough. I'm sure we could have found him useful in our investigations, but if we can get hold of that evidence we might just be able to crack this case ourselves."

"Such a shame" said Ophelia.

"Why's that?" asked Robert.

"I really like him. I sensed a lot of disappointment in his life and he's a bit of a worrier, but underneath it all, a good person."

Robert looked at Ophelia, slightly taken aback. "I always had you down as a strong independent woman, somebody who can stand on her own two feet and not worry about significant others."

"Oh I can do all of those things Robert, but despite what you might think of me, I'm not made of stone."

Robert wanted to laugh but decided that this might not be the most appropriate moment to do that. Ophelia was disclosing an aspect of her character that he hadn't seen before. Perhaps it was a private moment, a moment of trusting somebody to be discreet.

Chapter Nineteen

"No Robert, no, that's my final word."

"Oh come on Bill, this poor woman's dying of cancer and all she wants to do is clear her brother's name."

"Look, I'm very sorry for your miss .... miss ..."

"Her name's Becky, Becky Collerton."

"Miss Collerton, but I haven't got the resources. We're over-stretched as it is and our workload isn't getting any lighter. The last thing I have time to do is start investigating a cold case."

Robert had gone to see an old acquaintance called Bill Granger – or 'Inspector Granger' to his colleagues. Although they had a mutual respect for each other, they often locked horns when it came to matters of work. They had helped each other in the past. Robert had assisted with criminal profiling that led to the capture of a serious offender and Bill Granger in turn had been involved when Sue and Alan's daughter Ruth had been kidnapped, although even then they came to blows as to how the case should have been solved.

"Look, I'm not even asking you to give me a resource. Just let me get access to the box in the archive and I can carry out the investigation myself" protested Robert.

"Oh yes, and destroy vital DNA evidence in the process. It's not the same as giving your child a chemistry set at Christmas. There are processes to go through Robert, and if my superiors found out I was giving away evidence from a past case willy nilly to any old Tom, Dick or Harry that came along, my head would be knocked off my block, my P45 would be shoved down what was left of my neck and my sorry arse would be kicked out onto the street and I can say goodbye to any police pension."

"Oh come on Bill, I can get the evidence booked in with a professional DNA analyst no problem. I am familiar with procedures as I'm sure you're aware. We know who committed the murder, we just need to prove it."

"But you told me that the evidence from the actual case had been destroyed." Bill Granger looked at Robert puzzled.

"Yes, from the murder of Nick Putterill, but the evidence from his girlfriend's murder is still in the archives."

"So you want to carry out an investigation on one case with no evidence, believing that the evidence from another murder case will find your killer. Unbelievable! You really are starting to sound like a raving lunatic."

"The MO for both murders was the same, the blood group extracted from the defensive scratches and blood were both O positive. The ...."

"Robert, how many people are O positive? It's the most common blood group in the world."

"Yes, but with DNA it narrows it down to one individual .... or at least only a few individuals."

"Robert, it just wouldn't stand up in court. You really are chasing rainbows here."

"But don't you care that the real murderer is still out there – who knows how many people he could have killed."

"Evidence Robert, I need evidence. Cold hard facts .... witnesses, places, times, dates ..... you can't give me any of them."

"I can give you the date when both victims were killed."

"Yes, and my geeky brother-in-law could probably tell you what was no. 1 in the hit parade at that time as well. It means nothing."

Robert was about to say something when his phone rang. "Hello? Yes Alan, what is it?" What he heard next was unbelievable. "Arrested? What do you mean arrested?"

Even Bill Granger looked at Robert surprised.

"I'm coming over right away. This is insane!" Robert ended the call and literally ran out of the police station.

"Hang on, aren't you going to tell me what's happened ......?" Bill Granger's voice dropped away.

Robert's heart was pounding as he drove frantically back to Phyllis's house. The tyres screeched as he brought the car to a sharp stop and he ran down the path. Phyllis must have seen him as she was already standing at the door waiting for him with tears in her eyes.

"What the hell happened?" he said.

"Becky's been arrested Robert – on a charge of possessing drugs. The police were tipped off and managed to get access to her house. God only knows – but they found heroin in there with a street value of £250,000."

Alan and Ophelia came to the door as well. Ophelia was also crying and Alan looked seriously shaken.

"This is bullshit Robert, Becky would never do something like that. Somebody's set her up."

Robert paused for a moment. Alan glared at him.

"Don't you believe me?" he retorted.

"Of course I believe you Alan, I'm just trying to think. I'm trying to make sense of all of this."

"What's there to think about? First of all somebody tried to kill Becky and when that didn't work, they got into her flat and planted the evidence, then called the police. It's obvious."

"It sounds obvious, but how did they get into her flat? I made sure that place was secure. Did the police say there'd been any sign of a break in?"

"No but come on, if whoever did this can sell drugs with a street value running into the hundreds and thousands, I'm sure they can find a way to pick a lock for god's sake."

"Look, there's no point arguing you two. Let's all come inside and sit down to talk about this. We're being absolutely no help to Becky by squabbling." Ophelia's voice was firm but measured.

"Look, did the police say we can go and see her?"

"Not today" replied Alan. "They've got her in for questioning and will keep her in there until they can make a formal arrest. In the meantime, we need to get her a bloody good solicitor!"

"Well we could ask Martin" said Phyllis, completely unaware of what he had disclosed to Robert and Ophelia. The two looked at each other and fell silent.

"Well?" said Alan. "Why not?"

"He wouldn't want to get involved" said Robert.

"Well how do you know? I mean just because he and I split up all those years ago, I'm sure he wouldn't hold a grudge against either of you because of it."

Ophelia looked at Phyllis. "Sweetheart, it's not that simple."

"What do you mean?" Phyllis didn't like the fact that Ophelia seemed to have some understanding of the situation that she didn't.

"Oh Robert, we've got to come clean with Alan and Phyllis. It's no use hiding it from them."

Phyllis and Alan looked at each other and then both looked at Robert and Ophelia.

"Hiding what?" Alan and Phyllis said together.

"Sweetheart, can you make us some tea and we'll tell you what we know" said Ophelia.

"Oh, ok" said Phyllis, wanting to know immediately what this secrecy was all about but also understanding that the quicker she made the tea, the quicker they could all sit down and hear the strange revelations.

Shortly Phyllis came through with a large tray. She had two teapots on it – one filled with herbal tea, the other with ordinary. "There's also hot water if you want coffee. Alan, do you take sugar?" She asked more through nervousness than anything else.

"No thanks Phyllis, just milk."

Phyllis busied herself with serving everybody.

"Ok Robert" said Alan firmly. "What's this all about?"

Robert began to tell the story of what he and Ophelia had learned the other evening about Martin Smithson defending Thomas Collerton and how he was told to drop the case over threats on his childrens' lives. Ophelia filled in the gaps and when she saw how horrified Phyllis was that he could do such a thing, she emphasised the implications to Martin if he refused to co-operate.

"You can't blame him Phyllis, these people were being serious. Apparently one of them actually handed a note to his four year old daughter when she was in the playground at school telling her to give it to her daddy. That was their way of saying 'we know where your children are and we can act on our threats at any time.' I know you're probably disappointed in him taking that action, but let's be honest, who wouldn't co-operate with threats like that being made?"

"Ophelia's right Phyllis. If I'd been in the same situation and somebody had threatened Ruth's life, I would have backed down immediately. When you're a parent, your number one priority is your children. Everything else is completely irrelevant by comparison. You know for a fact that Sue would do the same."

This was probably a little unfair as it put Sue under the same umbrella as Martin, but Phyllis knew that Alan was right. Her best friend, Sue, who could seem quite harsh and even indifferent towards people sometimes, would move mountains to protect Ruth.

"This just goes from bad to worse" she said resignedly. "How on earth are we going to help Becky?"

"Alan, we're going to have to do something that could be a bit risky but it's the only thing I can think of right now."

"Oh, what's that?" Alan seemed slightly anxious at Robert's tone, but if this was for Becky, he was willing to do it. He couldn't let her down now.

"I don't know if they'll have her house taped off, but I've got a key to it. It's not a murder scene so I shouldn't think there will be any police guards there – or at least I hope not. The only thing I can think of is to go round there ourselves when it's dark and take a look around. We might find some clues."

Ophelia said what she, Phyllis and Alan were thinking. "But Robert, you could be taking a hell of a risk and if you were caught, you could both end up in prison yourself."

"I know Ophelia, but we've got to try something. We're getting nowhere fast. Martin Smithson doesn't want to have any further involvement, Bill Granger virtually told me I was a raving lunatic. What else can we do?"

The four of them sat in silence as they pondered on this thought.

"And what if there is a police guard?" asked Alan. "I'm not trying to squirm out of it Robert, you know I'd do anything to help Becky, but we've got to be realistic."

"A decoy" said Ophelia.

"What?" said Alan and Robert together.

"We'll set up a decoy. I'll go along with you and if there's a police guard outside the house, I can wait some distance away from it. I'll then let out the most ear-piercing scream you've heard and run in the other direction. With any luck the policeman will come running to see what's wrong. I can fall over and tell him I was being chased by somebody. I can make a fuss and add a bit of drama. It might not give you a lot of time, but you never know, you might have enough to look for clues. If one of you keeps guard by the door while the other investigates, you'll be able to see him coming back."

Phyllis, Alan and Robert sat in silence.

"Well?" Ophelia looked at them all expectantly.

"I don't like it ...." Robert began.

"But then again" continued Alan, "it's not a bad idea."

"The trouble is, he could call in the alleged attack and Ophelia could be taken down to the station, asking her to describe the assailant. It could all fall to pieces" said Robert.

"We've got to try something" insisted Ophelia.

"It's crazy."

"It's insane."

"It can't work."

"Ok, let's try it."

Chapter Twenty

"Are you sure you're up to this Ophelia?" asked Sue.

"I'll be fine Sue honest."

"But it's bloody dark out there and you really don't know who's hanging around."

"My guides are with me, they'll keep me out of danger."

Sue didn't look too sure about this. Up until now she'd been kept completely in the dark about what had been happening over the last few weeks and initially she was furious with Alan when he finally disclosed the whole story to her when she asked him why he was going out so late at night. At first she suspected that he may be going to see Becky secretly for a romantic liaison and even after Alan had told her what was really happening, she still didn't believe him. It was only when Robert, Phyllis and Ophelia verified the whole story that she accepted it.

"I'm disappointed with you Phyllis, I thought being my friend you would have told me." That statement stuck like a knife in Phyllis's heart. The last thing she would ever do was betray Sue.

"I swore Phyllis to secrecy" Robert interjected. "I got the distinct feeling that you didn't really like Becky the last time we talked and I didn't think it would help matters if we told you what we were doing. I swear to you Sue that nothing has been going on between Alan and Becky. We've just been trying to help her to solve the riddle of her brother's false conviction." He played one final card – one of emotional blackmail. "Sue, she's dying – we can't just tell her to get on with it. She needs friends."

Sue felt a little guilty when Robert put it like that. "I understand Robert, but I was under the impression she had friends in Cyprus."

"She does" agreed Robert. "But her brother's story is in England and that's where she needs to find closure."

Sue thought about this and nodded her head. "I'm not the complete cold bitch that you think I am Robert – and I would actually like to help."

"Well I appreciate the offer, but there's not a lot you can do."

"There bloody well is something I can do!" said Sue obstinately.

"Oh?" Robert was taken aback by Sue's dogged attitude.

"If you think you're going to leave Ophelia standing on her own in the dead of night on some street corner, you've got another thing coming. I'm surprised you even agreed to do it. Phyllis and I will sit in my car nearby so that if anything happens, we'll be on hand to help Ophelia."

"Actually Robert" said Phyllis, "that's a really good idea."

Robert didn't seem too keen on the idea initially, but the consensus of the group was that it would add an extra level of safety for Ophelia.

"How do you feel about that Alan?"

"Well ordinarily I wouldn't be too keen letting Sue out on her own at night like that, but if Phyllis is with her, it might not be a bad idea as an extra safeguard."

"Ok, but please try to stay out of sight. We don't want to arouse any suspicions" said Robert.

"It'll be fine" said Ophelia assuredly.

They discussed the plans as to what time they would set out, who would position themselves where and how they would give the signal to Ophelia if a policeman was on guard.

"I'm still not convinced about this" said Alan as he and Robert drove towards Becky's house.

"I'm not 100% happy with it myself Alan, but desperate measures are needed – we're not going to get anybody else's help with this."

Sue, Phyllis and Ophelia were also driving to Becky's house, but using a different route.

"I've seen how they pick up cars on cameras in these true life murder detective programmes" said Sue. If we're both going in the same direction and there are street cameras around, it could look highly suspicious." She'd also advised Robert that they should leave their mobile phones at home. "They ping off mobile phone towers so they can detect where you've been."

"Proper little Miss Marple our Sue" said Robert, winking

at Alan.

"Yes, well Miss Marple, even though fictitious, knew how to use her woman's intuition to crack the case, so don't knock it buster!"

Alan and Robert both laughed as Sue insisted on having the last word on the subject.

Robert made sure to park his car in a quiet side street where he felt it was unlikely that there would be cameras. Even so, he and Alan took the precaution of staying low so as to keep out of sight. As they approached Becky's house, to their dismay, a policeman was standing on duty outside the front door.

"Shit!" exclaimed Robert. "I thought this might happen."

"We'll have to give the signal then" said Alan.

"Afraid so" said Robert. "This is like something out of a cheesy detective novel."

"Don't knock it" said Alan. "If it works in the novels, maybe it can work in real life."

"Ok, here goes, wish me luck" said Robert.

"Break a beak" said Alan.

Robert put his hands to his mouth and made the owl call he'd been practising that day. Alan looked at him as if to give his approval. He did it again. Had Ophelia heard him or was she too far away? He wasn't sure. He was about to try another call when all of a sudden a piercing scream burst through the night. She'd heard him – and what a scream!

The policeman standing guard looked towards where the scream came from. At first he stood stock still, as if wondering whether to stand on guard or to go and see where the source of the scream came from. Shortly, his training kicked in and he ran towards the scream.

"Ok Alan, here's our one and only chance!" Both he and Alan ran towards Becky's house. Alan took the key and put it in the lock. He was apprehensive that the police may have changed it, but fortunately the door opened. "Right, if you stand on guard, I'm going to take a look around and for god's sake, if there's any sign of a policeman coming back, give me the signal and we'll have to run for it."

"Ok" said Alan and he stood behind the front door with

it slightly open so that he could see if the policeman returned.

While this was happening, Ophelia had turned and ran for her life, letting out intermittent screams as she did so. She ran around the corner towards Sue's car. Phyllis and Sue, meanwhile, had cooked up a little plan of their own which they hadn't told Robert and Alan about.

"They wouldn't agree to it if we told them" Sue had said to Ophelia and Phyllis. "It will also mean that Ophelia won't have to go down to the police station and answer any awkward questions."

"But what if we do some serious harm?" asked Phyllis.

"Don't worry, one of the girls at work is a fully qualified first aider and she told me how much force to use so as not to cause a serious injury."

Their plan was now in place. Sue stood behind a wall that separated a field and a car park. She could hear Ophelia racing around the corner towards her. She saw her zooming past her at speed and could then hear the policeman approaching to find the source of the scream. As he ran around the corner, Sue put her foot out and the policeman went flying to the ground. As soon as he fell, she took hold of the rolling pin she'd brought with her and gave him a smart whack on the head. He fell silent.

"Shit, Sue. You haven't killed him have you?"

Sue bent over and felt his pulse. "No, he's fine. He's still breathing. He'll be badly concussed but he'll come to." She took out some sanitiser and wiped his wrist where she'd felt his pulse. "Don't want to leave any DNA."

"Come on, we've got to go. I've just seen a light go on in a bedroom over there. We don't want anybody to see our car."

Ophelia was already sitting in the car waiting for them. Sue and Phyllis got in and Sue promptly started the engine.

"How hard did you hit him Sue?" asked Ophelia.

"Hard enough to keep him quiet" said Sue.

"Oh look" said Phyllis. "Somebody is coming out of their house to see what's going on. Hopefully they'll make sure he's ok."

"My guides have just told me he will be" said Ophelia. Sue wasn't sure whether Ophelia was just saying that to reassure her that she'd done the right thing, but Ophelia felt certain that no serious harm had come to the poor policeman.

"I know we used to call them pigs back in the sixties, but I do feel guilty about tonight" said Phyllis. "He was only trying to do his job."

"He was Phyllis, but this is the only shot we have at helping Becky" said Sue.

"Thanks Sue. I know it's not easy for you helping like this what with Becky and Alan's history" said Phyllis.

"That's ok Phyllis, we all want to do our bit."

While all this was happening Alan continued to stand guard by the front door of the house. He could hear Robert moving around, the beam of his torch moving from room to room as he searched for clues. The more he thought about it, the more ridiculous it seemed. Surely the police would also have looked for clues and taken anything away that seemed relevant. He began to think the entire exercise had been a complete waste of time. He stood waiting for what seemed like a lifetime, apprehensive that the policeman would return at any moment.

"Come on Robert, what are you doing?" he whispered to himself. He heard Robert coming downstairs.

"Found anything?"

"No, not really, but I just want to try one more room. I should have thought of it sooner."

"Which room is that?" asked Alan.

"The kitchen, the one room that we know he broke into the other night. You never know. It's got to be worth checking out."

Alan began to feel a little frustrated, thinking that this was a total waste of time. He was about to say so when he heard Robert say something.

"What's that?"

"Hold on a minute, I think I might have something here."

"What is it?"

"Just keep watching the front, we can't afford to get caught."

Alan grunted to himself. He continued watching the door while he heard Robert shuffling around in the kitchen. Eventually Robert came out of the kitchen to join him.

"I think I may have found something" he said.

"Oh? What's that?"

"Never mind right now, let's get back to the car and I'll tell you about it later."

"Ok" Alan agreed, though he couldn't imagine what Robert could have found.

Chapter Twenty-One

"You did what???????" Alan exclaimed.

"I hit him over the head with a rolling pin. Knocked him out. Well what else could we do? Let him catch up with Ophelia only to discover it was a false flag?"

"But we'd already discussed this beforehand Sue. Bloody hell, what are you trying to do, bring the long arm of the law down on us?" Alan glared at Sue.

"Oh come on Alan. Surely Robert you should know that the police are trained to read body language. They'd know that Ophelia was lying if she told them she was being pursued by an attacker. I thought if he was out cold, we could get away and nobody would be any the wiser."

"Jesus, I can't believe you ....."

"Hold on a minute Alan" Ophelia butted in. "Sue's made a good point. I'm not very good at lying and I'm sure if he had caught up with me and asked me to give a statement, my story would be so full of holes where I'd forgotten what I'd said five minutes earlier that ...."

"This is my fault" said Robert.

Everybody went silent and looked at him.

He gave a large sigh. "I should have thought about this more carefully. It was a stupid idea, it could have put us all at risk and I think Ophelia has made a good point."

"But you said yourself that we had no other option" pleaded Alan. "How else could we help Becky with no other options on the table?"

"Right, I think we all need to calm down. Phyllis, could I ask you to make us some tea and we can sit and mull over what we can do. It's late, we're all tired and on edge, so it's no wonder we're all going to be a bit tetchy."

"Of course Robert" said Phyllis, who was only too pleased to get the opportunity to go to the kitchen as the atmosphere became more charged.

"Now we have to look at it this way" stated Robert. "What's done is done. We can't change anything. All we can hope is that nobody saw the three of you, or your car for that matter."

"But what if they had?" asked Alan.

"If they had" said Robert, "Sue could just say that she was worried about her friend, gone out to look for her, saw her whizzing past and heard somebody following. Sensing danger, she tripped the person who was pursuing her and knocked him out."

"Oh of course" said Alan. "Doesn't everybody go about carrying a rolling pin in the middle of the night."

"Look Alan, Robert's only trying to give us something we can use if we are contacted, but to be honest, I don't think anybody saw us. I'm sure it will be fine" said Sue.

Ophelia was about to tell them that her guides advised her there that nobody had seen them and that there wouldn't be any repercussions, but she knew how Alan felt about her beliefs and decided to keep quiet. She may confide it to Robert later.

"Let's just put this aside for now" said Robert. "We have got something more pressing to deal with."

Phyllis came in with a tray.

"Do you need a hand with the cups Phyl?" asked Sue.

"Yes please love" she replied.

Sue and Phyllis went off to get crockery and biscuits. Phyllis had made some 'happy cakes' but she didn't think it would be a good idea to bring them out for everybody to tuck into, as nobody would be able to come up with any constructive ideas if they were stoned.

"Thanks Phyllis" said Robert and gave her a reassuring smile.

"No problem." She smiled back.

"Anyway, I think I may have something. To be honest, I'm surprised the police didn't see it when they were searching Becky's flat after the break in, but they were probably focussing more on the other rooms to see if something valuable had been taken."

"Oh, what is it Robert?"

"I thought at first it might be a gravy or jam stain when I first saw it, but something told me to inspect it closer and when I bent down it looked to me like dried blood."

"Dried blood? Where?" said Phyllis.

"By the kitchen sink. Although our intruder managed to

open the window without breaking any glass, I noticed there was a nail sticking out from the sink unit, possibly where Becky might hang a towel. Anyway, I would assume that he didn't want to switch a light on and when he put his hand on the sink, the nail pierced his hand. There were a few drops of blood on the floor. I inspected the nail and it definitely looked as though it had dried blood on it."

"You managed to get a sample?" asked Phyllis.

"I always carry my little swab kit with me. I've managed to put a couple of samples into two separate tubes. Tomorrow I'm going to get the fluid tested to see what blood group it is, but I'm pretty sure it's going to be O Positive."

"O Positive?" said Sue. "What makes you say that? That's my blood group."

"The blood found on the two victims was O Positive" said Robert. "We think it's Tristran Eldridge's blood. If so, I'll test it for any diseases and if it's clear, we can use it to give somebody a transfusion so they can see who our murderer is through the DNA Genetic Memory Modulation function on Ian's machine."

"I suppose I'm the most likely candidate" said Sue, not too pleased to be an unwilling volunteer.

"You don't have to Sue" said Robert. "We can always ...."

"Oh don't be silly Robert, of course I'll do it. It doesn't make sense to bring somebody else in. Who would volunteer anyway?"

"I'll have to warn you, you may see some pretty horrific incidents."

Sue burst out laughing. "Robert, I cannot believe you even said that to me!"

Robert looked at her puzzled?

Sue looked at him with a look of total disbelief on her face. "Don't you remember that I stabbed somebody to death back in 1978?"

Everybody in the room sat silent, not knowing where to look.

"Oh come on everyone, let's not beat about the bush. We all know it happened."

"Yes, but Sue it wasn't your fault ....." began Robert.

"Robert, I know it wasn't my fault. I'm just saying we know what happened. I'm not saying I relish the idea of going through with it, but unless somebody here can correct me, I'm the only one who is O Positive so that makes me the most likely choice.

Again, there was silence in the room as nobody could argue with Sue as she was pointing out something that happened to be true.

"Well ok Sue, but I don't want you feeling as though you're being pressured into this" said Robert.

"Oh don't worry Robert" said Sue, "after I've processed it, Alan can take me to a nice expensive jewellers afterwards and buy me a pretty rock as a reward." Sue was trying to lighten the mood, but all in the room remained somber.

"Well, if there's nothing else, I suggest we all try to get some sleep for what's left of the night and meet up again tomorrow evening. Phyllis, is it ok to bring the device here if all is ok with the blood sample?" asked Robert.

"Yes, of course. Ophelia and I will be on hand." She looked at Sue. "You must promise me sweetheart that if it becomes too intense, you stop it straight away, ok?"

"I'll be fine Phyll" she said. "We've all got to do our bit for the war."

The mood remained somber after this as everybody considered the process they were going to undertake the following evening.

"For all we know" said Robert as a passing remark, "it may not even be his blood. Becky may have cut herself and it could be no use at all." Was Robert hoping this was true? Only tomorrow would tell.

* * * * *

When the blood sample came back the next day and Robert was advised that it was all clear, the tests confirmed it was O Positive. Robert had mixed feelings – this was the result they were looking for but he was still apprehensive about the procedure they were going to carry out this evening.

Everbody was correct and present when Robert arrived with Ophelia at 7 o'clock. Robert was carrying Ian Pemberton's device and had also brought a syringe with the blood sample sealed in a little bottle.

"Now Sue, are you sure you're ok doing this?" he said, looking at her with some concern.

"I'm fine Robert. Let's just get it on with it."

Everybody sat silently as Sue rolled up her sleeve and Robert put the syringe into the bottle and filled it up with the reddish liquid."

"I've added a sedative to the compound to help you relax" he reassured Sue.

Sue nodded and sat back in the chair. Ophelia helped Robert attach the wires and he began to adjust the dials.

"Ok Sue, just try to relax. Take a few deep breaths and tell me what you're experiencing in your own time." Robert emphasised the last four words, speaking them slowly.

Sue sat silently for what seemed like a long time and twitched now and then. Her face went stiff at one point and Phyllis shot a worried look at Robert as if to beg that he stop the proceedings. He looked back at Phyllis and indicated that he would carry on until Sue decided to end it.

"I don't like this man" said Sue. "He's .... obnoxious, arrogant, entitled ...... and ...... oh hang on." She went quiet.

Everybody watched with eyes transfixed on Sue, hardly daring to breathe.

She began to breathe deeply, a fixed expression on her face, as if looking at something intently. After a while she sat back in the chair and began to take short, shallow breaths.

"Remember Sue, you can end this procedure any time you like" Robert whispered.

Sue raised her finger, as if to indicate to Robert that she needed to focus on what was happening. Her whole body stiffened, she was breathing faster now. Phyllis looked on, terrified.

"Oh Sue" she said quietly.

Sue no longer seemed to be in the 'present' but alternatively immersed in whatever she was experiencing. A few times Robert tried to ask her questions but she just raised her finger as if asking him to remain quiet whilst she continued to experience what was happening. Unbeknownst to Robert, the sedative was taking effect and it was helping Sue to deal with some of the horrendous images she was witnessing. She then started whispering something, but nobody could hear what she was saying.

"What's that Sue, we can't hear you very well" coaxed Robert.

"My name" she said, looking puzzled. "It's .... Seb .... Seb .... Sebastian ..... Blanchard."

"What's that?" asked Robert.

Again, Sue raised her finger as if to say "wait, give me time" and Robert took the hint.

"Listening, listening to our conversation ..... you were there. You heard everything."

The other four were dying to know what Sue was experiencing but she continued to focus on what was happening, making the odd statement here or there that meant nothing to the other four people in the room.

After what was just over an hour, Sue sat back on her chair, put her arms on the arm rests and began breathing steadily. Her eyes began to gently open and they flickered slightly as they adjusted to the light.

Phyllis, as always, was on hand. "Here you are love" she whispered. "Take a drink of water."

Sue took the glass gratefully and had several sips. "Thanks Phyllis" she whispered.

Robert was dying to know what she'd seen but didn't want to hurry her, so remained silent, waiting for Sue to disclose what she'd seen in her own time. Little did they know that at one point in the procedure, she was aware of this person standing in the bar talking to another man where she had met Chris and she was vaguely aware of Chris standing close to the bar, but this person wasn't paying any attention to him. That little detail she had decided to keep to herself, although she realised that Robert probably already knew it.

"Well, I can't say that was a pleasant experience" she said, strangely with a tone of calm. "But I have to say Robert, bravo for spotting that blood on the floor. I've learned a lot about our Mr Sebastian Blanchard."

"Sebastian Blanchard?" said Robert puzzled.

"Yes, that's the name of the person whose blood it was" said Sue.

"So it's not Tristran Eldridge then?" Robert was really puzzled now.

"No, all I kept hearing in my head was 'my name is Sebastian Blanchard, or Seb for short. Everybody called him Seb."

Robert frowned. "This doesn't make sense. I could have sworn it was the blood of Tristran Eldridge."

"I can only give you what I saw" said Sue, almost apologetically.

"Oh don't apologise Sue, you can only give us what's in the blood sample. I just can't work out why we've come across this Sebastian whoever he is and not Tristran."

"Well let's ask Sue what she witnessed. Maybe this Sebastian knows Tristran" suggested Phyllis.

Sue frowned. "I can't say. All I can say is what I experienced."

"Ok Sue" said Robert. "I'm going to switch on my digital recorder now if you don't mind telling us what you saw."

Sue confirmed their worst fears that this person, whoever he was, had indeed killed Nick Putterill and his girlfriend several decades ago. She experienced this murderer arguing with his father and being told that he needed to disappear for a while as his father could only protect him so much. He was walking through the cemetery looking at gravestones. Why was she seeing this? It seemed to be important for some reason. He kept fixating on different gravestones, paying particular attention to the date of death. He kept looking, searching ..... and then he stopped. He looked at the gravestone ..... he looked at the name and the date of death and he seemed to be pleased.

"I don't understand why he was pleased" said Sue puzzled. "Hang on" she said, as if trying to remember something. "Of course, of course."

"What is it?" asked Robert.

"I was experiencing the time after he'd commited the two murders. He was arguing with his father. His father was a very prominent man. Anyway, his father was extremely angry that he'd committed the two murders. He started shouting at him that he'd given this person, his son that is, every opportunity in life and that he'd blown it every time. The father was ranting at him that he was no better than a common street criminal and that he should let the law do its job and lock him away. But the son was crafty. He seemed to take great delight in pointing out to his father this if it was known in public that he was a murderer, it would damage his father's position and he would never be able to practice law ever again."

"But that sounds like Tristran Eldridge" said Robert. "I don't understand."

"Oh I understand perfectly now having processed the information thoroughly" said Sue. "It is Tristran Eldridge."

"But you just told me that his name was Sebastian Blanchard" queried Robert.

"I did Robert" said Sue.

Robert looked at Sue puzzled. "Sorry Sue, you've lost me."

"It's just come to me while I was describing what happened" she replied. "When Tristran committed these horrendous murders – and let me tell you – they were horrendous – his father told him that he could only do so much to cover up for him and that he suggested that Tristran leave the country so that he'd be safe from the law. But Tristran wanted to make sure that he disappeared totally. So he took a trip to the local cemetery, looked around the gravestones until he found one of a child that had died and was born around the same time that he was."

"Of course!!!" exclaimed Robert.

Phyllis looked at him puzzled. "I don't understand" she said.

"He most likely, no, he definitely obtained a birth certificate for the child and obtained a false passport using the child's name. I'm not sure what the situation is now with regard to obtaining somebody else's birth certificate, but back then it was relatively easily and it wouldn't be the first time a criminal had assumed a false identity using the birth certificate of a dead child" Robert explained.

"Oh" said Phyllis.

"Crafty, but bloody clever" said Alan.

"So in fact" added Ophelia, "our Mr Sebastian Blanchard and Tristran Eldridge are one and the same person."

"Exactly!" said Robert. "It makes total sense."

"And his father covered up his part in the murders and

when the police saw Tom standing over Nick's body, they thought all their Christmases had come at once. He was the perfect fall guy!" finished Alan.

"Got it in one Alan, got it in one."

"But how did he know where to find Becky?" asked Alan.

"I can answer that for you" said Sue.

"Oh?" Alan looked at her expectantly.

"By a strange coincidence, our boy Sebastian is involved in a drug ring operating in and around Cyprus. It's easy for him to smuggle the drugs into and out of the country. He manages to use the area known as no mans land – that's the land that's neither on the Greek or Turkish Cypriot side of the country. It's safe as it isn't heavily guarded. The authorities in Cyprus are aware of the problem, but it's hard to safeguard as it's quite a large area and both Turkish and Greek Cypriot authorities are stretched to the max in terms of capacity. They just don't have the resources to put troops on the ground there. Also, there are lots of drug routes around the mediterranean and he can get his contacts to smuggle in and out of the country as and how he needs. He's been doing it for years. He's aware that the authorities are doing their damndest to crack down on the drug ring, but the ring he's involved in is like an octopus with tentacles all over the place. Nobody could crack down on it with the best will in the world."

"Sue, surely you're not telling me that Becky's involved with this drug ring?" Alan looked at her with horror.

"Oh sorry Alan, I got carried away, no, not at all."

Alan breathed a large sigh of relief. "Glad to hear it."

"No, what happened was that one evening Becky was out at a Greek restaurant with her friends out there. She was telling them that she was going to pursue the investigation as to who was responsible for putting her brother away as he'd died recently and she wanted to get justice for him, even after death. She told them the entire story of what had happened and how her brother was wrongly convicted. She said she'd found some information that she thought might be helpful and was going to go back to England to pursue the investigation further." Sue paused briefly. "The only thing she didn't realise was that sitting at the next table to her was Sebastian Blanchard who overheard the entire conversation."

"Oh my god!" Phyllis's face froze in horror.

"Not only that" said Sue, "he actually followed her round for the next few days. He found out where she lived, what her movements were and ...." Sue looked at Alan, "he was sitting on the plane a row or two back from us when we returned from holiday and he heard the entire conversation that we had."

"Shit!" Alan's face was aghast.

"I experienced him walking off the plane, following Becky through the airport and getting a taxi to follow hers ...... right to where she lived."

"Jesus, so you were spot on Robert" said Alan.

"Looks like it" said Robert, with a tone that suggested he took no pride in his theory being correct.

"I'm guessing he was the one who put the poison in Becky's milk bottle, is that right?" said Alan, looking at Sue.

Sue nodded. "The trouble is, if he can follow Becky all the way back from Cyprus to her house, what's to say he didn't see you bringing her here Robert?"

Phyllis looked visibly horrified.

"Of course you were right Robert, he did cut his hand when he came through the window the first time he broke into the flat. Got quite a nasty gash too. He couldn't see in the dark and decided not to worry about clearing the blood up as nobody would be able to trace Becky's death back to him if she'd been poisoned as his DNA isn't on police files, so it would be nigh on impossible to track him down anyway."

"This man is just pure evil" said Alan, expressing exactly what everybody thought.

"The problem is" said Ophelia, "even knowing all of this, it doesn't help us in getting any nearer to him."

"Did you get any idea of where he's staying Sue?" asked Robert.

"He's moving about a bit. He stays in one place a few days and then moves on. He has connections in the UK and they can put him up but he's always on the move. He wants to stay one step ahead of the police."

"Which doesn't help us" stated Robert.

"And doesn't help us clear Becky's name either" said

Alan with more than a trace of anger in his voice.

"The only consolation there Alan is that at least Becky's safe while she's in custody, although god knows it must be really stressful for her" Robert tried to console Alan.

"So we have two tasks on our hand" concluded Alan. "One is to get Tristran Eldridge, Sebastian Blanchard or whatever he's calling himself out into the open and secure a conviction."

"And the other is to prove Becky's innocence" added Robert.

The five looked at each other, not knowing what to say. This was a task that nobody could anticipate knowing where to begin.

Chapter Twenty-Two

After the events of the evening, the five friends felt completely drained and decided to reconvene the following night.

"My head is beginning to throb" said Sue. "I was ok while I was going through the procedure, but now it feels as though my brain is trying to break through my skull."

"I'm sorry Sue, I'm beginning to regret that we went ahead with this" Robert apologised.

"Oh don't be ridiculous Robert, look at what we've learned tonight" she replied.

"Yes, but it doesn't get us anywhere nearer to Tristran" he argued.

Sue looked at him squarely. "I'm not sure that's true" she said. "Something keeps niggling at the back of my mind."

"Oh? What is it?"

"I don't know. Just something niggling somewhere. I'll sleep on it. I haven't got the energy tonight."

"Alan I know you're not going to like this suggestion, but I think Ophelia and I should do some healing work on Sue. She's been through one hell of an ordeal" said Phyllis.

"Actually Alan, I think I'd quite like that. Phyllis has done it before and I did feel much better afterwards" agreed Sue.

"Ok, if you think it will help. If you want to get a bit of night air Robert, we could go outside and wait by the cars for them."

"I could do with a bit of air" agreed Robert.

"We'll see you in a bit" said Alan to the three ladies as he and Robert walked to the door.

"Ok Ophelia, where do you want to start?" asked Phyllis.

"I suggest we get Sue a blanket and some cushions to lie on. I'll start at the head and you can start at the feet."

"Ok" said Phyllis. She fetched a blanket from upstairs and put it on the floor for Sue to lie on. "Rest your head on these Sue" she said as she plumped a few cushions.

"Thanks Phyllis" said Sue.

Ophelia put on some gentle harp music and the two

ladies began their healing session. Usually it helped to calm people down who had been through a trauma and indeed, it had done this for Sue in the past. This evening, although she seemed to visibly relax, there were instances where she twitched and her eyes seemed to screw up. Ophelia looked at Phyllis surprised. Phyllis looked equally puzzled, but they continued with the healing. Sue seemed to be muttering something and her head started moving from side to side.

"Easy Sue, just relax" said Ophelia in a soothing voice. It seemed to work – at least intermittently but then Sue would begin to twitch and jerk sporadically. Eventually Ophelia and Phyllis brought the session to a close and suggested to Sue that she should open her eyes when she felt ready.

Sue's eyes began to blink and eventually they opened fully. She looked at her two friends and smiled. "Thank you, that does feel better."

"What were you experiencing Sue? We both noticed you kept twitching and moving your head from side to side. Are you sure the session did any good?"

"Oh yes Phyl, definitely. It's just that I kept getting these images all the time. Two young boys – some sort of conflict or argument. I don't know where it came from. Very odd."

Ophelia frowned. "Has it happened before?"

"No" said Sue. "I've never seen that before in my life. It must have been some sort of dream."

"But you weren't asleep" noted Phyllis. "It seems a bit strange that you could have had a dream when you were still conscious."

"I don't know Phyl. Odd, but I'm not going to worry about it. I think maybe what I witnessed tonight has led to my brain playing tricks on me. I'll be fine, honest."

Phyllis didn't look very certain. "Well if you do need anything, make sure to call me ok. I don't care what time of the morning it is, do you promise?"

Sue went and gave her friend a hug. "Oh you silly old sod, what would I do without you Phyl? Honestly, I'll be fine. Now you two need to get some sleep as well, you both look shattered."

"We'll be fine Sue honest" said Ophelia.

The three ladies gave each other one final farewell hug and Sue and Ophelia walked to the front door.

"Now Phyllis I don't want to frighten you but will you make sure you lock your door tonight please?" asked Sue pleadingly. "And if you hear so much as a pin drop outside, you call me."

"I will Sue. Don't you worry, nobody can get in here. To be honest, if anybody has been watching the place, they probably would have seen Becky being taken away by the police so I shouldn't think they'd be interested in watching my house now."

"Even so, make sure to lock up."

Robert and Alan were waiting outside.

"Ready to go?" asked Alan.

"Yes Parker, you can take me home now."

"Very good me lady" said Alan in a mock Parker-Thunderbirds-esque voice.

"So tomorrow night the same time?" Alan asked Robert.

"Yes I'll see you then."

They said their goodnights with Alan and Sue in one car, Robert and Ophelia in the other.

Ophelia began to describe to Robert what had happened in the healing session and about Sue's 'dream'.

"That's interesting" said Robert. "I wonder if it was part of the genetic memory."

"That's exactly what I thought" said Ophelia. "It's obviously come up for a reason – almost as if ....."

"..... the memory is trying to tell us something" finished Robert.

* * * * *

Whatever Sue had experienced, it continued when she finally went to bed and switched out the light. She could hear Alan shuffling next to her and soon began to doze off.

Two children were running through a wood, one chasing the other. The smaller of the two was terrified of the other one.

"I'm going to get you Tristran Eldridge!" the bigger boy shouted.

"Leave me alone!" he screamed as he ran further into the

woods.

"Your dad sent my dad to prison, so I'm going to get you!"

"Your dad did a bad thing, that's why he went to prison. Leave me alone!"

"You're going to pay for it. I'll kill you and that'll teach your dad a lesson!"

"You're dad's a bad man, that's why he went to prison. That's what happens when you do bad things!"

"You're a liar Tristran Eldridge, when I get hold of you I'll show you!" the bigger boy screamed.

The chase lasted several minutes, although it seemed like a lifetime to the smaller boy who was running for his life, terrified of what the other boy would do if he caught him. As he continued to run ahead he saw a big cluster of trees. He ran towards them. He saw several clusters of trees huddled together. He could hide behind one of them. He came to a halt, trying not to pant too loudly so the other boy wouldn't hear him.

"I know you're here somewhere and I'll find you" the other boy shouted. "You can't hide from me forever."

Tristran Eldridge remained as still as he could. He had found a little hollow patch by the side of one of the cluster of trees. This seemed like a good hiding place. He could hear Sebastian Blanchard searching for him. Tristran's hiding place was in the shade and was easily obscured. If he could just remain hidden he would be safe. Surely Sebastian would tire of the hunt and go away eventually. Surely he would understand that his dad was a bad man and had to go to prison because he'd been naughty. Surely ....

"There you are you little pip-squeak. Now I'm going to teach you a lesson you'll never forget." Sebastian Blanchard towered over the cowering Tristran and pulled him out of his hiding place.

"Now you're going to get it" hissed Sebastian as he lunged his fist towards Tristran's face.

Whatever happened, be it instinct, quick thinking or just the desire to survive, Tristran managed to duck his head quickly and Sebastian's fist hit the bark of the tree.

"Aaaaaaaagggggggghhh!" The pain caused him to loosen his grip on the trembling Tristran and as he released it,

Tristran saw his opportunity to run. Run as fast as he could to get away. He ran towards the other end of the woods where there was an opening onto a field. He could hear Sebastian Blanchard shouting at him.

"When I get you, I'm going to kill you" he screamed.

In terror, Tristran Eldridge continued to run, ignorning the pain in his chest and the tightening of his lungs. He could see the opening onto the field. Hopefully it would make it easier to run, but then Sebastian would be able to see him more clearly. What could he do? He kept running, hoping that he would come back to the main road, but he was frightened and disorientated.

Sebastian's pursuit was now relentless. The pain had subsided slightly and he was more determined to teach this little runt a lesson. "I'm coming Tristran, I'm coming for you" he taunted.

As Tristran ran ahead, he could see a small bridge crossing a ditch from one part of the field to the other. As he ran towards it, he didn't see the branches growing across it near to the ground and tripped violently. As he fell he managed to grasp onto the railings and save himself. The shock stunned him into stillness, but hearing Tristran's voice again, he stumbled forward and continued to run. As he looked back he could see Sebastian approaching the bridge.

"I'm getting nearer Tristran. I've nearly caught up with ...."

Tristran continued running and glanced back in fear to see how near Sebastian was. He looked puzzled. Where was Sebastian. He was there a minute ago but Tristran couldn't see him. There was no way he could suddenly disappear like that. What had happened? He didn't dare slow down and yet .... and yet ..... he slowed to a stop. There was no sign of Sebastian at all. There was nowhere for him to hide. He cautiously turned and walked back to towards the bridge. He noticed that somebody .... Sebastian ...... was lying face down on the bridge. Was he pretending to be unconscious and waiting for Tristran to approach him before he leapt up? In his young mind Tristran couldn't understand why Sebastian wasn't moving. Was he playing a trick. He tiptoed gingerly towards the bridge and noticed a small pool of blood on the ground. He approached the motionless Sebastian and noticed a huge gash on his head.

Blood was pouring out of his ear.

"Sebas .... Sebas ..... Sebas ..... tian" he whispered.

He couldn't understand why Sebastian wasn't moving. He remembered that he had almost tripped and gone flying but managed to save himself by grabbing onto the rail. Had the same thing happened to Sebastian? If so, why didn't he grab onto the rail in the same way that Tristran had. His mind was confused. What could he do. He prodded Sebastian, but there was no movement. His eyes were wide open but he wasn't moving at all. What if somebody had seen Sebastian chasing Tristran? What if they came across him lying there and thought that Tristran had done something to him? He would get into trouble. He might go to prison with Sebastian's dad and his dad would be very cross and hurt him, just like Sebastian had tried to. He must try to hide Sebastian so that nobody knew where he was. If they couldn't find him they wouldn't be able to blame Tristran. Yes, that's what he must do – he must try to hide him. He pushed Sebastian's body off the bridge. As he did, Sebastian's body landed with a soft thud onto the tufts and bushes below. Now he must climb down and hide Sebastian's body under the bridge. Yes, yes – hide his body under the bridge. He gingerly climbed down off the bridge and landed right beside Sebastian. He pushed the boy's body under the bridge – it was almost impossible for the small boy to do it as Sebastian was bigger and heavier than he was. He decided to step over Sebastian's body and pull him under the bridge. It was still difficult but was slightly better than trying to push him under. Gradually, gradually Sebastian's lifeless body moved further under the bridge. When Tristran thought that he'd pulled it right under the bridge, he pulled off some of the tufts from the bushes and shrubs that surrounded the hollow by the bridge. He continued doing this until he felt satisfied that nobody would be able to see Sebastian's body. It was highly unlikely that they would be able to anyway but he wanted to make sure. He then managed to climb up onto the bridge, struggling to hold onto the rails as he pulled his body up. When he finally climbed back onto the bridge he was sweating and breathless.

"You won't ever bully me again, you won't every bully me again! I hate you! I hate you! You're a nasty boy! You're a nasty boy! Just like your dad!"

"Sue! Sue! Wake up!!"

Sue jerked up and her eyes shot open. She was gasping for air.

"It's ok, you've just had a nightmare" said Alan.

"No Alan, it was real. I'm telling you it was real!"

"Don't be silly, it was a dream."

"It was real Alan, I saw it, I'm telling you I saw it"

"What did you see?"

"It was him. It was Tristran!"

"Tristran? What was he doing?"

"He was a young boy, he was being chased through the woods by a bigger boy called Sebastian. The bigger boy was angry because Tristran's dad had sent him to prison so he was going to take his revenge out on Tristran."

Alan was now curious. "Go on" he said.

"Tristran was terrified but he managed to find a hiding place amongst a thick cluster of trees in the woods. He could hear Sebastian calling out to him that he was going to get him. Sebastian found him and was going to thump him but he managed to escape.

"And then what?"

Sue looked directly at Alan. "He ran out of the woods into a field with a small bridge crossing a ditch. He tripped and nearly fell but managed to cling onto the railing." She paused. "Sebastian wasn't so lucky. He tripped and his head crashed into one of the posts. I think ..... I think .... it killed him. Tristran came back and pushed his body into the ditch."

"Are you sure you're not imagining this Sue, especially after what ha ......"

"I'm telling you Alan, it's a vestige of his genetic memory. It was so clear, so real. He just ran and ran as fast as he could."

"So are you saying that ......"

"...... that Tristran Eldridge used Sebastian's death in order to obtain a false passport."

"And a new identity" concluded Alan. "Well, the only way to prove it is to make some enquiries as to when this Sebastian died and the circumstances around his death."

"I'm certain that it will corroborate with my story" said Sue.

"I don't disbelieve you Sue. The only thing is it doesn't help us in getting Becky released."

"I don't know. We seem to be getting snippets of information here and there and I can't help thinking that it's just a case of joining up the dots to see what the full picture is."

"Maybe" said Alan. "Maybe."

"Well I'm certainly going to mention it tomorrow night when we meet up again" she insisted.

"By all means, it can't do any harm. It's just ironic that the person who was responsible for the death of two other people was once the victim of a bully."

"I think it's far more common than you'd realise" said Sue.

Chapter Twenty-Three

Bill Granger glared at Robert when he walked into the police station. "Why do I just know that you've come here to give me grief, waste my time, make up crazy stories about imaginary criminals ..... or all three."

"Oh Bill, you give me far too much credit for having an active imagination when I haven't got anything of the sort. I'm afraid all I can bring you is truth" smiled Robert politely.

"Or your version of truth."

"Truth is truth my dear William, I can't change it, I can only bring it to you as it is."

"I'm a busy man Robert, I haven't got time to waste on you today."

"But here's the thing Bill. You're holding a lady in custody accused of possessing drugs and she's totally innocent."

"Oh I see" said Bill Granger sarcastically. "You mean we searched her flat and found heroin to the street value of god knows what and you're going to tell me she was stiched up."

"You see" said Robert, returning the sarcasm. "I knew you weren't just promoted for having a pretty face and a Charles Atlas set of abs."

"I'm not in the mood today Robert, now if you don't mind, I've got a shed load of work to do."

"So you're not interested in catching the person who could be the leader of a large drugs ring that stretches to the Mediterranean?"

"Well here's the thing Robert. Your Miss Collerton has told us how she goes back and forth to Cyprus, so maybe we've already got our culprit."

"Now Bill, Becky's a really nice lady. Also very smart .... but leader of a drug ring? Now who's got the imagination?"

"Ok, I'll do you a deal. Co-leader."

"Not happening on my watch Billy Boy."

"I'm the law around here and it's on my watch so I outrank you Mr Clinical Psychologist man. Go and do your Freudian analysis elsewhere."

"But I can even give you the name of our prime

suspect."

"Oh yes? Go on, give it your best shot. I'm all ears."

"Tristran Eldridge."

"Tristran Eldridge?" Bill Granger frowned. "I've heard that name before somewhere." He looked at Robert. "Doesn't mean to say I believe you though."

"His father was a judge. Retired now of course but still alive."

"A judge's son is the leader of an international drug ring? Jesus Robert, you need help. Hell, I think you need to be sectioned."

"I knew I was wasting my time telling you. I'd like to ....."

At that moment a smartly dressed gentleman walked in and introduced himself to Bill Granger.

"Good morning, I'm Miss Collerton's solicitor. I'd like to see my client please."

Robert's eyes nearly popped out of his head. "You're Becky's solicitor?" His voice went slightly higher as his excitement grew.

"Yes" the gentleman answered. "Sorry I don't think we know each other."

"Now don't you go telling him tall tales Robert. He's here to ascertain facts, not listen to some wild theories about drug rings and murderers."

"Excuse me Mr. er ..."

"Mr. Jansen" he replied.

"Mr. Jansen, I'm a clinical psychologist and a friend of Becky's. I have information that I think may be vitally important but my friend here doesn't want me to disclose it. Now I know that legally I'm not allowed to interfere with the case, but please take my card and give me a ring. Becky is innocent and I intend to prove it."

The solicitor looked at Bill Granger and then at Robert. He then looked back at Bill Granger. "You know this man? Is he a clinical psychologist?"

"Yes" grunted Bill. "But he uses his title to convince people that what he has to say is true and it isn't. Now I can't tell you what to do, but I would strongly advise you to stay well away from this man."

"Mr. Jansen, please call me. I will tell you what I know and if you choose to believe it's all nonsense, I promise you, I will never contact you again. But hear me out once."

"Robert! Go away! I'll have you arrested for perverting the course of justice."

"Sorry Bill, you can't do that. I know my law and I haven't technically done anything wrong. Please Mr. Jansen, give my best wishes to Becky and tell her that we're doing everything in our power to clear her name."

Mr. Jansen looked at Robert. He seemed to be very credible, articulate, intelligent .... why did the Inspector dislike him so much?

"Thank you Mr er ....." he looked at Robert's card and noted his credentials, "Mr Whitehead. I can't promise anything, but I have your number should I need to contact you."

"Thank you" said Robert and bade him goodbye.

Mr. Jansen believed himself to be a good judge of character and Robert definitely excuded respectability and ...... credibility. Could he have some information that might assist his client? As he heard Bill Granger begin to rant about Robert, a quote came to mind .... "methinks the lady doth protest too much" and Bill Granger was being very vocal in his derisory views of Robert.

Later that evening the five friends met again at Phyllis's house. Alan and Sue turned up first and Sue was about to tell Phyllis about her dream when Alan shook his finger.

"Wait until we're all here Sue, then you won't have to repeat it."

Sue looked at Alan and then at Phyllis. "Oh actually, that's not a bad idea."

Phyllis led them through to the lounge where Pywackit was sprawled across the sofa.

"Now darling, you're only showing off. You know that the guests need to sit somewhere and human beings need more space than you."

"Trust me Pywackit, we've got bigger derrières than you felines, so would you mind if we parked them please?" requested Sue.

Pywackit gave Sue his best sullen look, swished his tail

and moved to the chair.

"Thank you. I'll get you the biggest mouse you've ever had" she said.

Phyllis was preparing drinks and snacks when she heard the doorbell go.

"I'll get it" called Sue and she walked through the hall to open the door to Ophelia and Robert. "Pywackit may have taken his seat back in the time that I've walked out here to greet you so I hope you appreciate the sacrifice I've made."

Ophelia giggled and even Robert had a chuckle.

"Now you don't want to go upsetting Pywackit" he said. "I've seen the film 'The Uncanny'. Spoiler alert – it isn't a pretty ending!"

"Oh thanks Robert" said Sue. "I thought you were my friend."

"Just trying to warn you."

When they went through to the sitting room, Pywackit had not taken back Sue's seat but was then doubly-miffed when the mere humans expected him to give up the seat he was now sitting on. He walked up to the fireplace, turned his back on them and sat down, his tail swishing belligerently.

"That's done it" said Robert. 'The Uncanny' is going to take place tonight right here."

"Be quiet Robert" sue hissed. "You'll upset Phyllis!"

Robert smiled apologetically.

Phyllis came through, laden with tea pots, cups, plates, cutlery and napkins.

"Here let me give you a hand Phyllis" said Sue and followed Phyllis into the kitchen to collect the snacks that she'd prepared for them.

"Now Phyllis, you didn't need to go to all this trouble" said Robert. "There's enough here to feed the 5,000."

"I think you're exaggerating a bit there Robert" she said, smiling.

"Ok, 2,250 then" he added.

"Behave!" she giggled.

Sue helped Phyllis pour the tea when Alan decided to come straight to the point.

"Sue has some information to share with everyone. Well, we're not certain, but we think it's information."

"Oh?" said Robert.

"Well in the healing session last night, I kept getting flashes, images of two young boys, one running after the other. It wasn't very clear and I didn't think too much of it at the time."

"Go on" encouraged Robert.

"When we got home last night and went to bed, I had what I can only describe as a really vivid dream, but it wasn't a dream, it was too real." Sue continued to tell them the story of the two boys running through the woods, the bigger boy, Sebastian, chasing the smaller boy, Tristran, threatening to kill him because his father had been sent to prison by Tristran's father. The others sat in silence as she relayed the details of how Tristran hid in a hollow by a tree out of sight of Sebastian, only to be discovered, nearly thumped, and then managed to escape into an open field with a small bridge where he nearly fell straight into a post.

"Fortunately for him he managed to grab onto a rail, but his pursuer, one Sebastian Blanchard didn't have quite the same luck. He tripped, went flying straight headlong into the post. I can't say for certain but I got the impression that he died outright. Tristran, as small as he was, managed to push Sebastian's body down into the ditch, pull it under the bridge out of sight and cover it with branches and shrubbery."

"So are you saying that he left Sebastian there to ...." Phyllis faltered as she shuddered at the thought.

"........... die" finished Robert. "So it wasn't a random accident that he came across Sebastian's name on the gravestone and decided to take on Sebastian's identity. My Freudian colleagues would have a field day analysing that."

"So do we know if Sebastian was ever discovered?" asked Phyllis.

"We've made some enquiries today but will have to wait a few days to hear back. The local library have said they should be able to obtain newspaper stories from that time pertaining to the boy's disappearance."

"And Tristran Eldridge knew where he was all along and did nothing about it?" said Phyllis, looking disgusted.

"I know it sounds harsh Phyllis, but try looking at it from his point of view" said Robert. "If Sue's dream was in fact a remnant of the genetic memory procedure we underwent, and I've got good reason to believe that it was, then Tristran was obviously terrified of Sebastian and in his mind, he thought that if nobody ever found Sebastian, he wouldn't be bullied again by him."

"It makes sense" said Ophelia. "A child's first instinct is self-preservation and if he had been constantly bullied by this Sebastian, then he would have no reason for helping him .... whatever the consequences."

"I still find it hard to cope with" said Phyllis.

"Well, be that as it may, first of all, we have to decide if we believe it's a memory from something that happened to Tristran in the past, and if we do ...." Robert began.

"........ how does it help us in getting nearer to Tristran?" finished Alan.

"Exactly." Robert nodded.

"I mean we can hardly go to the press and say that an international drug dealer by the name of Tristran Eldridge is calling himself Sebastian Blanchard because he murdered two people decades ago and this is the only way he can move around freely without being caught and arrested" said Alan.

"Yes indeed" sighed Robert. "It sounds way too fantastic to be believable. Oh, and that's another thing." He took a bite of the cake he was eating.

"What's that?" asked Alan.

"I happened to bump into" he managed to say between mouthfuls of cake, "Mr. Jansen today when I was speaking to Bill Granger. Bill was his usual welcoming, helpful self, but this Mr. Jansen came in and introduced himself as Becky's solicitor."

"Wow, that's fantastic!" exclaimed Phyllis.

"Well, hold on Phyllis. Of course I jumped at the chance of introducing myself and telling him that Becky was innocent and I had what I believed to be vital information pertaining to the case, but Bill was really trying to make me look like some ranting lunatic and told the solicitor to ignore me."

"Oh no, that's no good" said Phyllis.

"Don't be too disheartened Phyllis. I got the impression he realised I was credible and I gave him my business card and asked him to call me. Now he hasn't called me so far but he may be interested in what we have to say. I'm sure it would have arisen in his meeting with Becky and she would encourage him to talk to us so I'm going to keep my phone close to me at all times."

"It might just be the break we need" said Ophelia.

"The only trouble is ……." Robert hesitated.

"What?" Phyllis looked concerned that Robert was going to put a dampener on everything he'd just said.

"Well, we can give him all the facts as we know them, but he would be bound to ask how we came across our evidence" said Robert.

"And telling him that we did it with a scraping of Tristran's blood injected into Sue and her coming up with all this information is not only going to sound ridiculous, but it certainly won't be admissible in a court of law" said Alan.

"You should have been a solicitor Alan" said Robert.

"No need to, I have a daughter who's one – and a good one at that." Alan couldn't disguise the pride in his voice.

"Everytime we seem to come up with a good idea, they only get bashed down again" said Phyllis. "It's so frustrating."

"So what do we tell him then, that is if he does call you?" said Alan.

"I'll have to think about that one, but it's not going to be easy" replied Robert. "Although ……."

"Although?" Ophelia looked at Robert. "What is it Robert?"

"I asked Bill Granger if I could obtain the clothes from the murdered girl in order to get DNA evidence. Well of course he told me no."

"Probably not in the most polite way either" said Ophelia.

"Quite" said Robert. "But if we can persuade Becky's solicitor to get access to the archive box and run a DNA test of the blood on the victim's clothes that belonged to the murderer as well as the blood that we collected the other night ….."

"Chances are it would be a match" said Sue. "And if it is, it makes our story more credible."

"Exactly Sue!" said Robert.

"Well we've got to get in contact with this solicitor" said Phyllis impatiently. "Is there no way we can find out what his number is?"

"You have to tread carefully Phyllis" said Robert. "As tempting as it is, we need to take baby steps otherwise he's going to believe what Bill said about me being a raving lunatic."

"Oh god, it's so frustrating. I don't like all this waiting around" retorted Phyllis. "Poor Becky's stuck in a rotten cell, probably feeling terrified, as well as being terminally ill and it just feels as though we can't do anything to help her. I don't like it!"

"Neither do I Phyllis." It slipped out before Alan could hold it back.

Sue tried to pretend that she hadn't noticed, but deep down she felt a little pang of jealousy. She changed the subject to pull away from the feelings she was experiencing. "Look, I don't want to put the kybosh on all of this as I honestly think it sounds like a great idea. But even if we do obtain DNA samples and they both match, we still have one problem."

"What's that?" said Phyllis, now beside herself with the ups-and-downs of solutions, problems, solutions, problems.

"I think I know what you're thinking Sue" said Robert. There's no DNA record of Tristran Eldridge on police records as far as we know and we have to physically get hold of him to prove that he's not only a murderer, but the person who broke into Becky's flat and tried to poison her ....."

" ....and then plant the drugs!" concluded Alan.

"Quite" said Robert.

"And we don't have a clue where he is, as we know he moves around constantly" said Sue.

"There's got to be a way of bringing him out into the open. Dangling a carrot .... something to tempt him ......"

Chapter Twenty-Four

The next few days saw the five friends making enquries, asking questions, Robert dodging the odd verbal bullet from Bill Granger as he dared to enter the sacred shrine of the Inspector's domain and ruffling feathers as much as possible. They were determined to get answers and time was ticking. Becky had told her solicitor everything that she knew. Feeling that he had come to a dead end, he had decided to call Robert to see what he had to say. He would try to keep an open mind, despite Bill Granger's protestations and ascertain himself just how credible this Robert Whitehead was.

"Mr Whitehead?"

"Speaking."

"This is Mr. Jansen. We met the other day at the police station."

"Mr. Jansen, thank you for calling back."

"Look, I'm going to be honest with you. My client has told me all that she knows and I can tell that she's innocent, but I don't have enough evidence to prove otherwise. I have nothing to offer the defence and I must be honest, I'm clutching at straws right now. With all due respect, this doesn't mean that I'm going to believe everything you might tell me, but I would like to hear what you have to say and work out for myself if it has any credibility."

"I would be more than happy to meet you Mr. Jansen. You just let me know when you're available and I can re-organise my diary accordingly."

"Would this afternoon at 2.30 pm be too short notice?"

"Not at all. Where would you like to meet?"

"If you could come to my office, I'll give you the address. Do you have a pen and paper?"

"Yes I do" said Robert, frantically scrabbling in his locker to find said items. "Ok, fire away."

The solicitor gave Robert his address and told him that his PA would put the appointment in his diary.

"Great. Thank you Mr. Jansen. I'll see you then."

Robert found it difficult biding his time until it came for

him to go and see Mr. Jansen. He tried to write down the facts in a logical order as he saw them. He decided to leave out the genetic memory procedure that they used to obtain the most vital information and realised that it would be difficult trying to disclose how this evidence was obtained.

It was 2.20 pm when Robert's car drove into the car park of the small firm that Mr.Jansen worked for. He had been slightly apprehensive as there had been a hold up due to an accident and was worried that he wouldn't get there on time, but the ever cautious Robert always tried to allow for any hic-cups along the way and set out earlier than would generally be considered necessary.

"Hello Mr. Jansen. Nice to meet you again" said Robert, shaking his hand firmly.

"I didn't mention this meeting to Inspector Granger so I would appreciate it if you didn't tell him I've arranged this meeting with you today."

"Mr. Jansen, I can assure you, you're singing to the choir. I have no wish for Bill Granger to know anything about this as he considers me an interfering busy body who pokes his nose into investigations with no evidence."

"And what would give him cause to think like that Mr. Whitehead?" asked the solicitor.

Robert smiled. "Just the type of question I would expect a solicitor to ask, and of course, you have every right to ask that."

"And your answer?"

"How can I put this nicely?" said Robert. "I have known Bill Granger for some years now and even helped on one of his cases profiling a criminal. They were able to use my information to track down the killer and he fit my description perfectly. Which pleased Bill initially because it meant the case was solved and it also made him look like the great case solver."

"Go on" added the solicitor.

"I also knew a few of the other policeman who were working on the case at the time. They started murmering things like he was impeding the case with his sloppy work and one of them virtually out-and-out told me that if it hadn't been for my profiling work, the murderer would still be out there. He told me that Bill had got all the credit for my hard work. Well my attitude was that I didn't care who got the credit, as long as the murderer was behind bars. But Bill got wind of this story and I think it stuck in his claw a little bit. He's been sour with me ever since."

"Would you care to tell me which case this was?"

"Yes. The Orion killer. Are you familiar with that case?"

"Am I familiar with it? Are you serious? It was all over the papers for weeks when he was caught."

"Indeed it was. Well Bill had a bee in his bonnet about the likely suspect – somebody who definitely wasn't the nicest character you'd wish to meet, but he just didn't fit the profile for the killer. We had arguments galore over it and were both very stubborn about which direction the investigation should go in. Anyway, I'm afraid I was a bit underhanded. I went behind his back to his superiors and put my case across as to why he had the wrong man. My profiling could even track down the area the killer lived in within 200 yards."

"Let me guess" said the solicitor. "It turned out you were right."

"I was" said Robert. "Since then, Bill has shall we say ....."

"Held a grudge against you?"

"Well let's just say he prefers it if I keep my nose out of any investigation he's involved with."

"Ok, well let's just say I believe you and it certainly gives you good credentials if that's true. How does this help Miss Collerton?"

Robert told the solicitor the story of how he had become acquainted with Becky through Sue and Alan and how he had rushed back to her house on the night she had been poisoned. He then described how Becky had been wrongly accused of possession of heroin, despite the fact that the drugs were found in her house.

"So how can you prove to me that it wasn't Miss Collerton?" asked the solicitor. "Whilst I'm convinced that she is indeed innocent, I have no hard evidence."

"Ok, I have a confession to make" said Robert.

"Oh?" Mr Jansen looked at Robert questioningly.

"I would appreciate it if what I am about to say is kept

confidential between us" said Robert.

"Depending on the nature of what you're about to say, I can't say for certain that I won't disclose it, but I will use my discretion as far as possible."

"Ok. Well we knew that Becky was innocent and we wanted to prove it. After the so-called drugs raid, we had a suspicion that there would be a police guard outside the flat but we decided we needed to do a bit of investigating ourselves."

The solictors eye-brows arched slightly.

"We went over to the house and managed to distract the policeman on guard. I had a key to Becky's flat as she'd given it to me for safekeeping. We looked around the property and noticed something that the police must have missed."

The solicitor now looked interested.

"We believe that when our suspect used the window to get in, he gashed his hand on a nail that was sticking out of the cabinet and there were traces of blood on the nail and the floor" said Robert. "I collected samples of it for my own use and I still have a sample. We believe we know who the blood belongs to."

The solicitor was writing notes down, occasionally looking up at Robert as if to coax more information out of him. "Go on" he said.

"We believe it's a man called Tristran Eldridge."

The solicitors eyes nearly popped out of his head. "Tristran Eldridge ...... as in son of Godfrey Eldridge?"

"That is correct."

"You're telling me that the son of a respected judge is an international drug dealer?" This was too much for the solicitor to take in.

"Not only that ......" Robert paused. "He's also the man who murdered Nicholas Putterill and his girlfriend." There it was – the bomb had been dropped.

The solicitor sat in silence, just staring at Robert. He'd stopped taking notes and dropped his pencil.

"I know what you're thinking Mr Jansen, but I believe I can prove it."

"How?"

"I met the solicitor who was defending Thomas Collerton at the time of his trial. He had strong evidence to show that Thomas could not have committed the murders."

"Yes, yes, that much I know. Miss Collerton told me how he was on the Isle of Wight when the first murder occured and that he was given a speeding ticket by the police at the very time that somebody was seen running out of the victim's house."

"So this is where it's going to sound completely ludicrous but I stand by this story and if you can help me, we can prove for certain that Tristran Eldridge is not only the murderer, but also the leader of the drug ring."

"That''s quite an ask Mr. Whitehead" said the solicitor.

"I'm going to be straight with you Mr Jansen. As you know, Becky has got cancer and I don't want her spending her last days in a prison cell as an innocent woman, in the same way that her brother spent years behind bars as an innocent man."

"So how do prove that Tristran Eldridge is indeed the person we should be investigating?"

"First of all, we need to obtain access to the archive box of Nicholas Putterill's girlfriend's clothes, the ones she was wearing when she was murdered. In both cases there were defence marks and some of the murderer's blood was left on the clothes."

"Yes, I know, O Positive as Miss Collerton told me, whereas her brother was A Negative. Sorry, I'm a bit confused. Why do you want access to that box in particular? I would have thought it would be much better to obtain the box for Nicholas Putterill, considering that Thomas Collerton was seen standing over his body and not his girlfriend's."

"That's just the problem" said Robert. "There isn't one."

"What do you mean, there isn't one?" said the solicitor, perplexed.

"The solicitor who was defending Thomas Collerton said that he was told to drop the case and that his children might not – how did he put it now – live to see a long and healthy life if he didn't drop the case and destroy the evidence."

"Really?" Mr. Jansen frowned disbelievingly.

"If you don't believe me, you can ask him" said Robert defiantly.

"Oh yes? What's his name?" asked the solicitor.

"Martin Smithson" said Robert.

"Martin Smithson!!!??" exclaimed the solicitor.

"You know him?" asked Robert.

"I know him very well. A very competent solicitor and a thoroughly decent human being. He's never mentioned this to me before."

"Well I guess people don't go around shouting their mouth off that they've been threatened by people otherwise they run the risk of getting killed themselves – or their children."

It was becoming evident to Robert that the solicitor was struggling to take all this evidence in. "And you say the evidence in the Nicholas Putterill murder was destroyed totally?"

"Every last bit. You ask Martin yourself, though he won't thank me for sharing this with you." Robert was both shocked that Mr Jansen knew Martin Smith and also pleased with himself that he'd managed to get his point across, using Martin's association to add to his credibility.

The solicitor picked up his pencil and began scribbling notes again. "I still can't believe that it's old Godfrey's son. It's just unthinkable."

"I met Godfrey Eldridge a few days ago at a bowling green. I have to say I've never met a more dislikable man in my life."

"What, old Godfrey?" questioned Mr Jansen.

"Yes, 'old Godfrey'" said Robert with a tone of disdain in his voice. "Thoroughly arrogant. The common law premise of 'innocent until proven guilty' is thrown right out of the window for him and he adopts a very Napoleonic law stand of 'guilty until proven innocent' and even then he'll quite happily throw away somebody's life ...." Robert paused to add extra emphasis. "Especially when it comes to protecting his own lousy son's life."

"So you're telling me that Thomas Collerton was a useful scapegoat to get his own son off the hook?"

Robert stared the solicitor directly in the face. "That's exactly what I'm telling you. I'm also willing to bet any amount of money that if you can obtain DNA from the girlfriend's clothing and compare it to the sample I have, you'll get a match. All we have to do then is track Tristran Eldridge down and get his DNA. Voila! You have the real murderer of Nicholas Putterill and his girlfriend as well as the leader of an international drug ring."

"Ok, I still have to remain objective, but let's just say you have a case here. Where do we find Tristran Eldridge? Do you know where he lives?"

"No, because he no longer uses that name. After the murders, his father told him to get out of the country as he could only do so much to protect him and just as a precaution, he ordered the birth certificate of a dead boy who was born around the same time as him and he took on that identity to get a false passport."

This was now stretching credibility as far as the solicitor was concerned.

"This is very detailed information Mr. Whitehead. How did you come by it? Who is your source?"

Robert paused. "That I'm afraid I can't disclose right now. I have to protect my source." He felt guilty – it wasn't exactly a lie as his source was a device that could assist in reading the DNA of a human being using their blood.

"You do realise though that if this ever went to court, I would have to demand solid evidence backed up by sources to put this case forward?"

"We'll cross that bridge when we come to it. In the meantime, we have to find Tristran Eldridge ... aka ..... Sebastian Blanchard."

"Sebastian Blanchard. That's the name of the dead boy I presume?"

"Yes" said Robert. He wasn't sure whether sharing the story of Tristran actually witnessing the demise of Sebastian Blanchard would be advisable at present – there was already a lot of information for Mr Jansen to digest.

"Look Mr. Whitehead, you've given me a lot to think about and it's going to take some time to consider your story fully."

"I appreciate that – it's a lot of information to take in."

The solicitor looked puzzled. "And yet it does seem to correlate a lot with what Miss Collerton told me. But I can't just go around throwing accusations all over the place. I have to make sure my research is absolutely on point. The slightest error takes away any credibility I have and I'm sorry if you think this is my ego talking, but I've spent too many years building up my reputation only to have it shattered overnight by investigating what, quite frankly, sounds like something out of a novel you'd buy at an airport to take on holiday."

"I fully understand. The only thing I'm asking of you is to obtain a DNA sample from the girl's dress and compare it to the one I have. If they match, you know that the murderer and the person who broke into Becky's flat are one and the same."

"I can't promise anything, but I'll see what I can do."

"Please Mr. Jansen. I'm usually a very resourceful man but I need your help. I need it for Becky's sake. I need to give her proper closure before ...... before ....."

"As I say Mr. Whitehead, I will do what I can."

Robert turned to leave. "Thank you for your time Mr. Jansen."

Chapter Twenty-Five

"So do you think he believed you Robert?" asked Ophelia.

"I can't say for certain, but he was definitely taken aback when I mentioned how Martin had been threatened to drop the case."

"You say he knows Martin?"

"Yes, small world isn't it."

"Which hopefully makes our story more believable as he holds Martin in such high regard."

"That's what I'm hoping."

"How long did he say before he'd get back to you?"

"He didn't give me any specifics, just said he would see what he could do. The trouble is he's got Becky's case to deal with and other clients I would assume."

"And yet if he was to look into the DNA evidence from the dead girl's clothes, it might help speed up the investigation."

"Not necessarily Ophelia. Remember, we still don't know where Tristran is, so even if we do have two identical samples, it means nothing until we catch up with him."

"That could take a long time."

"I wonder how Alan and Sue are getting along with their enquiry into Sebastian Blanchard's whereabouts."

"Funny you should say that, I think that's Alan's car approaching."

They both looked out of the window of Robert's lounge and sure enough Alan and Sue were parking their car just outside in front of Robert's house. They both walked down the drive to Robert's front door and he was on hand to greet them.

"Come on in" said Robert. "I might not be able to offer you a hamper of snacks like Phyllis does, but I can at least offer you both a cup of tea."

"That sounds perfect Robert" said Sue.

"Phyllis not able to make it?"

"No, afraid not. I think Pywackit ate something dodgy and apparently has been yakking up all night. I did offer to take him to the vet but she insisted she would prepare him a herbal remedy."

"I hope he's alright. I know we joke that he's the demon cat, but I wouldn't want anything to happen to him."

"I think he just sneaked a few of Phyllis's snacks and ate more than he could handle" said Sue.

"Well I hope you're right" said Robert.

Robert brought them into the lounge and Ophelia greeted them.

"I'll go and put the kettle on, be with you in a minute" said Robert.

Shortly afterwards, Robert was walking through with a tea tray, not quite as cosy as Phyllis's layout, but the tea was welcomed by all.

"So have you heard anything back from Becky's solicitor yet?" asked Sue.

"No" replied Robert. "We were just talking about it, but I'm not sure that we'll hear from him straight away."

"Bit of an odd coincidence that both he and Phyllis know this Martin Smithson" said Sue.

"Yes, but it does seem to be in the air at the moment. First of all Alan bumped into Becky, then Phyllis bumped into Martin. It'll be yours and Ophelia's turn to bump into old flames at this rate" joked Robert.

"Not likely Robert. Remember, the man I thought I may have had a love interest in I ended up stabbing to death on an occult alter."

"Now Sue, stop that. We've been through this before. It wasn't your fault" chastised Robert.

"Just saying" said Sue. "Unless he comes floating through the wall with a long chain and cash boxes like Marley's Ghost, I'm not holding my breath."

Alan looked at Sue disapprovingly. Sue looked back at Alan, offering him a cup of tea.

"One lump or two sweet cheeks?" she said, a tone of sarcasm in her voice.

"As it comes."

"How about you two? Did you manage to find out anything about Sebastian Blanchard and whether he was found?"

"We managed to get quite a bit of information, but

unfortunately, all of it is pretty negative. His body to this day has never been found, there was never any suspect and his mother is still grieving deeply, not only because she's never found her son's body, but also because, according to the reports, our dear judge Mr Godfrey Eldridge also did a number on her husband."

"What??!" Ophelia and Robert said together.

Alan nodded. "We found out that he'd been a bit of a petty criminal, nothing serious, but he was just a constant irritation to the police as they were always hauling him in and out of jail. Only for short stints. Petty theft, the odd drunken brawl, anti-social behaviour and crashing a car once under the influence. We think Godfrey was getting fed up of seeing his face and some sources say that he was stitched up with a big wad of cash that was planted. That's when they hauled him away to prison to serve a significant sentence and I'm guessing that ties in with the bullying of Tristran by Sebastian."

"That would make sense" said Robert. "So the poor woman not only lost her husband to a prison sentence, but then lost her son. What a horrible series of events."

"Is she still alive?" said Ophelia.

"Yes" said Sue. "She lives about an hour away from us. People say she never really recovered from the loss of her son, became a totally broken woman and rarely ventured out of the house."

"Did she have any other children?"

"Yes, a daughter who was younger than Sebastian. She doesn't really remember Sebastian that well as she was only young when he disappeared. Apparently she takes care of her mother but nothing's ever really given the poor woman any closure."

"That's awkward" said Ophelia.

"Awkward?" said Sue. "That's an odd thing to say."

"I only mean awkward in as much as we know where Sebastian's body is. We could tell the police where he is but wouldn't that look suspicious? I mean you're not exactly going to stumble across his body on a walk one day so they'd wonder how we knew he was down there."

"I see your point" said Robert.

"But it's the least we can do to give the poor woman

closure" said Sue. "God knows if anything like that happened to Ruth .... no ...." Sue shuddered.

"But you'd want to know wouldn't you Sue?" asked Ophelia.

"Yes, yes, of course I would."

"I'm just wondering ...." Ophelia's voice tailed off.

"Wondering? What? What is it Ophelia?" Robert looked at her quizically.

"Well, if a message was sent to the police anonymously that the sender could direct them to find Sebastian's body and that somebody was using his identity, it could alert the authorities to look for the imposter, which of course is Tristran, and they might be able to track him down that way. I mean he may have a bank account and credit card. They could monitor any bank transactions he had."

"It's not an unsound proposal" said Robert. "It's just that if the police know that we're tracking Tristran Eldridge and that this body is suddenly 'conveniently' discovered, they're going to ask questions." He stopped a minute and then nodded. "Yes, especially Bill Granger. I'm sure he'd love to put me in a cell on an historic murder charge."

"Oh Robert, don't be ridiculous, he wouldn't do that to you?" Ophelia argued.

"Ophelia, that man seems to think I am the biggest thorn in his side and if he could remove me permanently from the picture I'm sure he'd jump at the chance."

"We need to find a way to recover the body, have the bones identified and then get the police to make the connection somehow" suggested Alan.

"A tall order Alan, a very tall order" said Robert. "Besides, we don't even know where this field is."

"I've got a feeling I could locate it" said Sue. Mrs.Blanchard still lives in the same house and I wouldn't have thought Sebastian would have ventured too far away from it so the field must be in that area somewhere."

"But didn't they have police dogs searching it back then?" asked Alan.

"They may have done, but depending on how far they searched and what the conditions were like, other people could have gone over that bridge and covered any scent unbeknowingly" countered Robert.

"It's so frustrating" said Sue. "We're so near and yet so far."

"The only thing I can suggest is to speak to Becky's solicitor and see what he might suggest. I didn't tell him about the circumstances in which Sebastian Blanchard died as I think I'd already overloaded him, so decided to leave that little nugget out."

"The only thing we can do is wait for him to come back to you" said Alan.

"In the meantime" said Sue, "maybe we should start doing our homework to see if we can find where this field is."

"But where do we start?" asked Alan.

Ophelia looked at Sue with a quizzical expression. "Sue, how vivid was this event when you experienced it?"

"How vivid was it?" asked Sue, surprised at Ophelia's question. "It was like I was actually living it, I actually woke up with a start, it was so real."

"Hmmm, I wonder ...." Ophelia's gaze fixed just above Sue's head.

"What is it Ophelia?" asked Robert.

"Well, I do a lot of past life regression hypnosis with my clients and I'm wondering if I could put Sue into a light hypnotic trance to see if we can gain any more information."

"No, I don't like the sound of that" quipped Alan. "We don't know for one thing whether it would be accurate and it terrified the life out of Sue last night and I don't want her experiencing it again."

"Oh Alan, don't be ridiculous, of course we should do it" snapped Sue. "I might be able to get more information. I'm sure Ophelia knows what she's doing."

"I have had plenty of experience of doing this sort of thing Alan and I always ensure my client's safety and peace of mind are my top priority."

Alan was about to protest again when Robert interrupted. "Look, I think if Sue's willing to do it, we should give it a try. I understand your concern Alan, but if Ophelia makes you a promise that should Sue show the slightest amount of agitation, she will end the session."

"You can't say fairer than that Alan" agreed Sue.

Alan frowned slightly, but seeing that he was outnumbered, he admitted defeat, albeit reluctantly.

"Ok, ok, we'll do it, but you've got to promise me Ophelia, the first sign of Sue getting ....."

"I give you my word Alan" Ophelia reassured him in a soft, calm voice.

Alan shuffled in his seat as if to display one final show of protest before settling back into it again.

"Ok Sue, now are you sure you're quite happy to go through with this?" asked Ophelia. "I have to ensure that you are willing to do it, otherwise the whole thing will prove fruitless."

"I am Ophelia. You've done healing on me before and I trust you completely" said Sue.

"Right, in that case, if you'd like to sit back and relax and put your arms onto the arm rests and begin to take steady deep breaths."

Robert and Alan watched as Ophelia continued to take Sue through an induction into an hypnotic state. When she felt that Sue was deeply in trance, she began to ask her questions.

"Now then, I want to call Tristran Eldridge forward Sue if you wouldn't mind."

Sue shuffled a bit in her seat. Alan almost interrupted, thinking that she looked anxious but Robert looked at him and shook his head.

"What .... what do you want?" The voice was child like.

"Tristran, I don't want you to be frightened. I'm your friend and nothing is going to happen to you."

"How do I know that you won't hurt me?" A child's anxious voice came out of Sue's mouth.

"Because I'm a friend Tristran. I want to help you, but I can only help you if you tell me something ... a special secret."

"Secret? What secret? I don't know any secrets."

"Ok, would you like to hear one of my secrets Tristran?"

The childish voice suddenly sounded intrigued. "Oooh, what's that?"

"Well if I tell you my secret, will you tell me something?"

Sue seemed to frown as if she didn't like this deal. "What do you want me to tell you?"

"Well you see, I'm lost. I'm standing on a bridge and I've hidden something underneath it that nobody knows about. Would you keep my secret safe and not tell anyone?"

Robert was impressed. Rather than put the onus of responsibility onto Tristran, she was taking it herself so that the apprehensive boy would open up more.

"Erm, yes, yes, I will."

"Do you promise not to tell anyone? It can be our secret?" said Ophelia in that soft reassuring voice.

"I pro ... promise not to tell anyone." The child was nervous but answered with certainty.

"Thank you Tristran. It can be our secret. Now the only thing is I don't know where I am. I know I'm standing on a bridge in a field but I don't know exactly where I am or how to get back. Can you help me?"

"Yes, yes, I can help you." The small boy seemed to be pleased that somebody wanted his guidance.

"Thank you Tristran. Now I believe that we're close to a wood here. Can you tell me if we need to go back to that wood in order to get home again?"

Sue nodded. "Yes, yes, we need to go back the way we came. It's ok, we're safe now because Sebastian's not here. Come with me, I'll show you."

"Thank you Tristran. Can you describe the route as I follow you."

"Yes, yes. Follow me and I'll tell you where we are."

"Thank you Tristran. I'm following you know."

"Right, right. So we'll go back towards the woods. We follow the path. Can you see it?"

"Oh yes, I can see it."

"Good, so we follow the path right to the end until it comes out by the lake. Do you see the lake?"

"Oh yes, I see the lake. It's very nice."

"Now we walk around the lake and follow the path for a while. Now we can cross the train tracks."

"Ok, is it safe to cross them?"

"Oh yes, I've done it many times. You can hear the trains coming so I know when to cross."

"Now we carry on following the path and you'll see up ahead that it comes to the main road with houses on either side of it."

"Oh yes, yes I see" said Ophelia, although she had absolutely no idea where they were.

"Now we just cross the road. Unfortunately we'll have to walk by the road where Sebastian lives.

"And where does Sebastian live Tristran? What's the name of the road?"

Tristran's voice suddenly changed. "It's Becknall Road. He used to live there with his family but his dad's in prison now because he's a bad man. My dad told me he's a bad man so he has to stay in prison for a long time."

"Oh I see. Can you spell the name of the road for me Tristran?"

"Oh yes, I'm very good at spelling. My teacher says I'm one of the best in the class."

"That's good. You're obviously very clever. Can you spell it for me please?"

"Yes, it's B E C K N A L L R O A D."

"Thank you Tristran. Does Sebastian's mum and sister still live there?"

"Oh yes, but they won't see Sebastian or his dad ever ever again."

"No, I think you're probably right. Well I have to go now Tristran, but before I do, let's promise each other to keep our secret between us. We must tell nobody else. Do you promise?"

"Yes I promise. I won't ever tell anybody as long as I live."

"Thank you Tristran for keeping our promise, and thank you for helping me through the woods. I must say goodbye now."

"Goodbye nice lady."

There was a pause.

"Now that Tristran has left, I want Sue to come back. Sue, can you hear me?"

Sue's face moved from side to side as if trying to listen to something. "Ophelia? Ophelia?"

"Yes Sue, it's me. Would you please come back into the room? Tristran has gone away now and I would like you to come back into the room."

Sue continued to move in her seat for a while and her eyes began to flicker.

"Gently Sue, very gently, come back into the room, into the present."

Sue gradually began to open her eyes and looked around at the three anxious people.

"Here you are Sue, drink this water" said Ophelia, offering her a glass of water.

Sue took a few gulps. "I'm sorry, I wasn't very helpful. I think I just drifted off to sleep."

Ophelia smiled at Sue. "Oh no Sue, you've given us a wealth of information. We know exactly where Sebastian Blanchard is buried."

Chapter Twenty-Six

The following day Ophelia and Sue went over to see Phyllis to tell her everything that had happened the night before.

"And you don't remember anything Sue?" asked Phyllis.

"Not a thing" insisted Sue. "All I remember is Ophelia talking to me and I drifted off to sleep. The next thing I could hear was Ophelia's voice asking me to come back and when I woke up, I could see Alan, Robert and Ophelia staring at me. I had no idea what had happened."

"So Becknall Road, do you think Sebastian's mother still lives there?" asked Phyllis.

"From what I could research I think she does. I think her daughter goes to see her often as well. So if we can find out where it is, we should be able to find the woods and the field where the bridge is."

"The only thing is" said Ophelia "it might not be a good idea for us to go there as if people spot us and then Sebastian's body is suddenly discovered, people might get suspicious."

"But we have to give his mother closure Ophelia" said Sue. "The poor woman's been living in absolute torment for years. We have to let her know."

"Yes I agree" said Ophelia. "But we were discussing it last night and Robert said he'd think about the best way to go about it. I think we should wait to see what he thinks. We don't need the police pointing the finger at us."

"Well yes" said Sue, "but this is an old case, surely the police aren't going to accuse us of having anything to do with his death."

"Yes that's true, but then again, they would be suspicious as to how we knew the body was there. I mean let's be honest, if it's been hidden for years, it would seem very strange that we just happened across it" said Ophelia.

Sue didn't want to admit defeat but she could see where Ophelia was coming from.

Phyllis phone began to ring and Phyllis got up to go and answer it. "Oh hello Robert" they heard her saying. "Oh what's that?" A pause as Robert must have responded.

"Whatttt??????" she almost shouted. "Are you being serious?"

Ophelia and Sue looked up at Phyllis wondering what was being said.

"Oh god Robert, that's fantastic news. When is she being released?"

Ophelia and Sue looked at each other, both guessing the news that Robert had just disclosed to Phyllis.

"Tomorrow. Oh Robert that's fantastic!" Phyllis almost began to jump up and down and the receiver nearly flew out of her hand, though she managed to catch it. "What? Of course she can stay here Robert! She can stay forever." A slight pause. "No Robert, I mean it, if she wants to come and live here she's more than welcome."

Sue and Ophelia could second guess that Robert was trying to temper Phyllis's optimism, though they both knew it would be nigh on impossible.

"Ok, well you tell me when you're going to pick her up and I'll get eveything ready here. Oh my god, first of all a serious healing session. She must be absolutely traumatised after what's happened so Ophelia and I are going to absolutely spoil her!"

Nobody heard Robert's chuckle down the phone when Phyllis said goodbye to him and put the receiver down. She looked excitedly at Ophelia and Sue.

"They're releasing Becky tomorrow. All charges have been dropped!" The smile on her face would put any Cheshire cat to shame.

"Oh god that's fantastic news" said Sue. Her feelings of jealously had managed to subside as she felt compassion for Becky after what she had been through. She remembered something that Ruth had once said to her.

"Mum I love you dearly, but you can be a hard cow at times."

"Thanks for that vote of confidence dear daughter!"

"Oh mum, I know it's just a tough shell to hide a soft centre and I know you'd do anything for anybody who was really in trouble. But sometimes you need to tone down the bitch act!"

"So when did Robert say he can collect her?" asked Ophelia, breaking Sue's thought stream.

"I think about 10.30 am. They have to sign the papers for her release but Robert was saying that her solicitor was bloody good. Worth his weight in gold. He's done some research and has found out some amazing information."

"Which is?" asked Ophelia.

"Oh he couldn't tell me right now but said he'll reveal all tomorrow when he brings Becky over."

"That's great news" said Sue, who was surprised at how heartfelt she'd actually meant it.

* * * * *

The following day Robert went over to Phyllis's house to take some things that Becky had given to him.

"Robert, please, can I come with you?" Phyllis was almost tearful. "I just want to give her the biggest hug she's ever had. She's had a horrendous time and I know you've been a tower of strength, but sometimes a woman just needs another woman to give her a reassuring hug."

Robert was never usually one to succumb to emotional blackmail. There would be several formalities to deal with. He was planning to have a detailed discussion with Becky's solicitor and he wasn't sure that Phyllis's presence would be conducive to a constructive meeting. Finally he caved in.

"Ok Phyllis but you have to understand I need to have a discussion with Becky's solicitor. God knows she's in no fit state to take in all that he has to say and believe me, he has a lot to say."

"Don't worry Robert, I'll sit in the car with Becky while you talk to her solicitor. That's why I think I should go. If she's on her own in the car while you and her solicitor are having a lengthy discussion, she's going to feel pretty isolated."

"And how often do I have to take my medicine doctor?" he replied. "Is that one spoonful of emotional blackmail or two?"

Phyllis laughed. "Take the whole damn bottle, it'll do you good, Mr Formality."

"Come on then, we need to get there on time as they won't be impressed if I show up late. Not a good impression to put across."

When they arrived, Becky was sitting in a waiting area with her solicitor. When they saw Robert and Phyllis getting out of the car, Becky stood up and began to walk slowly towards the door, although it appeared that her solicitor advised her to sit down.

"Oh my god Becky, what the hell have they done to you?" said Phyllis, looking in horror.

Becky got up and attempted to run to Phyllis but was too weak. Phyllis almost ran towards her and put her arms around her, at which point Becky burst into tears.

"That's ok love, you let it out. Those bastards have got a lot to answer for. Now you come with me ok? Robert's got a few formalities to discuss with your solicitor." Phyllis, still holding Becky tightly, attempted to walk towards the entrance.

"Hang on Phyllis. I need to check with Mr Jansen whether Becky needs to remain here" said Robert.

"No that's fine Mr. Whitehead. We've gone through all the formalities and Miss Collerton is free to leave."

"Ok, thank you" said Robert. "It's ok" he said to Phyllis. "Can you take Becky back to the car and I'll be with you both shortly."

Phyllis nodded and gave Becky a reassuring grip as she helped her back to Robert's car.

"Thank you for getting Becky released Mr. Jansen. It really is a relief to all of us."

"Just doing my job" replied the solicitor.

"Well you must have done a hell of a job to get Becky released. They virtually had her sentenced on a drug trafficking charge."

The solicitor's face suddenly had an expression of disdain. "Can we talk outside Mr Whitehead? I don't really want to discuss things here."

"Yes, of course" replied Robert, slightly surprised.

They both walked out of the station and Mr Jansen beckoned Robert to a bench that was just to the side of the building.

"So I have to ask you, how on earth did you manage to get them to drop the charges against Becky?" asked Robert.

Mr Jansen let out a disapproving sigh. "They had no case!"

"What?" Robert looked at the solicitor in disbelief.

"I found so many holes in their so-called evidence that it really wasn't difficult to prove that Miss Collerton had been set up."

"Oh?" said Robert. "Do tell me more."

"I can't go into the details right now but I was able to inspect the package that had been removed from her flat. Whoever had planted it there hadn't been very careful. They'd obviously tried to wipe all the fingerprint evidence from it, but upon further inspection, we found quite a few prints of the same person – and that person definitely wasn't Miss Collerton."

"I knew it! I bloody knew it! Do you know who the person is?"

Mr Jansen shook his head. "No, however, I have been looking into this case more deeply. It's not straightforward at all."

"Tell me about it. I just don't know who is trying to frame Becky and why" hissed Robert. "She looks awful. I'm seriously worried about her."

"To be honest Mr Whitehead, so am I. I honestly think this whole ordeal has exacerbated her illness. That's why I've been doing some research to see if I can get to the bottom of all of this."

"Have you managed to find anything?" Robert looked pleadingly at the solicitor.

Mr Jansen looked around nervously. He then looked back at Robert. "Look Mr Whitehead, I shouldn't be discussing this with you, but after the information you gave me, I hope that we can trust each other. I know you mentioned that Inspector Granger didn't hold you in very high regard ...."

"That's an understatement" interrupted Robert with a sardonic chuckle.

"Be that as it may, after looking at how he's dealt with this case, I'm surprised he still holds the position he does."

"You mean he's bungled it?" Robert rolled his eyes.

"Well, that's not quite how I'd choose to describe it but ......"

"But if the cap fits ....."

"Indeed."

"So what have you managed to find out?" asked Robert.

"I have been making a lot of enquiries and pulling strings to see what information I can find and I've discovered some very interesting facts."

"Go on." Robert looked directly at the solicitor.

"I contacted Martin Smithson to ask him for information relating to the case. I explained to him that I was representing Miss Collerton on a drug trafficking charge and he was genuinely upset to hear that she'd been arrested."

"Well when I met him he didn't seem very willing to share any information, he just wanted me out of his office as quickly as possible."

"Yes, yes, I understand and I also know why."

"He told you that he'd been threatened if he didn't drop the defence case for Thomas Collerton?"

Mr Jansen nodded.

"Don't get me wrong, I can understand the fear of having your childrens' lives threatened" retorted Robert. "But surely he can't possibly imagine that they or his grandchildren would be in any danger now, after all these years?"

"It's hard to explain Mr Whitehead, and I'm not making excuses for him, but when powerful people make threats against you like that, it can leave a deep scar."

"I understand that but ...."

"Also I have some very important information for you but you have to promise not to disclose it to anybody. I could be struck off if it was found out that I'd told you."

"Ok" said Robert. This might mean that he couldn't share the information with Alan and the three ladies but that was a bridge he would have to cross later.

"I not only managed to obtain a sample of the female victim's clothing ...."

"You mean the girl that was murdered, Nick Putterill's girlfriend?"

The solicitor nodded.

"Yes, and did you run a DNA test?"

Mr Jansen paused for a moment. "Yes."

"And? Did you confirm that the blood group of the murderer was O Positive?"

"I could confirm that O Positive blood was indeed found on the clothing. I did check to make sure that it wasn't the victim's blood and was advised that it wasn't her blood type."

"Well that's a good start. So if I could give you a sample of the blood that I obtained I wouldn't mind betting that it's a match. I don't know what condition it would be in for testing purposes but I'm more than happy to give it to you."

"I would appreciate it if you could as that would help me clarify another matter."

"Which is?"

"Martin wasn't completely honest with you when he spoke to you that day."

"What about?" Robert looked at the solicitor suspiciously.

"He told you that he was forced to destroy all the evidence in the case for the defence, correct?" asked Mr Jansen.

"Yes, that's right" confirmed Robert. Where was this heading?

"He didn't destroy all of it. Some of it had been left at his house at the time when he took the box of evidence to court where it was 'conveniently' destroyed."

"You mean .... you mean some clothing still exists from the original murder enquiry?" Robert could feel his heart thumping.

"Correct" replied the solicitor factually.

"And has it been tested for DNA?" Robert was almost shaking.

"It has."

"And???"

Mr Jansen looked directly at Robert. "It's a match to the first victim."

Robert nearly leapt up off the bench. "I knew it, I knew it! When can I give you the sample I have Mr Jansen? There's no time to lose."

"If you can drop it off at my office tomorrow I can make some discreet enquiries."

"I certainly will. I know you probably can't answer definitively but if, as I suspect, that sample also matches the other two samples, is it a safe bet that we have our killer?"

"That would be a fair assumption" said Mr Jansen.

"So it definitely is Tristran Eldridge."

"Or Sebastian Blanchard as the case may be" added Mr

Jansen.

"Could we have the case re-opened if it is a match?"

"That's not so straightforward. There's nothing on the DNA database that matches – I've also carried out that check." Mr Jansen had certainly done his homework on this one.

"But if we could find Tristran Eldridge and take a DNA sample from him, that would be our smoking gun?"

"It would certainly be strong evidence against him. But there's the problem. Tracking him down. That is, if Tristran Eldridge and Sebastian Blanchard are as you say one and the same person."

"Oh they are, I can assure you Mr Jansen."

"But how can you prove it? You said that he took on the identity of a dead boy who was a similar age to himself. Where is the evidence for this?"

"Mr Jansen, I know you are going to find this hard to believe and again I can't disclose how I came across this evidence, but I believe I know where the remains of Sebastian Blanchard are."

The solicitor looked at Robert and frowned.

"I've also been doing some resarch and I discovered that his mother and sister have been trying to find his remains for years. The police never discovered where the body was when he disappeared and that remains the case to this day."

Now it was the solicitor's turn to coax Robert to give him more evidence.

"But I believe I know where the body is and if it's brought to the police's attention, they can run a familial DNA test alongside his sister and mother to prove that it is indeed the remains of Sebastian Blanchard."

"This is quite a claim Mr Whitehead. I hope you can back it up."

"I believe I can – and if I do – it proves that the person going around posing as Sebastian Blanchard is an imposter."

"An interesting theory."

"An interesting fact Mr Jansen."

"Well may I also give you something else to consider Mr Whitehead?"

"Go on" said Robert.

"I've made contact with the Greek and Turkish Cypriot

authorities. Now I don't know how much you know about Cypriot history but ....."

"I know about the outbreak of the war in July 1974 and how it divided the island."

"Yes, it certainly did and even to this day there it's an extremely difficult situation. Let's just say the two sides aren't always willing to share information."

"And how does this affect our case?"

"Well, I can tell you that both the Turkish and Greek Cypriot authorities have been following Sebastian Blanchard very closely for some time but he's a very slippery character. They are both very aware of the fact that he's headed up a major drug trafficking ring for several years now but they've never been able to catch him. When I spoke to both parties, they were quite eager to assist in any way they could, but they both wanted to guarantee that if he was caught, that he was handed back to both authorities."

"Well that would certainly be a challenge as you can't split him in two" observed Robert.

"Quite. But also if he was caught here in the UK and his DNA matched both the murdered victims and the blood sample that you recovered, then he would be tried for murder under UK law and the UK would not want to hand him back to either the Turkish or the Greek Cypriot authorities."

"God almighty, this is a hell of a discovery!" exclaimed Robert. "You really have been doing your homework Mr Jansen and I can't tell you how grateful I am that you have."

"Thank you Mr Whitehead, but again I must stress that I have told you this in the strictest of confidence. I haven't shared this information with Miss Collerton. To be honest, I don't think the poor lady is in any condition to worry about any of this. I honestly believe she's going to need constant medical attention. This period of incarceration has been extremely difficult for her and I don't think it's helped her health condition in any way."

"You're singing to the choir Mr Jansen, believe me."

"Yes, I thought you would agree with that point."

"So where do we go from here?" asked Robert.

"Well if you can submit the blood sample you have tomorrow, I can run a test to see if it matches the others. In the meantime, I can only leave the ball in your court as to the discovery of Sebastian Blanchard's remains and if you do manage to find them, I'm sure the police will run a DNA test against his mother and sister's DNA and then we can decide where we go from there."

"Will we be able to persuade the police that there's a connection between the murderer and Sebastian Blanchard's body being found?"

"Highly unlikely, but if we do discover the person who is posing as Sebastian Blanchard, he's going to have some very difficult questions to answer."

"Not before time Mr Jansen, not before time."

Chapter Twenty-Seven

The following day Robert was contemplating how they would be able to let Sebastian Blanchard's mother know where her son's remains were when his phone rang.

"Hello?" A voice asked to speak to Robert Whitehead.

"Speaking" said Robert.

"Hello Mr Whitehead, this is Mr Jansen here. I've had some news back from the lab this morning."

"Oh, you mean from the blood sample I gave you?" asked Robert.

"That is correct." The solicitor's voice was as formal as ever.

"And? Is it a match?" Robert waited with baited breath for the answer that he so desperately hoped he would hear.

"It is indeed a match. Not a very good one. The DNA wasn't in the best condition, despite it being a recent gash but they managed to replicate it and it came up positive. The technician did tell me the statistics – something like one in a billion, so that would mean possibly only eight other people having the same or similar DNA."

"That's remarkable" said Robert. "Would it be enough to take to the CPS?"

"I should think so. But please do bear in mind what I said before, as there is no record on the national DNA database to match it against, we still have the problem of connecting it to a specific individual."

"Yes, yes, I understand" said Robert. "So where do we go from here?"

"I need to prepare some reports in order to go forward with this. I may not be able to disclose all the information that I'm preparing for data protection reasons, but if perchance you are able to find the individual that you believe the samples belong to, we may be able to share information."

Robert understood this to mean that Mr Jansen was prepared to allow certain confidentialities to slip if Robert could track down the murderer.

"Thank you Mr Jansen, I really do appreciate the efforts

you've gone to."

"My pleasure Mr Whitehead. By the way, how is Miss Collerton doing?"

"She's still not great, but she's a lot better than when she was being held in custody. My two colleagues are taking good care of her."

"Well please do pass on my best wishes to her. I hope she does feel better, though I am aware of the severity of her condition. It's an extremely sad situation for her to be in."

"I will Mr Jansen. Thank you for your kind thoughts. I know we'll be in touch soon."

Robert put the phone down. Finally, perhaps, things were beginning to come together. If only he knew the whereabouts of Tristran Eldridge.

* * * * *

Two weeks later Sue was in the kitchen preparing dinner when Alan called through to her. "Sue, Sue! Come here – quickly!"

"Oh for goodness sake Alan, what is it, I'm preparing the ......"

"Quick, get in here now."

With more than just a hint of mild irritation Sue walked through to the lounge to see Alan transfixed to the TV. He pointed to the screen. "Listen to this" he said.

Sue wiped her hands on the towel as she still wasn't sure what all the fuss was about but as she continued to listen, she became as transfixed as Alan. "My god, my god Alan, it IS him!"

Alan said nothing but continued to stare at the screen, listening intently. He was watching the local news and the newsreader had just disclosed the story of the remains of a young boy who had been found hidden in a ditch under a bridge. The reader had a guest in the studio and asked her how they came to find the body. It was Lily Blanchard, Sebastian's sister. She had explained that she and her mother had been looking for her lost brother for years and that she had received an anonymous phone all telling her and her mother where her brother's remains could be found. The newsreader was transfixed with the story and went on to ask how Miss Blanchard felt when the DNA of the remains had been tested against her and her mothers and it came back as a familial match. At this point Sue and Alan stopped watching and stared at each other.

"So Robert made the phone call after all. I hope he didn't do it from his phone home or his mobile" said Sue.

"Oh don't worry" said Alan. "If I know Robert, he would make sure to use a phone without leaving any trace."

"Bloody hell Alan, we were right. It WAS Sebastian Blanchard that I saw!"

"Well Ian's device has never been wrong before, why should it be wrong now?"

"But this is huge. It proves that whoever is posing as Sebastian Blanchard is definitely an imposter."

"Well there's a slim chance that it could be a coincidence and that there are two people who share the same name – it's not uncommon."

"Oh come on Alan, you know that's not true. I mean, of course I know that a lot of people share both names, but a name like Sebastian Blanchard – it's not exactly John Brown or Fred Smith is it?"

"Can't argue with you there me old China!"

"We need to tell Robert ..... and Phyllis ..... and Ophelia ..... and ......"

"Slow down Sue. Before you start phoning every man and his dog, let's just give Robert a call first. He'll have a good idea of what to do going forward."

"But Phyllis and Ophelia have a right to know too" said Sue indignantly. "They've been involved in this investigation as much as Robert has."

"Yes I know – and I'm not implying we should keep it a secret, I just think we should tell Robert first and then see what he thinks is the best thing to do."

"I like Robert as much as you do Alan, but he's not some great leader."

"I didn't say he was Sue, but he has dealings with all sorts of people and he's been trained in handling sensitive matters, that's all I'm saying."

Sue grumbled slightly. Unfortunately she could see the

sense in what Alan was saying, but still felt that it was a slight on her two friends.

"I'll call him now while you continue to prepare one of your most excellent Michelin four- star meals, worthy of an expensive hotel" said Alan.

Sue glared at him. "Cut the crap buster, you're not getting round me that way."

"But if you don't, my poor stomach will think my throat has been cut and I shall starve and die right here in front of you."

"I don't know about me receiving a Michelin award for my cooking, but you sure wouldn't win any awards for that horrendous piece of ham acting I've just witnessed."

"But I'm withering away here as we speak!"

"Make that bloody phone call Baylock, and just hope that your gravy doesn't taste of bitter almonds!"

"Oh I always think that hemlock gives it a nice little bite to the sauce."

"PHONE! NOW!!" Sue went back into the kitchen as she heard Alan calling Robert.

"Oh you saw it on the news too. What do you think?" she heard him say.

"Yes, ok, I think that's not a bad idea. When did you have in mind? Ok, I'll let Sue know. I guess the obvious place would be Phyllis's? Right, it's going in the diary."

Alan put the phone down.

"What did he say?" asked Sue as she poked her head through the serving hatch.

"He said he also saw it on the news and he thinks it would be a good idea for us to catch up tomorrow if possible as he also has some information that he wants to share with us."

"Sounds intriguing" said Sue. "Did he give you any hints as to what that information was?"

"No, he was very candid, but that's our Robert" answered Alan.

"Yes it certainly is" said Sue, although she was thankful, knowing that Robert was well aware of what had happened between her and Chris. As far as she was concerned, Robert could be as candid about that as he pleased for the rest of his life.

Chapter Twenty-Eight

The following evening, Ophelia, Robert, Sue and Alan all descended on Phyllis's house. The usual meet and greet pleasantries were exchanged and everybody noticed that Becky looked considerably better than she had done just after her incarcertion. Sue, as always, helped Phyllis with the teas and coffees. As tea cups rattled, boiling water nearly scorched careless hands and various types of tea were offered out, Robert began to discuss what they knew so far.

"So we know that Sebastian Blanchard is actually Tristran Eldridge" he said. "The other thing is ....", he paused before disclosing the other bombshell that he had to reveal. Although Mr Jansen had sworn him to secrecy regarding his contact with both Turkish and Greek Cypriot authorities, he was not quite as guarded concerning the matching DNA samples.

"Go on Robert" said Sue, as she stirred her tea.

"Without going into too much detail, I can confirm that the blood we found at your flat Becky, plus the blood from the murdered girl's clothing are a match." Robert was extremely careful not to disclose the information that Martin Smithson had given his friend Mr Jansen. He knew that it was a sensitive subject and that if Becky knew about the existence of Martin Smithson and that it was he who had stepped down as her brother's defence solicitor, she would probably be happy to go to his office and kill him. As well as that, Mr Jansen had specifically asked Robert not to disclose this information to anybody.

"Oh my god!" exclaimed Phyllis. "So it's true then – Tristran Eldridge broke into Becky's flat."

The group suddenly went silent. It was Becky who broke the ice.

"Well it would make sense" she said. "After all, if he is indeed the murderer of both Nick Putterill and his girlfriend, he'd want to shut me up if he thought I was investigating the case. There's something else."

"What is it?" asked Phyllis.

"Hang on, hang on" she said. "Give me a minute.

"Something's niggling in the back of my mind. That name, Sebastian Blanchard" said Becky. "I'm sure I've heard it somewhere before .... but where?"

"Well it was on the news earlier" said Sue. "That's where you must have heard it."

"But Sue, you know I don't have a TV" said Phyllis. "Becky couldn't have heard it on the news."

"Sorry Phyllis, good point."

Becky looked directly at Phyllis. "Phyllis, could I be awfully cheeky and borrow your phone to call my friend in Cyprus? It's a long shot but I know I've heard that name before and it's really bugging me. She might be able to help me."

"No problem, go ahead" said Phyllis.

Becky took her diary out of her handbag and flicked through, looking for a number. She went into the hall and picked up the phone. The others sat, trying to make general conversation so as not to make Becky feel self-conscious that they were all listening in on her call, although they were all keen to hear what she may have to say. Within ten minutes she had said goodbye to her friend in Cyprus and walked back into the lounge.

"Any luck?" asked Ophelia.

"Well it's interesting. Penny said she'd heard of the guy through some of her social circles and by all accounts, he's not a very pleasant character. She didn't know a great deal but she had the impression that – how did she put it now – his professional credentials were slightly on the suspect side."

"Well if he is dealing in drugs, that's putting it politely" said Sue.

"The problem we have" said Robert, "is that despite the strong, albeit circumstantial evidence that Tristran Eldridge is the person we're looking for, we've no way of proving anything until we find him and get a sample of his DNA."

"And how do we do that?" asked Phyllis, a tone of defeat in her voice.

"Sue, is there anything you recall hearing that ....." Robert suddenly stopped. Becky was unaware of Ian's machine or the process they used to discover how Tristran Eldridge had come to murder Nick Putterill and his girlfriend, never mind realise that he was also a major ring leader in a drug trafficking system that stretched across the Mediterranean. Sue looked at Robert, realising why he had suddenly stopped.

"Well the information I managed to obtain through my research" she said, making it sound as though she'd stumbled on some documentation "didn't really give me a hint as to where he might be."

Robert gave Sue a quick smile as if to say "thank you" for bailing him out of an awkward situation.

"The problem is you'd have to have a criminal mind to understand his movements and I don't think any of us have" remarked Alan.

The situation was becoming awkward for the five friends as they all knew that Tristran had been listening to Becky's conversation in a Greek restaurant but didn't want to alarm her to this in case it scared her. Also, it would beg the question – how did they know such detailed information? It felt as though they were tip-toeing around glass, not knowing what to say so as not to raise Becky's suspicions.

"There's only one thing for it" said Ophelia.

The others looked up at her, puzzled.

"Sue, would you mind joining me in Phyllis's reading room?"

Sue looked puzzled but nevertheless agreed. "Yes, of course."

"Please don't think I'm being rude everybody, but I'd like Sue to come with me to her reading room. We have a little job to do."

Everybody looked puzzled.

"Right" she continued. "We won't be long. Phyllis, would you mind making more tea for everyone if they want some and we'll be back in a while."

The others looked perplexed as Ophelia and Sue headed towards Phyllis's reading room. They began talking amongst themselves to try and pass the time, wondering what on earth Ophelia was up to. Ophelia closed the door of Phyllis's reading room and asked Sue to take a seat.

"Right Sue, I'm going to put you into a light trance again if you don't mind. This time though I'm trying to find out where Tristran Eldridge might be staying so we won't be looking into anything sinister. Are you comfortable with that?"

"Of course I am" said Sue.

"Thank you. So as you did before, I'd like you to sit back and relax." Ophelia paused. "Take some deep breaths and relax your arms, relax your legs, relax your neck and just allow your whole body to relax."

Sue continued to follow Ophelia's instructions.

Ophelia took Sue through a short guided meditation before making a request. "I have some vital information that I'd like to share with Tristran Eldridge, but I don't know where I can find him. Can you help me?"

Sue shuffled in her chair, looking slightly uncomfortable. "Who wants to know?" she said with more than just a slight tone of suspicion."

"I have some news about Becky Cotterell, the woman who's been looking into the murders that took place several decades ago. I've come to give him a warning. I need to speak to him personally."

Sue still had her eyes closed, but her face turned towards Ophelia. "That bitch knows nothing and she'll find nothing. She can't threaten me."

"But her solicitor has cleared her of the heroin possession she was arrested for. They've found finger prints on the packaging. I need to give it back to you so that they can't trace it back to you."

Sue's body stiffened. She began taking short shallow breaths. "Well make sure that nobody can see you when you bring it. I don't want the police on my tail. I can sell it and make a packet on the street."

"Where shall I bring it?" asked Ophelia. 'Tristran Eldridge' was about to fall into her trap.

Sue's face moved from side to side, as if she was looking to see if anybody was listening. She whispered to Ophelia. "Bring it to 26 Becknall Road, but don't take long as I'll be moving on soon. I can't take the chance of staying in one place for too long. Make sure it's here before midnight."

"I promise I'll bring it straight away. Now then, if you don't mind, I'll leave you for now. Goodbye Tristran. Can I speak to Sue again please?"

Sue's body shuffled in her seat and her face twisted slightly.

"Sue, I'd like you to come back into the room, into the present" said Ophelia.

Sue's eyes flickered and gradually began to open. She looked at Ophelia and smiled.

"Any luck?" she said.

"Oh yes" said Ophelia. "And what a strange irony."

When they walked back into the lounge with smiles on their faces, Robert looked at them curiously, Alan looked at them anxiously and Becky had absolutely no idea what was going on.

"We think we have the address where he's staying" said Ophelia.

"What?" Robert and Alan said together.

Phyllis handed Robert the piece of paper. "Here it is."

Robert looked at Phyllis and then at Ophelia. "How did you get this?"

"I used a similar technique to the one I used yesterday" said Ophelia.

Robert decided it was probably a good idea to probe no further with Becky present, as she had no idea what methods they'd used to obtain the information. "Ok, well I could certainly carry out a vigil on this address, but we don't know what he looks like and even if he does come out, we can't exactly go up and say "excuse me, are you Tristran Eldridge, the murderer and drug trafficker?"

"That's true" said Ophelia.

"But we could wait for him to leave the property and search his bin for anything he might have eaten from or drunk out of" said Sue.

"Why?" said Becky, looking totally confused.

"DNA!" said Sue with a smile.

"You watch way too many forensic detective shows Sue Baylock" said Alan.

"But it's a damn fine idea Alan" said Robert. "Bravo Sue. Good thinking!"

"But won't it be dangerous?" said Becky. "I mean if you're sitting in a car outside he could see you and get suspicious."

"We could hide the car out of the way" suggested Robert.

"Trouble is" said Alan, "I don't mean to offend you ladies or whatever methodology you've used, but we can't be certain that this is where he actually is. It could be a complete waste of time."

"Oh trust you to put the kybosh on it Alan" said Sue.

"I'm just stating a fact" said Alan.

Robert, detecting an argument brewing between the couple, interjected.

"Look" he said. "I'll give it a couple of days and if nothing comes of it, we'll move on to some other ideas. But we have to start somewhere."

"I agree" said Sue, as if wanting to get the last word over Alan.

"So when do we start?" said Phyllis.

"Tomorrow" said Robert.

Chapter Twenty-Nine

The followng day Robert drove to the address that Phyllis had given him. He carried out a quick visual scan up and down the road to see if there was a discreet place where he could park his car. He noticed that there was one car already parked on the opposite side of the road and decided it might be an idea to park behind it and keep his head down. He had no idea if this was the address where Tristran Eldridge was staying and even if it was, he didn't know whether he was currently in.

As he continued to watch the house, somebody inside was cursing.

"Jesus Christ, this is all I fucking need!"

"Cool it Seb, you're being paranoid!"

"Paranoid? Are you out of your fucking mind? They've just announced on the news that they've dug that prick's body up after all these years and then given his name out! It'll be in the fucking papers next. I can see the headlines now. "REMAINS OF SEBASTIAN BLANCHARD DISCOVERED AFTER DECADES!"

"They won't make the connection, you'll be fine" said the other man.

"I don't believe you sometimes Garry, you really are thick! Don't you realise that when I go to the airport and check in at the desk, they'll see the name Sebastian Blanchard on my passport? The next thing you know it'll be a polite 'Can you just wait here a second Mr Blanchard, we need to check some details' and the next thing you know, the police are coming in to throw me into the bloody clink. This has screwed everything up. I'll never be able to bloody fly again!"

"So do what you did before. Go and find a gravestone of some young kid and get a new fake passport."

"Oh don't be bloody stupid, it's not as easy as it was back then. Identity fraud has become the new hot issue and the first thing they'd do if I produced a birth certificate would be to check if the person's dead or not!"

The other man thought about this for a moment. "So what are we going to do?" he said.

"Fuck only knows. My cover is well and truly blown. Shit, it was working so well for years. Now I'm back to square one. Jesus I don't believe this."

"What are we going to tell our connections?" the second man said.

"You tell me Garry, you just tell me because I haven't got a fucking clue. My ass is well and truly whipped."

"But they can't nail anything heavy on you, I mean it's not as if you murdered the bloody kid."

"No, I didn't – but having my name in headlines like that is going to attract all the wrong kind of people. The Cypriot authorities on both sides of the island have been watching me for years. You can bet your bottom dollar that if they get wind of this, they're going to be sneaking around asking a lot of questions and I sure as shit won't be able to come and go as easily to Cyprus as I have done for years."

"I don't know what to suggest" said the other man.

"Neither do I. Shit, I can't stay here. I'm going out."

"Where are you going?"

"I don't know. I need time to think. I'll see you later."

With that he stormed out of the house and got into a car. Robert sat bolt upright. Was this the man they were looking for or was it a friend? Should he remain watching the house or should he follow this individual?

"Come on Whitehead, you've been trained to think on your feet. What should you do?" A little voice inside his head told him to follow the car. He waited until the other car had set off to allow some distance between the two. Then he turned the ignition key, put the car into gear and followed.

"I just hope he doesn't manage to lose me at a traffic light" he said to himself. As if to tempt fate, this very nearly happened, but Robert managed to jump the light just as it was turning from amber to red. "Naughty boy Robert, slapped wrist, but needs must."

He followed the man into town and watched as he turned into a car park. A car came from the other direction and Robert had to wait but continued to indicate to turn into the car park. As the car passed by, Robert turned into the car park and managed to find a parking space. It had an automatic plate recognition in place so he didn't have to worry about getting a ticket. He watched as the other man got out of his car and headed towards the main shopping precinct. He followed carefully, making sure it wasn't obvious that he was watching the man, although he needn't have worried as the other man was on his mobile, seemingly talking to somebody and by the looks of it, it wasn't a pleasant conversation. The man walked into a cafe and sat down at a table. Robert watched from inside a shop on the opposite side of the precinct. He continued to watch as the other man ordered a coffee.

Robert suddenly felt a tingle of excitement. "Oh please, please go on, drink the coffee." He continued watching as a member of staff brought the man a cup of coffee. As if by autosuggestion, the other man began to take sips of the coffee. It was obviously still hot as he only took small sips to begin with. He continued dialling several numbers, making more calls, possibly to his connections. As he became more focussed on his calls, he took larger gulps of the coffee.

"Can I help you?" said the shop assistant to Robert.

"Er no, I'm fine thanks" he replied. He didn't dare take his eyes off the man in the cafe.

The shop assistant eyed Robert suspiciously but decided to leave him alone. Perhaps just by giving him a suspicious look, she was subconsciously saying to Robert "I'm watching you, so don't think of stealing anything!"

The man in the cafe made one final call and then got up to leave. He paid for his coffee and walked out of the cafe. Robert's heart leapt into his mouth. Now was the time to move. He waited until the man had walked a safe distance away and then virtually ran into the cafe. He noticed one of the staff pick up the coffee cup and ran over to her.

"Excuse me" he said. "Can I please have that cup? It's important."

The staff member looked at him oddly. "What do you want it for?"

"I'm a clinical psychologist and I'm working with the police. We think the man who was drinking from that cup is a murderer and it's vitally important we obtain his DNA." Robert may have blown his cover and he wasn't completely telling the truth, but it was the best he could do on the spur of the moment.

"Well it's highly irregular, but I'll have to ask the

supervisor." She called over to her supervisor.

"Yes, is there a problem Kim?"

"This gentleman wants to know if he can take this cup. Says he's a psychologist working with the police and thinks the guy who had the coffee is a murderer."

The way she stated it didn't sound totally convincing so Robert added the details about the DNA and that it was important that he took the cup. "Look, I'm quite happy to pay for the cup. Here's my business card." He handed the supervisor his business card. "If you want to check on my credentials, please feel free to call Inspector Granger at the police station. I have his number."

The supervisor looked at the card and then at Robert. Of course if the supervisor had called Bill Granger, he probably would have been told to send Robert packing, possibly with a firm boot up his backside, but he had to take that chance.

"Ok, it can't hurt, though if the police come in here asking questions I'll point them right back to you as I have your card ..... that is if it isn't fake."

Robert pulled out his driving licence and a credit card. "Is this enough proof for you?"

The supervisor looked at the photo of Robert on his driving licence and the name on his credit card. "Looks ok to me" he grumbled. "Kim, give the gentleman the cup."

"Thank you" said Robert and took out a handkerchief from his pocket to avoid getting any more fingerprints on it.

"You want the saucer as well?"

Robert thought quickly and vaguely remembered that the man hadn't touched it. "No, just the cup is fine thank you."

"Ok."

With that Robert said a final "thank you" and left.

He returned quickly to the car. He placed the cup carefully inside his glove compartment. Before leaving, he decided to quickly go over to the other man's car and take down the registration plate – that is, if the car was still there. Fortunately it was still parked and Robert looked around quickly to make sure nobody was watching him. He took a quick picture of the car on his mobile phone and headed quickly back to his own car, after paying his parking fee. Before he set off he needed to make a quick phone call.

"Hello?" said the voice on the other end of the line.

"Is this Mr Jansen?"

"It is."

"Hello, it's Robert Whitehead. I think I may have made a major breakthrough and need to bring you something for DNA analysis as soon as possible. Can I come over and see you today?"

Mr Jansen paused a second. He seemed slightly taken aback but agreed to let Robert come and see him. "Very well Mr Whitehead. I need to go and see a client at 2 o'clock but if you can bring me your evidence before then, I can arrange to have it examined."

"Thank you Mr Jansen, I'll be right over." Robert thrust his key into the ignition and turned it with such vigour that it nearly twisted in his hand. He reversed out of his parking slot and drove out of the car park.

When he arrived at the solicitor's office, he was greeted by a very surprised PA.

"Er hello, I've arranged to come and see Mr Jansen. He's expecting me. My name's Robert Whitehead."

The PA looked suspiciously at the handkerchief that Robert seemed to be holding with great reverence.

"Erm, please take a seat Mr Whitehad, I'll let Mr Jansen know you're here."

She walked off and shortly returned with Mr Jansen following her.

"Hello Mr Whitehead. We meet again. You said you have some evidence for me."

"Yes, here it is. Please treat it very carefully, I don't want to contaminate it any more than it already has been."

"How many people have handled it?" asked the solicitor.

"As far as I know, only one or two members of staff at the cafe and the other person I believe is Tristran Eldridge."

Mr Jansen looked at Robert surprised. "Goodness you really have been busy. How did you manage to find him?"

Robert suddenly realised that in explaining how they came upon his whereabouts, tales of street maps, pendulums and 'crazy witches' as Alan described them came to mind. "It's a long story which I'm willing to tell you later at some point, but it really is a matter or urgency that we get this cup analysed for

DNA."

"I can assure you Mr Whitehead I will make the call straight away and arrange for it to be carried out. I have to be skeptical of course – I'm afraid it goes with the territory of the profession as I'm sure you'll understand, but I'll endeavour to do what I can to assist you."

"Thank you Mr Jansen, if this DNA sample is a match and we catch him, I will be forever in your debt."

"I know people think we solicitors are only in it for the money, but I do actually get job satisfaction in preventing people from carrying out acts that hurt other people in some way."

"Our jobs, although different, are not dissimilar Mr Jansen."

The solicitor smiled. "Good day Mr Whitehead, I'll be in touch."

Robert left the solicitor's office. He was a grown adult, he hadn't had the easiest life and he lost his wife several years ago – a woman who he loved more than he realised until she died. Nothing had excited him in life for a very long time. Nothing had made him feel as though he couldn't sleep because of sheer anticipation. Yet now, for the first time in a long time, he could feel butterflies in his stomach.

Chapter Thirty

Godfrey Eldridge returned from his Tuesday game of bowls and walked slowly up to his front door. He turned the key in the lock and opened the door. Was that smoke he could smell? He'd stopped smoking years ago and his cleaner didn't smoke either. He suddenly felt a slight tremor of anxiety. If there was an intruder, would he realise that the old man was about to make a hasty retreat and stop him in his own hallway? "No" he thought to himself. "Confront the problem head on if there is somebody in his house." He walked into his living room and looked across at a man sitting on his sofa.

"What the hell are you doing here?" he hissed.

"Hello daddy dearest. Long time no see."

"Get out! If you don't leave right now, I'll call the police."

"And tell them what? That your prodigal son has decided to return but you're not in the mood to offer him the fatted calf? Most un-Christian of you father."

"You've got a nerve talking about Christian values with the things you've done in your life, you thieving, murdering, pilfering little ......"

"Oh dear – ever ready with the accusations – and this coming from a man who would convict people on the turn of a hairpin."

"Yes, and it was just as well for you that I did, otherwise you would have been the one to be rotting away in prison for the rest of your life. If it wasn't for me ....."

"Yes, yes, yes, if it wasn't for you, I'd be behind bars and probably dead right now."

"Yes, apparently just like the person who I convicted in your place."

"Oh really? And where did you come across that little nugget of information?"

"Somebody came to the club asking me about that particular case – and they certainly seemed to know about you."

"And did you get their names?"

"His name. No, I didn't! Does that make you feel

anxious that somebody is looking into the case after all these years?"

"Well why should it? All the evidence was destroyed, my DNA is on no database, there's no way they could prove me guilty after all this time."

"All the evidence wasn't destroyed – they still have the clothing from the victim's girlfiend, no doubt with your blood on it."

"That's as maybe, but they already convicted that poor sucker for it, so I shouldn't think they'd be coming after somebody else after all these years."

"Oh really? Well it seems as though some relative of this convict is looking to re-open the case, and if they do, I'm certainly not going to protect you. You're big enough now to fight your own battles."

"I could disappear in a whisper and they'd never find me. After all, I've done it before."

"With my help, may god forgive me."

"Oh what's this, suddenly in old age you're developing a conscience? Worried about not getting your wings and harp when you walk up to the pearly gates?"

"You won't even get that far when you die. You'll be smelling the pits of sulphur with your last dying breath!"

"Touchy today aren't we daddykins. What's the matter – cleaner refused to let you get your wrinkled, knarled old hands around a certain part of her anatomy? Poor poor daddy!"

"Shut up and get out! If you've just come here to throw insults, then you might as well leave. I've got better things to do than listen to you – and I will call the police if you don't leave."

"Oh, I'll leave alright, but first there's something I've come to collect."

"I've got nothing to give to you."

"Oh, but that's where you're wrong, you have."

"I wouldn't give anything to you if my life depended on it."

"Well perhaps maybe your life does depend on it. After all, nobody else knows I'm here. I could easily ...... cause you to have a mishap and then leave the scene before anybody notices."

"Go on, do your worst, I'm not long for this world anyway, so do your damndest!" shouted the old man.

"No daddy dearest, too messy, too time consuming and – gee whizz, I don't think I'm in the mood to murder anybody today" he said sneeringly. "Not good for my biorhythms you know."

"You talk such rot!"

"Well let's do less of the talking and more of the doing."

"What do you want?"

"I've come to collect my birth certificate."

"I don't have it! I threw it out years ago!"

"Oh yes you do, daddy-o. Once a judge, always a judge. They never throw away evidence or documents of any kind."

"The only evidence your birth certificate proves to serve is that I should have used contraception nine months before you were born!"

"Now you'll upset my poor little feelings daddy dearest, that's no way to speak to your loving son."

"You make me sick!"

"Be that as it may, I've come to collect my birth certificate and I'm not leaving until you give it to me."

"Even if I did have it, I wouldn't have a clue where it is."

"Just as well I've got a good memory. Let's see now – mother used to keep all the family documents in this bureau here. Bless her, she was always so well organised."

Tristran Eldridge walked over to the bureau and opened one of the drawers. He shuffled through various piles of paper. "No, not in here" he said. He opened the other drawer and began shuffling through that one and suddenly stopped. "Ah, what do we have here – a birth certificate if I'm not mistaken and ..... wouldn't you know it ...... it's got my name on it!"

"Take the damn thing and go, for whatever good it will do you. I take it that you're in some sort of trouble and need it to get you out of a tight spot."

"You see, that's the one thing I always admired about you. You always were quite perceptive." The tone of sarcasm in Tristran's voice was very apparent.

"Just go. I never want to see your face again. Your mother would be turning in her grave if she could see how you've turned out. I swear it was all the stress you caused her that sent her to an early grave."

"Oh yes?" Tristran Eldridge looked his father squarely

in the eye. "And I suppose the number of tarts you brought back here to fuck when she was out at her WI meetings had nothing to do with it? The fact that several times she came back early and caught you screwing had nothing to do with it? My god, what a hypocrite! You really are a piece of work old man!"

"GET OUT!!! GET OUT!!! You've caused your mother and me enough suffering. We tried to give you everything and this is how you repay us!"

"Oh that old story. And you don't think that maybe you could have made my life hell."

"Your life hell?" laughed the old man. "You had everything, how could your life be hell?"

"I was despised at school because everybody knew I was old man Eldridge's son. The equivalent to a modern day Judge Jeffreys. The other kids always used to clamp up when I was around for fear that I would snitch on them. That kid that's just recently been on the news – the one whose remains they found. He used to bully me mercilessly because you put his old man in prison. I thought you were doing the right thing at the time but I found out later that the guy was a petty criminal and wouldn't have the balls to pull off a job the size of the one that you convicted him of doing."

"Oh yes, and did you murder the boy to get rid of him!"

"I DID NOT MURDER HIM!!!!" Tristran stopped to take a breath and calm down. "Oh yes, I was present when he died but I didn't cause it. He tripped running across a bridge and his head smashed into a post. That was the only crime I was guilty of – not telling anybody."

"And you say that I'm callous?"

"Yes, but my reasons for doing so were self-preservation. As long as he was lying hidden in a ditch, he wasn't bullying me! You can't criticise me for that!"

"Perfect little angel weren't you Tristran. Butter wouldn't melt. You're rotten to the core."

"Chip off the old block hey daddy-o? Chip off the old block. Anyway, I can't stay here to exchange pleasantries all day, I have things to do. No doubt we'll never meet again so I'll bid you a fond farewell and hope you enjoy what's left of your sorry life."

"Go to hell! You've squirmed out of your

misdemeanours thus far but they'll catch up with you one day."

"Well if they do I'm sure you won't still be around to get the satisfaction of seeing me get my just desserts."

"But get them you will. Get them you will. Now get out of here."

"On my way. Goodbye father. Make sure that Beelzebub saves me a nice warm spot when you finally slip off this mortal coil and meet up with him!"

Godfrey Eldridge said nothing but glared at his son as he watched him leave. As he heard the front door slam he slumped down on the sofa and begin to sob. "May god forgive me for some of the things I've done and even worse – the things I should have done."

Chapter Thirty-One

"Well that's a real turn up for the books" said Robert. "I've had confirmation from Mr Jansen that the cup I gave him with Tristran Eldridge's saliva is a match for the blood samples he tested!"

"So there's our smoking gun" said Alan. "Positive proof that Tristran Eldridge aka Sebastian Blanchard is not only the murderer of Nick Putterill and his girlfriend but also the man that you saw in the cafe Robert."

"It is indeed" said Robert. "The only problem we have now is that it's public knowledge that the remains of the real Sebastian Blanchard have been discovered so he'll be looking for a new identity."

"I should think it would be a bit more difficult to fake one nowadays with identity fraud being such a big thing" said Alan.

"Precisely" said Robert. "That's why I think he may have defaulted back to his own name."

"What do you mean?" Alan looked at him, thinking he knew what Robert was getting at, but wanting it confirmed.

"He'll probably get a passport using his real name. After all, Tristran Eldridge has never officially been convicted of any crime, so he's not going to worry about using his own name on any official documents."

"But we've proved that he's the one who committed the murders and so all the police need to do is arrest him, take his DNA and convict him" said Becky.

"All well and good in theory Becky, but we've got to catch him first" said Robert.

"But we know where he is. Ophelia and Sue worked out the location he was staying at" she replied.

"'Was' being the operative word. We know he moves around a lot and I should think that the discovery of Sebastian Blanchard's remains have spooked him quite a bit so he'll want to be on the move again" said Robert.

"So we're back to square one" said Becky, the desperation and despondency in her voice clear for all to hear.

"Well the first thing we have to do surely is inform the police to alert all the airports. Look out for somebody on the passenger list named Tristran Eldridge and make sure he doesn't get on the plane" said Alan.

"Yes, that's good logic Alan" said Robert. "Phyllis, can we use your phone? I know he won't be very pleased to hear from me, but if I tell Bill Granger to put all the airports on the alert, if he tells me to bugger off, I'll promise him that he can take all the credit for all the work we've done."

"That's a bit bloody unfair Robert" retorted Sue. "We've all done our bit to bring this scumbag to justice and you're willing to let some third rate inspector take all the credit?!"

"If it means apprehending him Sue, I'm willing to do anything – even if that entails letting him have all the glory."

"Well I bloody well like that, encouraging him to be a ……."

Before Sue could finish her sentence there was a knock at the door. All six of the group looked at each other and frowned.

"Who could that be?" said Phyllis. "Surely not ….. you know who."

"Tristran Eldridge? I wouldn't have thought so. What would he be doing here?" said Sue.

"Supposing he's found out that Becky's here and wants to …… oh god, we've got to hide her quick. Come on Becky, I'll take you upstai ……."

"Hold on Phyllis, don't panic" Robert reassured her. "If I was Tristran Eldridge, the last thing I'd be thinking of right now was any sort of vengeance. I'd be trying to get the hell out of the country as quickly as possible."

"But who else can it be?" said Phyllis. "I never get visitors."

"What about the Jehovahs witnesses. Don't they come round sometimes?" suggested Sue.

"Not any more" said Phyllis. "The last time they came I told them that according to their religion, there's only room for 144,000 of them in heaven, so if they want to stand a chance of getting in, they'd best fuck off quickly and try to get in before the Pearly Gates are slammed on them."

Becky let out a smirk.

"Look, we may as well see who it is and find out what they want" said Sue. She started walking towards the door before anybody else could. When she opened the door, the others heard the voice of a man.

"Can I help you?" said Sue.

"Sorry I appear to have the wrong house. I was looking for a lady called Phyllis Brewer."

"Who wants to see her and what for?" Sue's tone was curt.

"My name's Martin Smithson. I have some information for her."

Phyllis overheard the conversation and recognised Martin's voice. "That's Martin" she said and walked swiftly to the front door. "Martin? What are you doing here?"

"Hello Phyllis. I've come to speak to you and Mr Whitehead. Do you know where I could find him?"

"He's right here. Come in." Phyllis made way for Martin to come through.

Sue looked at Phyllis puzzled. "Who's he?" she whispered

"It's a long story Sue."

Martin was surprised to see the group of people in the living room and upon recognising several of them, felt more than a little intimidated.

"Mr Smithson, what brings you here?" said Robert.

"Erm, I wasn't going to come but a friend of mine who I think you've met, Tony Jansen contacted me. He wanted to obtain some information on the Thomas Collerton case from me."

"Thomas Collerton?" Becky looked at Martin Smithson puzzled. "What do you know about the case?"

Robert could see a potential melt down from Becky if she discovered who Martin was and tried to interject, but it was too late.

"I'm Martin Smithson, I was the original defence lawyer for Thomas Collerton."

Becky looked at him ..... Becky glared at him. "You" she hissed. "You". Her entire body stiffened. "It was you who was responsible for sending my brother to prison for life."

Before anybody could do anything, she'd leapt on the unsuspecting solicitor and began attacking him, thumping, hitting, scratching, kicking, all the time screaming "MURDERER! MURDERER! MURDERER!"

Robert pulled her off as quickly as possible and even though he was quite a strong man, he had difficulty containing Becky. Alan could see he was struggling and went to assist.

"LET ME GO! LET ME GO!!" she screamed. The quiet friendly Becky had suddenly turned into some demonic animal.

Martin Smithson looked physically shaken and there were several deep scratches on his face. There was a deep gash just under his eye though Becky hadn't actually damaged the eye itself.

"Calm down Becky, calm down!" Robert almost shouted.

"Noooooooooooo! I'll kill him, I'll kill him! Let me kill him!" She was screaming and crying at the same time with Ophelia, Phyllis and Sue looking on, helpless.

Phyllis went to hug her. "Come on love, you've got to calm down" she said softly. This didn't appear to do the trick. Even Ophelia looked helpless.

Meanwhile Martin was trying to apologise, as he also began sobbing. "I'm sorry but I couldn't do anything else. They threatened to kill my children if I went ahead with the case. One of them even handed my four year old daughter a note at her school to give to me so that I knew in no uncertain terms that they'd harm her if I continued representing your brother. God knows my consicence has never let me rest since I did it, but what choice did I have?"

"YOU FILTHY MURDERER, I HATE YOU, I HOPE YOU ROT IN HELL!" Becky was still screaming.

It was Sue who intervened. She'd been listening to the conversation intently and as soon as she learned that Martin's children were at risk, she took firm action. She went up to Becky and slapped her firmly across the face and hissed "BECKY! LISTEN TO ME!"

The shock made Becky stop and she stared at Sue in disbelief.

"I'm sorry Becky, I didn't want to do that but I need you

to listen to me." Sue paused.

Becky continued to look at her, although Robert still wasn't confident that he should loosen his grip,

"Becky" Sue said in a softer voice. "Now I'm not in any way trying to justify what this man did and I can understand why you're angry with him. God knows if I was in your shoes I'd feel the same way. But first and foremost Becky, I'm a mother. I have a daughter who means more to me than anything else in this world. Now a year and a half ago she was kidnapped. I cannot begin to explain to you the torture I went through not knowing if she was alive or dead. It was the worst period of my life and I wouldn't wish that on any parent. Now this man has just explained that his childrens' lives were threatened and if I'd have been in his shoes, I'm sorry Becky, but I would have done the very same thing to protect my children."

Becky looked at Sue, first with a look almost of hatred, but then of puzzlement. She was battling with her thoughts and wanting to kill Martin and then being told that when childrens' lives were at risk, it added a dynamic to the situation that would test the morals of the saintliest person on earth.

"Sue's right Becky" added Alan. "And I'm sorry to say it but I would have done the same as Sue. Ruth is the most precious thing in our lives and god knows when you're a parent your entire thought process revolves around the fact that you worry if they don't come in on time – you think the worst. Somebody's taken them, done harm to them ....."

"It's horrible Becky, it really is. You love them so much that you would even give your own life to protect them" said Sue. "I know that what this man did was morally and legally wrong, but I'm afraid that when you're a parent, those considerations suddenly take less priority."

Becky stood there looking first at Sue, then at Alan, then at Martin. She started crying again – as if defeated. She didn't want to understand what they were saying, but she had no choice. Sue seemed to be able to read her mind.

"Let's put it this way" she said. "When you were younger, if you'd had a responsibility to do the right thing and somebody told you that if you did that, they would harm Tom, what would you do?" It was a cruel blow, but Sue knew it was the only way that Becky would understand what she was trying to say.

"It's not fair! It's not fair! He died in prison and he didn't deserve that! He was innocent." She was sobbing now and Phyllis pulled Robert's arms from around Becky and held her.

"Come on love, sit down!"

Phyllis guided Becky to the sofa and held her as Becky continued to sob. Sue also sat down with her. "I'm so sorry Becky, it's a shit rotten world and your brother didn't deserve that. The only thing we can try to do now is bring him justice."

This seemed to have a calming effect on Becky.

"I'll go and get some tea" said Ophelia.

Phyllis smiled at her. "Thanks love."

When the situation had calmed down a bit, Martin, although still apprehensive, spoke to Becky directly. "I can't justify what I did Miss Collerton but I truly am sorry for what happened. Your brother was a decent man and didn't deserve that sentence. I know it's too late to offer any consolation but when I spoke to Tony, er, Mr Jansen, we took the liberty of making some phone calls."

Becky was still in no fit state to take in what anybody was saying. Phyllis was cuddling the sobbing woman, rocking gently back and forth, as if holding a frightened child.

"Phone calls?" asked Robert.

"Yes" said Martin Smithson. "When the DNA test came back positive from the cup you managed to obtain – and I must say Mr Whitehead, that was very impressive detective work – when we could confirm that the DNA was indeed a match, we decided to call the police and tell them to alert all the airports countrywide."

"Oh thank the lord for that" said Robert. "We were actually just about to do that when you knocked on the door."

"We also received news that Tristran Eldridge had indeed bought a ticket for a flight back to Cyprus from Stansted."

"Really?? When?" said Robert.

"This Friday. The police will be undercover there ready to catch him and arrest him."

"Did you hear that Becky" said Phyllis. "They're going

to catch Tristran Eldridge. He'll finally be brought to justice."

Although Becky was still dazed, she managed to give Phyllis a weak smile.

"Finally, after all these years, the bastard will get his comeuppance" said Sue.

"Not before time" said Ophelia as she handed Becky a cup of herbal tea.

Chapter Thirty-Two

"But I want to see the bastard get arrested" cried Becky.

"Becky, it could be dangerous. Even with his new passport, he could be wary and he may even be carrying a weapon" said Alan.

"Alan's right Becky" added Robert. "They've stepped up security in case anything happens when they go to arrest him. He could be very volatile."

"But surely he wouldn't try anything, he'd be so woefully outnumbered there's no way he could escape" she insisted.

"They've got to take every precaution they can. You don't know if he's going to be on his own or if he's going to have any other members of his gang with him. It's too risky. Far safer to stay here" said Robert.

"But you're going" Becky protested.

"I'm the only one who got a good look at him and can identify him positively. That's why they want me to go along."

"Robert's right love, it's best if the less people go, the better. They'll get him and he'll be brought to justice" said Phyllis in a consoling tone.

"Look, we're going to have to set off shortly. Alan's going to drive me to the airport – I don't think he saw me the other day, but it's best if we don't take my car in case he did catch a glimpse of it. We don't want to arouse any suspicions."

"Well good luck Robert, both of you" said Ophelia. "Just make sure you don't put yourself in the way of danger."

"Oh don't worry about that Ophelia, I'm going to stay well hidden" said Robert.

"Goodbye Alan" said Ophelia. "Get back safely."

Alan smiled. "Don't you worry, I know better than to get back late and see Mrs. Baylock here standing at the door with a rolling pin in hand."

"Rolling pin? Oh no, far more sophisticated these days. Thumb screws to start with, then the stretching rack" said Sue.

Both Alan and Sue were trying to make light of what was a tense situation. Although everything had been planned carefully, there was still a sense of unease about the whole situation.

"Right, we're off then" said Robert. "We'll call you to let you know when they've caught him."

Alan and Robert said their final goodbyes and headed towards Alan's car. The four women waved them goodbye and waited for the car to disappear round the corner before finally closing the door.

"Well then" said Sue. "Now we just have to sit and wait."

"This is going to be the hardest part" said Becky. "I won't feel easy until they finally arrest him."

"They will love, they will" said Phyllis.

* * * * *

Alan and Robert arrived in the airport car park in good time before the flight was due to leave.

"I'll sit and wait here for you Robert, but give me a call if you need me for anything" said Alan.

"I will Alan. Thanks."

Robert got out of the car and headed towards the airport terminal. He was casually dressed so as not to bring attention to himself and tried to look relaxed as he walked into the main lounge of the terminal. He spotted three policemen there that he'd met earlier when they were finalising their plans. He made sure not to make eye contact just in case. Each man in his turn acknoweldged that Robert had arrived, but did so in a way that would not arouse suspicion.

One of the policeman appeared to be standing in a shop, pretending to browse through magazines. Robert stood several feet away and spoke in a low voice.

"Any sign yet?"

"Not yet."

Strange, thought Robert. He should have appeared by now. Most of the passengers had already boarded the plane and from what he could gather, they were just waiting for any late comers, although they wouldn't be able to leave it too long as the runway was needed for other flights. He walked out of the newsagent and went to buy himself a coffee. He noticed another policeman standing not far from there. He glanced at him quickly as if to gesture for the policeman to follow Robert, to see if he had any information.

"Just a filter coffee with milk please" said Robert to the Barista. The policeman was standing behind him. "Do you think something's gone wrong?" he asked.

"Not sure" said the policeman in a low voice. "I would have thought he'd have left in plenty of time to get the flight if he thought the law was after him."

This was strange. Robert suddenly had an uneasy feeling in his stomach.

* * * * *

"Oh my god, look at how young he was there" said Sue. "I don't believe it. My god, look at how slim he was."

Becky had pulled out some old photos that she had of Alan when they were both teenagers in Cyprus. She didn't want to show them to Sue initially as she thought Sue might feel resentful, but the situation was becoming more tense and they needed something to make the atmosphere lighter.

"He was pretty fit as well. He could jump over the fence at school and that wasn't exactly low. Mind you, didn't do him any good eventually as one day when he jumped, he had a horrendous landing and sprained his ankle badly."

"Oh yes, I remember him telling me about that" said Sue. "No doubt he was trying to show off."

Becky laughed. "You know it" she said.

The atmosphere was becoming more relaxed when Phyllis brought more tea in. As she put the tray down there was a knock at the door.

"Strange, wonder who that could be. Don't tell me they've forgotten something" said Sue.

"I'll go and see" said Phyllis.

"I wonder if the police have contacted them to say they've already arrested him and they don't need Robert to identify him" said Becky.

The three ladies carried on talking when Phyllis walked through to the lounge with a strange look on her face. Following her in were two men.

"Good evening ladies, what a pleasant surprise to find you all here" said the first man. "And sadly, no men friends to protect you." The tone was sarcastic, smug, self-satisfied.

"Who are you?" said Ophelia, looking at both men, trying to take in what was happening.

"Oh sorry" said the first man in a mock-dramatic tone. "I'm forgetting my manners. Ladies, let me introduce myself. My name is Tristran Eldridge and this is my good friend Garry ....."

The other man looked at him and frowned.

"Oh I do beg your pardon. My friend here doesn't like me giving his name away. He's very shy you know."

"What do you want?" said Sue, a slight tone of panic in her voice.

"Well it's very simple. We want to leave the country, but as you can imagine, it's slightly difficult for us at the moment as I'm sure every airport countrywide has got my name on it's most wanted list and is just waiting for me to fall right into their hands."

"Well as none of us are pilots I'm afraid we can't help you" said Sue, trying to take the tension out of the situation.

"What a shame" said Tristran, again in that sarcastic tone. "But fear not, for we still have a use for you ....." he turned and looked at Becky. "Or at least one of you."

"What are you going to do?" said Phyllis with panic in her voice. "You'll never get away with it, the police will be looking for you for the rest of your life."

"You have a point there, but in the short term we can take a hostage that will, shall we say, give us some negotiating power" concluded Tristran.

"Leave her alone, she's ill. You can take me instead" said Phyllis boldly.

"Oh such chivalry madam. Very impressive indeed. A veritable knight in shining armour. But I'm afraid I will have to decline your offer. You see, this lady has been the source of all of my problems. As soon as I overheard her saying she was going to look into the case of her late brother's wrongful conviction, I knew it could cause me problems. You see, my dear father was very successful in, shall we say, 'persuading' your Mr Smithson to destroy all the evidence, but you see, I was very silly when I got into your flat and jabbed my finger. Bloody painful and of course I didn't think there would be an issue with them using it for DNA because I expected you to be dead Miss Collerton. Alas, you obviously didn't swallow enough of the little liquid gift I left you and so I knew you'd probably ramp up the hunt from thereon in." Tristran Eldridge's face changed to a look of pure malice. "And oh dear was I right. I thought planting the drugs would do the trick but then your smart arsed solicitor got you off the hook."

"Well you obviously aren't as smart as you thought you were" sneered Becky, "because you left fingerprint evidence on the package."

"Don't taunt him Becky" cautioned Ophelia.

"You would do well to heed your friend's advice Miss Collerton. I'm not the sort of person you want to get on the wrong side of. As you are all too painfully aware, I've already killed two people in this country. As for what I did in Cyprus ..... well ...... doesn't bear thinking about."

"You don't frighten me. I've got terminal cancer so I'm going to die anyway. There's nothing you can do to intimidate me. I'll be a thorn in your side until my last dying breath."

"Be that as it may. In the meantime I may need a hostage to negotiate with and I think you're the perfect applicant for the job. Consider yourself hired Miss Collerton."

"LEAVE HER ALONE, TAKE ME. SHE'S ILL FOR GOD SAKE. HAVEN'T YOU GOT ANY HUMANITY IN YOU?" shouted Phyllis.

"Very touching dear lady, very touching, but as I say, I have no gripe with you and also, if you don't mind me saying, you're a touch on the ample side whereas your friend here is of slight build and therefore easier to transport around."

"I won't let you take her, I'll ......"

At that moment the other man pointed his gun towards Phyllis. "Do what the gentleman says lady, otherwise there will be nobody displaying any chivalry here tonight ...... or ever." The last two words were emphasised for effect.

"It's ok Phyllis" said Becky. "Thank you, but this is my battle, not yours. You've already done more than enough for me, and unlike this low life scum bag, you've proved to me that there are still some bloody fine human beings on this planet and

I count you as one of the best."

Tristran chuckled. "Sticks and stones, dear lady, sticks and stones. As it is, we have no time to waste so I'd like you all to lie on the floor face down while my good friend here ties you up. Don't worry, there will be no deaths here tonight. Not because I think anything of you because I don't. I just don't want to give myself any more problems nor the police any more reason to come after me."

The four women lay down on the floor, face down as instructed and the second man took out several ropes that he'd been carrying and proceeded to tie each of them up. As he finished, Tristran Eldridge indicated for him to lift Sue up and tie her to one of the armchairs. Phyllis was then lifted up and tied to the other armchair. The second man then looped large pieces of rope around the seated cushions on the sofa and forced Ophelia to lie down on it, tying the ropes aroud her. Tristran Eldridge inspected his handywork.

"Very good Garry. You see, all those years in the cub scouts came in handy after all." He indicated to his friend to pick up Becky.

"Go gently with her. As much as I dislike the woman, I don't want to cause her an early demise as she's still useful to me. Once we've caught the boat and are safely away, we can dispose of her."

Ophelia, Phyllis and Sue all felt a sharp stabbing pain inside when they heard this.

"Right, two final things. First hankies for their respective mouths. We don't want them bringing attention to themselves do we now. And while you do that Garry, I'll cut the phone cord. Can't be too careful."

The second man gagged each one of them as Tristran Eldridge cut the telephone chord.

"Right dear ladies, we will be on our way. A shame we can't stop for tea, but duty calls. Say farewell to your friend – it will be the last time you ever see her."

Becky managed to turn one more time, tears in her eyes as if to indicate a final goodbye to the three people who she'd come to view as true friends.

"Come on, stop stalling, we've got to go" said Tristran Eldridge. Both men left, taking Becky with them and they heard the door close.

What could they do? They were helpless. Each tried to struggle against the knots that held them bound, but to no avail. The struggle became increasingly frustrating as they tried more and more to the point of exhaustion. Ophelia had managed to force herself to fall off the sofa, still tied to the seat cushions. She landed with a 'thud' and both Sue and Phyllis squirmed, worried that their friend had injured herself. Ophelia wriggled and wriggled with the other ladies looking on, wondering what she was trying to do. As Ophelia struggled more and more, it became apparent that she was working herself loose from the seat cushions. The struggle was long and hard, but she persisted. She usually gave people the impression that she was probably quite a delicate person with not the strongest constitution, but neither Sue nor Phyllis had seen such determination and strength. She kept struggling relentlessly and she soon managed to start pulling the bottom cushion downwards until it became free of the ropes. This seemed to give Ophelia a renewed strength, whereas Sue and Phyllis could only look on in wonderment. Eventually after a further struggle, the second cushion came free. She stopped to catch her breath and managed to sit up. What she was going to do next was anybody's guess. Sue and Phyllis could only look on, perplexed by what was happening. Ophelia managed to squirm her torso back onto the sofa with the rest of her following. She was now in a sitting position on the sofa. She gingerly attempted to stand up, although at first almost lost her balance. She steadied herself and soon became acclimatised to this new way of standing. She attempted to take baby steps and went at a tiptoe pace towards the kitchen. Sue and Phyllis could hear her opening a drawer. They heard cutlery rattling and assumed she was looking for a knife. Phyllis desperately wanted to call out "Don't hurt yourself sweetheart" but her gag wouldn't allow her to warn her friend.

Things suddenly went silent and both Sue and Phyllis were worried that Ophelia had cut herself seriously. Then suddenly they could hear a rhythmic cutting sound. Was Ophelia managing to free herself of her bonds? The noise continued for some time and they then heard a loud gasp.

"I've done it" called Ophelia. "I'm free. I just need to

cut the ropes from around my legs and then I'll be able to free you."

Just as she said this there was a knock on the door. Initially Ophelia felt a sense of panic. Was it the two men returning? Surely it couldn't be – why would they knock if they thought the three women were still tied up? She cut the knots free as quickly as possible and came back into the lounge. She cautiously peeped from behind the curtain and let out a small gasp. She signalled to Sue and Phyllis that she would be back shortly. They heard her opening the door and could hear a man's voice.

"They've got Becky" they heard Ophelia say. "They tied us up. I managed to get free and now I need to get Sue and Phyllis free. But you've got to alert the police. They obviously didn't go to the airport and they mentioned getting a boat."

"Are you alright?" they heard the man's voice again as he walked through to the lounge with Ophelia to see Phyllis and Sue tied to the chairs. It was Martin Smithson.

"Yes, we're fine. Don't worry about us. Just call the police and let Robert and Alan know that he's not boarding the plane. He must have booked that ticket as a decoy knowing that it would alert the authorities."

Martin Smithson took his phone out of his jacket and pressed several digits. "Hello, hello, police please. This is a dire emergency."

As he continued to give instructions, Ophelia cautiously cut the ropes that bound her two friends. Both woman took large gulps of air and rubbed their wrists.

"Those bastards! Jesus that rope was tied tightly. They certainly didn't want us to get free" said Sue. She turned to Ophelia. "How the hell are we going to find them?"

"I dont' know Sue" said Ophelia, unable to hide the desperation in her voice. "I'm sure Martin will think of something."

They overhead him saying something about the A120 but had been so focussed on trying to re-orient themselves that they didn't take in the full conversation.

"Sue, what's Alan's mobile number?" asked Martin.

Sue quoted Alan's number and he proceeded to make a second call.

"Hello Alan? Alan, this is Martin Smithson. Listen, he's not taking the flight. Buying that ticket was a decoy. He's got Becky and he's taking her somewhere by boat. I don't know what he's planning – whether he's going over to France to get a flight from there or otherwise, but I've called the police. You and Robert may as well come back here. I'm going to try and figure out a plan."

When Alan ended the call he literally ran into the airport and looked frantically around to see Robert. He caught a glimpse of him near one of the boarding gates.

"Robert!" he called out. Several people looked up to see who it was but he was completely oblivious to any attention he was getting. Robert looked at him and frowned.

"Alan, what the hell are you doing, you're going to blow our cover ...."

"Robert, I've just had a call from Martin. He came round to Phyllis's house to say that the flight plan was a decoy. He's not getting on the plane."

"What?" said Robert.

"He's not getting on the plane Robert" repeated Alan frantically. "And what's worse, he's got Becky."

"Becky? How?"

"There's no time right now. Tell the police to call off the plan. We need to do some quick thinking. Come on!"

Robert followed Alan back to his car.

Chapter Thirty-Three

"You mentioned a boat Ophelia, is that right?" asked Martin.

"Yes, yes. He said that all the airports would be on alert and would reprimand him on sight so decided to take a boat instead. He took Becky with him as a hostage for security. The trouble is once he feels he's safe" said Ophelia, her voice now quivering, "he said he'll dispose of her."

"Jesus, I should have known this was going to happen" said Martin.

"But how could you know?" said Ophelia. "You can't blame yourself Martin, it's lucky for us that you got here and that you've alerted the police. At least we know action is being taken."

"But as soon as I learned that he'd booked a flight under his own name I should have worked it out. I had a case several years ago where something similar happened. The criminal managed to give the police the slip by booking a flight and then skipping the country by boat. Why on earth I thought he'd go ahead and take the flight, it was stupid of me."

"You can't beat yourself up about it. He's been giving the Cypriot authorities the run around for years from what we've heard" said Sue. "But the problem we have to focus on now is Becky. How the hell do we save her?"

"Well I don't want to get anybody's hopes up, but I've thought about this strategically and only one or two options make sense" said Martin.

"Oh?" said Sue. All three of the women looked at Martin with anticipation. They desperately needed to hear some good news about Becky.

"Well the way I see it, and I'm trying to think like a criminal now, the A120 runs alongside Stansted airport. That goes directly to Harwich. They could get the boat there, though I doubt it as it's a major port. The other alternative would be to follow the A120 until it connects to the A133. From there they could either go to Clacton-on-Sea or Holland-on-Sea."

"Which is the more likely do you think?" said Sue.

"I would think Holland-on-Sea as Clacton is pretty built up and has the funfair and amusement arcades there, so they wouldn't want to be in such a busy area."

"But by the time the police get there they could be long gone" said Sue despondently.

"We've already alerted the Essex police and they're going to get some helicopters up there."

"I just hope you're right" said Sue. "Jesus, I don't mind admitting that when I first met Becky I was quite jealous because of her and Alan's history, but I'm worried bloody sick about her." Sue began to blink back tears.

Phyllis put her hands around Sue's wrist. "We all are love. All we can do now is wait and hope the police get to the boat before it leaves. I'm sure they will." Was Phyllis saying this to reassure Sue or herself? Either way, she didn't feel convinced.

"I'm going to call Robert and Alan to let them know. I did tell them to come back here but I'm now wondering if it would have been better to tell them to go the other way" said Martin Smithson.

"Well it's not too late" said Sue. "Give Alan a call."

Martin called Alan's number. "Hello Alan, sorry, you're driving. Can you pass me over to Robert?" He paused. "Hello Robert, it's Martin. Listen, I think I know where the boat that's picking them up might be. We think either Harwich along the A120 or alternatively Holland-on-Sea which is just off of the A133." Martin paused as Robert replied. "Oh you are? Oh good. Well the Essex police have been alerted and they're also sending out helicopters to search the coastline. The only thing I would say is be careful. They're armed. I know you want to save Becky but let the police do their job, they know how to handle these situations. Ok, ok, give me a call if you have any other news and I'll do likewise." Martin ended the call.

"They're already going down there aren't they?" said Sue.

"Yes" said Martin. "I've told them to let the police handle it though. Tristran Eldridge wouldn't hesitate to use a gun if he thought it necessary."

Nobody wanted to think about that as they all knew too well that Martin was right.

* * * * *

"Oh come on for god's sake, bloody move it!" Alan ranted.

"You can't get the car to go any faster Alan" said Robert. "Besides which, you don't want us being chased for speeding and stopped. That would only make it worse."

"I know but why is it that when you're in a hurry, everything seems to slow down?"

"Always the way, but Martin's informed the police and they'll be there long before we will."

"Yes, but that lunatic's got Becky ..... and a gun!" Alan couldn't hide the desperation in his voice.

"I know Alan. But we can only hope that as he's taken her for insurance, he's not going to hurt her."

"I wish I could believe that" said Alan. "He's already murdered two people that we know of. How do we know he hasn't murdered others?"

"We can't – what we can do is focus on getting there as quickly as possible. I honestly can't see how he can escape if he's got helicopters searching for him. I shouldn't think it would be that difficult to find him with the lights from the helicopter."

"Well let's hope so" said Alan as he continued to push his foot on the accelerator which refused to go down any further. "Trouble is we don't even know where the boat is."

"We don't, although Ophelia had a pretty strong hunch that it was Holland-on-Sea."

"Oh not all that bloody pendulum malarky" grunted Alan.

"Look Alan, I don't believe in all of that any more than you do, but she did find where Tristran Eldridge was – to the exact house, so if she's done it once, there's every chance she's done it again."

"It's all weird though, I don't like it." Alan couldn't argue with Robert but didn't like the fact that what Robert said was true. She had found the exact house and it had led to them not only to finding Tristran Eldridge, but more importantly, getting his DNA.

"Right, here's the turn off to the A133" said Robert. "Not far now."

Alan continued to follow the road for what seemed like eternity until Robert suddenly altered him to something.

"Look! Up there! It's a helicopter! It seems to be hovering in one spot! I'm sure they must have found them."

Alan continued to drive, looking for somewhere to park the car. Up ahead he could see a group of police cars. "Look Robert, over there."

Alan drove towards where the police were parked. A few of the policeman looked at the car suspiciously and signalled for him to pull over.

"Would you mind turning around sir, we have police business here and we don't want you getting into any danger."

"Like hell I'll bloody turn around!" snapped Alan. "That psychopath has got my ex-girlfriend on board and I'm not going anywhere until she's back on safe land and that murdering lunatic is put behind bars!"

The policeman looked at Alan, uncertain as to whether he should believe him.

"Look constable" interjected Robert. "My friend here is telling the truth." He produced his card. "These are my credentials and we are seriously worried about the lady who's been taken hostage. She's got cancer and Tristran Eldridge has a gun. He's already murdered two people. Now if you could let one of your officer's know we're here, I may be able to assist."

The policeman looked at Robert's business card, looked back at Robert and paused. "Wait here" he said.

He walked over to the police cars and spoke to one of the other policeman there. They both walked back to Alan's car. Robert and Alan explained the situation again and the other policeman stood silent.

"Look, it's Martin Smithson, a friend of mine, who called the police to alert them to this abduction."

Suddenly they heard a gunshot.

"Right!" said the policeman. "You're exposed here so park your car behind the police cars and stay well out of sight."

Alan didn't need to be told twice. He started the engine and pulled behind the police cars as he'd been instructed. The only thing he wasn't happy about was being told to stay in the car.

"Look I know it's frustrating Alan, but we'll only be hindering the police if we got in the way" said Robert.

"But didn't you hear that Robert? It was a bloody gunshot. How do we know he hasn't shot Becky?"

"We don't Alan, but the problem is getting more people shot isn't going to help."

They heard a voice over a tannoy. They couldn't hear exactly what was being said as the car window was closed but it was obvious that the policeman making the request was telling Tristran Eldridge to give himself up. Before Robert could do anything, Alan had quietly opened his door and crept out of the car with his head down.

"Alan!" he hissed. "Don't be a bloody idiot!" It was too late – Alan couldn't hear him. Robert could see him creeping beside the police car, trying to get as near to the front of the car as possible, without the police seeing him.

"Shit, you idiot" said Robert and decided that if he couldn't beat him, he might as well join him. He slowly opened his car door and crept low, making sure that nobody could see him. He slunk around the side of the police car until he could see Alan's shadow crouching by the side of one of the police cars. "You bloody idiot!" he whispered. "You should've stayed in the car!"

"There's no way I could have done that, not when Becky's life is on the line" Alan replied.

Robert knew it was futile arguing with Alan and he crouched silently behind him.

Another shot rang out.

"Get down!" screamed one of the policeman, and several policemen took cover. One was crouched on the other side fo the car.

"YOU CAN'T GET AWAY!" announced the policeman with the tannoy. "TURN YOURSELF IN. EVEN IN THE HIGHLY UNLIKELY EVENT THAT YOU DID MAKE IT ACROSS THE CHANNEL, THE AUTHORITIES HAVE ALREADY BEEN ALERTED!"

They heard a voice shouting back. "NOT AS LONG AS I'VE GOT THIS BITCH AS A HOSTAGE!"

Suddenly they heard a woman's voice crying out.

"Don't worry about me, shoot the bastard! At least I can go to my grave knowing that this lowlife piece of dirt has paid for what he did to my brother."

The policeman didn't understand what she was talking about, but at that moment his only concern was to get her back to shore alive.

Another shot rang out.

"Running out of bullets aren't you?" mocked the woman. "This cat's nine lives are coming to an end."

"Shut up bitch, or the next bullet's got your name written all over it!"

"Go on – put your money where your mouth is, you over-prilvileged little shit!"

Alan was crouching by the car, praying for Becky to stop goading Tristran. "Becky, don't, he'll kill you." Her voice was faint but he could still hear everything that was being said.

What happened next seemed to cause panic to both those on the boat and the policeman. There was a sudden gust of wind and that, together with the waves being created by the helicopter blades, caused the boat to sway violently to one side and there was a sudden 'splash'. Alan's stomach turned over in knots. "God if that's Becky ...."

"Heeeeeeeeeeeelp!" A man's voice called out in desperation. "Tristran help me, I can't swim!"

Tristran's companion continued to splash about as he struggled to keep his head above the water. "Tristran .... help .... help .... help .... me!"

Even Alan and Robert squirmed as they continued to hear the man fighting for his life. Thug though he may be, hearing somebody trying to save themselves from drowning had a disturbing effect on the two men. Although neither of them could see what was happening, they got the distinct impression that the victim was being pulled further away from the boat by the waves and the wind. His voice was getting fainter .... and fainter .... and fainter ...... until ....

"The policeman with the tannoy spoke out again. "GIVE YOURSELF UP NOW, YOU'RE ONLY PUTTING YOUR OWN LIFE IN DANGER. COME BACK TO THE SHORE BEFORE IT'S TOO LATE!"

"NEVER!" screamed Tristran.

Alan was clenching his fists, both in rage and frustration. "For fuck's sake, what the hell does he think he's going to achieve? He can't get away and at this rate, they'll both end up going overboard!"

Robert felt completely helpless knowing there was nothing he could say to convince Alan that everything was going to be ok.

"COME ON TRISTRAN. IT'S OVER. WE KNOW WHO YOU ARE AND WE KNOW ABOUT THE TWO MURDERS YOU COMMITTED AS WELL AS THE DRUG TRAFFICKING. YOU'VE GOT NOWHERE LEFT TO GO!"

"NICE TRY COPPER, BUT IT'S NOT GOING TO WORK. I'VE GOT MYSELF OUT OF WORSE JAMS THAN THIS ONE!"

"Jesus Sarge, this guy is seriously deluded" Alan heard one of the policeman say to his superior. "He can't seriously think he can get out of this one?"

"He's a psychopath Evans. They don't understand the word 'danger'."

"Doesn't seem like it, that's for sure" replied his companion.

"NOW GET THAT BLOODY HELICOPTER OUT OF HERE OR SHE GETS A BULLET!" screamed Tristran.

There was a pause. The helicopter had its light beaming right down onto the boat. If it was to turn around, the boat could disappear into the darkness.

Alan couldn't believe what happened next. The helicopter motioned to turn around and leave. Had somebody radio'd to the pilot to do as Tristran instructed? Surely he could get away. Surely he could disappear into the ....

Suddenly there were two loud screams.

Alan's heart leapt into his mouth and he jumped upright. The policeman saw him and was about to ask him what the hell he was doing there when two loud shots rang out into the night. The helicopter turned around again and seemed to rotate several times in the same spot. One of the policeman shouted to some of his men who started running down towards the shore. Before he could help himself, Alan was running after them.

"What the hell is that bloody idiot doing?" shouted one of the policeman.

Robert stood upright. "I'm sorry, but if you're going to arrest him, you'll have to arrest me too." With that he ran after Alan towards the shoreline.

The helicopters beam blinded him momentarily as it continued to rotate around, the waves rushing frantically towards the shore. In the middle of the chaos, Robert could see the boat frantically bobbing from side to side, almost capsizing at one point. Where the hell were Tristran and Becky?

"I can see them Sarge!" shouted one of the men.

"Well then for god's sake get on that bloody boat and rescue them!"

The helicopter moved away, still keeping it's light on the troubled vessel. The other boat moved towards it, it's main beam scanning the water. "OVER THERE!"

It moved around the side of the boat and seemed to stop. Alan was running into the water and had to be tackled by two policeman!

"I've got to save Becky" he screamed. "She's drowning!"

The two policeman managed to pull him back to shore. An irate policeman came running furiously towards him. "Get this bloody idiot out of here! I'll deal with him later."

Robert was torn between wanting to help Alan and looking to see if the police boat had found Becky and Tristran. As he continued to scan frantically, he could see the police boat appearing from the other side of the troubled vessel. He couldn't see anybody aboard apart from the two policeman that were steering the boat. It began to head towards the shore. He could feel the knot in the pit of his stomach. Surely they couldn't have floated that far out to sea? Why didn't the boat continue to look for them?

"GO BACK!" he screamed. "GO BACK AND LOOK FOR THEM AGAIN!"

The policemen in the boat looked towards him with what he thought appeared to be a puzzled expression. Why couldn't they understand what he was saying? He wasn't that far away from them? Why were they heading towards the shore?

"GO BACK! YOU'VE GOT TO KEEP LOOKING FOR THEM!"

As the boat changed direction, he looked again and ....

he could see two people sitting in the back of the boat. He didn't want to get his hopes up but was it ...... could it be .... "please God" he said to himself. As the boat got nearer, he began to shake uncontrollably until he could see ..... sitting in the back with blankets around them were .... Becky and Tristran. He heaved a huge sigh of relief, pushing aside the wave of nausea he'd felt only moments ago. His only concern was that Tristran wasn't being guarded. Whilst he was certain that he would no longer have the gun, Robert couldn't help feeling concerned that he would pull some sudden stunt. But as the boat got nearer he could see that Tristran was handcuffed to a beam that ran across the boat's width.

Alan was still struggling against the two policemen. "Becky! I've got to get to Becky!"

Robert could hear the commotion and ran up to the three figures. "It's ok Alan, stop struggling. They've got her. She's fine."

Alan looked at Robert, an expression of weary disbelief on his face. "Robert, don't lie to me, I ....."

"Alan, it's ok. They've got her. She's safe."

Several policemen managed to pull the boat up to the shore and two of them assisted Becky in getting out. Two others assisted Tristran to get out of the boat after unlocking his handcuffs, though not with quite the same delicacy as they'd treated Becky.

Alan managed to pull himself free and ran up to Becky.

"Becky, thank god you're alive. I thought he was going to kill you!"

The two policeman ran after Alan in an attempt to restrain him again but one of the policeman who had assisted her in getting off the boat signalled for them to stand down. "Leave the poor guy alone, he's not doing any harm."

Robert stood watching as Tristran was taken to a police van and Alan held Becky for what seemed like eternity. He walked towards the pair.

"Come on Alan, we'd best get a move on. I'm going to have a hell of a job persuading the police not to throw your sorry backside into jail tonight. I don't think Sue would be very impressed."

Alan looked up and smiled at Robert. "It was bloody

worth it" he said.

"Are you ok Becky?" asked Robert.

Becky smiled, although she looked tired and cold.

"I think you need one of Phyllis's world famous cups of hot herbal tea ...... followed by a snotty glance from Pywackit for nicking his chair!"

It was just the perfect line to break the tension and Becky burst out laughing. "Oh Robert, that's not fair. Pywackit loves me!"

"That's what you think" he continued, relieved that his joke had eased the tension. "As soon as you're out of sight, he'll get his voodoo doll out and stick pins in every inch of it."

"Never mind the bloody voodoo doll" said Alan, joining in the humour. "He'll be standing over his bloody cauldron casting spells and curses."

"Will you two stop it" said Becky. "You know how much Phyllis loves him. That's not very nice."

The three of them watched as Tristran Eldridge was shuffled into the police van.

"Well if Pywackit is capable of casting spells" said Becky, "maybe he's responsible for getting that scumbag locked up where he belongs!"

Chapter Thirty-Four

"Are you sure this is a good idea Robert? I mean, I know the old goat has had this coming for years, but you know .... being old and .... well ......" said Alan.

"No Alan, I'm not sure at all. It goes against all my professional ethics and yes, what you alluded to as well without saying it – that he's an old man and could keel over at any moment and then I'd be left with a guilty conscience. However, I've decided not to go and see him myself."

"So you're not going to go round to the bowls club then?" replied Alan, looking relieved.

"Well I didn't actually say that Alan. I'm taking Becky over there. I've talked to her about it and she's promised not to go into some raving tyrade but will put her point across succinctly and to the point – and then leave."

"Hmmmm, all within earshot of the other members" said Alan, raising an eyebrow.

"I guess that's unavoidable."

"A bit like saying that grass is green."

"The thing is Alan, I've learned over the course of my career that not everybody is evil because they had their teddy bear taken away from them at an early age or because they were abused. Of course in many cases that still holds true, but there are people who have had fairly decent lives and still turn out to be evil. I'm afraid in the case of Godfrey Eldridge and his son, they prove the point."

"And you want them to know that they fall into that category" said Alan.

"Not for me to say, although I can understand why you think that. I'm just trying to look at it from Becky's perspective."

"Oh?"

"Well it goes without saying that nothing will bring her brother back. What's done is done, you can't turn back the clock and sadly nobody can change the fact that an innocent man served a life sentence in prison for a crime he didn't commit."

"And on the other hand?" said Alan expectantly.

"On the other hand, there are what I'd call mitigating circumstances in this instance."

"Oh now you're speaking lawyer talk" quipped Alan.

Robert laughed. "Heaven forbid. No, the way I look at it, and sadly I wish we didn't have to, but we have to face facts, Becky doesn't have a lot of time left. It saddens me deeply because even in the short time I've known her, I've become very fond of her. Oh no, don't get the wrong idea, not like that. I just mean that this has obstructed any chance she had in life of living for herself. Everything she's done has been for her brother – sadly with no happy ending. That's why I think we need to allow her to find closure in whatever way she can."

"Well Tristran Eldridge has been caught and will no doubt serve a life sentence" observed Alan.

"Without a shadow of a doubt" agreed Robert. "But let's be honest, if it hadn't been for old man Eldridge pulling the strings behind the scene, he would have gone to prison years ago."

"And Tom might even still be alive" finished Alan.

"There's every possibility that that's exactly what might have happened. He could have had a family, children, grandchildren …."

"As could Becky" added Alan.

"Exactly. But old man Eldridge took all of that away from them. So if she wants to go along to his comfortable little bowls club and make him look less than perfect in front of his friends and peers ……"

" ……. you think we at least owe her that much" said Alan.

"I do."

"Well, don't be too long as I promised her I'd take her to Tom's grave with some flowers afterwards. She wants to say her final goodbye to him."

"I think that would be a very fitting end to the occasion" agreed Robert.

* * * * *

Two hours later Robert and Becky were driving towards

the bowls club.

"Now please Becky, you promised me you wouldn't cause a scene there. I know he deserves it, but he's an old man now and the other members could keel over with a heart attack if World War Three breaks out."

"Don't worry Robert – I've always agreed with the old saying 'revenge is a dish best served cold' and his pudding is going to be ice cold."

"And I see you've brought the local paper along to rub his nose in it."

"He's been a bad dog and dumped on the carpet, metaphorically speaking, so he deserves to have his nose rubbed in it."

"Hell hath no fury ....."

" .... like a woman who is getting revenge for the sentence passed on her brother."

"Quite" said Robert with a wry smile.

Robert parked his car just outside the bowls club. "Remember Becky ......"

"Calm, cool and collected" said Becky, a sudden smile coming across her face.

She walked into the reception area beaming brightly, putting on her best 'sweetness and light' personae. "Turn on the charm and then deliver the poison" she said to herself.

"Hello, can I help you?" asked the receptionist.

"Erm, I hope so. I just need to have a quick word with one of the gentleman in the club. It won't be a minute, but I do need to get this message to him rather urgently. It's his son you see." Well, she thought to herself, she wasn't lying.

"Oh no, I do hope it's not serious" said the reception looking concerned.

"Well I'm rather afraid it is" said Becky, feigning the concerned citizen look.

"Well erm, it's not usual policy to let non-members in, but if you could be quick, I'm sure he won't mind."

"Thank you, I do appreciate it" said Becky, giving the receptionist her sweetest smile.

As she walked towards the group playing bowls she managed to pick out Godfrey Eldridge from a photograph she'd been shown. He looked quite a bit older now, but she could tell by that dour look on his face that it was him.

"Er, hello, is it Mr Eldridge?" she asked, maintaining her overly-sweet smile.

"Yes" he said.

Becky realised that using the 'softly softly' approach hadn't stopped him from keeping his guard up. 'Oh well', she thought, 'might as well deliver the package anyway'.

"You don't know me Mr Eldridge but you knew my brother."

"Oh?" he said, looking to his friends for moral support.

My word he really did have his guard up, thought Becky.

"Well yes" said Becky. She made sure she had everybody's attention whilst keeping her composure and delivering her speech with the sweetest smile and softest tone. "You see, I couldn't help noticing this article in the local paper a few days ago. Very interesting Mr Eldridge. You see, a man by the name of Tristran Eldridge who I believe just happens to be your son, was caught trying to escape the country in a boat, only to be captured by the police." She paused. Of course he could start shouting and protesting but she was adamant she was going to deliver the full message. "Now he just happened to have me as a hostage at gun point in that boat, but thanks to the good work of the police, he was caught and luckily for me, I'm still ailve. If you don't believe me, you see, it's on this page here." She opened the paper up. "This is a picture of your son, and this is a picture of me." Her tone was that of a mother reading a fairy story to a young child. "But why do you think he would do such a thing?" she continued, a tone of wonderment. "Well wouldn't you just know it, but over three decades ago your son murdered two people and my brother was framed for both murders – even though he was out of the country when the first one occured and it's since been discovered that the DNA of the murderer on both murdered bodies matches your son's exactly. Now isn't that a turn up for the books Mr Eldridge?"

"If you've come here to ....."

"Oh now don't you fret, dear man. I haven't come here to upset you in any way. I just want to point out some facts. Like the one that the original defending solicitor was told to destroy all the evidence otherwise his children would seriously be harmed. Oh I can prove it, he told me so. Of course I wasn't happy about the fact, but as my friends explained to me, when children are brought into the equation, people seem suddenly happy to comply with any methods of persuasion."

"You'd better leave right now or I'm calling the police!"

"You'll do no such thing" one of the other club members suddenly barked.

This was an unexpected turn of events for Becky.

"Now you listen to me old man" said the elderly man. "I've been playing bowls in this club for years and I've seen the way you behave, as if you own the place. What you don't know is that I've talked to friends. Friends who've talked to other friends and what I've heard about you isn't very nice old man. I've never been able to prove it, but it seems as though this young lady can and I want to hear her story!"

This took Becky back a bit. She had her entire speel ready to deliver but this sent her off course slightly.

"Erm, thank you Mr, er, Mr ....."

"You can call me Richard. Now please, I want to hear what you've got to say."

The other club members darted a look at Godfrey Eldridge as if to say 'button it' and then looked back at Becky expectantly.

"Well, er, where was I?"

"Evidence" said Richard. "You were talking about evidence."

"Oh yes, thank you." She smiled appreciatively. "Well there were several pieces of evidence that were destroyed. First of all the speeding ticket which was issued to my brother not long before he arrived at the victim's house lying on the floor dead. Oh yes, it looked damning but several witnesses said they'd seen somebody running out of the house minutes before my brother got there and the culprit was much taller. Then there was the blood evidence. The murderers blood was O Positive in both cases and my brother was A Negative." Becky had picked up her pace again. "But as my brother was standing over the body of the victim, who also happened to be his best friend, well it wrapped the case up nicely for the police. In the meantime, Tristran Eldridge, erm I believe that's your son" said Becky with more than a hint of sarcasm, "obtained the birth certificate of a boy who had died years ago called Sebastian Blanchard."

"Hang on" said one of the club members. "Wasn't there a story in the paper the other day about the remains of a boy with the same name being discovered?"

"There was indeed" nodded Becky. "I believe he used to bully your son because you also sentenced his father for a robbery that he didn't commit" finished Becky. "It does seem as though you liked sentencing innocent people for crimes they didn't commit.

"There was nothing innocent about either of them. Keith Blanchard was a thief and a drunkard ...."

"Er no, Mr Eldridge, he was a petty criminal and yes he was a drunkard, but the robbery you sentenced him for was way out of his league. It was big time ..... he was known as being the small fry thief, that's apparently what his friends used to call him."

"Oh and I suppose you're going to accuse my son of killing the boy are you? When he was only five years old himself?"

"No, not at all. That was a tragic accident, your son had nothing to do with it. Who'd have thought he'd become a murderer ...... oh, and the leader of a major drug ring in the mediterranean as well."

"Absolute rubbish. You're going into fantasy land now."

"I don't think so Mr Eldridge." Becky's tone was losing its softness and was now becoming stern. "Both the Turkish and Greek Cypriot authorities have been trying to catch your son for years but he's always given them the slip."

"Oh and I suppose that now he's been caught they're drinking from the rafters?" he sneered.

"Quite the opposite Mr Eldridge. From what I've heard, they're positively raging. They both wanted the British authorities to hand him over. Not only for the drug trafficking but also for a murder that they believe he may have been involved in. The problem is of course that as it's been proven beyond reasonable doubt that your son murdered two people in this country, they intend to keep him on terra firma in this country permanently. He's going to rot in an English prison ..... a bit like my innocent brother did after thirty years before dying in it."

The mood of the other club members had changed from light-hearted banter when Becky originally came in to one of silent glares, all aimed at Godfrey Eldridge.

"Can I take a look at that paper miss?" asked one of the club members.

"Yes, you can have it. I bought several copies when it came out last week."

"Thank you" replied the elderly gentleman. He scanned the pages as Becky finished off her story.

"My god Eldridge, you really were a piece of work. How many people have you wrongly convicted? How the hell do you sleep at night?"

"It's fine for you to cast aspersions, but you don't know what it's like to be a judge and to find out your son's a murderer. What the hell was I supposed to do? Turn him in? My own son? And what would that have done for my reputation?"

"Well you never know old man" said the other gentleman sardonically. "Maybe people would have had some respect for you for having the balls to treat your own son in the same way that other common criminals and murderers are treated. But not you – not the righteous pillar of the community Godfrey Eldridge."

"I don't need to stay here to put up with these insults and abuse, I'm going." Godfrey Eldridge picked up his jacket and headed towards the reception area.

"And if you've got any moral compass, you'll never show your face in here again" called back the elderly gent.

There were a few "here here's" from the other men in the group.

"I always knew he was a bad egg" said the elderly gentleman to Becky. "But I didn't realise he would stoop that low."

"I can't deny the fact that I've had some satisfaction at seeing him humiliated after all this time" said Becky. "After what he did to Tom, I just wanted to see him squirm."

"Well squirm he did" said the gentleman. "I shouldn't think he'll show his face here again. Come inside, let's get a cup of tea. I'd like to talk to you a bit more about this case."

"Oh er, I have a friend waiting in the car for me" said

Becky hesitantly.

The elderly man smiled. "Invite him in. Us old'uns can sometimes lend a good ear and you might just be interested to hear what I have to say about the old codger."

Becky thought for a moment and smiled. "Ok" she said. "Hold on, I'll go and get him."

Becky went to the car and managed to persuade a very reluctant Robert to come into the club.

"I saw him leaving, I assume he didn't like what you had to say to him" he said.

"Oh it wasn't what I said to him" replied Becky. "It was what one of the other club members said to him."

"Oh?"

Becky and Robert walked into the club to be signalled to join the group of men sitting in a cluster of tables.

"Weren't you here a little while ago?" one of them asked Robert.

"I was" said Robert.

"That's right, you spoke to the old goat didn't you? You definitely got him well riled. Ruffled his feathers good and proper." The elderly gent chuckled.

"Well, at least I've done something good in my life" chuckled Robert.

"Oh and that's just the start of it" replied the gent.

Chapter Thirty-Five

Alan and Becky walked through the cemetery slowly.

"I promised myself I wasn't going to cry" said Becky. "But I can't help it Alan, I still feel so guilty about not ....."

"Becky, we've been through this" said Alan. "You did everything you could, you were fighting against people who had a vested interested in keeping Tom in prison. There was no way they were going to let the truth out. Reputations and livelihoods depended on it."

"Don't I know it." A tone of bitterness arose in her voice. "Even so, I still think I could have done something ...."

"Right Becky, you have to make me a promise" said Alan.

"What's that?" asked Becky.

"Today you're going to put your flowers on Tom's grave, you're going to say farewell to him and tell him that you did your best. I'm sure he knew that anyway, but you've got to let this go." Alan could feel himself getting upset. "Shit I don't want to address the elephant in the room, but let's face it Becky ...."

"I know Alan. I haven't got long left to go, you don't have to avoid the subject."

"But that's why I want you to try and enjoy what you've got left of this life. Christ only knows it hasn't been kind to you. I mean look at me, I've got Sue and Ruth, but you ....."

"Are you happy Alan?"

"What?"

"Are you happy Alan?"

"This has got nothing to do with me. This is about you."

"Even so, I want to know that you're happy before ... before ......"

"Yes I'm happy." The deep sigh betrayed his answer.

"I do wonder how things would have turned out if we'd kept in touch."

"So do I Becky, so do I. But that's water under the bridge now."

"Time and tide wait for no man."

"No they don't Becky, and that includes a brother who you need to say goodbye to. Come on."

They walked silently towards the slab that marked Thomas Collerton's life. "Nothing but a bloody criminal's stone, as if he was insignificant."

"But you've ordered the new gravestone and it will take pride of place to replace this one" said Alan.

"You're damn right it will" said Becky.

"Come on love, make your last time with Tom a memorable one for the right reasons."

Now it was Becky's turn to sigh. "You're right Alan, you're right."

She knelt before the grave. "Hey bruv, I've come to see you one last time before I go back to Cyprus. I'm so sorry that I never managed to ..."

"Becky, please ..."

"Sorry Tom, it's Alan. He's telling me to lighten up." She let out a small chuckle. "He'd find that funny and agree with you."

"He definitely had a sense of humour" said Alan.

"Anyway Tom, I've come to tell you that they caught the murderer. It was Tristran Eldridge, that bastard judge's son. But you'd be proud of me Tom. I made the old man look two inches tall in front of all his bowling buddies. Neither of them will have much of a life now, what's left of it for both of them." Becky's words broke into sobs. "Just like you didn't have a life. But listen, I'll be joining you soon. I haven't been very well and ..... let's just say I'll be with you, mum and dad before too long. I love you Tom. I'll see you soon and I promise you, I'm getting this rotten slab changed for the gravestone you deserve." Between the sobs she let out a laugh. "You'll be boasting to all the other poor buggers in here that you've got the best gravestone in the cemetery."

"Yup, that's about right" chuckled Alan.

"And it will be Tom, it will be." Becky knelt down and kissed the meagre slab stone. "Goodbye Tom, rest in peace, until we meet again."

Alan put his arm around Becky as she continued to sob. She was just standing up when a robin flew down from a tree and stood on top of the slab. It looked at Becky for what seemed like forever and then flew off. Both Alan and Becky looked at each other. Neither of them knew what to say.

*****

"Oh I wish you weren't going back to Cyprus" said Phyllis as she hugged Becky for what seemed like forever.

"I know Phyllis and in a way I wish I could stay here too, but I promised my friends I would go back to see them and I want to tell them the good news."

"But didn't you phone them and tell them?" asked Phyllis.

"Yes I did, but we're going to have a little celebration in Tom's memory."

"Well as much as I really don't want to see you go I can't blame you" said Phyllis. "You will promise to keep in touch won't you? I know people usually say they do but ....."

"Phyllis, there is no way on god's earth I'll loose contact with any of you. I honestly don't know how I could have managed the last few weeks without you. It's not easy leaving, I can tell you. I've got good friends in Cyprus and now I've got good friends here."

"Yes, but Cyprus has sunshine and that would definitely trump it for me" said Alan.

"Oh I don't know about that, being stuck on a hot plane for ages" added Sue.

"Becky, I want you to have this" said Ophelia. She walked forward and put a necklace around Becky's neck. "It's a healing pendant and I want you to wear it."

Becky hugged Ophelia. "You know I will Ophelia, and thank you."

There was the sound of a car horn.

"Oh that's Robert. He's probably worried that I'll miss the plane. I'd better go. God knows I'm torn but ......"

Toot! Toot!

"Ok I'm coming Robert."

"Take care Becky and please come back anytime, there's always a room for you here" said Phyllis.

"Thanks Phyllis I will. Well goodbye everybody. Thank you all for everything, from me and Tom. I mean it."

"Goodbye Becky." Sue gave Becky a hug. As she turned to look at Alan, there was a look on his face ...... what was it? Sadness? Regret? Loss?

"Bye Becky" he said meekly. Even Sue could hear the tone was unusually sombre for Alan.

"Bye Alan. Look after him Sue, he's very special."

She walked towards the car and got into the passenger seat. Robert started the engine and Becky waved at them as the car sped off towards the airport.

Alan, Sue, Phyllis and Ophelia walked back into Phyllis's house.

"I feel suddenly deflated" said Phyllis. "I just hope she's going to be alright. I know she's got friends out there, but I can't help feeling she'd be better off here with us looking after her."

"I agree" said Ophelia. "She looked so frail and tired."

"I know. I just wish the future had more to offer her" replied Phyllis.

"Yes Phyllis, so do I" said Ophelia. "The only consolation she has is that she's had some closure with her brother."

"I think it meant a lot to her" said Sue. "Think what it would have been like if she hadn't found out about Tristran Eldridge before .... well ..... you know ...."

"Don't worry Sue, we're all thinking the same thing" said Ophelia. "Maybe it was meant to be this way. It seems so cruel, but I think this will give her some peace."

Phyllis suddenly looked sombre. "I wonder ...."

"Wonder what Phyllis?" said Ophelia.

"I just wonder how many innocent people have been wrongly convicted and sent to prison."

"Too many" said Ophelia.

"It's an imperfect system and sadly it fails for many" added Sue.

"It does Sue" said Ophelia. "But the only consolation we can take from all of this is that at least in this case, finally, justice was served."

"I know Ophelia, but what a price Becky had to pay."

"What a price indeed."

A taster of David Dhekelia's follow-up book "The Curse of Samael's Grimoire"

Chapter One

"Do you want me to get that Phyllis?" asked Ophelia as she heard a knock at the front door.

"No that's ok Ophelia, I'll get it. It's probably Robert."

Phyllis walked to the front door and opened it. Sure enough, there stood Robert.

"Come in Robert" she said somberly.

Robert followed her through to the lounge. "Hello Ophelia" he said.

"Hello Robert."

"Take a seat Robert, I'll make some tea" said Phyllis.

"Thanks Phyllis."

Robert and Ophelia sat in silence while they heard Phyllis in the kitchen making tea.

Finally Robert spoke. "Have either of you spoken to Alan and Sue?"

"Phyllis has" said Ophelia.

"How did they take the news?"

"Not well, although according to Sue, Alan is holding a lot in from what Phyllis said."

"Oh dear, that's going to be difficult" said Robert.

"Yes Robert, I think you're right."

Phyllis came through carrying a tray with fresh cups and her usual two pots of tea. One with herbal tea and one with normal tea. "Here you go Robert."

"Thanks Phyllis."

Robert stirred his tea as the three of them sat in silence.

Phyllis tried to put on a brave face but couldn't hold it in any longer. She began sobbing. "It's not fair" she said. "Just when she'd finally got closure for Tom, that bloody awful disease took her. She didn't deserve that."

"I know she didn't Phyllis, I know she didn't." Robert felt helpless. There was no way he could console either her or

Ophelia. They'd received the news of Becky's death several days ago and even though they all knew it was inevitable, it was still a shock when she finally passed.

"It's hard to feel spiritual at times like this" said Phyllis. "I know it's an imperfect world, but it really hits you when it's somebody you know."

"It's not just a case of knowing her, I think we all felt protective towards her" said Ophelia.

"Yes you're right Ophelia. She was like a kid sister to me. I couldn't help feeling protective towards her."

"Does anybody know when the funeral will be? Is it going to be in Cyprus or are they flying the body back to the UK?" asked Robert.

"She's going to be buried in Cyprus. That's where most of her friends lived so her last wish was to be buried there" said Phyllis.

"Apparently there's a letter on the way" said Ophelia. "Becky wanted to write us a farewell letter before she ...... before she ......"

Phyllis's phone rang and she jumped up to answer it, more as a distraction from the subject than to see who was calling.

"Hello? Oh hi Sue. How are you ...." Phyllis paused as Sue was relaying information over the phone. "Oh really? Oh that was quick, I didn't realise ......"

Robert and Ophelia both looked up attentively, although Phyllis was in the hall so neither could see the expression on her face. They could only guess what the conversation was about from Phyllis's replies to Sue.

"Oh well, yes, I can understand how you feel about that. What has Alan said? Oh not yet. Oh ok. What do you think he'll do?"

Ophelia and Robert became impatient, wanting to know what was being said. However, it wasn't too long before Phyllis ended the conversation.

"Well look Sue, why not come over later, on your own if you like. Just to give yourself time to think. Please love, I think it might help. Ok, well you know where I am. Take care."

Phyllis walked back into the living room. She could tell by Ophelia and Robert's expectant looks that they wanted the run down on the conversation she'd just had.

"That was Sue" she said.

"We gathered as much" said Ophelia, almost in the tone of somebody saying, 'no need to state the obvious'. "What did she say?"

"Well, it was a bit awkward. Apparently Alan and Becky had been emailing each other and one of her friends found Alan's email address and decided to write to him direct."

"Oh?" said Ophelia.

"It would seem that this friend told Alan that Becky had held a torch for him for years after they split up, but didn't try to contact him again because she felt ashamed for losing contact when she did."

"But we know it was because of what happened to Tom" said Ophelia.

"Yes, yes I know" said Phyllis. "But I suppose she felt it would be hard to explain. Anyway, the bottom line is that the funeral is in a week's time and they wanted to know if we wanted to fly out for it."

"A week's time? That rules me out because I've got seminars to present for the next two weeks. I'm behind my schedule and need to catch up with the paperwork and that's going to take me at least five days" said Robert.

"I can't go either" sighed Phyllis. "I promised my friend Elspeth I'd go and stay with her for a week or so because her mum died recently and I'd already cancelled on her twice. I haven't got the heart to do it again."

"I'm afraid it's the same here" said Ophelia. "I'm helping to set up the new Mind, Body and Spirit Festival. They used to run years ago but died down after a while. I've been contacted by two of the people who used to run the original ones and they told me there's been a renewed interest and they've decided to hold a few small ones locally. If they do well, they're going to expand further afield and they asked me if I'd go and give them some guidance. I promised them I would which means I'm going to be occupied for the next month at least."

"What about Alan and Sue?" asked Robert. "Will they be going?" He could tell by the expression on Phyllis's face that the answer wasn't going to be straightforward.

Phyllis sighed. "Well, I get the impression that Becky's friend is keen to meet Alan because Becky used to talk about him a lot. But the problem is ....."

"Sue doesn't want to go because she'll feel like a fish out of water ......" added Robert.

"...... and I think there may still be a small tad of jealousy there" said Ophelia.

"Oh I don't know about that" protested Phyllis.

"Oh Phyllis, look, we're not being derisory about Sue in any way at all. It's just that I could pick up the signals quite a lot when Becky was here" said Ophelia. "Oh, please don't take that the wrong way, I know that Sue was genuinely concerned for Becky after she was nearly poisoned and fell ill, but I just got the feeling that things weren't the same between her and Alan when Becky showed up."

"But that was years ago ......" Phyllis tried to argue.

"I'm sorry Phyllis, but I agree with Ophelia" said Robert. "Just little facial tiks, expressions, looks ..... and as for Alan."

"Alan?" asked Phyllis.

"He tried to suppress it, but everytime he was near Becky he was like a little puppydog who'd found a new owner. If he'd had a tail to wag, they could have used it to power up several generators by the energy it would have produced."

Ophelia let out a little giggle and instantly regretted it. "I'm sorry Phyllis, I didn't mean to be glib, it's just that I can see exactly what Robert's saying. Couldn't you feel the energy in the room when they were in each other's company?"

"Well they didn't seem particularly sexual to me" said Phyllis.

"No Phyllis, we're not talking about sex, we're talking about two people who genuinely love each other. It was quite plain to see." Ophelia looked sadly at her friend, not wanting to disillusion her.

"Well I can honestly say I didn't pick up on anything" said Phyllis, feeling as though her psychic abilities were being challenged.

"It's no comment on your gifts at all" said Ophelia. "It's just that your loyalty to Sue blocked any unconscious signals that were being given off."

Phyllis wasn't sure she liked this observation.

"Look" said Robert trying to change the subject. "The fact is either they go or they don't go. My guess would be that Sue probably doesn't want to go and not because it's being in any way disrespectful to Becky's memory. I just think she would feel uncomfortable in that situation, and I wouldn't blame her for not going. Alan on the other hand ....."

"...... would probably give his right arm to go" finished Ophelia.

"Succinctly put" said Robert.

"Dilemmas dilemmas" said Ophelia. "What to do?"

"Well I've told Sue to pop over tonight for a chat if she wants to. I'm hoping she will. I think she needs a bit of space away from the home right now, somewhere where she'll feel free to say what's on her mind."

"Do you think she'll come?" asked Robert.

"Yes, yes I think she will" said Phyllis. "I do get the feeling she needs some support right now."

"And there's nobody better than you" said Robert, smiling at Phyllis.

Phyllis blushed. "Don't be silly Robert."

"It's just the truth" said Ophelia matter-of-factly. "Sue knows she can come to you in a crisis."

"Well just in case she does, I'll bid you both goodbye and catch up with you when we're all less busy" said Robert. "You both have my number so if anything happens ....."

"And goodness knows these days things certainly do seem to be happening" said Phyllis.

"All the more reason to keep my number to hand" said Robert.

"Thanks Robert. To be honest, I think we'll all be so pre-occupied there won't be time for any incidents to happen."

"Don't say that Phyllis" countered Robert. "That's just asking for trouble."

"Robert's right" added Ophelia.

"Ok Robert. Well don't work too hard and I hope your seminars go well. I'm sure they will."

"Thanks Phyllis. I hope your friend is ok as well. Sounds like she'll definitely need your support if she's just lost her mum. Good luck with your festivals Ophelia."

"Thanks Robert. I'm sure we'll catch up again soon"

said Ophelia.

With that, Robert said his last goodbyes and headed towards his car. As the car disappeared into the early dusk, Ophelia watched the tail lights disappear. "Sooner than we think" she whispered to herself.